HOW TO SELL YOUR BLOOD

& FALL IN LOVE

D.N. BRYN

HOW TO
SELL YOUR BLOOD
AND FALL IN LOVE

Guides for Dating Vampires
Book Two

D.N. BRYN

Printed in the United States of America
First Printing, 2023

Print (paperback) 978-1-958051-09-2
Print (hardcover) 978-1-958051-08-5
Ebook 978-1-958051-07-8

For information about purchasing and permissions, contact D.N. Bryn at dnbryn@gmail.com

www.DNBryn.com

Cover design by ThistleArts.
Cover and spine typography by Houda Belgharbi.
Page Breaks by Татьяна Олина on vecteezy.com.
Published with The Kraken Collective.

This work is fictitious and any resemblance to real life persons or places is purely coincidental. No vampires were harmed in the making of this story.

This book contains multiple memories and strong feelings of guilt related to the violent death of a parental figure, the nearly continuous smoking of anti-pain meds for chronic pain, and one scene of a rather sexual nature.

To me and my Justin.

Every unsatisfying kiss is only
serving to make your lips taste better.

1

CLEMENTINE

Dr. Clementine Hughes did not deserve this.

He could feel the blood pulsing through the neck of the lab technician who sat three desks away from him. His gaze yanked to the exposed veins on her wrist as she tapped her pen. As though his fangs had a mind of their own, the venomous canines slipped free. He retracted them in a panic. The few humans lingering in their research lab's communal office space seemed not to notice.

This time.

It had been three months since Clementine turned, and with each slip-up he was more and more certain *someone* would take note. When they did, he could only hope that they killed him before they tried to fire him. That sounded like a much nicer progression. No severance pay, but at least he'd never have to tell his parents that Vitalis-Barron Pharmaceuticals, frontrunner in medical research and therapeutics, had sacked him just as they were considering his promotion to their microbio department's senior research associate.

Clementine ran his tongue over his front teeth—no more fangs, thankfully—and tried to ignore the lab tech as she walked behind him. He held his breath. She passed by. He exhaled.

And his fangs slipped out again.

Dammit.

Clementine didn't know much about vampires, but he knew he didn't deserve to *be* one.

The first few days had been a waking nightmare of pain and sweats. Many people died during the transition, but after living through it he was pretty sure he *had* died. That was where the myth of the undead vampire came from, he was certain. He had died, and this was hell.

Except Clem was also certain that in the real afterlife, he wouldn't be having quite this hard of a time, seeing how he'd done absolutely nothing wrong in his entire life. That wasn't arrogance, and it wasn't delusion. Dr. Clementine Hughes, chemist of the year, potential Nobel Prize winner, secret writer of five million words of slow-burning, emotionally smutty and incredibly gay Star Trek fanfic, had exerted a great deal of energy in order to live this perfect a life.

And now his meticulously sculpted existence was falling apart around him. Because of a tiny, itty-bitty disaster, one that hadn't even been his fault. He was *pretty sure* about that. He'd analyzed it fifty times already that evening, and after another fifty he was prepared to bump *pretty sure* up to *mostly sure* before the whole process started again tomorrow.

It *hadn't* been his fault, right?

When he could remember so little of what had happened to him, it was hard to be certain…

"Clementine!"

Clem flinched so hard that his vampiric strength knocked his chair into his desk.

Dr. Anthony Hilker leaned toward Clem's shoulder, watching him with his brow raised. The man had his blazer slung over an arm and his brown hair was pulled up in a bun today, revealing his undercut and the long slope of his neck. Blood pulsed faintly beneath the skin there, but Clementine's general annoyance with Anthony made it a bit easier for him to drag his gaze upward.

A few wisps of gray were growing at his temples.

Clementine hadn't even turned thirty yet and he already swore he was finding some silver mixed with his own hair, though the natural gold of his curls did a better job of hiding it. Working for this company seemed to have an aging effect on people. Or perhaps that was simply the result of fighting for promotions against Anthony's aggressive enthusiasm.

Clem forced a smile. "Good evening, Anthony."

"You're in… what is this, early for you?" Anthony wrinkled his nose. "I still can't believe you've shifted so many of your hours to a night schedule. That would wreak havoc on my ability to sleep."

The fact that their level of the lab sat two stories underground was the only reason Clementine could stand the few day shifts he'd kept, and even then he had to time his coming and going to avoid direct sunlight. "The empty lab

3

helps me think," Clem replied. "Dr. Blood approves of it. She suggested we form a full night team. It would be almost like having two labs running without the need to build a second location."

Anthony's eyes tightened. "That sounds... capitalistic. But I can't imagine Vitalis-Barron would implement it. It would make it far too easy for vampires to slip into our midst."

"We could use it as a new hunting tactic." Natalie Deleon wrapped an arm around Anthony's neck as she slipped in behind him, her chin tucked against his shoulder like a rabid PDA announcement. "Lure them in with a job offer and don't let them back out again."

A tremble worked itself up Clementine's spine at the thought of the secret, lowest level of their research complex's underground labs—the basement—where they kept the vampires they used in very specific and very secretive parts of their research. Vampires who looked like they were inches from death, hollow-eyed and locked in cages. Vampires who people from Natalie's team had gently pressured into 'volunteering' for the cause.

Vampires, like Clementine.

He'd always known that some of their microbio projects used compounds produced by vampires, but he'd assumed they were acquired on a more ethical basis until Vitalis-Barron had recently deemed him worthy of visiting the basement lab. There was nothing technically illegal about using vampires as lab rats, not when lawyers could argue that the research ethics laws currently in place were written specifically for humans. None of it would have sat right with Clementine even before he'd turned, but now the chance of getting another job anywhere half as respectable with a quarter of the paycheck would be out of question. One daytime interview in a well-lit room and they'd usher him out the door like his painful sun-induced shakes were contagious. No more respectable job, no more apartment, no more family approval, no more life.

He just had to keep his head down and his work consistent and hope that no one noticed his fangs.

"Nat," Anthony cooed at his girlfriend. He was too old for her, and the feigned childishness made it even more obvious. "Don't tell me you're bored already."

She waggled the tip of her dark braid against Anthony's lips. "Not bored, just frustrated. I think I have a lead though, finally, some vampire who's been helping the two who murdered Matthew. If I can get my hands on them…"

"And then you'll be ready to let this vengeance nonsense go?"

"Then I'll have closure." Natalie pecked him on the cheek. The mark of her red lipstick remained on his skin like a brand. "And the boss will be happy. The basement is low on subjects again."

Clementine tried to roll his chair away, staring anywhere but the woman's neck. "Our research on vampires is at the forefront of modern science." He repeated the line from their tour, trying to beam *pro-vampire torture* from every cell of his being.

"I'm not sure we can claim we're truly progressing our pharmaceutical research when everything we do is based solely on where the money is," Anthony put in, playing with Nat's braid. "How much more would we learn if we stopped caring whether anything turned a profit and instead followed the science, wherever it led?"

"Right now the science is leading me back to the lab," Clementine replied, scooting his chair further away from the incessant lovebirds. "If you would excuse me."

As he tried to leave, Anthony called after him. "You heard about the break-ins at our blood bank, right?"

The slightly darker, entirely unhuman blood in Clem's veins went cold.

"Yeah," the man continued as though Clem had acknowledged him. "Apparently someone's been stealing from it, maybe for months. They're putting up cameras now."

"Are they? Cameras?" Clementine's voice sounded distant to his own ears, echoing back at him across a great plain of his own panic. "Good. Good on them." Good *on* them? Those couldn't have been his words.

Fuck it, he needed to get out of here. But more than that, he needed to work, because taking his shifts at night, without the rest of his team, had already put him behind on his current projects. And if what Anthony had said was true, and his bagged blood supply was suddenly disappearing on him, he would have to find a new source.

Most likely, a live one.

Clem ended up in the bathroom, both hands pressed to the back of a locked stall as he focused on breathing. Through extensive tracking of his own consumption, he'd deduced that a moderately sized adult vampire such as himself was meant to drink approximately 44 milliliters—a shot glass, hilariously—of blood a day, but for the past month he'd been trying to hide his stealing by diluting his intake down to half that, as though he might wean himself off the horrid stuff entirely. Which wasn't actually possible. He assumed. It wasn't as though he had anyone to ask, exactly: the only real vampires he'd ever seen outside the news had been the ones locked in cells and strapped to tables three floors beneath him.

But just setting foot on that level would raise the entire building's alarms since the bizarre break-in shortly after Clem was turned. There had been a vampire in the lab then too—a vampire who was healthy and strong, who had held his human partner's wrist and leaned toward his ear without his gaze catching on the man's neck even once. An escaped new arrival, perhaps? Or a thief?

Clementine should have run after him. He'd been too slow on the uptake, too convinced that the nightmare of his vampirism would somehow work itself out. That since he didn't deserve this, it would have to go away.

But it hadn't.

He shoved the bathroom wall with a muffled growl. The tile cracked beneath the pressure. Cracked, like him, from reasons beyond his control. Undeserved.

Thirty minutes later, he finally returned to the now much quieter office space. He put his headphones in, blasting the soothing tones of orchestral metal into his skull, and threw on a lab coat, descending into work until everything else faded away.

By the time he collected his leather satchel and donned his tweed coat, the 7 a.m. lab staff were already arriving with coffee and yawns. He checked the sky for the first signs of dawn as he stepped out into the dark winter morning. The air was unusually chilly—a mid-thirties that might almost have brought snow, if the precipitation would ever make its way past the white-capped eastern mountains. Three months ago, it would have made him tug up his collar and hurry to the car, but since turning, he never felt particularly cold. Instead, he tugged up his collar in an attempt to block the appetizing scent of the incoming wave of staff and hurried to the car to keep any of them from trying to talk to him.

As he slipped inside his electric sedan, his phone buzzed with an incoming call. He hated those, hated how disconnected they felt, how the participants were expected to understand the full scope of emotion being conveyed without any facial or body language cues, and, worse, to convey their own emotions *back* using tone of voice alone. Even the best calls left him feeling tired and jittery.

He almost tossed his phone over the obnoxious beach umbrella that took up his center console—an emergency precaution he hadn't had to use yet—but the caller ID stopped him. His sister couldn't wait; family was a priority, at least in his family. Alongside the priorities of financial growth, academic acclaim, and all-around prestige.

Clem hit answer a moment too late and cursed as he struggled to call Odysseus back while turning on the car. Its Bluetooth clicked over, Odysseus's voice booming out as clearly as though the woman was in the vehicle with him.

"Clementine, honey, is this not a good time? I can call back."

"Sissy, hey." He raised his voice, then regretted it as his sister audibly recoiled. Softer, he added, "No, no, this is fine. Do you need something?" *Need something.* Clem cringed. That was too forward. Pushy even.

Odysseus sighed. "No—yes. It's just Reggie. He's coming back into town next month and I thought we'd throw him a little thing." *A little thing* had also been Sissy's way of describing the New Year's party she'd hosted last week: a five-hundred-guest gala with a seven-course meal and a million-dollar charity raffle. Between that and heading a prestigious law firm, she had covered everything her family could possibly want from her. And here was her younger brother, secretly dreading the fact that a promotion to senior associate would take him further away from the mundanity of routine lab duties and feeling burnt to hell and back from the few hours he'd spent at his family's holiday functions.

9

"Oh just a *little* thing, then." As he said it, he realized he'd sounded not only pushy but annoyed, too. In person he could have smiled it off, but now he was stuck. Would an *I'm just joking* work? Suddenly he couldn't recall if that was a thing people did.

The other end of the phone went quiet for a moment. "Are you all right, Clem?"

What a day. "Yes, fine. I'm great." Clem tried his best to grit his teeth and beam through the phone. "Dr. Blood is thinking of taking up my idea of a full night shift, and the drug we pushed to clinical trials last month is already giving us positive results."

"Which of the many drugs you won't tell me about is this?"

"Alas, I am sworn to secrecy."

"Still afraid I might steal your compounds for my law practice?"

"I just hope you never have to prosecute us." Clem finally pulled out of his *associate of the year* parking space, but all he could think of were Vitalis-Barron's cells full of vampires. If only they'd let him keep his phone during that tour…

Sissy laughed, all sparkling wine and biting logic. "Why I'd never. Conflict of interest! But you had better be working on something for my poor wrinkles. I'm thirty-seven and I look like the Grim Reaper. Not even the hot, boy toy version. It's disgusting."

Odysseus had presented as a hot, boy toy version of herself for most of her life, but the last five years she'd finally transitioned into a literal goddess instead. Their parents had initially put on a show of distress, but once Sissy proved that she was just as capable a businesswoman and lawyer as she had been while using her birth-assigned pronouns, they had grudgingly offered support. Really, Clem figured none of them should have been so shocked when the sibling who'd feminized what their parents had always claimed was a gender-neutral 'Odysseus' into 'Sissy' had turned out to be a girl. It was like the universe had programmed itself to fit her needs ahead of time.

Clem cringed. That was too harsh of him—the universe had put his sister through a fair helping of emotional and surgical trauma to get her to this place—but he still envied how optimistically and effortlessly she'd handled it all.

"Unfortunately no," he replied. "But we are working on a pill that takes away the headaches your old, decrepit sister gives you, and I plan to get a lot of use out of it."

"You are such a hoot." Sissy chortled. "Now, I have hot yoga to catch and a client at 9:30. You sleep well, Clem! Buh-bye."

The call ended before he could give his own farewell, which was for the best, since it sat a little sour on his tongue. At least this way he didn't have to deal with the eternally awkward back and forth of 'how many goodbyes is appropriate' and trying to figure out who should be the one to hang up.

As he pulled past the parking lot's security gate with a wave, his gaze caught on the guard's neck. He swore he could see the blood pounding beneath her skin. Calling to him. His stomach ached like a black hole and his fangs slipped free with such force that he had to struggle to pull them back in.

He could feel his empty fridge taunting him already, his last stolen blood bag finished this morning. Before he left for work next, he'd have to find a new source of blood, or else risk sinking his fangs into his Vitalis-Barron coworkers.

Which meant that Dr. Clementine Hughes, faltering phenomenon and broken vampire, would have to hunt his first human tonight.

2

JUSTIN

Justin Yu deserved this.

He had done such a significant number of things wrong in his life that he'd lost track, and now he was finally paying back his debt. There was, at least, no better community to be indebted to. The fourteen square blocks that composed Ala Santa were his home, and he had no desire to be free of them.

He loved the cracked pavement where the little weedy yellow flowers would pop up in the spring. He loved the tired apartment buildings sitting atop little old shops, weathered from years of life and love but still just as personable and unique as the day they'd first opened, the balconies above them draped in overgrown potted plants and a colorful array of flags with the occasional rope of drying laundry. He loved the chipped stucco and the murals that had been coated one atop another every decade since the walls had been built, and he loved that the little scattered graveyards tucked into the alleys and side streets were old enough to hold the immigrant great-grandparents of the people still cooking their family recipes and celebrating their traditions. He was even a little fond of the smell: every kind of grime mixed with the lingering wafts of frying oil and spices. It was the oldest and often the roughest part of San Salud, but it was—and always would be—home. After the hell he'd put it through in his youth, he owed it this penance.

Which was why, as the chronic pain between his shoulder blades mounted at the end of a long day of odd jobs, instead of returning to his apartment, he perched himself atop the large angel monument at the front of the micro-cemetery that felt more like home to him than his own apartment. He sat on the statue's shoulder, one leg lounging over its side and the other tucked against its unfurled wing. The individual feathers had been sculpted out in perfect detail once, but now most of them bled together, chipped and worn. He related to that.

As he smoked his back pain away with long puffs of his custom under-the-counter drug blend, he scanned the area for anything amiss. The sky was just darkening to purple, the old lamps from the main street casting everything they touched in a slightly golden hue while the alley, with its eternally broken lighting, remained dark and haunting. For the moment, everything seemed quiet—everything except the constant buzz from his phone. He swiped open the top string of text messages.

Isaiah
God I forgot how much I hate trains.

I know they're more efficient and America should build a bunch of them, but they're consistently overloud or weirdly quiet and people eat food in your presence.

Hello, batman, are you reading this?

Activating bat signal NOW!

(I would just like my misery acknowledged, that's all.)

Justin

Lmao you're so getting off on this.

You know I was tempted to not answer and see how long it takes your attention deficit to break my phone.

Isaiah

You are so rude.

And please don't kink shame me.

You know I get off on that too.

Justin refrained from continuing the gag, for both their sakes. But mostly Isaiah's. It wasn't fair to joke about the things they both knew Justin could never actually offer him.

Isaiah

I suppose flying comes with most of the same cons but at least it would have been faster. And Priscilla WAS willing to pay.

Justin

But they wouldn't have let you bring your blood. And I don't want you burning up in the sun if your plane gets delayed.

Isaiah

Yeah I do suppose that might have been a little bit inconvenient.

Justin

So how was the wedding?

Isaiah

It was nice! Pretty chill. The cake looked magnificent, I took so many pictures. Priscilla also looked good, I have lots of those pictures as well. (James was fine I suppose. Totally average. I still think Priscilla could have done better.)

Believing Priscilla could do better was ironic coming from the vampire who couldn't seem to accept that Justin wasn't worth his dedication. Soft and strong and more beautiful than was probably good for him, Isaiah could have had anyone. And Justin desperately wished he wouldn't waste his time pining for the worst option imaginable.

Justin had gone a decade without dating, and he'd keep that trend going as long as his neighborhood stood, his vampires walking the streets at night and his debt to them eternally unfulfilled.

Isaiah
I miss you, though.
My tall, dark, and lonely.

Justin's heart broke at the line. No one else would have called him lonely; no one else knew him that well. Dark, probably. Bitter, angry, and tense, absolutely. For all the penance he paid Ala Santa—and all they eagerly accepted from him—that darkness still remained. Maybe that was why the neighborhood could call his name in greeting and welcome him to their tables after he'd filled their fridges and cleaned up their streets, and he still felt like there was an invisible wall between himself and them. Despite their love and forgiveness, they were first and foremost the people he'd hurt in his youth, and their community was all that remained of the leader he'd taken from them. He had to make up for that before anything else.

Justin
Missing you too, tol.

He threw in the platonic Tagalog term of affection at the end for good measure, though he suspected that by now if Isaiah hadn't taken his hints—and more explicit denials—to heart, there was a chance he never would.

Justin

How are things going with your new suburban friends? Wes and Vincent?

Isaiah

Changing the topic on me I see.

It's not going anywhere since (a) I haven't been home, and (b) they have some asshole hunter who's trying to get to them through their contacts, so they're staying away from other vampires whenever possible right now. Besides, I was mostly just finding them vamps to offer their spare room to, which the hunter is complicating anyway.

Justin

Ah, that sucks. Keep me informed about the hunter though. If they come poking around here, I'll send them packing.

As he sent the message, three college-age teens slipped into the wide alley, looking shifty as they nudged each other. They huddled around the bike rack on the corner, two of them standing guard while the last knelt with a pair of pliers. One of them wore a shirt with the logo of the city's tiny but somehow still obnoxiously loud anti-vampire group.

They weren't his neighborhood kids—Justin would have recognized them if they were, and they would have known better than to try this kind of shit.

And they would have known to look up.

Justin

BRB found some punks.

Isaiah

Don't you dare.

Batman please.

You need to take a break already.

Next time our friends get married, you're going to come with me, even if I have to half-drain you and smuggle you onto a train in a duffel bag.

Don't think I won't do it!

Justin stopped reading, quietly sliding his phone back into his pocket. His joint had dimmed his usual nerve-tingling pain back down to a low, ignorable ache. It flared between his shoulder blades as he stretched out his back, highlighting the gnarled tissue around his spine, like he was some mythical fallen angel with severed wings. Symbolic, really.

"Faster!" one of the watching teens snapped.

Her kneeling companion scowled. "The blade's dull."

Justin stubbed out his joint and carefully perched the remaining coil of it in the angel's cupped palms. He leaped to the alleyway pavement, his black boots scuffing on the worn cement. A fresh flare of pain attacked his back as he straightened, but he grimaced through it.

Hooking both thumbs into his pockets, he barked, "I think that's quite enough."

The gazes of the three teens snapped toward him.

He made one hell of a sight in the waning light, he knew. His dark hair swept back from his tight, monolid eyes and his plethora of tattoos peeking out from the collar of his ripped denim jacket and descending across the back of his knuckles. He'd considered buying a mask just for these interactions. A cape too, maybe. Subtlety was not his style.

As the teenagers watched, he circled around them like a stalking tiger, scanning them up and down. "Now, I'm not against all theft—some people have so much more than they need, they won't even notice."

Justin knew the people who owned these bikes couldn't replace them so easily. Tai had saved up for that black sporty one for six months so he could ride it out to the lake to sketch the birds, and Roberto's rickety pink thing might have been a hand-me-down from his boyfriend's sister, but the collection of pride stickers he'd covered it with was all his. Justin himself had pitched in to buy the blue one for Ana Lee, the vampiric single mother of four who worked in the back of the Chinese bakery across the street.

"But if you steal from Ala Santa," he said, "It'll be the last thing you ever take."

The teenagers should have run. Most kids from the surrounding neighborhoods would have. But not these, wielding their Caucasian ancestry and designer labels like shields as their expressions hardened.

The teen with the dull chain cutter lifted it like a weapon. "Don't come any closer."

From the other end of the dim alley came a sound like a breathless curse. Justin ignored it.

"Some kind of initiation, is this? Or do you think you're being cool?" He was baiting them, of course. But some habits died hard, died like vampires, taking you down with them, bite after bleeding bite.

The punk with the anti-vampire shirt stormed forward like he was reenacting a scene from a movie, his grip on his chain cutter too high and tight, his feet too close together and his chin lifted in a way that was all ignorant courage. Justin stepped lazily to the side and knocked the kid across the jaw with his elbow. He tried not to put the full force of his considerable strength behind it, but he didn't try particularly *hard*. The punk toppled to his knees, and Justin shoved him back with a firm nudge from the ball of his foot.

The space between his shoulder blades shrieked at him for that, but he'd appease it with the rest of his joint shortly.

All three punks scrambled back, cursing. They glanced to the street, then at him. Movement came from deeper in the alley, the shifting of shadows so fast and subtle that by the time Justin glanced toward it, everything seemed fine again. Probably just a car coming down the little backstreet that ran behind the apartments.

He bared his teeth at the punks. Though they were flat and human, there was still something in the depths of every person that felt the danger in the threat of a bite, even from those who couldn't tear flesh or draw blood the way a werewolf or vampire might. It was incredible that smiles had

21

arisen in tandem—aggression and joy as interwoven concepts. He could still feel the lingering roots of that connection.

The teens finally did the smart thing and stumbled out of the alley, tripping over each other as they fled back down the street the way they'd come.

Justin relaxed. "And stay gone—"

He didn't get to finish his threat, because someone grabbed him from behind.

He was yanked by two fistfuls of his jacket, dragged roughly backward with the strength that only a nonhuman possessed. His instincts kicked in, jerking him free of the hold.

His attacker *hissed* a tight, hot, "Sorry," then gurgled like they'd tried to swallow the noise. They grabbed Justin again, and as they pushed him into the angel monument, he finally got a good look at the man.

Not a man at all, but a vampire, or possibly some Greek god incarnated into the wardrobe of a preppy English professor. His golden hair curled delicately around his angular face, and his slight nose wrinkled up as his lips pulled back to reveal thick, dagger-like fangs, large and sharp. He smelled lovely, like vanilla and almonds and a kind of wood only the wealthy bought. And Justin, pinned against a statue, had absolutely no right to be noticing *that* of all things.

Not that, and not how the vampire's Adam's apple bobbed as he swallowed, not the heat of his thigh pressing up the inside of Justin's, not the way his hand darted into

Justin's hair to push back his head, his gaze locked on Justin's throat. It was almost enough to drown out the ache in his back.

"I promise I won't kill you," the vampire muttered in that same hot, low voice.

Any second now, Justin was going to pull away. That was the reasonable thing to do when being cornered by a strange vampire in an alley. Any second now.

Any—

But as he reached his arms up, intending to knock the vampire's hold off and duck out from under him, those oversized fangs sunk into his skin and his world tilted. It had been over a decade since he'd let a vampire feed directly from him, and that day had been a nightmare of his own making, his anger and pain overflowing into the lives of those he loved in ways even his previous aggression and abuse hadn't managed. That time had felt nothing like *this*, this wave of dizzying bliss. It was just a toxin, he knew, a soothing agent to keep him calm and content in exactly the way he was caving to now, but it felt like lightning in his chest and a pleasant throbbing in a place that might have been his soul or might have just been his dick, like the rush of a first crush without any of the fear, like the victory of a well-fought battle without any of the blood or strain. It felt like the one thing he didn't even know he'd been missing from his life.

And then in a snap, it vanished.

The vampire let him go, jolting backwards. "How the hell am I supposed to do this?" he muttered, fingers floundering through his curls and setting them out of line in a way that only made him all the more breathtaking. "I can't—I just can't."

Justin slumped down the side of the statue onto the dirt, hissing from a wave of back pain. Blood trickled down the side of his neck. He pressed a palm to the bite. "Hey?" When it didn't have any effect, he raised his voice, "Hey!"

The vampire looked at him and somehow managed to pale even further in the twilight. "God, I have to, though." He drew in a breath, taking one step back toward Justin, then another. "I'm sorry, I really am. It'll only be a minute." He looked downright nauseous, but he sprang into a crouch in front of Justin with such speed that Justin could only flinch in response.

He tried to scramble away as the vampire lunged for his neck once more, but his back shrieked in pain, and he barely made it half a foot around the base of the angel monument. The vampire grabbed his collar again.

With the sky fully dark and the lamps from the street barely reaching into the alley, no one would see them tucked behind the hulking monument. If he wanted help, Justin could always shout for it, but he wouldn't dare endanger his neighbors. He dealt with Ala Santa's other problems himself; he would just deal with this one too.

This problem, however, didn't seem exactly sure what it wanted to be yet. The vampire appeared locked in place by a mixture of hunger and disgust, his fangs out and his breathing shallow, every muscle prepped to spring. But he didn't move. Didn't bite.

Taking the most straightforward approach possible, Justin asked, "What's wrong now?"

The vampire's brows drew together, and by the way he kept staring between Justin's eyes, it seemed as though he was trying *not* to look down. "Aren't you afraid?"

Justin probably should have been. Vampire attacks were rare, and when they happened they were often driven by an extreme hunger that impeded even the most upright vampire's sense of morals. But this particular vamp was conscious enough of his actions to keep staring at Justin in confusion. Justin grinned at him. "Afraid of what?"

He seemed to consider that for a moment. "I suppose, that I'll turn you? Or kill you?"

"I've got a genetic disposition against vampirism, and you just said you weren't planning to kill me."

"No—I—" The vampire paused, gnawing on the side of his cheek. His grip on Justin's collar loosened, and his thumb brushed the side of Justin's neck.

It made Justin think, ridiculously, of the vampire's fangs pressing into his veins, of the way it had felt.

The vamp shook his head, and for a moment he looked like nothing more than a scared, lost man. His attention leapt to Justin's neck, then away.

Justin sighed. "Are you going to eat me already?"

"Can I go find a straw?"

This was getting ridiculous. "Fuck it," he grumbled.

Finally letting go of his gently oozing wound, Justin wrenched free of the vampire's hold and shoved him back with both palms. He locked one fist in the vamp's vest—damn, that wool was soft—and spun them both, pinning the vampire on his ass against the back of the statue. The vampire's yelp drowned out Justin's own grunt of pain as his back protested. The vamp struggled. Justin held him fast, straddling his hips and locking his arms in place, using superior skill to make up for the fact that his pain was going to start fizzling at the corners of his vision if they had to keep this fight going much longer.

As the vampire seemed to realize he was trapped, he went still, tense and weary. His Adam's apple bobbed. Served him right for attacking someone in Justin's neighborhood. And for being that beautiful while doing it.

Justin was ridiculously tempted to grab him by the hair just so he could get his fingers in those golden curls. Instead, he bared his teeth, giving a hiss that could rival a vampire's. "Are you paying attention?"

"Yes," the vampire whispered, his gaze fixed on Justin's neck.

Justin could still feel the bite mark oozing there. "At this rate I'm going to lose all the blood I can spare if you don't at least close the fucking wound while you psych yourself up."

The vampire glanced away, then back. "And you'd like me to...?"

Justin couldn't tell if he was too embarrassed to say it or if it was a straight up question. "You've never done this before, have you?"

Vampires weren't known for their tight-knit dynamics the way the werewolves were rumored to be, but never had Justin met one who hadn't been informed of at least some part of the process by the vamp who turned them. The fact that this one seemed capable of biting in the first place was probably down to his instincts and nothing more. He was a baby, a vamp pup, a fresh turn.

"I'm getting the hang of it," the vampire muttered. "It's not my fault there's a learning curve." He sounded utterly put-out.

"Lesson one: when you do bite people—preferably people who consented to it first—lick the damn wound closed after."

"Okay." The vampire dragged in a breath then let it back out. He kept watching Justin's neck, leaning forward a little. Another breath, and a little closer. Another breath. Justin would be dead by the time this poor fool acted.

"If you don't, it's like sex with no orgasm."

The vampire jerked back hard enough that he smacked his head on the base of the monument. "Why would you compare it to that?"

Clearly, he'd also never been properly bitten before he was turned. Justin wanted to find the vampire responsible and string them up for their negligence. "Just lick it already."

"I'd really prefer not to. It's humiliating and unsanitary."

"You were the one who bit my neck in the first place!"

"I was desperate then."

Justin shoved him lightly into the monument once more, leaning in as he gripped the vampire's clothing—soft fabric and taut muscles beneath—until he was certain the vampire could feel his breath, his bleeding neck inches from the vamp's mouth. "I'm about to make you pretty damned desperate *now*."

"Please…" The vamp gave a whimpering sound. "This is all very uncomfortable."

"Fine." Justin let off a little. But not too much. The vampire deserved some discomfort. "Lick *my* fingers instead, I'll do it myself."

"God, no that's worse!"

Justin couldn't make out the vampire's exact skin tone well enough in the shadows of the alley, but he could have sworn he was blushing. "Can you at least lick your *own* fingers?"

"Not while you're sitting on my lap!"

Justin blinked. Quietly, he shifted backward, settling into the dirt in front of the vampire. It wasn't quite as nice, but it seemed to make the vamp relax a little. Justin sighed. "Better?"

"Yes. Thank you."

"And *now* can you…?"

In response, the vampire pressed both his fingers to his own tongue in the least sexual way imaginable. "Li' 'is?"

God, why was Justin still finding it hot? Was this vampire that beautiful, even half in the dark, or had Justin just become *that* much of a lonely, self-denying asshole? On second thought, he didn't want that question answered. "Like that, yes. Now press them to my neck."

The vampire did as he was told, so calculating and clinical that Justin could almost believe that the way he stared at the wound as he did so was a purely professional experience and not born of a terrible hunger. There was something ethereal about his poised precision, like he was one of the legendary immortal vampires that had only ever been a myth. That was, until he pulled the fingers away, a smear of blood on them, and plopped them directly back into his mouth.

Now *that* was *absolutely* sexy.

Justin closed his eyes, trying to crush down the image before it could do unhelpful things to his dick. Too late. He groaned internally.

They stared at each other.

The vampire's gaze traveled back toward Justin's neck again, and he shook his head, shoving himself to his feet fast enough that he bumped his shoulder into the lowest edge of the angel's wings. Justin stood too, trying not to jar his back as he did. He held out his hand to steady the vampire. The vamp waved him off. They both stared at each other, tense and awkward in a way that made Justin want to bare his teeth again, whether as a threat or an invitation, he wasn't sure.

At the front of the alley, the bike rack rattled as Ana Lee tugged open her lock. The pudgy vampire glanced once down the alley, and when she found their silhouettes in the gloom, she looked momentarily startled, before smiling wide enough to press her eyes nearly shut. "Goodnight, Justin," she called.

"Say hello to the twins for me," he returned as she pulled back onto the street.

Three cars passed behind her before the strange vampire finally spoke.

"Should I keep apologizing? Because I most certainly can."

"I'd rather have a name from you, seeing as you did put your fangs in me. Though if you hadn't been so fucking apologetic"—and goddamned beautiful—"we'd be having a very different conversation right now, so kudos."

"Of course, yes, sorry. I'm Clementine." He held out his hand—the one he'd licked the fingers on, Justin noted, though he wasn't sure why his brain went there. "Dr. Clementine Hughes."

"Justin Yu." He locked his hand with the vampire's and pulled him closer as he added, "If you go hunting on my streets again one of us *will* end up dead, and it won't be me."

"Right. Sorry. It won't happen again." Clementine chuckled, but it sounded off-kilter and he wiggled himself out of Justin's touch.

Good. Justin wanted the vampire reasonably afraid of him. Every potentially dangerous party who entered his neighborhood should be. "How did you end up here in the first place?"

"I tried to pick an inner-city area between my home to the south and my work near the financial district. I'm heading there after—to work, I mean. In hindsight, my appearance makes me stand out a bit."

Justin gave his outfit another once over. Even in the dark, his silhouette was obviously fancier than most Ala Santa residents outside of Sunday services. "A bit, yeah. And you thought you'd just snack on someone in a dark alley and leave after?"

"If you could direct me to the nearest convenience store that stocks blood, I'd be more than happy to—"

"Right, okay, you don't have a lot of options, I get that."

"Indeed." Tension twisted in Clementine's shoulders as he crossed his arms. "Well this has been... informative. Thank you." His gaze shifted to Justin's neck, then away.

"You're still hungry."

"Yes, well, I haven't gotten a full blood meal since I turned." The smile that tugged at his thin lips had an edge to it. "One more day won't kill anyone."

"It better not," Justin said, and like the rest of his existence, it came out harsher than he meant it.

Clementine grimaced. He pushed his hands into his pockets, his chin held high. "I suppose this is where I leave and never come back?"

That should have been exactly what Justin wanted from him—a rich, prissy vampire who knew so little that he was a danger to those around him, with a tall, poised presence that was all kinds of distracting. Justin should have nodded and told the vamp to scat.

But he was here, in Ala Santa, and any vampire in Ala Santa had been Jose Mendoza's once, to nurture and protect, before Justin had let his self-centered teenage rage and pain take him over and he'd ruined that for all of them.

So while he stood in these streets, that made the vampire Justin's instead.

Justin glanced back at the bike rack and thought of Ana Lee and the dozens of others in Ala Santa he wished he could do more for, vampires and humans alike. Maybe they could both win tonight: this vampire pup and the neighborhood he'd dared hunt in. Clementine Hughes did look wealthy; soft, high-end clothes and luscious hair and that self-assured, almost pretentious way he spoke, like he'd been spit right out of a prestigious university with a hotrod and a ten-million-dollar loan from his parents. Justin could use money like that. All of Ala Santa could.

Clementine seemed to interpret his hesitation as a farewell, taking a few steps backward.

"Wait," Justin called.

The vampire lifted one brow. "Did you forget to reprimand me for something else?"

Was that *sarcasm*? It was so hard to tell. Justin put on a smile, which he was pretty sure just read as another baring of teeth, equally threatening as any that had come before it. "I have a proposition for you."

Clementine looked suspicious. "Yes?"

"You have money, I have blood." Justin widened his grin. "How would you like to buy it?"

3

CLEMENTINE

This was not going as intended. Which was hard for someone who had formed shockingly little of a plan in the first place. What he'd landed on had been a mix between logic and fanfiction—neither of which were reliable sources of vampire lore, but trusting them was preferable to googling five variations of 'how do vampires find blood' and having hunters appear at his door twelve hours later.

All he'd needed to do, really, was find a human a bit off his beaten trail, tucked away enough that he wouldn't immediately be spotted, and take a bite. One bite. A few minutes of feeding. Clementine felt like a monster just for considering it, but with how distracting the veins of everyone around him were becoming, he figured he had to get this over with while he was still in control of his body. And, somewhere in the back of his mind, he couldn't quite put aside the idea that this would be like the start of the tragic vampire x human fic he'd stumbled onto once for the Chekov and Sulu Star Trek pairing. Logic didn't exactly contradict that—mouth-to-skin and chest-to-back with a good-looking stranger while trading them intoxication for blood—that had to be just a little bit sexual, right?

But then he'd put his mouth on the man's neck—on Justin's neck—and it had been the exact sum of its parts: his mouth touching the flesh of a random person, a potentially grimy person, weirdly tepid and gross and uncomfortable in a hundred ways he hadn't even known to anticipate. At least it wasn't as terrible as kissing, even if there was still a foreign bodily fluid involved. Altogether, the whole experience should have led to Clementine fleeing back to his car and having a ten-hour breakdown while debating a full identity change just to be sure Justin never found him again.

Instead he was being given the offer of a lifetime.

Buy Justin's blood.

Clementine stared at him—this man who smelled and tasted human but had strength to rival Clem's vampiric enhancements—and tried not to openly gawk. "You'd like to sell me your blood?"

Clementine lifted his fingers to his hair, then pulled them back down as he realized how anxious and confused that made him look. Which was, ironically, less anxious and confused than he actually felt.

His voice rough, he asked, "Isn't that illegal?"

"Are you planning to tell any cops about it?"

Clementine was planning on telling absolutely no one, seeing how no one in his life knew he was a vampire to begin with. "Would it come in a bag, or will I be biting you directly?"

"I'll need the venom from your bite to regenerate my blood. Besides, you shouldn't carry bags of it through the city. That's also illegal without the right permits."

"Right." Clem glanced out of the alleyway to the scattering of pedestrians and the gentle stream of cars. At least no one had bothered them, here in the darkness. That was where monsters lived, after all. "People hate vampires. How could I forget."

Perhaps hate was too strong a word. It was mostly indifference. Indifference in the face of systematic oppression, and acceptance of all the benefits that provided them. And Clem had been one of those indifferent humans, had been too preoccupied to notice how much of their pervasive ideology had entrenched itself into daily life, all the ways they made traditional schooling impossible for vampires and jobs harder to secure and keep, made blood so difficult to acquire that even with all Clementine's money and connections, here he was now, illegally buying it in the street. From what Sissy had told him, even prosecutions and death counts were higher for vampires. Humans were victims. Vampires were asking for it. A tale as old as bigotry itself.

Now in the roil of his thirsty gut and the constant subtle fear of discovery that wracked his bones, he'd been forced to remember his society's distaste for vampires twenty-four seven; no weekends, no vacations. Not that he took vacations outside the five-day trips Reginald and Odysseus dragged him on every few years, and those were generally less relaxing than his job, because Reggie and Sissy were determined to force all three of them through a ridiculous number of loud and chaotic activities that left Clementine locking himself in the bathroom whenever he could get away with it. They were both convinced he had IBS.

"What does blood run, then? Eleven? Twelve?"

Justin laughed, a short, harsh sound that matched so much of him a little too perfectly. "Dollars?"

"Hundreds," Clem clarified with a grimace. "Am I way off?"

"Oh, no, blood *is* expensive," Justin grumbled. He seemed to consider something, a thoughtful dip in his brow. "Fifteen hundred a pint should do nicely. We can't really measure it, but that's about ten days' worth of regular feedings for a vamp your size."

Fifteen hundred, paid every ten days. Clementine felt nauseous as he did the math. He had paid off his new car in full just before he'd turned, which left his savings quite diminished. If he used what he was putting monthly into that account, along with the surplus he usually funneled to one of Odysseus's favorite charities, he'd be able to afford half a dozen pints from the money he still had lying around. After that, he'd be down to two a month, and the same incessant hunger he was fighting now.

Unless he asked his parents to pitch in. They had loaned Odysseus the money for her firm's startup, and Reginald had run off globe-trotting with his full inheritance during his sophomore year of college—and was now making it back twice over. If Clementine asked for funds though, they would want to see something come out of it, and he doubted a 'vampiric lifestyle' qualified.

But there was the senior associate position coming up. That pay raise would heft him nicely into the necessary three pints a month, with a bit of change still left over. And with a consistent supply of fresh blood keeping his mind sharp, getting the promotion was far more likely.

"Fifteen hundred a pint," Clementine confirmed. He could feel venom fill his fangs as he thought of it, no rationing or weaning down: just as much blood as he needed, when he needed it. He glanced at the main street once more—same calm stream of passersby happy to ignore their little alley where the lights were all out.

Justin seemed to catch onto his worry with an unusual speed and an even more unusual compassion. "We're hidden enough here. You're safe."

Clementine nodded. He wasn't sure he believed it, but he closed the distance between them all the same, each step back into the darkness making him feel a little less like a businessman and a little more like a predator. He could smell Justin's drying blood, and despite all his higher senses telling him it was about as enticing as plain, tepid oatmeal, it still drew him in. He didn't mean for his voice to go so breathless, but there it was, parched and husky as a desert with a thirst. "I think this is where you give me your vein."

Justin's throat bobbed. "Do you mind if I finish my smoke while you bite?"

Whatever the man was putting into his body, the blood-to-drug content would likely be minuscule, and Clem would be drinking relatively little of the stuff. "Be my guest."

Justin plucked something small and long from the angel's cupped fingers. He ignited the end with his lighter before motioning to the ground. "Sit. It'll be more comfortable for you."

Clementine obeyed, settling at the monument's feet once more.

For all of Justin's earlier agility while fighting, he lowered himself down like an old man. The streetlamps cast one side of his face in a golden glow, leaving sullen shadows on the other. His thick brow curved like little shark fins, and his soft features turned hauntingly pointed in the harsh lighting. A few delicate tattoos peeked from beneath the collar of his shirt. His slim eyes were piercing, not just from the richness of their brown but from the sheer depths of expression in them. Clementine didn't have to want him sexually in order to notice.

"Wrist all right?" Justin asked, startling Clem out of his daze.

Clem nodded. He took Justin's extended arm as gingerly as he could. His jean jacket was tough, and Clem rolled the cuff back methodically, his fingers gliding into Justin's palm and over the lines of delicate tribal ink that traced along his wrist. He almost dropped the man's hand entirely when Justin's thumb grazed the back of his knuckles.

Clementine breathed in, then out, and lifted Justin's wrist to his mouth.

He could feel the moment his fangs broke skin, the way Justin tensed, then loosened as the venom hit his system. Blood slipped across Clem's tongue. It wasn't that bad, truly—just bland and a little thick, with a chemical aftertaste—and his body responded to it so desperately that it kept his fangs engaged and his mouth gently sucking against Justin's skin. Drinking it warm was certainly better than the cold bagged stuff. Still, the constant reminder that there was flesh beneath his lips and a heartbeat pumping the blood to him made his stomach twist.

As soon as Clem began wondering if it was time to stop, an odd tingle of satisfaction sprung in the back of his mind. He almost pulled away out of habit, but his instinct took over, urging him to lick his tongue along the little fang marks.

Justin *sighed*.

Clementine dropped the man's hand. He wiped two fingers over his lips to check for anything unsavory on them, and swallowed the final remains of the blood in his mouth.

Digging out his wallet, he quickly counted his hundreds. He held the bundle out. "I only have seven on me. I'll bring the rest during the next ten days."

Justin lowered his joint and released a wave of oddly-scented smoke as he took the cash. It was the same almost sweet chemical smell that lingered on him and tickled at the edges of his blood. "Taste was okay?" He sounded oddly hopeful.

The back of Clementine's mind told him to lie, to say what the man wanted to hear and not have to deal with the backlash if he didn't approve, but then he reminded himself that he was a vampire buying blood in an alley, and Justin would keep selling to him regardless. "Honestly, you taste perfectly average. Commendably regular."

He seemed genuinely disappointed. "Sorry about that. I thought maybe…" He shrugged. "Usually vamps don't care what their bagged blood tastes of, since they can just mix it with other things."

Clementine wasn't sure why it shocked him so much, and he was embarrassed that he'd spent so many months drinking his stolen blood cold and bland, straight from a shot glass.

"But feeding directly from a human," Justin continued, "is a… it's an intimate thing, for both parties. That's why most vampires don't do it unless they have a partner. That, and having your fangs in someone leaves your back exposed. I imagine it's a much nicer experience when you actually like your food."

Clementine could not tell whether he meant *like* as in taste bud enjoyment or a crush, and frankly he didn't want to know. "It's been three months and no blood I've tasted has been particularly great. I wasn't expecting anything better." Twenty-nine years and no lips had ever tasted right, either. That connection made his stomach sink. Maybe *he* was the problem, not the blood. He was *not* broken, he tried very hard to believe that, but with so many cards stacked against him…

Justin's brow tightened. "You've been like this for months, and you've never fed on a human?"

"I had a source at a blood bank until now."

"And you've been alone all this time?"

"I'm not alone. I have kept up a full and pleasant life since turning."

"That's not what I meant."

Clementine knew that well enough, thank you. But what Justin had meant hit too close to home. Because Clem *had* been alone, not just without another vampire to guide him, but without anyone that he felt comfortable enough telling he'd been turned. He had his family, his coworkers, a few online friends from the Star Trek fandom, yet he had no one he trusted to see his pain in this, to wipe his tears, to give him stoic, logical comfort the way Spock would for Kirk, or shout and cry for him the way Kirk would for Spock.

Clementine was alone in every way that truly counted. Everything in him screamed to hide that fact, to not let this bizarre, beautiful man—this man who'd been attacked by Clementine only to turn around and offer his own blood as salvation—know that Clem was this pitiful. Yet there was also something about Justin, or perhaps simply about the way they'd met, how Justin had already seen Clementine desperate and out of his comfort zone and still offered him help, that made it feel like, for once, maybe he could let on how he was feeling. At least a little.

"It's been… rough." There, see, he'd done it. Emotional vulnerability.

"No wonder you're hopeless." Justin laughed. "Clementine the lemon. Cuh-*lemon*-tine."

Actually, fuck emotional vulnerability, Clem could *feel* the blood draining from his face. "Oh god."

"Don't worry, Lemon, my puns will only grow more disastrous from here." But as Justin watched him, he blinked, the humor sliding off his face. "I thought it was a funny nickname, kind of cute I guess, but if it bugs you—"

Ignore it; Clementine should just ignore it. Finish their interaction and pretend that nothing fazed him. But it did faze him. Too many blows at once and he'd tumble. "It's the context, you know—lemons are duds, and I've been a dud of a vampire, I admit, but I'm not usually as hopeless as all that."

In the dim alley under the distant shine of the streetlights, Justin stared at him like he was picking apart each wrinkle and fault and insecurity with his gaze alone. Like he was trying to see into Clementine's soul.

"I don't really know you, Clementine," he said finally. "But I imagine there are lots of things you're pretty damn great at. And if no one taught you how to be a vampire, it's not like you can be expected to understand everything it entails all on your own. Hell, there are vampires who've been around the block and back but are still figuring their shit out.

Humans too. That's just living, I think." He smiled. "I didn't mean to imply you *were* a lemon. But if you were, I don't believe there's anything wrong with that either."

"That's..." Something welled in Clementine's chest, thick and warm. "Thank you. I suppose this nonsense with turning has just left me feeling, perhaps, a bit like... like..."

"A bit like you're making a mess of something, and anyone else would have known better?"

The perfect way Justin encapsulated his feelings took his breath away, a gut punch and a moment of wonder. "Exactly like that."

Justin shrugged. "Some people enjoy a good lemon, you know? How else do you get lemonade?"

"Oh, so now I'm not useless, just sour?"

"You make my lips pucker, Lemon." Justin pursed his lips dramatically at the end.

Clem snorted. This felt... almost comfortable? The way he imagined being teased was meant to, like an inside joke instead of a barb. "I'm going to pretend that was not an innuendo."

"That's fair, it wasn't particularly good anyway." A smirk slipped across Justin's face. "Be careful though, if you pretend too much, you may become a tangerine."

"Now *that* was abysmal and you should be ashamed of yourself."

"Oh, I am." His face fell as he repeated the words, much softer, his gaze sliding away from Clementine. "I am."

Clementine's gut reaction was to bring the old smirk back. "It *is* a cute nickname, in the proper context. Usually people simply call me Clem, which is far more boring." He couldn't believe the words coming out of his mouth, but somehow he meant them. "I think I can bear the shame of being a lemon, for once."

Justin perked back up. "You're sure?"

"Absolutely."

"Lemon it is, then." His sharp grin returned as he said it, and it felt as though the world had been set back into place. Clementine wanted to keep it that way, and he was oddly happy to realize that he would get the chance. A lot of chances indeed, if his feeding schedule had anything to say about it.

"I think *this* is where you give me your phone number." He only realized how much it sounded like a line from a fanfic *after* he'd said it, and he was almost not embarrassed by that connection, except that the specific fanfic line it sounded like was far too flirty for his intentions.

And Justin was staring at him again. "Ansabe?"

Was that English? "Your number, so we can arrange our next meeting. Does every other night work? That should be often enough to keep my hunger at bay."

"Right. Yes, that's fine." Justin retrieved a business card from his wallet. He handed it over between two fingers, like he was passing a joint.

Justin Yu, it read, then *Ala Santa* with a phone number. No job description. On the back a gorgeous but raggedy pair of wings had been sketched.

Justin laughed. "A friend made them for me as a joke. They come in handy, though."

"Thank you." Clementine stood, wiping his hands on his vest. His whole outfit would be going in the wash immediately. "Well, have a good night." After all that had happened in such a short time, there should have been something more significant to say.

But Justin seemed happy with it, his smile brighter and a little less bitter than before. "Goodnight, Lemon. I'll see you again soon."

And for the first time in a long time, Clementine found he genuinely wanted that.

4

JUSTIN

Those few blissful minutes of Clementine's feeding still lingered like a soft buzz in the back of Justin's mind. That was the best money he'd ever made, even easier than what he'd stolen and beaten for in his teenage years, and the first half of the payment was already more cash than he'd held at one time since he'd developed a conscience. That conscience bucked, reminding him that he was vastly overcharging Clementine in order to make this much. But what the vampire didn't know wouldn't hurt him.

And some of that money could buy blood for the vampires in Justin's neighborhood, few of whom had human partners to support them, while still allowing Clementine to get the help he needed.

Help, and nothing more, Justin reminded himself. However hot the vampire was and however much Justin relished his bite, he would have to keep their interactions purely professional. He was in no place for anything else.

Justin leaned against the wall to finish his joint, pulling up a short cooking video on his phone to give his brain something to focus on that didn't have fangs and luscious curls. By the time the YouTuber's cake sat on their counter, the final twinges of pain between his shoulder blades had turned back to an ignorable ache. It wasn't as dulled as he would have liked, but he could survive for a few more hours before sparing another dose. The amount he had already been forced to smoke this week meant the bony tumors around his spine were worsening. A bitter taste roiled in his mouth.

Justin swallowed it down and headed for the little family-run convenience store on the next block.

As he stepped inside, he still swore that he could catch the decade-old whiff of Jose Mendoza's cologne. Justin could almost believe that the middle-aged vampire would appear from behind a shelf, his smile bright and his heart open regardless of how many times teenage Justin had used him as a punching bag for his growing aggression—the one person he knew he could plant a metaphorical knife in over and over again and never break. If only he'd kept to metaphorical ones, hadn't tried to remove his pain by inflicting it on someone else. Someone his arrogant young mind had sworn would never perish beneath it. Then maybe his own heart wouldn't crack and ache like this, his voice breaking for just an instant before he managed to shove it into something reasonably cheery.

"Mrs. Mendoza!"

The old, squat woman with wrinkled brown skin glanced up from her romance novel. She formed a grin that always reminded Justin of a fox, or possibly an imp—something small and devious and entirely too lovable. She'd forgiven him for her son's death, no matter how many times he'd made it clear that she shouldn't. "Mister you-stocked-the-top-shelves-wrong!" she teased. "How dare you walk in here with that look? Shame. Go away, we're closed."

Justin knew better than to obey her; if he left in the next ten minutes he'd be hearing about it for weeks. "Then what would I do with this?" He asked instead, slipping a worn paperback out of his jacket and salaciously flashing the cover. The two illustrated women on the novel posed in traditional illustrated romance fashion, one of them peeling off the other's historically inaccurate but lavishly pretty dress while making an orgasmic expression.

The wrinkles around Mrs. Mendoza's eyes accumulated as they narrowed. "You bring that here this instant."

"Are you sure? I could leave. You do seem awfully busy." Justin motioned to the empty store.

Mrs. Mendoza scoffed. "Only because you stock the top shelves wrong!"

"A ladder would fix that."

"Why buy a ladder when I have you?"

She had him, and not Jose. She'd tell him he was wrong to think like that. And one of them certainly *would* be wrong, but it wouldn't be him. He handed over the book. "I can't stay, I just need a few things."

"Bah," the old woman grunted. She folded a tissue into her first book in order to take the new one with a

49

mischievous grin, setting it on the shelf behind her where her late son and husband's photos stood surrounded by those of her close friends and extended family. Justin had stolen the pictures of himself from the collection twice before realizing it was futile.

As he filled his basket with eight people's worth of meal supplies and a heaping number of nonperishables, he found a worn set of salt and pepper shakers tucked in the top shelf of aisle three, wearing a 99 cent price tag. No one else in Ala Santa would spend that on an oddball set of eclectic crabs with top hats, but it wasn't about the monetary cost; it was the fact that Mrs. Mendoza had seen them somewhere, knew he'd want them, and was letting him accept them the only way he knew how. He returned with them wrapped securely between the toilet paper, a box of diapers tucked under one arm, and pressed two of Clementine's hundreds across the counter. "No change."

She clicked her tongue, but she slipped the bills into the register without question. If she was determined to forgive him, this was his penance. "You want to hear the gossip?" She asked.

"It's not gossip if they know you're going to tell me."

"You're a busybody—it's gossip." She clicked her teeth. "They're saying there's a suspicious woman with holy silver asking questions about the vampires in the neighborhoods around us. Marcus, he hid from her in a bar bathroom coming home last night! So unsanitary!"

"Mrs. Mendoza! Marcus could have been killed, and you didn't text me?"

"Do not Mrs. Mendoza me, anak. Could be nothing." She looked pointedly at him, emphasizing the familiar term in a way that just served to remind him of the real son he'd taken from her. "You *worry* over nothing." And like this really was just the daily gossip, she plunged on to her next topic. "There is lunch after mass on Sunday. You will be there?"

"To the lunch? Absolutely."

Mrs. Mendoza harrumphed his exclusion of mass itself, but she didn't press it.

Justin wasn't ready to be pushed on that yet. As though the crimes of his younger life weren't enough, the wider religion had disowned him for the perceived worse sin of being interested in anyone who wasn't a cis woman. Someday, perhaps, with a congregation that was more affirming, and a soul he wasn't half convinced would burn in hell for reasons completely outside his sexuality, he'd be ready to sit in the pews again, but that day was still years off, if it came at all. Until then, he was happy to quietly believe alone and on his own terms. Of all the aunties who chided him to attend, at least Mrs. Mendoza, as a late-blooming lesbian who'd discovered her sexuality years after her husband passed, understood that.

The fussing over it was just her way.

"Well, you come," she said finally. "We will feed you."

"I am a grown man, po. If you tell me I'm too skinny—"

"Jesusmariosep! You are a child. A skinny child, who can't stock a shelf!"

Justin sighed and shook his head, but his smile remained. "Goodnight, Mrs. Mendoza."

"Bring me another of these books, hah?" she shouted after him.

He laughed. "I always do!"

The humor didn't last through the door though as he juggled a packed grocery bag in each arm. His back only protested a little. It always protested at least that much.

His mind funneled back to the woman with the holy silver who was apparently stalking Ala Santa's outskirts. There was always some shithead or aspiring vampire hunter poking their head around the inner city. Most were punks much like the ones he'd scared off earlier. With holy silver at her disposal though, this woman could do real damage to the vampires she came across.

A number of vampires *had* been vanishing from the city at an alarming rate over the last few decades. Someone out there clearly knew exactly what they were doing and had been doing it with intent. It seemed he'd have to add in a few additional hours of patrolling tonight. The thought felt a little daunting, but it was his job—his sentence—regardless of the wear and tear. He'd just have to fit it in after the groceries he'd be handing out and the stop he planned to make at Ana Lee's to help her cook. He'd try to pick her up a blood smoothie on the way; she'd looked pale earlier, and he knew her bag from last week was getting low.

Then Isaiah was getting back, and Justin had wanted to chat with him in person. *Not* to tell him about Clementine. Nothing was going to happen between him and the rich, if devastatingly hot, vampire, not the least of which was because of people like this hunter for whom he now had to watch out. Fighting people like her was the only physical contact he could allow himself the time for.

And if she stepped foot into his neighborhood, she'd find that Ala Santa's vampires weren't so defenseless as the rest.

5

CLEMENTINE

For the first time in months, Clementine went a full evening of work without his fangs trying to slip free or his gaze pulling to the nearest exposed vein. He could focus again, and it was doing wonders for his productivity. If things continued like this, he might even get his life back on track, reviving its upward momentum, born of his sweat and labor and not marred by a ridiculous accident that hadn't been his fault in the slightest.

Because his turning *hadn't* been his fault, it couldn't have been. And he would keep believing that.

If only all his problems were so easily solvable. Avoiding the sunlight would only grow harder as the spring approached, and his body reacted poorly to takeout now, along with many of his frozen and pre-packaged meals and his favorite brand of chicken strips. The one ingredient they all, hilariously, had in common was garlic, but Clementine hadn't felt comfortable testing for how much his body could consume without a reaction—and whether those reactions would get worse or better with exposure. Perhaps Justin could help him with that...

Clem slipped out of his shoes at the door to his apartment and opened his texts again, as though this time he'd actually write something. 'Dear Justin Yu, I am sincerely a lemon, and I have no idea what I'm doing.' It was insane that he'd even consider that kind of admission. But his lack of ability still felt a little safer with Justin—with someone who had no other connections to Clem's work or family and no bearing on his life, someone who had already seen him fail miserably once and seemed to think no less of him.

Still, Clementine's fingers froze over the keys.

He'd just ask in person. Or he'd not ask in person, and he'd keep living as he was until he died. They both seemed like equally agreeable options to him, or equally miserable ones at least.

Clem flicked through the rest of his notifications as he meandered along the hallway, dropping his keys in their place on the end table and his jacket over the hook on his bedroom door where yesterday's already hung. He answered the work emails that had come since leaving the lab, fretting over his wording in the final one to Dr. Anthony Hilker for ten minutes before finally sending it. The man was so hard to read these days, with his constant weirdly-specific probing and comments about Vitalis-Barron's scientific impact, like he perhaps didn't quite believe in what they were doing to the vampires on their lowest basement level. Like he was trying to tell Clementine something. Or convince Clem to tell it to *him*.

He shuddered.

Shifting his focus, he replied to Sissy's new pictures of the crows in her backyard with a smiling emoji and a *do they attack your enemies yet?*, then his mother's newest inquiry into his not-yet-happening promotion with an explanation on how the current senior associate was still in the process of retiring. His mother knew his boss better than he did—she would be well aware that Dr. Viktoria Blood would fill the position in her own time and no amount of ass-kissing could change that. No matter what he told his mother, though, she would follow up with a million pointed questions that made his lack of promotion his own fault, until his father also chimed in through the same group chat with an inspirational story about how Clem's grandfather had done twice what Clementine hadn't managed yet, but in half the time.

He grabbed a beer from the fridge. At least he could bet that Grandpa Hughes had never successfully immersed himself in writing alternate universe, werewolf-inspired Star Trek romance so completely that he'd forgotten his drink in favor of the tension between Kirk and Spock as an earthquake trapped them in a malfunctioning elevator during heat. It was his pre-bed routine for the days when he came straight home from work, but he needed this now more than ever; needed to vicariously live through Kirk and Spock as they felt their crush's movements like they were tuned exclusively for each other; the subtle tug of lips, the pulse of a jaw, the weight of each other's breaths, the scent of their lust thick in the stale air.

Despite everything that life hadn't seen fit to give Clementine—namely any sort of attraction of his own—he still wanted that. He wanted it so bone-deep that he'd never felt comfortable identifying as strictly asexual; even if he'd never had those feelings, he yearned for them. He wanted to feel that nearly-irresistible draw to another real person the way he did to fictional characters, to have his gaze pulled to them not because of the blood in their veins but because it was *their* blood, because their body called to him and their soul clicked with his. He wanted to *want* someone.

A soulmate.

Or, at least the kind of person could be that for him in a soulmate alternate universe fic.

He thought about Justin Yu. Perhaps the man was a bit gruff and rude and bitter going down, yet the aftertaste of him—not his blood, but the impression that lingered in Clem's thoughts—was something bright and soft. Licking closed the little fang marks on his wrist had felt almost natural, despite the fact that it was a complete stranger's flesh under his tongue. Tender, vulnerable flesh that Justin had trusted Clementine with. The man had sighed after, like it was a treat instead of a tax. And he'd offered Clementine genuine kindness after Clem had been an asshole and a fool.

Justin was someone well worth wanting.

And yet Clementine felt... nothing.

At least, not physically, and not with a flutter in his chest, not for his more or less average blood. All they had between them, from Clementine's side anyway, was the early forming of a friendship. It hurt just how strongly that disappointed him.

Regardless of his feelings—or lack thereof—for his new prey, Clementine's stomach still buzzed with anxiety as he climbed into his car two evenings after his first meeting with Justin. He pulled his scarf like a hood over his head, put down his car's sun visor flaps, repositioned the oversized beach umbrella poking onto his console, and forced himself to drive. Despite the fabric's protection, he still shook faintly by the time he'd parked. Sharp twinges of pain shot through his muscles as he walked down the twilight streets toward their alley meeting point. Sun exposure worked like that: about thirty minutes after, the effects would finally hit him. Some kind of delayed metabolism, the light producing a compound beneath his skin that then needed time to be converted into the poison that now ached in his joints. Which meant that someone could, theoretically, produce a medication to prevent it.

If anyone actually cared about helping vampires, instead of using them as lab rats.

For how often—and horribly—Vitalis-Barron was doing research *on* vampires, there was so much research that no one was doing *for* vampires. Hell, no one even knew what in a human's blood was so necessary for vampires to live, or whether there might be a way to synthesize it. No one in research positions bothered to care, and those who could didn't have the funding.

But Clem didn't want to think about that right now, not Vitalis-Barron's basement with its hungry, hollow-eyed vampires or Anthony's constant check-ins or the mysterious way he'd turned. Which obviously meant his brain was on an imminent spiral down that path.

He was saved by a call of, "Lemon!"

Justin sat atop the angel monument, one leg hiked up and the last stub of a smoking joint dangling from his fingers. He bared his teeth in a smile that held more threat than joy. The collar of his rugged jean jacket had been pulled up, and it would have covered his tattoos if not for the way he'd unbuttoned its front down to the base of his low V-neck, revealing slim tribal-style ink in delicate, geometric lines that gave an almost lacy appearance from a distance. A long chain with a silver crucifix on the end bounced against his sternum. His grin widened as Clem's gaze rose to meet his.

Fuck. How was he this lovely, yet Clem's heart did nothing? It *did* nothing, right? He searched for even the slightest hint of targeted longing, and felt only the hollow sense that he was meant for more than this.

Justin landed quietly as a cat beside him, clapping him on the shoulder. Clem looked away, but he could still feel the tingle of the momentary contact amidst his light shaking. His head swam. Curse that damn sun-exposure, making his body so overly sensitive.

Justin steadied him with a firmer touch, more solid this time. "Easy," he said, low and rough. "Did you drink enough last time? You can take more if you need it."

"No it's—" Clementine shook his head. It was kind of Justin; not just the offer but to see that Clementine was struggling and provide help instead of judgment. "Too much sun, I think. But thank you."

As Justin let him go, his signature smile appeared again, bitter and dangerous. It seemed to put Clem back together with the same speed it dismantled him. "The blood will help with that," Justin said, waggling his wrist in front of Clementine's mouth.

"You don't have to taunt me," Clementine grumbled, grabbing his arm, his strength turning the motion more aggressive than he'd meant it.

Justin laughed. He came closer, re-angling his body as Clem leaned over the tender flesh at the base of his palm.

His fangs slipped free like they'd been waiting for this moment for two days—and however much Clem had been dreading all the ways he might make a fool of himself again, and the blandness of the blood, and the fact that he had to put Justin's flesh in his mouth to receive it—he had also been anticipating this. Hoping, just a little, that it would be nicer than his first feeding. That it would be like the fairytales, or the horror stories anyway: the vampire craving the delicacy of a certain human's blood until the desire consumed them or they consumed the human. A ruthless, dangerous lust, but lust all the same.

In the dimming twilight, Clem's eyes floundered between the monochrome of his vampiric night vision and the distant glow of the streetlamps blinking to life on the much busier main street. The lights shone down on a few pedestrians passing, cars and bikes beyond them, a woman yelling at a teenager on a skateboard and a small gaggle of elementary kids with backpacks. The lights in the alley themselves were off again tonight, or perhaps just broken, but Clementine still tucked himself behind the bulk of the angel monument, hiding them both from view.

He cradled Justin's wrist just as carefully as their first time, but less scared, less awkward. When he'd last bitten Justin, he hadn't taken a good look at the lines of ink that wrapped down the man's arm to the back of his hand. They came in a series of unique rows, with something resembling fern fronds reaching toward his knuckles at the end. Above it twisted lines like different varieties of scales, from simple diamond configurations to striped triangles and ornamented squares that looked floral up-close, all the thin, delicate lines impeccably symmetrical. They were elegant and timeless and perfect.

Clem rolled his thumb along the ridge of one before he realized what he was doing. His heart skipped, and he covered the tender act by tapping loosely at Justin's pulse like he was double checking before biting. It was odd that he could tell exactly where to bite without seeing the veins or knowing the way they ran through the body. He tried to think about that, instead of how smooth Justin's skin was there, or how Justin's fingers gently curled when Clem lifted the wrist to his lips.

He bit down.

Justin made a sound so soft that Clem almost missed it, but then the man's life was in his mouth, hot and thick. He cringed from the slight bitter hints in the blood, the chemical taste oddly sweet as he swallowed it. He fought back his disappointment. This wasn't much better than last time. A bit less bland perhaps, but still boring and awkward, and while his body instinctively reacted to it, his soul yearned for something more.

At least it was less terrifying now. A little safer, a little surer. He could do this. He could keep doing it. It was survivable, and perhaps that was enough.

Just as he settled into this newfound resolve, his concentration was broken by a group of people tromping along the front of the alley. Their guide was already shouting over the bustle, her voice chipping into the sound of the passing cars and the sudden hammering of Clementine's heart as she explained that they were reaching a particularly haunted micro-cemetery. "But not by ghosts, oh no, the truth of these graves is even uglier!"

"What the fuck," Justin whispered. He jerked his wrist out of Clementine's mouth too fast for Clem to close the pair of large fang nicks he'd caused.

He made a sound, then tried to unmake that sound as he heard the tour group close in on the other side of the monument. "I thought you said we were safe here?"

"Fucking ghost tours. They usually back off until the tourist season." Justin bared his teeth like he was preparing to bite the offending group's heads off. He held his arm back out. "Lick."

Clementine licked—that came easy now, at least. The way Justin grinned after left odd goosebumps along his arms, like a chilled breeze.

"Fair warning, I'm about to be an absolute menace." Justin pulled his jacket off to reveal his full tattoo sleeves, intricate tribal line-work on his right turning to more typical black-and-white ink of thorns and feathers on his left.

From beyond their angelic cover, the guide had continued explaining in a theatrical voice, "This spot is the final resting place of the victims of the angel of death, a winged being who killed by draining the life of his prey, leaving them mummified corpses. The people of San Salud stabbed their angel of death through the heart with a sharpened crucifix of holy metal, pinning him to the earth long enough to burn off his wings, but legend says that he left behind an unborn child and his descendants still—"

Justin's not-grin grew wider and so dangerous that it looked like he might sprout fangs. Then he leaned bonelessly against the back of the angel statue, one hand gripping the monument's base like his life depended on it, and *moaned*. It was a low, rough sound that by all accounts shouldn't have echoed above the tour guide's voice the way it did, but the alleyway seemed to amplify it, bouncing it back at them.

Surely they couldn't see much more than his lower arm and the back of his head, but the group began shifting uncomfortably, a few teenagers giggling as parents tried to tug their younger kids out of the alley's entrance. The guide stumbled over her retelling in an *um, so, yes.*

In response, Justin rolled his body, tipping back his head against the angel's hip as he continued with a series of breathless, sensual noises. "Fuck, yeah. Oh god, oh god."

The proper version of Clementine—the one who nodded politely at his parent's charity galas and talked of his future promotion like it was something destined—wanted to die, right then and there. But the whole scene felt so familiar somehow, so fucking familiar that it took him a moment to place why.

He'd written this before.

Spock and Kirk in a park, limbs tangled and clothes half off, touching each other with such gusto that their enemies had run straight by. It was a trope as old as time, and it was *hot.* Clementine had been so wrapped up in writing it that he'd burned with every ounce of the couple's restrained lust, and while Justin didn't stir the same feelings in him—not

64

desire, anyway—there was still something whirling in his gut, aching deep and low. Want, not of the kind he might have felt had he wished to crash his body against Justin's and grab those gasping lips between his own, but a subtler, less sexual yearning for the unabashed amusement Justin seemed to be having. To have a taste of this, even if he'd never achieve the full deal.

Justin winked at him, and where Anthony and Natalie's blatant public displays of affection made him want to crawl out of his skin, this platonic play-acting felt right; limitless and electrifying. It felt like an open doorway begging to be entered.

Before his proper Hughes side could convince himself just how very badly this could ruin him, Clementine pushed forward, leaning into Justin's space with what he hoped was all the sexual prowess he'd spent a decade writing. He didn't quite touch the man, hovering far enough away that either of them could still pull back, but he could feel Justin's body heat, smell his sweat, bitter and sweet all at once. He slid one hand beside Justin's on the monument, their skin brushing as he clutched there too. Pressing his forehead to the angel's wing, he hid the top of his face with the stone, the rest of his body in shadow. His mouth hovered near Justin's ear.

He could have sworn the sounds Justin made shifted then, just slightly.

It was weird how easy the performance was. Or perhaps it wasn't. He'd spent his whole life acting; acting like the perfect student and son and employee, acting like most conversations didn't feel like half nonsense and half incompetence, acting like he wasn't secretly terrified that someone would find out how often his heart raced and how overwhelmed he commonly felt. This scene, at least, was the kind he'd written a thousand times before, a role he knew by heart even if he hadn't ever found someone with whom to truly fulfill it yet.

When he let his gaze detach, he could almost feel a shudder along his spine from the ragged way Justin groaned. Could pretend he sensed a thickening between his legs, his dick awake enough to catch his attention. Could imagine a scenario where this was real, where he wanted the man whose hot breath crested his neck and husky pleas filled his ears.

It was all a fiction—no more built from genuine, real-life attraction than all the times he got himself off with fanfiction or imagined characters, and no more likely to lead anywhere—but it was still exhilarating.

And the tour group certainly thought it genuine. He heard snatches of something just homophobic enough to ping a reaction of anger and fear in the back of his head. Clementine wasn't attracted to real men—no more than he was to anyone else—but with how much he'd thirsted after his favorite Spock/Kirk fanfics, the cruelty still drove deep. To spite them, he focused on matching Justin's pleasured sounds with grunts and taunts.

When Clementine spoke, his voice came out not quite as he'd meant, darker somehow, and rumbling with a sound like a vampiric growl. He could feel his fangs out—had he ever put them away?—and he was suddenly aware of the lingering hints of Justin's blood in his mouth. "I want you to scream for me."

Justin's tone shifted to match his, so graveled and desperate that it seemed to latch itself into Clementine's brain like a leech. "God, fuck yes."

And whatever Clementine did or didn't feel for the man, in that moment Justin Yu was intoxicatingly handsome.

JUSTIN

Justin swore he'd never seen anyone more beautiful than Clementine in that moment.

He'd known from the instant the vampire had grabbed him that he was attracted to Clem, but this was proof like nothing on earth—Clementine so close their chests nearly brushed, fangs glinting in the orange light streaming through the gap between the angel's torso and wings, his voice a growl and his demand—oh *god*. If the vampire had wanted to drag him further back into the alley and make good on that promise, Justin knew by the tightening of his pants and the ache that came with it that he'd have let him in an instant.

It wouldn't have gone anywhere, of course. Justin didn't have time for a relationship, especially one with the vampire he was knowingly taking advantage of, who could only ever be his for short flashes. But a single good fuck? Maybe he'd been depriving himself too long...

Clementine wasn't interested in him though—he found Justin's blood bland, after all. There was a reason they were only acting, not quite touching, not quite grinding or kissing or biting or any of the dozen other things Justin's body begged for. No matter what Clementine's presence was doing to Justin, this was still all a show.

But the tour group was buying it hook, line, and sinker. As Justin gave a long, deep howl of pleasure, their guide had reached her limit. She ushered them frantically back onto the main street, running through apologies as she hurried them along. "There's a better site for pictures up ahead! It's too dark in there anyway."

Someone laughed awkwardly at that.

The sound of their uncomfortable chatter quickly died down, and Clementine pulled back, his throat bobbing. The absence of his body so close to Justin's felt like a hollow, but that lack wasn't enough to keep Justin from slumping against the statue's base as he laughed. The joy seemed to wash over Clementine, spreading out across his features until he was laughing too, so light and high that it was barely a sound. But it was there, sparkling in his eyes and loosening his shoulders. In the odd lighting, he appeared, for a moment, almost relaxed. It was an intoxicating look, and Justin wanted more of it.

Clementine leaned against the statue at his side, tucking his hands into his pockets. "So?"

"I didn't expect—" Justin shook his head, descending back into laughter. "That was *hot*. You're a great fake fuck, Lemon."

The statement brought a smile out of Clem—small, and still shades of serious, but as bright as the rest of his expression.

More than the fictitious moaning and the physical nearness, it was this that curled up inside Justin's chest and made an aching home beside his heart. He wished he could let himself want Clementine, fully, emotionally, like the moon did the sun. And if Justin had been anyone else, with any other set of responsibilities...

Clementine fiddled with his scarf, the very edge of his lips perking up. "I haven't done something quite that outrageous in a long time. Or ever, actually. I've *never* done anything *nearly* that outrageous." He laughed. "Is this an effect of vampirism? You lose your sense of propriety?"

"I think that's an effect of spending too much time with me," Justin admitted. "It's not entirely my fault though. I blame all my best chaos on growing up with Isaiah, and Marcus, and Ana Lee."

"Who?"

"My people—they're all vampires, actually. Ana Lee is raising her kids by herself now that she's turned, so she hasn't had time to be wild in years, but Marcus and his platonic partner Paola are always down to do something bonkersly stupid. Isaiah's just a beautiful disaster, and I say that with all the affection possible. He dances from one mess to the next like that's what he was made for." The way he'd been helping his new friends in the suburbs find vampires to host in their spare room seemed to be doing him good though. It was a shame an obsessive hunter was getting in the way.

Clementine watched him, searchingly. "And you... support that?"

"I support *him*. He'll figure his shit out someday. But even if he doesn't, I won't judge him for it. Would *you*?"

"No, of course not." Clementine inhaled, then paused, like he was weighing his options. "I just haven't experienced much of that myself, I suppose. When my brother was momentarily the family disaster a few years ago, all my parents could talk about was how much potential he was throwing away, how disgraceful he was being. Even my sister, as much as she claimed she'd always support him, said nothing in his defense. But then he stumbled into being a full-time travel influencer who makes almost as much as both our parents combined, so crisis averted, I guess." He scoffed, but the emotion turned quickly to a cringe. "Sorry, I didn't realize how much that still hurt." As though he could escape the pain by plunging forward, he added quickly, "You said you grew up around here, right? Or implied, anyway."

"You're allowed to have emotions, Lemon." Justin's tone came out so soft, he could have been speaking to a friend. But here was this vampire, this almost stranger with his gorgeous face and his tangled emotions and his money ripe for the taking, and suddenly Justin couldn't stop himself, like all of Clementine was a perfect intoxicant. "But yeah, I was born five blocks from here in a bathtub. This neighborhood raised me, like it raised my mom and my grandpa before her."

"Were your parents…?"

"My dad was never in the picture and my mom passed when I was young; saved a couple kids from a fire while high out of her mind. If you ask around about her, you get a lot of conflicting portrayals. She's a bit like me that way." His voice didn't catch at the end, and for that he was grateful.

"If she was much like you, then she must have been fairly incredible." Clementine said it so frankly that it caught Justin off guard.

"I wasn't always the stunning beacon of charity you see before you." He bared his teeth on instinct, like the right smile could scare away his debt.

It didn't scare away Clementine. He patted Justin's arm the way Justin had done to him earlier, but more hesitant, like he was figuring the motion out. "But you are now."

Now wasn't all that mattered. Despite the ways he'd improved himself, the lives he'd made better, it would never compensate for the ones he'd destroyed. The one he'd taken. He couldn't just say that though; he had a feeling that Clementine's answer would be much like Isaiah's, with his constant use of the *Batman* nickname and his conviction that Justin was doing more than he had to. But Isaiah didn't have to carry his guilt. He had stayed at Justin's side in an effort to pull him back, never throwing the punches or wielding the knife. He hadn't been there when Jose breathed his last.

From the alley's entrance came an obnoxious clap of metal on metal, so loud that Clementine visibly cringed.

"I saw your fangs, vampire!" a woman shouted. "I just want to talk."

She stood in front of the micro-cemetery, her dark braid pulled over one shoulder, and she held a pair of foot-long metal sticks a similar length and size to the Filipino *bastons* they practiced with in the rag-tag Eskrima martial arts gym seven blocks away. The light of the main street silhouetted her from behind, making the silver of her weapons gleam around their etched crucifixes.

The fire flaring in Justin's chest felt like a physical thing, his hatred and determination turning to metal at the back of his throat. This had to be *her*, the suspicious woman with the holy silver—not just the small charms that most hunters got their hands on, but two full bastons worth. And she wasn't just another hunter in the city. She was here, now, targeting *his* vampires. He was sure as hell going to do something about that.

Clementine tucked his body against the angel monument in horror, staring at Justin like his life depended on him. If the hunter had any great skill, it very well could.

Justin mouthed the words, "I got this." Teeth bared, he burst fully into the light with all the nonhuman haste and agility his peculiar genetics granted him, hoping the hunter would see his speed and decide he was the vampire she sought, not realizing that his particular nonhuman genetics didn't include fangs or a weakness to holy silver until it was too late. "You summoned?"

The hunter looked him up and down, her nose wrinkling. "I'm looking for a specific vamp who lives around here. Darker-skinned pretty boy, friends with Vincent Barnes and Wesley Garcia Smith."

Those were the names of the couple Isaiah had been helping. "Why do you care?" It was a threat more than a question.

"Barnes murdered someone close to me. I'm just trying to make things right."

"How about instead you fuck off and never return?"

"How about *you* watch yourself?" The hunter's lips pulled into a grin. She spun her bastons and her trench coat flared with each step she took toward Justin. Her smile widened the longer he stood his ground. "You know what these are, you bloodsucking freak?"

"Roman silver, celestial silver, *holy* silver," Justin spat the name like a curse. "Whichever you want to call it." He lunged the final stride between them.

She didn't blink, swinging her weapons in a sweep toward his chest.

Justin caught them.

"Then you know what they do to your kind?" She asked, pressing their joint ends against his sternum. As his grip held fast, her amusement wavered, confusion setting in.

"I know what they do." He couldn't see his own grin, but he could feel it like a miasma, palpably toxic. "See though,

I'm not a vampire." With a great shove to her bastons, he threw her backward. The pain that shot through his back only enhanced his anger.

As she floundered in shock, he kicked her in the gut. She stumbled. Holding her weapons as a shield, she retreated warily each time Justin stepped toward her.

"What I am is the devil. And the vampires here, they're mine," he growled. "If you touch them, it'll be you the angel of death takes next."

The hunter swallowed, her eyes narrowing, and for a moment it seemed like maybe this would just make her all the more angry. But then her expression settled. "You're not the only one with friends," she spat, still slowly stepping away, glancing over her shoulder every few steps. "We'll be back."

Justin stopped at the alley's entrance, shoulders hunched and trembling. "Bring it. I look forward to fucking you *all* up."

CLEMENTINE

The moment Natalie's voice had rung through the alleyway, Clementine's blood had gone cold.

It wasn't his fault that Natalie had shown up here—it couldn't have been, right? She didn't know what he was. She didn't have any reason to be following him. She must have been nearby, attracted by the tour group's commotion long enough to poke her head in and see... his fangs.

Fuck.

But that had been all she saw, wasn't it? She hadn't called him out by name, hadn't questioned when it was Justin who emerged. In the shadows behind the monument, Clementine must have looked like any other tall, light-skinned vampire.

Still, he had stood immobile through their encounter, pressed against the angel like it might come to life and protect him. He could feel an uncomfortable power radiating off Natalie's weapon even from twenty feet away, as if the metal of her holy silver was the sun magnified. The exposed skin of his face had prickled the one time he'd tried to peek out, and he'd tucked his arms close after, burying his hands in his sleeves.

Even with his strength and speed, if Justin had not been there, he knew without a doubt that he could have done nothing to stop Natalie.

But Justin had stood in Clementine's place and returned Natalie's aggression tenfold. Her flight set loose something in Clementine that he hadn't realized was so badly clenched, like a knotted muscle finally massaged free. She *deserved* to be fucked up. After all the pain she caused bringing vampires into Vitalis-Barron's labs, all the hours Clem had spent analyzing each exchange he'd seen between her and Anthony, trying to figure out how much they knew, how much danger it put him in, Clem was glad someone was standing up to her. Even if Clem had done nothing to deserve his own fate, at least he could take comfort in knowing some parts of the world were still fair.

Justin returned slowly, his breathing heavy and his body taut. He leaned against the monument beside Clementine, looking pensive and distracted.

Clem tried out a soft smile. "And you thought *I* was hot?"

"You got my good side." Justin muttered, but his lips quirked.

"That woman…" Clementine struggled to find the right words. *She's from my work, where they torture vampires like me for profit* and *yes I am still angling for a promotion there, please don't judge me.* But from what Natalie had said, she wasn't here because of Vitalis-Barron. Or, she wasn't here *just* because of them. And she hadn't been lying—Clementine only knew bits and pieces of the story, but her mentor *had* been killed a few months back.

"I can deal with her, don't worry."

With *her*, he could. But if she brought her friends next time, Clementine wasn't so sure. "Just be careful, all right. She works for Vitalis-Barron, and anyone who joins her might too." There, that hadn't been so bad. "They've been taking the vampires. Whoever she's after now will probably end up in Vitalis-Barron's labs, and I doubt they'll be coming back out."

Justin went still, his voice tightened like a drawn bow. "You're certain?"

Clementine wanted to say no—it felt safer, like it was what Justin hoped to hear. But if the truth would make him more cautious, keep him out of danger, then he had to know. "I'm positive. I, um, I'm a research associate for them. I've seen it firsthand—just once, but that was enough. It's all very hushed up though, so I don't have any proof, and I can't access their department unsupervised, can't do anything about it, as much as I hate it. You can believe me or—"

"Shit, I believe you. That must be where they're getting all that holy silver from." Justin exhaled like he was struggling to keep himself contained. "But god, you quit, right? You're not working for them still?"

"I *can't* quit." Not with his life teetering on the edge of decimation and this position the only thing keeping him from that impending disaster. "It's a precarious situation, I admit, but if I left—if I had to go through the same sun-lit interview process and background checking that all the prominent companies are doing these days, at best my application would be quietly dismissed, and at worst the over-exposure could kill me. I'm sticking with the devil I know, and all that."

"You have other options, now," Justin objected. "You could come here. It wouldn't be lavish or prestigious, but—"

"It's not about *status*." How was he supposed to explain this? The way losing this job would crack whatever respect his parents had left for him, total his finances beyond repair, send him into a spiral that would ruin all the decades of raking himself over the coals to get there. Besides, he would never be able to pay for both blood and rent again. "The risk of staying is still worth it to me."

"I just hope it doesn't lead to your funeral." Even in the dark, Justin must have seen the effect those words had on Clementine. He sighed. "Look, so long as you're here, I can help if something happens. If you're not..." His usual bitter smile turned sad. "I understand the choice, I do, but I don't support it. The first sign someone's onto you, I hope you run like hell."

"I'll keep that in mind." Clementine didn't know if he could make himself follow the advice though. And if Justin's protection only extended to the edge of Ala Santa, then he needed to know enough to take care of himself. All the questions he hadn't found a way to ask yet still cluttered the back of his mind, but this one was easy enough. "What makes her silver burn like that? I haven't had issues with the metal before now."

Justin took the change in topic with poise. "It's a special alloy, not real silver at all. The Church called it holy silver in the medieval period as propaganda, similar to their myths with crucifixes and holy water, except whatever's in this particular metal actually burns." As he spoke, he rolled himself a joint, looking far stiffer and more exhausted than he had just minutes ago.

Clementine watched, admiring the shape of his fingers, the flutter of his dark lashes, the way his tattoos snuck out from beneath his jacket cuffs and the deep v-neck of his shirt. This wasn't attraction—he knew what that was meant to feel like, had been down that road with fictional characters more than enough times—but it was still nice, warm and pleasant and natural.

Justin glanced his way, and even in the dim light he seemed to catch Clementine staring. "I won't let that hunter hurt any of my vampires, though, don't worry."

Clem's cheeks warmed. "*Your* vampires?"

"Yeah." Justin lit his joint, drawing in one long drag before explaining, "In these nine square blocks, there's about a dozen of them. They come because they know they're safe here, that I've made this place safe for them."

"Oh." There was something lovely and alluring about that. However much Clementine wasn't willing to give up his job and his life for it, he could still find hope in the way Justin cared, so sharp-toothed and dangerous but with that threat always aimed only at anyone who might hurt those less fortunate.

Justin's lips quirked. "Whenever you're here, you're included in that number."

Clementine had to remind himself of the qualification. *Whenever you're here.* This wasn't his place; Ala Santa was only a way-stop for him. He was here so that he could go back to living his own life as close to the way it had been before he'd turned. Which meant he had to ask more questions. With the gentle way Justin watched him now, maybe putting himself out there wouldn't be so uncomfortable after all. "Then help me understand my vampirism, please. Teach me. I don't know what I'm doing."

Justin hesitated. "It would be better if I introduced you to one of the other vamps. Isaiah is really cool, disaster notwithstanding, and he loves helping out other vampires. I'd be happy to—"

"No." Clementine surprised himself with his own ferocity. "No, it has to be you." How did he say this, and not look pathetic? Maybe he was already pathetic, and the avoidance would only highlight that. "I'm a little embarrassed for other vampires to know how ignorant I am." *A little* being the understatement of the century.

Justin nodded slowly. "All right. I know enough that I can get you jump-started."

"That's perfect." It felt like a weight off his shoulders. He could do this. He *was* doing this.

"If this is going to take more of my time though, then maybe..." Justin rubbed his fingers together in a sign for money.

Clem grimaced. They *had* entered this arrangement as a business agreement. And this wouldn't be a permanent cost, at least. He could still afford it for the moment... so long as he got the senior associate position soon. "I can pay you for as long as it takes me to learn. How is another hundred to each pint?"

A wicked grin filled Justin's lips, not quite making it to his eyes. Clementine had to remind himself that this was the same man who had just defended him from Natalie, even if he was also still here for the money. "Perfect." His expression dropped to a scowl at the ring of sirens in the distance, too far off to tell which way they were moving. "But not today. One of those damn tourists might have called the cops."

Clem stood.

Justin clamped a hand around his arm. "Be careful at your work, Lemon. The rest of the city isn't as safe as Ala Santa." *The rest of the city doesn't have me,* he seemed to say. Which meant Clementine didn't have Justin either.

"I will." He squeezed his fingers over Justin's before gently peeling them off.

Justin could offer Clementine a place among his vampires all he wanted, but so long as Clem walked out of Ala Santa and back into his old life—the life where he pretended to be a human working at a place that experimented on vampires—he would still be on his own.

Alone, with his family bearing down on him, with Anthony vying for the position that Clementine desperately needed, and Natalie hanging off his shoulder during the day and coming after Justin's vampires at night.

At the thought of her, Clementine's stomach turned with a whole new terror. The rest of the city wasn't as safe as Ala Santa. But the faster he learned about vampirism, the better he could hide.

CLEMENTINE

Clementine knew he couldn't rely on Justin's protection.

It was all the more reason for him to learn how to work around his vampirism as fast as he could and concentrate on returning his life to the stability and progress he'd maintained as a human. For the rest of the night though, his thoughts seemed to have other, more irksome ideas, returning to Justin when his focus should have been on work.

Nearly an hour before dawn, he found himself sitting vacantly at his work desk staring at the man's business card as he considered it, his protocol notes all but forgotten. It gave him no new clues about the man, bearing only Justin Yu's name over that of his neighborhood, with the wings on the back. Who the hell was he? Beating up punks, selling his blood, calling himself the devil.

The devil wasn't real, and Justin seemed practically human outside his unusual speed and strength—his blood tasted human, anyway—yet his honeyed bitterness clung to

Clementine's mind like magic. Clem twisted the card back and forth in one hand, tapping his pen with the other.

"Good morning!"

He was so absorbed that he didn't notice Anthony coming up behind him until the man was already leaning over Clem's shoulder. His hair was pulled back in a French braid that exposed his undercut, one of Natalie's colorful scrunchies at the end. It bobbed against Clementine's collarbone.

Clem flinched, dropping the business card.

Anthony retrieved it for him, and something twisted in Clementine's stomach to see his fingers on it, like his skin might contaminate the places Justin had touched. Which was ridiculous. It was just a business card. As Anthony handed it back, though, his gaze caught on its front. His eyes widened.

With growing horror, Clementine realized his mistake. But there was nothing he could do about it now.

"What a small world!" A chilling smile spread across Anthony's face. "Natalie was telling me about this *Justin Yu* from *Ala Santa*. He's not too tall, pretty dark, and incredibly handsome—her description, not mine. He does sound like a catch, though, if you're into that."

Clementine's heart felt like it was ricocheting through his rib cage, but he forced himself not to show it, slowing the tap of his pen to a steady rhythm. It was just a business card. Anthony could make all the assumptions he wanted, but Clem having met with the same man who confronted Natalie last night wasn't proof of anything. "Is he?" Clem chuckled, the sound echoing in his ears. "He's a friend of a friend, honestly. I don't really know him."

Just a person Clementine didn't really know, but couldn't get out of his head.

"Really? I hear he has a soft spot for vampires," Anthony said.

Clementine's pen snapped in his grip, spilling a gurgle of ink like oozing black blood over his fingers and across the paperwork he was meant to sign for one of his lab technicians. He cursed.

"Ah, here." Anthony scooted into Clem's space to pat at the spill with an absorbent wipe.

Clem resisted the urge to yank away from him. Like prey in the sightline of a predator, he froze instead, letting the man dab at the pooling ink. When he tried to take the wipe for his fingers, Anthony grabbed his wrist. It took all Clementine's willpower to refrain from breaking the hold with vampiric strength. A display of that now could be his downfall. If he wasn't already doomed.

"Working so many late shifts is wearing on you, I see." Anthony circled his grip like a noose around Clem's wrist, but the stroke of his paper towel was unnervingly gentle and meticulous as he cleaned the ink from Clem's cuticles.

A shudder ran up Clem's spine.

"I'd thought you'd be gone already. The sunrise is getting earlier each day, after all." Anthony lowered his head to

Clementine's ear, his breath hot. "Dr. Blood can't promote you to senior associate if you burn up."

Clem's instinct told him to run, now, before Vitalis-Barron's security arrived with guns and tasers and Natalie's holy silver. But whatever he did in this moment could save or condemn him. "I think I can handle a winter sunburn." Clem swore he was trembling from the center of his bones, but his voice came out flat and annoyed. He curled and extended his fingers, like he was scrutinizing the lines where the ink remained on his skin. "I may have lost a little color, but I'm not *that* pale."

"My mistake, I suppose." Anthony bundled the unused side of the wipe and bent Clem's finger to dab at the remaining stains between the wrinkles of his joints. "Besides, vampires don't actually burn up, do they? They get the shakes, and the pain, and then, after too long, they just die like anyone else. They're really so much easier to kill than in the myths."

Clementine had a flash of Justin's dangerous grin and the confident, ruthless way he'd respond to this: *"Easier to kill, but also deadlier."* He'd run his tongue over his canines suggestively, his smile growing wider and more threatening with each second of delay. *"A little sunshine won't hurt us, and no one needs to grant us permission inside."*

It was a nice thought, to rattle Anthony in the same way he was successfully rattling Clem. But Clementine couldn't risk pushing his colleague that hard, not with everything he had to lose. Perhaps Vitalis-Barron would let him live to bear the trials of being a vampire in a new city with no job options or income. If he went to the press or the law, his money might be enough to make a minor fuss, but with no proof of Vitalis-Barron's immorality that would be a battle of power and checkbooks, and theirs were still infinitely deeper than his own. But the most likely outcome would be the nightmare he'd had all throughout his first month as a vampire: Vitalis-Barron's basement security snatching him from his office, covering up his disappearance as they must have for so many other vampires.

Clementine had too few options; his life was in the palm of Anthony's hand. And Anthony was right: the sun was about to rise.

The early shift workers were already arriving around them, the gentle buzz of *good mornings* meeting with the thrum of computers and the distant gurgle of the coffee maker in the breakroom.

Anthony continued making a show of cleaning the ink, his grip firm enough that he could tighten it at any moment. "See, I've been learning a lot while dating Natalie. Killing a vampire is easy. You have the garlic allergy, of course, along with the sunlight, but a bullet or a knife works just as well. Or there's holy silver if you're lucky enough to know how to get it."

Clementine could feel the metal before he saw it, the little bat-shaped bracelet charm slipping free from a band beneath Anthony's cuff with a flick of his other hand. Clem flinched away from it, but Anthony lowered the charm determinedly.

As it pressed to Clem's skin, it burned with a white-hot pain. Clem hissed and his fangs slid free. Everything in him begged to fight back, but there were too many people here, too many witnesses, and Anthony knew it.

As quickly as he'd forced down the holy silver, Anthony removed it. He let go of Clementine entirely, leaning back to prop one hip on the desk with a smirk, his gaze shifting from the bright red welt on Clem's skin to the room's entrance.

Natalie strolled through it.

While Clementine had been afraid before, that fear had been a broad thing over the fate of his future as a whole and every way Anthony might choose to screw it up, but at the sight of the hunter all his panic condensed to a single point. Whatever Anthony was up to, all he had were his words—words that could still ruin Clementine's life or throw him into the basement, but words all the same. Natalie could use the chair he sat on to break every bone in his body. At that moment his body very much wanted to avoid shattering, and it had a million nerves telling him so.

She waved, and Anthony lifted a hand in return.

The man's eyes never lowered, but with two fingers, he tugged down the sleeve of Clementine's shirt to cover the holy silver's mark as he shouted to Natalie, "Grab me a coffee, babe?"

She made a face but turned for the kitchen.

Natalie didn't know yet. Anthony hadn't told her, thank god. And it seemed—at least for the moment—he wasn't planning to. Clementine released a breath, some of his terror sliding off him, but it left his muscles weak and numb.

"You know," he managed, "killing me would be easier if you hadn't informed me that you knew what I was first."

"I had a hypothesis. I needed the confirmation," Anthony replied, like this was any other science experiment to him. "But I don't want you dead, Clementine. Whatever you might think of me, I respect you. You do good science, you don't make drama and you haven't eaten anyone I care about. So long as that trend continues, then I don't mind if you're a little… less normal."

Clementine fought back the flurry of dread in his gut. As much as Clem wanted to believe that Anthony wouldn't hold his vampirism against him, he knew there had to be more. His skin crawled. "What *do* you want, Anthony?"

Anthony tipped his head toward Natalie where she stood just inside the kitchen door, pouring creamer into a steaming mug of coffee. "My girl over there, she might not look it, but she's a lot torn up that someone like you caved her mentor's head in. Well, not entirely like you. From what I'm told he was a homeless ruffian—a feral. He's protected right now, but he's made connections to a vampire in your friend Justin's neighborhood of Ala Santa."

Connections to a vampire in Justin Yu's neighborhood. He could see where this was going. He could see it like an impending train crash, with nowhere to jump or run or hide.

"Ala Santa—Is that saintly wings or holy feathers? My Spanish courses were decades ago." Anthony shrugged.

"Holy feathers in the city of saint health—Vitalis-Barron really did a number on this place in the early days, didn't they?" He grabbed the back of Clementine's chair, turning him ever-so-slightly back toward his desk, and leaning down once more to bob his head above Clem's shoulder as he tapped the front of Justin Yu's card. "I'm going to make you a deal."

Clem stared at his half-cleaned desk, the ink-sullied wipes bundled in a pile. His fingers clenched. "Go on."

"Natalie is looking for a way to get back at the vampiric low-life who killed her mentor in cold blood, and the one vamp who might offer her that vengeance is hiding somewhere in Ala Santa. Except this Justin Yu has decided to stand in her way. He's as strong and as fast as a vampire without the limitations, and he won't let Natalie in. He clearly lets *you* in though, with your little fangs and that pesky sun allergy."

"*Whenever you're here, you're included in those vampires.*"

Whenever Clem was there. But not while he was at Vitalis-Barron, not so long as his goal was to keep his job, his life, the stability he'd worked so hard for. Justin had made it very clear that whatever hardship Clementine faced in staying, he'd be facing it on his own.

Clem owed him nothing, technically; nothing but the substantial amount of money he was paying. But Justin was kind to him when he shouldn't have been, had teased him and smiled at him and made him feel like his vampirism was more than just the hardships it brought on, had accepted the little moments of vulnerability Clementine had managed with a soft hand and an unreasonable amount of wisdom.

"I won't help you hurt anyone in Ala Santa," Clementine replied, uncomfortably aware that it was as close to a refusal as he could muster.

"Someone is going to get hurt, Dr. Hughes. I can't stop Natalie's vengeance, and frankly, I don't care enough to. But I care about *her*, and every time she goes chasing a vamp through those streets trying to get information is a chance for Justin Yu to hurt her. I just want this to go down with the least harm possible. All I need is the information Natalie would have to fight them for: how many vamps Justin has, what their lifestyles are like, who they're helping, if they're biting anyone, simple things like that. Enough to point her in the direction of the vamp she wants and keep her out of conflicts with anyone else along the way."

Just information, information she'd be beating out of Justin's vampires—or Justin himself—otherwise. Clementine knew what her holy silver did from a distance. If she caught one of Justin's vampires without him present… the end result could be horrific. Still, giving in felt dangerous, felt like a betrayal. Especially since Justin couldn't know. He'd hate it, not simply the information handed over, but the fact that Clementine was doing it in order to stay at Vitalis-Barron.

"The first sign someone's onto you, I hope you run like hell."

Clementine wished he was in a place where that was possible, where it wouldn't mean throwing his life away just as cleanly as if Anthony had turned him in.

But then Anthony kept talking, and a whole new twist came into Clementine's gut, jealous and hopeful like a deep, soul-level craving. "If you do me a solid here, I can sweeten the deal for you. Not only will I keep your secret, but I'll cover for you. Your weird shift hours and your new habits— I'll set up projects that accommodate, make up bullshit reasons an experiment needs to run for twenty-four hours straight, throw them off your trail. If they grow suspicious of *me* it won't matter. They can put me in the sun all they want."

No more fear of his schedule seeming too weird as the sunnier spring months approached, no panic over Vitalis-Barron finding him out. And the more he could relax here, the better his chances of promotion were.

"I don't want you dead, Clementine." Anthony smiled, and his baring of teeth held none of Justin's threat. But it didn't need to. Clem knew what was at stake. "In fact, I have a proposition; whoever makes senior associate, we work together on a little project, right under Vitalis-Barron's nose. For decades this place has been using vampire research for their human pharmaceuticals. Wouldn't you like to start doing research on vampires, *for* vampires? *That's* the kind of science I want to be doing. Groundbreaking territory no one else has dared step into. We could make that finally happen."

The idea of risking his job to use Vitalis-Barron equipment, Vitalis-Barron money, to do personal projects without their go-ahead should have sounded terrifying. But what Anthony described was freedom. And Clementine wanted it. Needed it. "Could you turn me back?"

"Who knows, but we can try. We'll shoot for the moon, attempt what no one else has dared, make vital discoveries just for the sake of knowledge… help some people like you along the way?"

Information in exchange for his job, his safety, his life, and someone willing to conduct proper research on his vampirism, research that could transform the way vampires existed in society. Surely whatever Clementine collected would be no more than what Natalie would beat out of the Ala Santa vampires on her own sooner or later—and this way he could pick and choose the less invasive facts, just give over enough to make Natalie feel like she was moving closer to her vengeance with as few innocent bystanders getting hurt in the process as possible. And if she did find the vampire she was looking for, then Clementine could give Justin a heads up. They'd have a decent chance to fight back and a protector who was willing to stand up for them.

"Well, Clementine?" Anthony asked.

"I'll get you the *information*, but that's all."

"Perfect." Anthony drew back and his voice shifted to a louder, upbeat tone as Natalie appeared with his coffee. "I knew I could always count on you, Dr. Hughes."

"Always," Clem parroted, the full weight of their deal finally hitting him.

He barely registered Natalie and Anthony kissing, their hips brushing as Natalie pressed the coffee into Anthony's hands, still far too close to Clementine's desk for comfort. Already he felt nauseous. Nauseous and giddy, guilty and excited.

But he'd taken the only option that could be expected of him; the one that traded the most benefit for the least pain; he couldn't blame himself for it. Justin and his vampires would be fine—better than fine, without Natalie to harass them.

And Clementine would get his life back.

9

JUSTIN

Clementine worked for Vitalis-Barron.

Justin still couldn't believe it.

Vitalis-Barron. It was a name that got passed around the city with the same regularity as cemeteries—and sometimes in the same breath. They were San Salud's two most prominent features, after all: the esteemed pharmaceutical company that founded the city with their sanatoriums, and the high density of graves those medical and research facilities were—whether inadvertently or not—responsible for in the early twentieth century.

Beyond that, the only things Justin had known about Vitalis-Barron were that they'd brought prosperity to the city as they expanded to become a global power—prosperity that took the form of cheap immigrant labor and wealthy local managers in a trend that would impact generations—and that they wouldn't partake in any pharmaceutical development that wasn't likely to make them money. Rare disorders for not-quite-humans like Justin were so far off the table they might as well be in the sewers.

And now he knew they had vampires in their basement. *Vampires*, tortured and turned into profit.

It made him feel sick, and weak, and tired. If only he could do something for them, be enough like the superhero vigilantes of fiction that he could take care of the whole city instead of just his little portion of it... but he wasn't that strong, didn't have that kind of time or reach, and the moment he stepped out of Ala Santa was the moment a hunter could step in. As much as Isaiah teased him about being the city's Batman, he was not. Batman was selfless and compassionate, his focus reaching to every crack and corner of Gotham—or at least, that had been the Batman of the extensive Batman x Superman fan fiction he'd been following during his mid-twenties and had always meant to pick back up if he could ever find the time again. But Justin was not that Batman.

He was just a man with a debt.

A debt he was currently taking a short, pre-dawn break from, perched on the rooftop above his micro-cemetery with a lace patchwork tutorial playing on one knee. Not that he'd ever actually sewn anything himself. The DIY video habit had started as a way to pick up new skills to bring to his neighborhood, but now he just liked the relaxing nature of it, the soothing voices and the coming together of something beautiful.

He almost missed Isaiah's approach until his friend sat down, swinging his legs over the edge of the building as gracefully as a cat. His baggy sweater pooled off both shoulders tonight, revealing a generous amount of smooth brown skin, and his small, coiling locs were piled on his head in clips. In the glow of Justin's screen, his dark eyeliner accentuated his wide, gently curving eyes, emphasizing the elegant combination of his Filipino and Black heritage.

"Oh, is this a *Leather and Lace* video? I have *such* gender envy for all their clothes. It's not quite my style but the aesthetic is incredible."

As they watched the phone screen, his friend's fingertips fell against Justin's back, making gentle circles across his aching shoulder blades. Isaiah was the only one who knew the right amount of pressure to relieve some of the pain without producing a fresh backlash. Probably because he was the only one Justin wouldn't murder for trying to touch him there, the only one beside Mrs. Mendoza and Jose who'd seen the gnarled flesh that lay beneath the skin along his spine.

As good as it felt, he didn't deserve it. Didn't deserve anything from Isaiah. Maybe that was why his disabling pain was getting worse again, the universe proving to him just how much he was worth.

Justin tried to slide away from the rewarding touch, but Isaiah only scooted closer.

He brushed a hand through Justin's hair and gently guided Justin's head to rest on his shoulder. "Come here."

"No, I—"

"I *miss* you, so come *here*."

"Fuck your guilt tripping." But he gave in, finally, an unwitting sigh escaping him as Isaiah returned to his gentle massage of his back. He shouldn't have. He should have told Isaiah that he was giving so much more than Justin could ever give back, and that he had to move on.

Yet another thing to feel guilty over.

Had relationships always been this hard? He swore things were suddenly different, but the only change in his life was Clementine.

Clementine. Justin had fought so hard to keep his thoughts from constantly circling back to the vampire. To the tender brush of his fingers on Justin's wrist and the smooth slip of his fangs into Justin's vein. To his body wrapped nearly around Justin's as they'd faked a sexual climax together. To the softness of his voice when he'd tried to protest that he was more than just a useless lemon at their first meeting and his little burst of frustration at his family's treatment. To the way just thinking about him like this made Justin's heart beat faster.

He had to stop.

He had to stop this right now, before the feelings churning inside him turned lethal.

Isaiah paused the current video. "You're tenser than normal. What's up?"

Justin stared into the alley, memorizing the lines of the angel's wings four stories below them and thinking of the way Clementine had looked crouched beneath their majesty. Finally he said, "I think I want a vampire."

Isaiah hummed. "That's tough. I could recommend the pet store on 32nd Street, but really the best vampires all come from the pound."

"Punyeta."

Isaiah laughed at the insult. He twirled his fingers through Justin's hair. "For real though, do you want a vampire as a pet, a partner, or a fling?"

"Why would I want a vampire as a *pet*?"

"Some humans do. Some humans want a partner who *is* a pet, and some vampires just want to be obedient to the person they love."

Justin chose to ignore the last comment like that might make it go away. "You know the kind of human I am! And you know my kinks, too."

"A pretty vamp can always hope."

"I won't actually be *having* a vampire regardless of what I *want*—you know that. Not as a partner or a pet, anyway, and not as a fling if they're someone I'm supposed to protect, someone I already happen to love." He tipped his chin, pressing his lips to the side of Isaiah's head. He did love Isaiah, a deep, steady love that had been there since they were kids and would remain until the day he died. And it was a love that could probably come with their mouths pressed together, their bodies merging into one, if he opened himself to it enough.

But when he imagined a vampire in his life, his thoughts went instantly to Clementine.

"What I'd really want—if I wasn't me, if I was allowed that kind of distraction—is to be *distracted* by someone. I want them to bare their teeth at me in the grocery store while the clerk isn't looking and I want to taunt them with the turn of my collar." There were other examples his mind went to: wandering hands and the heat of Clem's breath. Because try as he might to replace him, it was still Clem who filled Justin's fantasies, Clementine's fangs and his gentle fingers and his beautiful, quizzical stares.

"You want to be teased," Isaiah concluded, a grin in his voice, but something sad there too. "I'll put the word out for you. One tense Batman, looking to be teased by one non-female vampire from outside Ala Santa."

"You will *not*. My god, Isaiah, if you start telling vampires I want them to come *tease* me I swear I'll—"

"You'll what?" Isaiah smiled for real then. "You'll bully me, will you? You know my kinks—"

Justin pushed him so solidly he almost fell off the roof. Isaiah grabbed hold of him to steady himself, still smirking like a fool.

"Ah yes, I forgot, you like to make your own announcements. *In public.*"

"I can shove you harder." Justin grunted, crossing his arms and trying to ignore the fresh lance of pain that the last push had flared between his shoulder blades. It had been worth it, though. The way Isaiah was eyeing him, it could be worth it again…

Isaiah laughed as he stood. "I should go. Tomas Santos said he had a dawn delivery I could help with, if it comes in before the sun gets too high."

As upbeat as he sounded, Justin knew the tension beneath the words; all the time Isaiah had taken off for Priscilla's wedding had cut into his usual work schedule, and the less he worked, the less he'd have to purchase blood with after rent came due. Justin was pretty sure Isaiah was paying five-fifty a pint these days, but his friend had cut him out after Justin kept trying to buy it in his place.

While he was turned away, Justin tucked a hundred-dollar bill into Isaiah's back pocket, receiving a muttered, "You could always squeeze that," for his trouble. It wasn't until Isaiah had slipped over the side of the building, dropping from one dark ledge to the next like a true creature of the night, that Justin noticed the little figurines he'd left behind. Freshly painted salt and pepper shakers, two black and white cats that fit together into a sexually explicit position.

Justin chuckled, carefully tucking the shakers away. He'd have to swing by his apartment to drop them off when he'd finished patrolling.

His phone buzzed.

Lemon
Is it all right for me to ask you questions over text?

For how formal a request it was, it should not have made Justin feel the way he did.

Justin

I don't see why not.

BTW you still owe me nine hundred dollars by the end of next week.

Lemon

Of course. My apologies. I had it on hand but the situation with the hunter sidetracked me. I'll bring it tomorrow.

You're sure no one is monitoring these messages?

Justin

I'm sure no one gives that much of a fuck.

But we can always talk in code if you'd rather.

Do you know how ciphers work? You seem smart enough to understand shit like that.

Lemon

I had half a mind to text you back in morse code for implying that I'm merely 'smart enough' to understand 'that shit', but then I realized you're not worth the effort.

Justin

How cruel. I *am* answering your questions after all.

Lemon

God, sorry, I didn't mean it like that. I thought I was being funny.

How cute was that? Justin had to close his phone for a moment to recalibrate, taking a deep breath, then popping the thread back up.

Justin

Relax, I took it in a 'omg is he flirting with me' kind of way. Except in a platonic business partner style.

Lemon

Is that another compliment?

Justin

Lemon, you're too sour for compliments.

Lemon

Ha ha.

Does this mean I should insult you more often?

You indignant, foolhardy fiend. See how much extra attention I pay you in order to show that you're worthless!

Well, damn, I can see where you get the flirtatious interpretation from.

Justin's stomach fluttered. This wasn't *actually* flirting; he had clarified that himself. Platonic business partners could banter too. There just happened to be one platonic business partner here who was biding his time with bland blood and second-hand knowledge, and another who was savoring every moment until he had to go back to denying himself again. That was okay.

Justin
It's not my favorite form of teasing but it's a decent second.

Justin waited as Clementine's dots appeared, then vanished, appeared then vanished. A response never came. He preoccupied himself with strolling up and down the streets, popping into the family-run shops as they began to open for the day to see which needed help with their nightly restocking, and assisted with unloading a delivery at Mrs. Mendoza's convenience store until his back ached with such waves of agony that he had to sit on the curb and smoke through the pain just to see straight. By the time he could focus on his phone again, Clementine had replied.

Lemon
Am I truly allergic to garlic now?

Justin
Yes, and that includes garlic powder.

Lemon
You're killing me.

If I keep trying to eat it, will it progress to anaphylaxis?

It went like that, on and off through the morning, alternating between casual joking and basic questions. Justin patrolled two hours longer than he would have—than he should have, judging by how much his feet were dragging and his eyes blurring when he finally collapsed into bed— just for an excuse to keep talking. There was not a lot, it turned out, that he wouldn't do for one more message from Clementine.

Justin woke to find that Natalie had returned while he slept, bringing her promised friends with her. No one had been severely injured, thankfully, but only because the vampire they'd targeted had managed to flee into a manhole. Natalie had left before Justin got there, but he'd discovered two of her friends still hanging around, poking at an old vampire den behind the alley of 16th Street. He'd sent them limping out of Ala Santa, one with a set of broken fingers and the other with a concussion that had probably killed their few remaining brain cells.

It had been well worth the pain now setting in.

"You're going to give these hunters an excuse to bring in the cops," Isaiah hissed at him when he found Justin after.

Justin wiped the blood from his cracked lip and smiled, the ache in his back forming a constant blinding buzz behind his eyes. "Good. I'll fuck them up too." A flash of anger rushed through him, but the agony that tore between his shoulder blades was enough to quench it, along with a significant amount of Justin's consciousness.

Isaiah swore, catching him as he stumbled and lowering him gently to the ground before scrounging through his pockets. "Where are your drugs, my love?"

"I can't," Justin protested, trying to grab for his friend's hands and seeming to always be a moment too late. "I won't have enough."

Isaiah pulled free his little tin and began rolling a joint. "You will, because you'll be resting after this." He lit the joint, pressing it between Justin's lips with a tenderness that would have been intrusive from anyone else. "Breathe."

Justin obeyed. The first drag did nothing, and the second seemed to make it worse instead of better, the motion of his lungs straining his back muscles, but after a minute of steady inhales, he could see through the pain. He leaned his head on Isaiah's shoulder, feeling pieces of himself relax back into their proper place—his emotions included. "Thanks."

Isaiah ran a hand through his hair. "Don't scare me like that." His fingers pressed soothingly along Justin's back, and

Justin could see them gauge every flinch and exhalation. "We can help, you know."

"They have too much holy silver. You'll just end up beaten and burned."

"There must be nearly two dozen of us here now. If we work together, they can't incapacitate us all."

Nearly two dozen. It felt like more than that, but as Justin ran through their faces—Isaiah and his roommates Whitney and Mya, Marcus and Paola on Eagle Street, the shy teenager who lived above Tomas's shop, Ana Lee with her four human kids, the couple of older vampires who had survived this long by keeping low profiles, the loner who used to sleep in the sewer below Mrs. Mendoza's before she gave them a job and a cot in the supply room, and the new arrivals who'd been scared out of surrounding areas over the last month. His vampires.

His vampires, one Clementine short.

"No, not—not yet," Justin insisted. "I can still manage."

He stayed up the rest of the night, and through most of the morning, passing the time he spent walking the streets by texting Clementine intermittently. Just when he'd assumed Clem had asked all his vampire-related questions, their conversation shifted, growing more personal. Clem wanted to know about Justin's relationships to his vampires, how many had been living in Ala Santa, how he'd maintained the place as such a safe, vampire-friendly neighborhood, and what it was like for those who lived there. It was adorable.

And a part of Justin, a terrified part that knew he could never have Clementine as more than a friend but desperately wanted it all the same, wondered if perhaps he was asking because he had reconsidered joining them.

He would only be coming because he wanted the safety of Ala Santa, Justin reminded himself. Safety that *he* was responsible for providing. So he kept patrolling.

But the hunters didn't reappear. They were waiting, probably, recuperating and planning. Natalie had said she'd be back, and he couldn't imagine her goons having had one bad run-in with Justin was enough to scare her off. He knew her type—obsessive, relentless, oh so much like himself—and she'd return.

He just had to wait and watch and stay alert.

But as the days passed and the hunters didn't set another foot onto Ala Santa soil, waiting seemed like all he was going to be doing; waiting and agonizing over Clementine. And texting Clementine. And seeing Clementine. And dreaming of him.

At first, Justin dreamed only of his golden curls and his pink mouth, of letting Clem nuzzle lips into the crook of Justin's neck and feed to his heart's content, of the nearly orgasmic rush of venom that would follow, tingling like a high in his veins and clouding his mind with a light-headed bliss. But the more he grew to know Clementine, the more those dreams widened, encompassing all of Clem's fascinating, meticulous mind and his quiet scrutiny, and his rigorous curiosity. There were so many pieces to

Clementine, intricate and beautiful, fitting together to form a person Justin didn't fully understand, but whom he very much wanted to.

But he couldn't oblige himself—not when he had Ala Santa to take care of. Not when he could never deserve Clementine.

For the next week, he checked his texts sporadically as he went about his rounds, certain, somehow, that Clementine would message him less now—as though the vampire would have nothing to say after spending all his free time on Justin.

Answering Clementine's questions would have been worth the effort even without the incredible monetary payout and the near daily doses of the vampire's blissful venom. There were the other things he was getting out of their business deal, too: the way Clementine's lips crooked at the edge when he was deep in thought, the little snort he gave the moment before he launched into an elaborate explanation, the adorable formality of his texting, the care he took when he counted out his hundreds, like he was suspicious one of them might give Justin a papercut.

By the end of their second week of texting and feeding, Justin's crush was only growing stronger, and Clementine harder to ever consider saying no to.

10

CLEMENTINE

Clementine was learning.

Between Justin's facts on vampirism and the information he was coaxing free for Anthony, Clem felt like he'd opened a less destructive Pandora's box—a thing full of horrified wonder and harsh realities and an expanding kernel of guilt over his part in the hunters' schemes. But what he was doing for Anthony had kept Natalie's hunters out of Ala Santa, just like Anthony promised, and the more Clementine learned about his vampirism, the more settled he began to feel. Not resigned, certainly, but more stable for knowing exactly what would harm him—predominantly garlic, the sun, holy silver, and going too long without feeding, though blood loss and organ death were still on the table.

Justin had also confirmed all the basics of vampiric life, from their incredible immunity, to their only slightly longer but significantly more ageless lifespan, to all the fabrications of asked entry and water crossing and coffin sleeping that had arisen over the centuries.

Clementine

But there's still a chance that I can control bats, yes?

Please say that I can exude some form of bat pheromones to bend them to my will.

My sister is ardently attempting to wrangle the crows that live near her house, if I can one-up her on this then I may finally have achieved true success.

Justin

Not that I know of. But hey, anything is possible. If you want to find a cave and give it a go, I'm happy to watch.

Justin followed it up with an image of a winking cartoon bat, which Clementine had to admit was rather adorable, even if his feelings for Justin were still purely platonic. It was so adorable, in fact, that he ended his next fanfic chapter with Kirk sending Spock a winking cartoon wolf. Clem still occasionally found himself staring at Justin, his heart in knots and his brain whirling. They were just friends, he was certain about that—friends and business partners. And what Clementine truly needed from Justin most wasn't lust or love, but information.

For all that he'd learned so far, there was one question he still hadn't found the courage to breach. He knew as much about vampires now as most other vampires were likely to, but still he couldn't figure out how he'd become one. Particularly since he'd never been bitten.

Clementine

Can we meet again tomorrow night?

Justin

Always.

Always. That made Clementine smile to himself. If only his good humor could stay that way.

11

JUSTIN

Justin arrived at the micro-cemetery to find Clementine already leaning against the dirty stucco at the side of the alley, staring distantly toward the empty shopfront across the way. His slacks had been tucked unevenly into his boots, and his scarf had come half unwrapped from his turtle-necked sweater, falling farther off each time he ran his hands over its hanging edge.

"You lost, Lemon?" Justin nudged Clem in the shoulder, brow lifted.

The vampire shuddered like he was coming out of a stupor. His curls bobbed as he shook his head, the cast of the nearby lamps turning them a gilded auburn. "Only in my head, I suppose."

The giggle of a child echoed from down the road and a black cat sauntered across the dumpster to their right, but their little bubble of the neighborhood seemed lost in time, a hollow, quiet place that pulled the sound away and drained the color into deep black shadows and the orange sheen of the streetlamps. Clementine was beautiful in it: a timeless god, pulled not from a laboratory or a campus, but from the threads of legend. He still didn't look at Justin, his eyes fixed on an angelic mural whose wings stretched over the vacant shop. Half the golden ichor that dripped from its wings gleamed as though freshly painted while the other half drowned in a darkness like the night.

One of Isaiah's many masterpieces. If the dark-haired angel's face had turned toward the light, he suspected he knew who they'd resemble. It was a terrible likeness. If Justin had wings they'd be too stained in blood to drip anything but red.

He slumped against the wall at Clem's side. "Something wrong?"

Clementine startled. He drew a thick breath, and when he let it out again, he seemed emptier than before. "No."

There were no fangs beneath his lips, just their gentle curves, the little dip in the middle accented by the shadows that turned his slight frown mysterious and intriguing. If Justin could only run a finger along Clementine's mouth, it seemed he might ease the strain. He could almost feel the softness of Clem's skin, the clean shave of his chin, the ridge of his Adam's apple and the curls at his temple, the way the coils of hair would feel if he grabbed them and pulled Clementine's mouth to his own. The thrall of that desire bundled sharp behind Justin's teeth, so thick he had to roll his tongue over it. If only Justin was free to ask that of him, worthy of letting his worship become touch.

Clem closed his eyes. "I've been thinking a lot about my own turning, and I need to know how humans become vampires."

"Yeah, sure," Justin replied automatically. "Whatever you want, I'm here for you." So long as it didn't distract him from his debt, the back of his mind reminded him.

Clementine nodded. "Could we have this conversation in private, please?"

"Of course." Justin smiled, trying to soften the normal sharpness of his teeth, but with the guilt still swirling in his gut he wasn't sure he managed it. As open as his neighborhood was to having vampires in their midst, it didn't make them all equally accepting of discussions like these. Taboo, some called it, like they could stop themselves from accidently waking up a vampire if only they refused to recognize how it happened.

He headed, wordlessly, across the street. Approaching the old shop didn't hurt the way it once had—he'd been in and out of it so many times since Jose's death that the sharpness of the ache had lost some of its hold—but visiting still tugged at all his buried guilt. Of the three keys he kept on him, the one for the vacant storefront was the oldest and most worn, a piece of history he should have returned weeks ago but couldn't bring himself to give up. It still slid into the lock—no new owners had come to replace them yet—and the stiff door creaked open.

"This place was a thrift shop for decades," Justin explained.

He hadn't been in since they'd cleared out most of it before Christmas, but nothing had changed in those few weeks. The emptiness turned the place from a hazy, musky fantasy world to a haunted space of long forgotten things silhouetted by the orange lights from outside: a lampstand with a shattered bulb beside a bare display case, a pair of plush teddy bears bleeding fluff on a high ledge, a bookshelf where only stray papers remained. It had held such beauty in his youth, then such despair as his pain and anger had developed into a storm throughout his teenage years. He could still pick out windowpanes he'd broken at fifteen, the crack in the only shelf that had survived his drunken seventeen year demands for money, the nicks he'd left in the arched wood ceiling six months later as, high out of his mind, he'd tried to stick a duffel bag of stolen knives into it, not caring what or who they fell on as he stood beneath. Jose had always been there to quietly mend things after Justin's violence, to offer Justin the same care and tenderness with which he treated the rest of the world.

It was a love he'd never deserved, even before his final act of depravity.

"It was owned by a vampire once," his voice went tight, and even the distance of the epithet couldn't stop him from seeing Jose stacking his mother's old romance books on the shelf and hearing his laugh catch in the high ceiling like it was infectious. At least his blood had been wiped from the floors a decade ago. "He got this place to thrive, but no one else has really managed to turn a profit since. It officially collapsed a couple months ago." Mrs. Mendoza had threatened to give it to him, claimed Jose had always hoped he'd take it over, but even if he'd had the time, he didn't have the right to a place he'd abused so thoroughly. "The building has such personality, though. I hope something good comes of it."

"It's lovely," Clementine replied, his gaze drifting as he stood there, backlit by the orange glow of the street.

Justin had to move his feet to stop himself from staring. He meandered along the center of the room, all too aware of Clementine following him. Clem's strides took him ahead of Justin, but he paused at a back table to pick up a pair of small objects. Justin quickly recognized them: a set of shakers, one a lemon with a large slice cut out and the other the slice itself, delicate and sturdy all at once.

Clementine snorted, twisted the bigger lemon between his fingers. "I suppose no one wanted these."

"Ah, no, I did, actually." Justin tried not to feel embarrassed as he stopped beside Clementine. "I had set them aside when we went through everything in December, but then… I don't know, I guess I got distracted." He picked up the little slice. "They're charming in their own way, aren't they?"

"I suppose." He was standing so near to Justin now, their shoulders practically touching, and he lifted the larger whole of the lemon shaker up to the side of Justin's. His fingers slid under the base of Justin's shaker, skin brushing skin in a stuttering rush of sensation that Justin could have sworn

Clementine had to feel, but he seemed too focused on lining the two pieces up. They fit.

Clementine turned his head then. The presence of his mouth this near to Justin's neck and the electric touch of their hands made Justin ache, deep and hollow, like there were places within him that needed to be filled, places beyond the physical—though he'd have approved of that too in a heartbeat. It was wrong of him to even dwell on it, he knew; every moment here distracted him from Ala Santa. He didn't deserve any part of Clementine that wasn't bringing money back to his vampires. And yet...

Justin shuddered the desire away and set the shaker down.

"So, vampire turnings," he said, sitting himself on the edge of the table. "How much do you remember of your own? It generally works best when you're drained near the point where death would be inevitable without a transfusion, and then when the pain hits it tinges whatever memories you have left, so I know a lot of vampires forget most of their experience."

Clementine leaned against the table beside him, staring out across the shop. "Let's assume I remember nothing."

He presented it like a hypothetical—an experiment by a scientist who viewed much of life under an analytical gaze—but when Justin lay the suggestion out beside everything else he knew of Clem and everything Clem *didn't* know of vampirism, his stomach turned. Most turnings were horrific, of course; the transformation killed people nearly as often as it let them live, and those who survived traded sickness and wrinkles for dependence and hatred. Few humans went into it unless they had no other choice, often forced there as a final effort to cure an otherwise fatal illness—or debilitating pain—or from the bad luck of partnering with a vampire who didn't understand what they were doing until it was too late—or worse, one who just didn't care.

But to not remember any of it, perhaps not even the identity of the vampire involved, was a trauma that Justin didn't want to contemplate.

Justin nodded slowly, hoping his horror wasn't written across his face. "What have you heard, then?"

"The usual rumors." Clementine's tone was detached, as though he was surveying this as a distant myth and not a thing that influenced the way society perceived him before they even knew him as a person. "The most common belief I've encountered is that any number of vampire bites may result in a turning, but the arguments of which ones and why are varied. Some paint it like a viral infection, others like a curse. Many associate it with multiple bitings, particularly of a more sexual and consensual nature, but some act as though merely touching a vampire might bring about the change."

Clementine went quiet then, but it was with a familiar contemplation that Justin didn't feel right interrupting.

Finally Clem rewarded him, his arm brushing the side of Justin's knee for just an instant as he continued. "But these all seemed superstitious to me. Curses aren't real, and no virus—if it is a virus, which has yet to be proven—is random in its infection. I assume there is some transmission source we've yet to discover, and that it bears rules of its own, but rules nonetheless."

It was exactly the thoughtful, logical answer Justin expected from him. "I certainly don't know its rules on a chemical level—"

"Molecular, most likely," Clementine interrupted. "Though the chemical components determine the... this is irrelevant, I apologize."

"Irrelevant but cute."

Clementine hummed to himself in such a low, contemplative tone that Justin couldn't tell if Clem had even noticed.

"Anyway," Justin went on, "there *is* a consensus throughout much of the vampiric community. Not an exact science, but still two things that make it far more likely for the turning to be initiated. First is blood loss. Almost all turnings happen when the human has lost a significant amount of blood. If a human actively seeks to turn, they'll always be drained near to death."

"Huh," Clementine said, and no more.

"The second is the venom. The more of the vampire's toxins there are in a human's system, the more likely they'll end up turning."

"It's in the venom? Can a human turn from one and not the other? Extensive blood loss but little venom, or extensive venom but little blood loss?"

"I'm not sure. I've heard some vamps—older ones, usually, with senses more honed than your average vampire—talk about their venom itself feeling wrong when they've supplied too much of it at one time. At some point during a long feeding, a vampire gets a bit loopy too, so it's no wonder that most wouldn't notice it, but these reports describe it as though they've run through their fresh venom supply and hit the dregs. Like they're using venom that's old or gone bad or—"

"*Turned*," Clem supplied. "Incredible. There's so much left to study here. If laboratories like Vitalis-Barron would only work with vampires to help them learn more about themselves, instead of using them as lab rats."

Justin grimaced. Vitalis-Barron's disregard had turned his stomach even before he'd learned what they were really doing. It was discomforting enough when one of the most profitable pharmaceutical companies constantly recruited vampires for research they had no intentions of ever using to help the vampiric community. He was glad he'd managed to provide his own vampires with enough blood and lodging to keep any of them from volunteering. "That's the problem though: that it would still be humans doing the studying, humans deciding what to do with the data. The knowledge itself isn't the issue, but rather the people who control it, and the likelihood that they will choose certain things. If it was the humans who knew the ins and outs of how vampires worked, then they could use it to forcibly eradicate whatever causes vampirism. To eradicate the future of vampires altogether."

A sound came from Clem, so soft and tight that the large space nearly swallowed it up. "Wouldn't that be a good thing? If we could learn how to replicate a vampire's immunity and longevity in humans, we could retain everything good about it—all the knowledge it might bring us to forward humanity—then stop vampirism from infecting anyone new. Isn't that the best outcome for the world? For the people like—like me—who didn't want this?"

"I'm sure some vampires would agree that it is." Justin spoke gently, without judgment. Clementine didn't need his righteousness; he had been hurt by his vampirism—was still being hurt—and his frustration and desire were normal, as was the fact that, through the blinders his own experience had placed on him, he could see no better world than one without vampirism. "Few vampires chose this life happily, but for many it has become a large part of who they are, and they don't want the things that make them different to be sterilized and handed over to humans while the remaining vamps are left to die out. They want sunblock that works and blood that isn't illegal and a society that doesn't fear them. They want to live in a world that is worth offering their strengths to, not to be used and abandoned after in favor of some sparkling utopia built on the graves of who and what they were."

"Oh." There was a long, incomplete silence, Clementine so deeply in thought that he went still as a statue, seeming not even to breathe for a long series of moments.

Justin gently pressed his palm to the vampire's arm.

Clem stiffened, then he patted Justin's fingers, resting his hand just below it after, the side of his pinky brushing Justin's thumb. "It's hard to imagine a world like that. But I can see how it would be a better place than the one where we ended vampirism entirely. If I could go out in the sun, and I could keep my job, and the people I knew thought no less of me, then being this monster—it wouldn't hurt me so monstrously anymore." He inhaled, sharp and breathless like a laugh. "I'd like to enjoy the blood I was drinking, of course."

Justin smiled. "I can't fix any of those others, but there's still a chance you'll find blood you like if you keep looking. It's something you crave, right? Like an empty shelf in your soul waiting to be filled."

"It is." The statement hung in the air, as though all the emptiness from earlier had been released, and it laced between Justin and Clementine like cobwebs. It made Justin's heartbeat pick up. He felt his weight shift toward Clem as the vampire continued. "It's exactly like that."

"Then it's out there." He squeezed Clementine's arm. "You'll find it."

If only it was Justin's blood. He swore he could feel Clem's gaze fix on his neck: an unwavering hold, like the quick thrum of his pulse was luring the vampire in. Like

Clementine might suddenly sink his fangs into Justin's skin, dragging all of Justin's desire blazing to the surface with a touch of his venom. He was too afraid to glance over and find himself wrong.

Instead he swallowed. With a mind of its own his thumb brushed up and down Clem's arm, as though needing to feel more of the vampire.

Clementine shifted, his arm drifting beneath Justin's grasp. But he didn't pull away.

Justin did finally look at him then, and his face nearly collided with Clementine's shoulder. He caught the line of the vampire's gaze just for an instant, peering down at him. At him, at his neck, at the lack of space between them, who knew. Clem pulled away so quickly that it could have been anything, if not for the way his fangs were still flagrantly out, the tips glistening with such swells of venom that he licked them in a way that seemed almost instinctual.

"My own turning…" He cleared his throat, his voice settling back to a light whisper, not the least bit tense or husky or predatory. "Do you want to hear about that?"

Justin felt breathless as he answered. "Please."

12

CLEMENTINE

Somehow, Clementine hadn't predicted how easy this would be.

For all his days texting with Justin, meeting him beneath the angel's wings, learning what his vampirism meant to him, and finally gathering up the courage to broach the topic of his own turning, he had never imagined that the sensation in his chest as he spoke of it wouldn't be anxiety, but excitement. But he also, somehow, hadn't factored in just how nice Justin smelled in a confined space, how the added darkness and enclosure of the thrift shop would make him feel nearer, physically and emotionally, how the weight of Justin's attention would settle on him like a comforting blanket. How safe it would all make him feel. How much he'd want to lean closer, to share this piece of himself with Justin and Justin alone. With his friend, tried and true.

When Clementine started his explanation, it was as easy as breathing. "I say that I remember nothing, but that's not entirely accurate. I was in the lab when it happened—when I assume it happened. I'd been there for fifteen hours by then, but I was waiting for the results of the test. And I fell asleep. When I woke, I had a few bruises and needle-sized cuts. But they didn't look like fang marks. I would have *noticed* had they looked like fang marks. I felt so terrible; I'm not sure how I made it home in one piece. I didn't even know I was turning until I woke up a few days later."

"Oh, Lemon. I'm so very sorry." Justin sounded it, soft and genuine, even his usual bitter edges tapered down. "And you couldn't figure out why? Were there no other clues?"

"None," he spat, the pain boiling up. "I just—I want to know why *me*. I did nothing. I was safe, I was at my job, I wasn't out letting vampires feed on me for my own benefit." He cut himself short, realizing what he'd said. "No offense."

"Offense absolutely taken, but go on."

"No, you're right, that was an awful thing for me to imply. I only meant… well, I guess it doesn't matter what I meant. It was rude and steeped in bias. I'm sorry. That you've allowed me to drink from you is an honor, truly."

"Thank you." Justin sounded sincere, if a little shocked. His lips curled. "I do like to be appreciated by the vampires I'm giving up my blood for."

Clementine's gaze went to the crook of Justin's neck, where he could suddenly feel that very blood pumping beneath the surface like it was a part of him. Had Justin always smelled this heavenly? Maybe it was a new cologne… But it was so distinctly *Justin*, bitter as a dark, earthy tea and laced with the odd chemical sweetness of his drugs. Clementine had the oddest desire to press his nose against

Justin's vein, to see if that deepened the scent. That thought finally triggered alarm bells in his brain.

Something had to be terribly wrong with him tonight.

He swallowed down the impulse and nudged his leg into Justin's foot instead. "I know I've never drained you far, but there's no risk of me accidently turning you, right? When I attacked you, you implied you couldn't be?"

"You don't give me nearly enough venom for it either." The way Justin looked at Clementine when he said it made Clem's fangs drip again. God, why was this happening? Something *was* terribly wrong with him indeed. At least Justin seemed not to notice. "But you're right, I can't turn. I think it's because I'm not human enough. I'm a lot human, don't get me wrong, but I've got some pieces of the genetic code that makes other so-called 'non-humans' stronger and faster."

So that was where his near-vampiric physical abilities came from. It made sense. Clementine knew that almost-humans like Justin were incredibly rare—people who had extra-human traits, but who could pass as humans with no change to their regular lives. For the most part, society seemed happy to forget about them.

It had always struck Clementine as philosophically bizarre that the line between *human* and *not-human-enough* was so indeterminate, yet carried so much weight if you happened to exist a hair too far to one side of it. They were all from the same large gene pool. Vampires in the south and werewolves in the north were just humans whose bodies had been modified later in life, yet they were the least respected, the least "human," as though the fact that anyone might become one made for all the more reason to push them into their own category.

"How do you know that you *can't* turn, though? Some almost-humans still can, right?"

"I... I tried it once, about ten years ago, in this very building, in fact. It did a fantastic job of almost killing me, but all I got out of it was a hospital bill I couldn't afford and enough guilt to fill a mausoleum."

"You *wanted* the life of a vampire?" Clementine tried not to sound horrified. "I'm so sorry for whatever you were going through."

"Don't be." Justin's voice went dark, his expression pinched with a pain Clementine couldn't understand but wanted suddenly, desperately, to find a way to ease. "I didn't deserve to live through that attempt."

However he tried, Clementine couldn't seem to reconcile that statement with the man beside him—this compassionate protector, who'd so clearly thrown himself in harm's way for the most oppressed people in his neighborhood—but it didn't feel right to ask, only to keep believing in him. "I'm glad you did," Clem whispered. "Whatever the case was then, I'm glad you're here now." He wanted to lean closer, to wrap an arm around Justin's shoulders and take away the strain he held, wanted to press his nose to the side of Justin's head and tell him just how much everything he'd done for him had meant. Wanted to offer him the venom that kept blooming behind his fangs until Justin felt nothing but its bliss. God, he wanted that, wanted so much to make Justin happy that he spoke again before he could help himself. "And I'm glad you still have human-enough blood for me to drink." He was instantly worried that he'd made light of a heavy topic, but the way Justin's smirk crept back into place, his body shifting toward Clementine and his face turning up like a plant to the sun, left Clem warm and melty inside.

"You can feed now, if you'd like." The way he said it, it sounded almost like *please.*

"Well..." Clementine's gaze immediately caught on Justin's neck, and he forced it lower, down to Justin's cradled wrist. He rolled his tongue over his fangs, and something in him seemed to snap into place.

He *wanted* this.

He wanted to *bite* Justin.

He wanted—

The realization scared him so much that he almost backpedaled, but Justin was sliding his hand against Clementine's, wrist turned over to reveal the veins. Every little movement Justin made, every breath he took, the scent of him, stronger and fuller than it had been before, it all made Clementine woozy with desire.

He cupped the back of Justin's wrist, massaging the muscles in gentle rolls along the pressure points, tanned skin and dark ink beneath his fingers, and within that the gentle thrum of his pulse. Clem lifted the vulnerable spot to his lips, letting himself inhale one long, precious breath.

Justin went loose, making a sound like he'd been dosed with venom despite Clem's fangs still barely touching him.

Clementine was pretty sure he had only two options then: to flee and never come back… or to commit.

So, he bit down. The yearning in the center of his being turned to a tingling warmth, as though the blood that met his tongue was satisfying something deep within him. When had the flavor turned this bright and bold? It seemed to have happened while his eyes were closed, not shocking exactly, but still overwhelming in the newness of it. He drank, not like it was a necessity, but by taking each pull with care, savoring the earthen bitterness that filled his mouth and relishing the slight honeyed sweetness it left behind. He traced one thumb through the grooves of Justin's palm as he did, and rubbed along Justin's forearm with the other, making the blood flow in languid pulses.

Justin released a long, musical breath. He eased forward, draping himself against Clementine's shoulder. This near, Clementine could imagine Justin settling into the crook of Clem's neck, sighing his little happy sounds against Clem's own pulse. The vision felt right, soft and surely platonic, but he couldn't find the courage to make it a reality. Instead he drank deeper, feeling a larger dose of venom slip into Justin's veins in the process.

Justin gave a soft whimpered sound that was almost as delicious as his blood.

Then his arm tugged out from beneath Clem as Justin nearly tumbled off the table he was sitting on.

Clem withdrew his fangs on instinct, jerking forward to catch him by the waist. Justin grunted, steadying himself. "Fuck, I relaxed too much."

"Are you—"

"I'm fine." He sounded less fine, and more downright intoxicated. He held out his wrist with a sloppy grin. "You going to deal with this?"

Clementine recognized it as one of the first things Justin had said to him. It should have brought a wave of embarrassment to be reminded of that day—of how much he'd gotten wrong. Instead it warmed his chest to know that Justin had seen that and not given up on him; had kept letting him return despite his early mistakes. For a price, anyway.

Clem wound his fingers through Justin's to turn his arm gently, cautious not to tweak the man's elbow as he licked up the lifeforce still seeping from Justin's fang nicks. They closed beneath his tongue. He licked again, cleaning the rest of the blood away, letting it linger on his lips after: not bland, not average, but delicious blood, bittersweet as dark chocolate, deep and full and incredible.

And Dr. Clementine Hughes had no idea what to do with that knowledge.

13

CLEMENTINE

Clementine liked Justin's blood.

That should have been a blessing, not a problem, he reminded himself for the thousandth time. But it *was* a problem, because it utterly and completely terrified him. Despite his desire to find blood that tasted the way it was spoken of in fiction, actually receiving it was far more distressing than the yearning had been.

Because now he had a target for that vague yearning, rendering it pointed and specific, like his soul had tuned itself to the exact frequency of Justin's heartbeat and could no longer hear anything else. And he wanted to run from that, to run so far that he never had to face whether Justin would taste the same next time—could taste better, even—or if this was just an odd blip in his broken palate.

And if Justin really would continue to taste this incredible—regardless of how platonic Clementine still swore he felt toward the man—then would Clem spend the rest of his life making trips to Ala Santa because no one else's blood would satisfy him?

He swallowed. The tips of his fangs pressed against his tongue. He drew them back up, glad the darkness around his car hid his flush. That would be another problem; that and the fact that he had the sudden instinct to let his fangs be free any time Justin was near, to bare them at him just to see Clem's desire mirrored on Justin's face and released in his breath...

Clementine swerved as his phone's ringer filled the silent car with orchestral metal, and the extra-large beach umbrella perched against his center console bumped against his elbow. Such a large part of him retaliated to the thought of answering the call that he almost pressed reject. Almost. Instead he turned the speaker's volume down and grudgingly accepted.

"Hello, Odysseus." He managed to sound far more chipper than he felt at the thought of talking to her, now, over the dreaded phone of all things, while so much of his mind was still wandering the inked skin above Justin's veins and trying to recreate the bitter tang of his scent. "How are the crows?"

"Clementine!" His sister's voice boomed uncomfortably despite the lowered volume. "They're immaculate as ever. I've been putting vitamins for feather health in their treats. You'll have to come do one of your little science projects about it to tell me if it's working."

"My *science projects* have to start *before* you give them the supplements, you know." He was getting grumbly again, only thirty seconds into the conversation. Clem swore there

134

was a time before his turning when every exchange he had with Sissy didn't make him want to snap at her. A time where he could adequately pretend her parties were the best things he'd ever experienced, that he'd have been there sooner if not for work, stayed later if he didn't have to get up so early again, drunk more if only his stomach hadn't been acting strange that week, or danced harder if the lab hadn't given him such a migraine. But lately it took more and more effort just to come across as her usual dutiful middle brother, always ready to rival Reggie's enthusiasm.

"Hm, yes, I do remember you telling me that, but I also figured I could get you to waive the usual protocol for me."

If he were in any better a mood, with any potential to visit her crows during the day, he probably would have. As it stood, he had other, better reasons to say no. He just couldn't tell any of them to Sissy. "You can't lawyer your way out of science this time."

"Perhaps not. But I can lawyer you into coming to Reggie's party. On pain of *I'll tell mother if you allow work to steal you away again.* Dr. Blood has to let you out of the lab *occasionally.* I'm going to send Vitalis-Barron a restraining order if you keep missing all my get-togethers."

Reggie's party, what was that—an evening two weeks from now? Fuck. "Work is fine, I think time has just been getting away from me. Your New Year's celebration still feels like yesterday."

"What about the garden party last Tuesday? That wine-tasting weekend I held in November?" She huffed, and her

135

voice went soft. "You missed Christmas, Clem. I understand you've been too busy for casual visits lately, but these were special."

"I'm sorry," he muttered, trying not to feel the weight of her hurt. They had all required too much time in the sun, too many opportunities for his family or their friends to notice something was different about him, too much of the kind of stress that broke him to pieces. "Things will calm down if I get the promotion." *Once* he got the promotion. That would have been a better way to phrase it. Now he looked as though he was trying too hard and it still wouldn't be enough. It had to be, though. No matter how much he would hate the change, he needed the money.

Odysseus didn't respond for so long that Clem wondered if they'd lost connection, or worse, she was judging his authenticity, seeing through his excuse to all the ways he was failing right now. "Well, don't work yourself too hard in the meantime," she said. "And find someone to bring to Reggie's party! I know you're not dating at the moment, but you could get a friend or two to come."

When he'd told Sissy he was *taking a break* from dating, he'd meant he couldn't handle putting himself out there just to be disappointed over and over when his partners grew more into him yet he felt nothing in return.

"You do have friends still, right?" Sissy asked. "You're doing *something* outside that damn lab?"

"I'm driving in my car, which, last I checked, was outside the lab, yes."

"Driving where?"

"To work," he responded instinctually. He *was* driving to work, moving out of San Salud's financial district with the shimmering expanse of the lake to his right. Though now that he thought about it, he didn't have to be. He was caught up on most of the projects he'd let slip while starving. The only thing there for him right now was the soothing routine of it all.

"It's Saturday," Sissy said, as though standing inside his brain.

"I'm just popping in for a moment," he justified. "And I'll probably even go out after." To pick up a bottle of something harder than beer and bring it back home. That still counted as *out*.

"Oh, I think the Fishnettery has a trivia thing tonight! That sounds just up your alley."

"My brain's a little too dead for facts at the moment." Hopefully she couldn't hear the cringe in his voice. Trivia, he liked, but the thought of it happening in a bar's busy atmosphere with the uncomfortable lighting, loud music, and crowded bodies made him feel queasy. But maybe that *would* be enough to get Justin out of his head. Softer, he added, "I really do need a drink, though." And a friend.

"Oh, Clem." She made a sharp sound. "Tell me where you're going and I'll be there."

"No—Sissy—" Panic swept through him, and he realized his fangs were out again with a curse. He could *not* risk her seeing that. But he also couldn't risk her feeling pushed away, or she'd throw an impromptu family vacation to the Caribbean or something in an attempt to cheer him up, and then he'd have to quickly choose whether he wanted to die from sun-poisoning or the shame of being a terrible brother. They both sounded about as painful, but to his knowledge one took extensively longer.

"There's something you're not telling me." Sissy's tone hardened. "So spill it."

"There's nothing to spill." There were a lot of things he wasn't telling Sissy, a whole life's worth that would make him look like a pathetic hermit who couldn't handle social situations and didn't know how to properly have fun. But those had built up slowly and secretly over a childhood of watching his family bloom under the spotlight and knowing he couldn't fall short of that. The one plaguing him at the moment had hit like a lightning bolt, far more volatile and still dancing around his chest with electric tingles.

She sighed. "I'm phoning in Reggie."

"No, god, please," he rambled as the other line began to ring. The only thing worse than a one sibling phone call was two siblings on the same call. "I mean it, I don't need an intervention, Sissy, it's just a—"

"Yo, Sis," Reggie answered at the same moment Clem exclaimed, "A crush!"

They all went silent. An incoming car honked at him, and he veered out of its lane with a curse. The umbrella clattered again. His heart thrummed in his ears, turning the rest of the world distant.

It *wasn't* a crush—god, why had he said that? Or perhaps it was, but rather it was a *blood* crush. That sounded right; all the tingling feelings, the yearning, the inability to direct his thoughts anywhere else—they were all over the blood of a man he was absolutely, positively, not otherwise crushing on.

But that wasn't something he could clarify to Odysseus and Reginald. So he'd just have to *pretend* the feelings were romantic.

He hated that he was telling them *any* of this in the first place, letting them judge how broken his attraction was for themselves. But he wasn't getting out of it now, and he knew it; his siblings would show up at his doorstep with roses and chocolates if he hung up, which would be a feat seeing how Reginald wasn't even in their time zone at the moment. He had to pretend that what hadn't worked for him all these years was finally clicking into place when in reality it was just blood he craved, not Justin's body, not his mind or his soul— even if he did adore those things, too. Platonically.

He mentally apologized to Justin as he repeated, "I, um, I have something *like* a crush, I guess."

"Oh," Sissy whispered.

Clementine cringed. He could see the Vitalis-Barron entrance gate from beneath the bridge of the freeway, the city sparkling with a thousand lights in his rearview mirror. This wasn't a conversation he wanted to have in his work's parking lot though, not while his head felt this light and his fangs kept sliding down at the mere thought of Justin. He pulled off the road into a dirt lot for the beach-side hiking trail instead. A van of young people were lounging and laughing on the other side, but he parked under the shade of the pine trees that turned to a deep forest the farther south the lake curved.

Still, Odysseus and Reginald said nothing else. This—this was why he hated these calls. It was already hard enough to tell what anyone was thinking while they were standing right in front of him—he didn't need the added anxiety of not being able to see their faces, having to increase the volume until it hurt just to make out the finer details of their tones.

"Hello?" he ventured.

"Clem has a crush!" Reggie whooped. "This was worth the early wake up."

"Spill it *now*, Clem." Odysseus's voice should not have been able to get that low anymore, damn her.

"It's not *really* a crush, okay," he clarified again.

"But it's *something*?" Sissy asked.

"Maybe." Clem dropped his head into his hands. "There's this… guy."

He lingered over the word, half terrified and half excited. It felt *right* to want something intimate from another man, even if it was just this one small thing. After all the time he'd spent obsessing over Spock and Kirk's every canon glance and writing them with sexual tension up to their ears, the fact that it was a man's blood that he craved made sense. *Just* his blood. Just his skin beneath Clem's lips and his vulnerable little sighs and the taste of him on Clem's tongue. That was definitely gay, but not a sexual kind of gay.

"No shit." Reggie reacted faster than Odysseus, clapping twice slowly. "I *told* Sissy—"

"You shouldn't try to predict people's sexualities or genders, Reginald, it's rude," Sissy said, incredibly matter-of-fact. "But yes, Clem, you're into men, we know."

"I'm not, though! That's the problem." Clem wanted to sob, but he tried to keep his voice even. He couldn't break down with them. He couldn't let them know just how much this was distressing him.

Sissy paused. "Explain, Clementine. Just explain it to us."

"I've never *been* interested in anyone. Everyone I've dated—I've kept things as slow as possible and dropped it when they pushed for more because the more—the romantic dinners and the physical aspects—they've always felt wrong." There, he'd said it. Flat out, irrevocable. Already his mind was screaming at him to try to take it back, nausea building so heavily that he almost cracked his window open for the fresh air. His throat felt raw from the words. This was the most vulnerable thing he'd told his siblings in years—in all their lives perhaps. And he had to keep going. "I thought maybe I was aromantic and asexual, but I've always *wanted* that kind of attraction, it just hadn't happened for me. It's like when you're craving a certain ice cream but all you can find are the flavors you don't enjoy, and you keep trying them hoping the next one might work out, but it never quite satisfies." So many years of that, so many disappointments.

But now he had *something*, even if it wasn't the full thing. He felt himself smile at the thought, sad and scared, but excited, too. "Then I met this *guy*, and I didn't think he was my flavor in the beginning. He *wasn't* my flavor. At first he tasted just as bland as everyone else."

"By taste," Reggie interrupted, "is this saliva or cum or—"

"My god, Reggie, it's a metaphor!" Clem ran his hands down his face, groaning into them. If only blood had been included on that list.

"You know it was just too good to pass up!"

"Reginald Hughes, who let you on this call?" Sissy snapped.

"Sorry!" he grumbled, his connection crackling for a moment. "Ice cream metaphor again, go."

Clementine rolled his eyes. He ran his tongue under the point of one of his fangs. "I've been getting to know him for a couple weeks, though, and suddenly... it's different." Suddenly he tasted like a better flavor than Clementine could have imagined. Suddenly Clem's gaze didn't know what to do with itself, and his heart made indecent music in his chest, and the thought of licking this particular man's skin made him think not of germs and the gross sheen of saliva he'd leave but of the sensation of it and the way it lit up his nerves. "Am I batty?"

"Not unless you've been *biting* him." Reggie giggled at his own joke, clapping again. "Get it, because vampires, bats, biting?"

"You can't explain the pun, it takes the joke out of it," Sissy said before Clementine could, and his nearly identical comment lodged in his throat. He dropped his forehead onto the wheel. What was he becoming? Odysseus inhaled so loud he could hear it over the phone and added, "Clementine, are you sure you're not just demisexual?"

"Oh shit, that's a form of ace, isn't it?" Reggie asked, sounding weirdly genuine. "I dated an ace girl while I was in Australia last summer. Biromantic, asexual, she said, so she's romantically into both women and men but not sexually attracted to them." He paused. "Did I get that right?"

"You're a good little ally, Reggie," Sissy cooed. "Now shut up and let the queers speak."

"Right. Muting myself." And he actually went quiet, which was somehow the weirdest part of Clem's day.

"Demisexual is the one where you have to know someone first, before the attraction comes?" Clementine asked, less a question and more a verbal contemplation. He wanted that—he wanted to *be* that, to claim it and hold it close and make it his own because it felt so much like who he wanted himself to be. But he wasn't *actually* attracted to Justin, just to the man's blood. He tried not to let that disappointment drown him. If this had occurred with blood, maybe it could with sex. Justin had implied that there was a connection between them. "It sounds nice, but I've been close to plenty of people in the past"—a few people, anyway; he *had* been good friends with a couple of his past partners, particularly the ones who hadn't pushed him for anything—

"and I've never had that—I mean *this*," he corrected, "happen before. Can I still be demi if there's only one person I'm demi for? Am I demi *and* gray-ace, or—" He wanted to say, *or am I just a weird, broken asexual who's wanting something so bad that he's seeing it where it doesn't exist,* but he'd shared enough of his failings already that night. His siblings didn't need to know exactly how insecure this all made him. "How do I know if that's me?"

"You don't know, Clem. You just have to take the evidence you have, and you argue it with yourself, and if the facts fit strongly enough with the definition, then you win the case." It sounded like something Sissy had said before, over and over again, if only in her head. "If the term feels right, then it's probably right, and even if it isn't, you can run a retrial any time you choose. Unlike our terrible court system."

Clem steadied himself. He had to ask the question, even if he already knew the answer. He had to hear it for himself. "And even if I don't fit a category, or what I think is my sexuality changes again—then there's still nothing wrong with me?"

Sissy's voice went as warm as it was stable. "Whatever you are, Clementine, there's nothing wrong with you."

Clem tried to smile, but his fangs clinked into his lower teeth. If only she knew. Unlike their parents, Sissy had never said a cruel word against vampires, but her pity for them had always been clear. In her eyes, they were impaired, and perhaps that wasn't the vampire's fault and it shouldn't have been up to them to fix themselves or make a better place in the world, but that view didn't come without a sliver of judgment. Of disappointment.

The silence between them was broken by a harsh speaker pop, followed by a clatter and Reggie's shouting.

"Fuck! You can hear me now?" He called into the phone, his question so loud by the end that he seemed to have his mouth directly on the microphone.

"Yes!" Both Clem and Sissy shouted back.

Reggie laughed. "I actually muted myself! And then I forgot I did that. Anyway: there's lots of things wrong with you, Clem, like your choice in music and that pair of shoes with the buckles. But like Sissy said, this is definitely not one of them."

"Thanks, Reginald," Clem mumbled, rubbing his temples. His baby brother seemed, at least, to be trying. Maybe though, he'd been trying more often than Clem had given him credit for…

"You can like any flavor of *ice cream* you want, my guy," Reggie added, so much emphasis on the *ice cream* he had to be winking through the phone. "Some tastes are just acquired is all."

Or maybe Clementine wasn't judging him harshly *enough*. "God, I don't even want to know what you think this metaphor represents now."

Sissy laughed like maybe she was crying on the inside.

Reggie didn't miss a single beat. "So you're bringing this tasty guy to Sissy's party?"

"I thought it was *your* party?"

"It is his party," Sissy said, while Reggie answered, "No it's definitely for Sissy."

"Traitor," Sissy muttered. "It's for all of us. We deserve an excuse to have fun for the night."

"Whoever's party it is, I'm not bringing him," Clem replied firmly, trying his best to leave no room for argument. If he gave them a crack, together they'd tear down the whole wall. They seemed especially good at that tonight. "First, he and I are not that close yet, and I don't even think he'd come—it's not really his scene. And second, I imagine Mom and Dad will be there, seeing how your invite says it's at their house. I'm not exposing someone I actually like to their scrutiny so soon."

And Clem would not be able to take his eyes off Justin's neck or stop licking his fangs, which didn't bode particularly well for either of them. Unless he could convince Justin to let him feed in a closet or something. That sounded a bit thrilling, actually, like a scene he'd written last week involving a blow-job under a table and Kirk's inability to mask his emotions.

Clem shook his head. He could not talk himself into wanting to bite Justin under his parent's nose if Justin was never going to be under his parent's nose in the first place.

He put the car into reverse. "But I'll be there. Six-thirty on Friday, right?" He'd have to put in some day hours at the lab first, but he could pull the curtains closed and nap in his

146

managerial office on the third floor in the morning—it might as well have a use.

"Six-thirty, and not a moment later."

"Right. I can't wait," he lied. But maybe this time he could conclude the stressful outing by returning to Ala Santa for something less exhausting, something quiet and bitter and sweet all at once. Clem forced himself to bundle his flutter of excitement back up. He still had to confirm that this whole thing wasn't in his head, that Justin's blood actually did taste as good as he remembered. And hope that didn't scare Justin off in the process.

Twilight hadn't properly set in yet when Clementine arrived, his scarf hooding his head and his hands tucked into his pockets. He almost missed Justin, perched on the angel monument's shoulder. Its wings obscured his back and one of his arms was slung atop its head as he stared off across the street, the smoke from his joint wafting into the pink and indigo sky.

Clem hesitated at the base of the statue. He had thought of a million and ten ways to say this: *It's the strangest thing, but I like your blood now* and *it probably means nothing, but I think your bitterness is growing on me* and *did you change your diet, because you taste different suddenly,* or maybe just to say nothing at all and let the world keep on spinning, Justin none the wiser. That was the safer course of action. He didn't fit in Clementine's life, not permanently, and Clem couldn't ask him to. *Feed me forever because everyone else tastes gross* wasn't an acceptable request, no matter how much Clem was paying him.

And he *was* paying Justin, just as he was selling out information on Ala Santa's vampires for a future that included the money to keep living and feeding instead of being thrown into a basement of torture. The deal between himself and Justin had nothing to do with whether Clem craved Justin's blood or whether Justin enjoyed Clem's bite—it was a transaction, nothing more. As long as Clem kept paying and gathering information for Anthony, then they *could* just go on like this.

But Clem wanted more. He *wanted* to bite Justin, not with cautious professionalism but predatory desire. And he wanted Justin to want it too.

He just had no idea how the hell to say that.

Clementine cleared his throat.

Justin's expression widened as he looked down. A slight smile spread across it: no teeth bared, only the twitch of lips and the gentling of his brow. His voice was unusually soft and even. "Hey, Lemon."

He shifted like he meant to leap to the ground, but before he could, Clem grabbed one of the angel's arms and swung himself up, setting part of his ass seamlessly on its shoulder across from Justin. He smiled back. "Hello."

"That was beautiful," Justin said, as though it was just a normal fact and not something that made Clem's heart leap oddly and an anxious flutter rush through him.

"I *am* a vampire, and I can't change that. So when I can, I might as well enjoy it?" The question sounded like a series of real words in a sensible order, even if they echoed a bit between his ears.

Justin's lips quirked farther. "It suits you."

Would every compliment from him feel like a blow to the chest now?

Clementine tightened his grip on the angel's head. He could do this; he could tell Justin, not just that he tasted good, but that the yearning to feed on him made Clementine feel feral. That he wanted the romantic push and pull of a vampire and their prey, even if he wasn't romantically interested in Justin himself. And after all he'd already shared with Justin, that should have been easy.

Potentially devastating to his emotional state and absolutely uncharted waters, but easy.

Justin dropped his remaining joint onto the angel's outstretched hands and turned toward Clementine. He crossed his arms over the top of the statue's head, one wrist—the wrist he always gave to Clem—languidly splaying into Clem's space, the vulnerable flesh there exposed. The elegant tribal tattoos that wrapped it broke in beautiful triangular points around a geometric sun framed at the top and bottom by ferns. They had become so familiar to Clementine that he could replicate them on post-its, which he now had at least three of tucked into various notepads and the side of his computer monitor. That had come before he'd realized how good Justin tasted. A sign from his subconscious, probably.

Clementine perched between the angel's shoulder and wing, so low that Justin's bare arm dangled almost carelessly in front of Clem's chin. It drew Clem's fangs free and made his mouth thick with hunger as he fought the impulse to tuck his fangs into the vein. He ached behind his jaw and in the crook of his gut with the need to be just a little closer to Justin's skin. To feel him. To taste him. To *take* from him, and to take in a way that gave back in bliss.

"Well?" Justin asked, his teeth bared. He leaned close enough that Clementine swore he could feel his breath, hot and thick, and the pounding of his heart through his V-necked shirt.

Restraining himself with everything he had in him, Clem traced the lines of Justin's tattoos with one fingertip. He turned his head, nearly knocking his nose into Justin's. "Well, indeed."

Justin looked caught in a high beam for a moment, like he was dangling on the edge of a knife-point. Flight or fight. His lips parted.

Slowly, he bowed his chin, prostrating himself until he all but laid over the angel's head, his chin pressed to the stone and one arm stretched vulnerably before him. His swept-back hair brushed against Clem's lips. It smelled as he tasted, like an aged tea, earthy and bitter, and something chemically sweet beneath. The drug he smoked, Clem realized; it had a lingering scent a bit like that. Clem breathed it in.

There were people on the street, the laughter of a Sunday evening spilling into the alleyway. People who could look up and pick him out among the monument's hulking silhouette: a vampire luring in his prey. But that was exhilarating somehow, adding a spark of tension that fueled the fire already building inside Clem.

He turned his chin until it bumped against Justin's arm. His lips brushed Justin's skin with the lightest touch. For once, the contact of mouth to flesh didn't put Clementine off, didn't make him cringe away. Because Justin's blood sang beneath it. That was the only reason why. Looking for a deeper one would only tangle his heart into knots.

As he lingered there, Justin didn't make a sound, as much as he *stopped* making sound for long enough that it became a noise of its own. Clementine grinned just to show off his fangs, catching Justin's gaze out of the corner of his eyes.

"You're like the world's most predatory puppy today." Justin's smirk infused his voice, but he leaned backward. His arm slipped away a bit too.

Clementine grabbed Justin's wrist, his hold gentle but firm. "This is mine, I think," he grumbled, and it came out like a breathless growl.

Justin went limp for him, his grin turning almost sloppy. Not a threat, but a lure. Though perhaps that was a different kind of threat all on its own. "Are you going to bite me already, or is this just a tease?"

Clem lifted his shoulders, trying not to look like a child caught with his hand in the cookie jar. He slipped his fingers along the underside of Justin's wrist, circling his pulse.

Justin's blood sang to him; he didn't have to taste it again to know that. And maybe... maybe he didn't want to taste it, not yet. If he only got one bite a day—every other day, when either of them were busy—then he was going to make it count. "I'll feed, but I'd like to run an experiment first. If you're up for it."

"Will I like this experiment?" Justin's words were barely more than an exhalation.

Clementine smiled. For all the social engagements he'd found hard, taxing, and terrifying in the past, pressing Justin in this way felt like breathing. And oh, how he wanted to keep doing it. "That depends... Do you *like* to be teased?"

14

JUSTIN

Did he *like* to be teased.

This goddamned vampire—he could have pulled the entire earth out from under Justin and it would have done less nonsense to his stomach. He could still feel the way he'd shuddered as Clementine bared his fangs, the way Clem's hair, his skin, his very *soul* had smelled as he leaned so close to Justin that his heat seemed to radiate from him like the sun. Justin was a cat who wanted to curl up in the vampire's light for a thousand years.

And Clementine—this beautiful, timeless urban deity with his golden curls and his elegant turtlenecks and silken scarves and his smile that just barely quirked the edges of his lips—had told Justin he wanted to keep doing this, to keep teasing him this way.

It was absolutely going to lead to Justin's self-destruction once he had to finally turn the bulk of his attention back to Ala Santa, but at the moment he couldn't find it in himself to care.

Clementine's shoulders straightened, and he stared across the street as he continued. "I'm aware that when you agreed to this, I had likely given the impression that I wanted your blood with as little theatricality as possible. But I'd like more than that now. If you're willing, I'd like to continue this experimental exploration of my vampirism. I understand that it's a higher level of engagement than you agreed to, though, so I'm willing to compensate you accordingly."

Somehow even with the professional wording and the poised, stoic way Clementine delivered the question, it still churned something loose inside Justin. *More than that. If you're willing. Exploration. Engagement.* He could not help himself—Justin wanted to hear the vampire say it. "Explain what this will entail?"

Clementine's pale skin seemed to glow faintly in the night light. His Adam's apple bobbed. "Well, that's—I can't give you an exact list. I'm making this up as I go."

"Then we'll put vampiric instincts at the top?"

"Yes, that's—Yes," he agreed. His fingers traced up and down his own forearm, drawing Justin's attention like a moth to the flame. "And I'd like to touch you more. Your arms, especially. As I was doing, soft but well, grabby, I suppose?"

"Grabby," Justin repeated. If Clementine noticed how hoarse and breathless Justin had gone, he didn't show it.

"Momentarily restrictive."

"You want to momentarily restrict me and touch me."

"Also the crook of your elbow. I'd like the crook of your elbow, please."

If Clementine decided to so much as turn his head he would see the effect this was having on Justin. The tender skin along the inside of his arm tingled, its little flutters seeming to roll up his veins and into his chest. "Would you be having my neck too, while you're at it?"

"If I may?" Clementine kept gazing toward the street, but he appeared not to be seeing the cars that rolled slowly by, much less the pedestrians that paused to eat outside the Chinese bakery across the way. "From your jaw to the nape of your neck—"

Justin's imagination was going wild now, picturing Clementine's fingertips caressing his jawline and fiddling with the short hair at the base of his skull.

"—to the tips of your shoulders and along your collarbones, if that's acceptable."

"I should put my chest up for auction too, at this rate," Justin teased.

Clem pulled in his arms and his attention dropped to his lap. "I'm sorry. I'm being ridiculous."

Justin almost told him to fuck right off with that nonsense, but then Clem absentmindedly fiddled with the fabric of his slacks, and Justin's brain turned to putty trying to picture what else lay between them, what it might be like to reach over, despite the people walking innocently below them, and slip his palm between Clementine's pants and his

155

briefs and make him fight to stay silent as he rode the edge of an orgasm.

Fuck. Justin needed his head above water. He needed to say no to Clem, was what he needed to do. Just hearing Clementine describe what he wanted to do with Justin was distracting enough, regardless of how scientifically he'd presented the offer and how unlikely it was that his thoughts were going to the same place as Justin's. Those fantasies alone made Justin lightheaded and giddy, though, like he was fifteen again, learning what it felt like to have another boy breathe against his lips and tug at the rim of his pants.

But this was no more a relationship than any of his toxic teenage flings had been, and now he was an adult with a hundred different jobs to do and a neighborhood to protect. He couldn't give in to his desires; he knew where that road led. He had started this partnership with Clementine to make more cash for Ala Santa, and that was how it would stay.

If he just *had* to let Clem touch him in order to get that money... Well, wasn't that worth the sacrifice?

Guilt rose in the back of Justin's throat but he swallowed it down, baring his teeth in his best grin. "Dammit, Lemon. You don't pay me enough to tease me like this."

"Ah, right." Clementine turned his face away, shifting to pull out his wallet. "I think I owe you the five hundred now? Do you need more for the... for letting me..." He seemed to struggle over his phrasing, each new attempt making Justin's chest tighter. Clementine dropped his wallet back into his lap twice as he tried to dig through it. "I can do, let's see… three hundred now? That feels insufficient. But tacked on to the regular fifteen and the extra hundred, that would make this nineteen hundred, every ten days. I'm not sure how long I can keep that up for…"

Justin snorted. "Am I finally bleeding you dry? You could throw in that black sweater with the gold stitching around the wrists and we'll call it even." God, it would probably smell like him and everything.

"You could exsanguinate me, and I'd just keep paying." Clementine whispered it, so soft that Justin wasn't sure it was meant for his ears. It sliced into him like a dagger all the same, tearing straight to his heart. Clementine slowly folded the three bills and tapped them to the top of the angel's head.

Justin slipped two of his fingers around them. His skin grazed Clementine's.

Finally Clem looked up, looked so deep into Justin's eyes that he seemed to be searching for something hidden within them. "Is this all we are? Business partners?"

"No, of course not. You're my friend. You're…" Justin's mind cartwheeled through every lust and longing he'd had for the last half hour—fuck, the last two weeks—and *friend* seemed insufficient a word to cover a single one of the things he'd felt. To him, Clementine was infinite. But he *was* also a payday, a highly overcharged one that Justin couldn't bear to give up now, and someone he could never have—never deserve—even if he wasn't. His mouth felt dry suddenly, and his jaw ached.

A flash of something sparked through Clementine's expression, half hidden by the darkness. He tugged at the cash in Justin's grip. "Then I suppose you don't want this?"

Justin held onto it, half impulse and half something else; responsibility. Self-destruction.

Clem let go so abruptly that it unsettled Justin. Pain flared through his shoulder blades as he straightened. He forced himself to retrieve his half-smoked joint from the angel's palms, the folded hundreds still tucked between two fingers. The little flame from his lighter cast Clementine's face in harsh angles, setting creases into the dip between his brows and frown lines around his lips.

In the split second before the fire died, Clementine's eyes leapt away from Justin's and his chin lowered. The shift changed the look entirely: no longer harsh but soft, not angry but scared and confused. Not a timeless deity but a poor man who'd woken up one day branded as a monster and was still fighting to find happiness in that.

"I'm sorry," Clementine whispered. "I don't fault you for wanting the money. It was all we ever agreed upon."

Justin exhaled a long breath, letting the smoke drift out before him. It hung for a moment in the orange beam of the streetlamps before dissolving into the night. He knew the truth: Clementine could bleed *him* dry, and Justin wouldn't stop him.

But he had Ala Santa to protect. He owed his life to them. He deserved that debt far more than he deserved

Clementine's fingertips on his skin or Clementine's venom in his veins.

Even if just the thought of that made his determination waver, made him wonder if the two might overlap, if only for a night. Just one night, with whatever it happened to bring. Maybe then he could return to focusing on his neighborhood.

"Do you want to know what I spend my money on?" Justin asked. "Come. I'll show you."

15

CLEMENTINE

Clementine hadn't known what to expect when Justin had said he'd show him what he spent his money on, but it had not been this: a little convenience shop with a grumpy old Filipino lady who occasionally shouted at Justin over her incredibly explicit paperback novel as he piled up too many groceries for one person. Clem was still reeling from his own shifting emotions; the high of Justin accepting his more predatory displays, and the low of it being all about the money, then the confusion of it not actually being all about the money, *maybe*, all the while Justin had sat across the angel's head from him, smelling like black tea, smoke, and honey and having his veins so deliciously on display beneath his gorgeously inked skin. And now this.

Clem tried not to stare at him too much, but when Justin dragged his own fingernails up and down his neck while surveying the bottled drinks, Clementine thought he might lose his mind. He bumped his elbow into Justin's as he passed, reveling in Justin's intake of breath. Justin directed him to retrieve a large box of rice, and as Clem hefted it up, he let his fangs come down far enough to lick one of them.

"That's not fair," Justin grumbled. He loaded an armful of instant ramen from the side of the cart that made him squeeze in close, his neck cocked in a way that couldn't have been entirely necessary. "You haven't even bitten me yet."

"You were the one who agreed to this being less… conventional."

"Oh, fuck off. And get a few cases of pull-ups," he added, his lips pursing in their direction.

The switch from food to household supplies made Clementine even more confused. Justin didn't have a toddler—Clementine didn't *think* Justin had a toddler. The more seemingly random items Justin piled in, the more Clementine's bewilderment broke. These weren't for Justin; at least not all of them.

"You're going to clear me out!" The woman at the counter shouted as they finally emerged, their cart so full that Clem had to hold one side to keep things from falling out. "Who will restock? Makes my shop look bad to be so empty!" She squinted at Clementine. Her tongue clicked against the roof of her mouth and she nodded slowly. "This one is plenty tall, he could do. Smart looker. Good fangs too, I think."

Clementine stiffened, a chill running through him.

"She's safe," Justin said, patting his arm.

The touch felt oddly like sunlight and a Santa Ana wind, and it left a flutter in Clementine's stomach.

But that was only from being so near Justin's blood. What he felt for Justin was purely platonic, and clinging to the idea of more would be making mountains out of mole hills, setting himself up for disappointment in the long run. Simply because he *wanted* to be demisexual didn't mean he *was*.

The old woman poked her lips toward Justin. "This one needs somebody with good fangs, hah, keep him in check."

We're not like that, Clem wanted to protest. Whatever his heart might have wished, his feelings *were* still platonic. He wasn't even technically one of Justin's vampires. But a part of him wanted to be Justin's *something* so badly that he felt the words slipping from his lips: "I'll take care of him, don't worry."

Justin suddenly looked very interested in his money. When the three hundred didn't cover the bill, he began digging through his pockets for tens and fives.

Before Clementine could stop himself, he pulled out his credit card. "Put it all on this," he said, handing it directly to the woman.

Justin's brow lowered. "You're not just a payday, Lemon."

"And this isn't part of our deal," Clem objected. "Besides, I'm curious now, and I'm certainly not helping you put any of your hoard back on the shelves."

Justin shrugged, looking so nonchalant that Clementine almost missed the subtle pink in his cheeks. "Suit yourself."

He grinned. "In that case, you can keep his change too, Mrs. Mendoza."

Mrs. Mendoza muttered under her breath.

The evening only got wilder from there. Clementine steered the cart along the precarious pavement, past broken bus stops and an angel mural so gorgeous he found himself slowing to stare.

"Isaiah's," Justin explained with a nod.

They made their way around two other micro-cemeteries, both smaller and less impressive than the one they regularly met at, past tall, rusty fences and front stoops overflowing with potted plants and windows with music so loud it thrummed through the glass. They seemed to pause at random, Justin pulling up in front of a townhouse or apartment like he was following an emotional metal detector. At each stop, he selected what to bring with ease, choosing whether to knock and leave or wait for a response. Every door that opened met him with smiles and warmth, people who welcomed him like family. He quickly but gently turned down each of their offers to come inside.

As lovely as these people seemed, Clementine was grateful that Justin didn't try to linger. Each new introduction felt as though Clem was emptying his emotional shopping cart at nearly the speed that Justin was emptying their physical one. But the effort was worth it just to watch Justin clap hands and joke and ask all the right questions, easily carrying through the kind of small talk that seemed ridiculous to Clem. The speed with which he took

163

over at the first sign of Clem's discomfort was like a breath of fresh air after a lifetime trapped in a stale room of *and how is your job going* and *are you seeing anyone.*

For all of Justin's many distractions, though, he never stopped paying attention to Clementine. Clem had been more reserved with his predatory teasing since the convenience store; a casual flash of fang here and a soft brush of his fingers there. It was hard, but not for the reasons he'd anticipated. The call of Justin's blood was still a gentle pulse beneath the man's skin, luring Clem closer, but it was how he interacted with his people that made Clementine thirst; how he genuinely helped them.

And they *were* helping people. Not in the stuffy way that Clem's parents begrudgingly contributed to charities, or the lavishly generous donations that Sissy provided the local queer organizations, but with a life and love that reached deeper and held on stronger. The goods Justin offered seemed to matter just as much to these people as the fact that he had known what they needed without being told.

And seeing this—seeing the care and affection his money distributed among the neighborhood—settled thick and tight and deep in Clementine's chest. He had never doubted that Justin was good, but knowing the depths of his selflessness turned every bundle of hundreds Clem had given him into something beautiful. If he was going to drain his bank accounts dry, this was a worthy cause. Justin wasn't just a man selling his blood and beating up punks and hunters.

He was a guardian angel.

Maybe Clementine didn't believe in strictly classified religion, but he believed in that.

As they traveled back toward the convenience store with their now empty cart, Justin pulled out the tin he kept his joints in. He gave a scowl that seemed more confused than upset and tucked them away again.

"Do you need something?" Clementine didn't know how much more he could offer to buy Justin when the money for his blood was already dwindling so low, but after watching Justin give so much away, Clem wanted to offer.

Justin shook his head slowly. "I don't—that's what's weird. Usually at this point I'd be dying for a smoke, but I guess you pushing the cart makes a big difference."

"What did that change?"

"I just get a bit of back pain normally. All the pushing and carrying can intensify it, but you... you helped a lot." Justin's attention drifted to him slowly, but once it settled, it stuck there with an intensity that warmed the chilly winter night. "So thank you."

"Always—any time, I mean."

The streets had quieted, and the low lights of the side alley they were moving down left them both washed out, the shadows deep in every stoop and building gap. No one was watching them. Clementine draped his arms over the cart's kid-shelf and watched Justin, parting his lips just enough that he knew his teeth would be visible, flat pearly-whites with two longer pointed canines.

One corner of Justin's mouth quirked and he played with the collar of his jacket where a few swooping waves of his tattoo peeked up, folding it neatly then flipping it back up entirely.

Clementine huffed. He shifted his hold on the cart to one hand, giving it an extra shove when it caught on the uneven cement. Quicker than was humanly possible, he slipped in close to Justin and tugged at the collar himself, picking at the fabric with his nails. "Here."

His skin brushed Justin's pulse once, then again, so soft it sent sparks through him.

Justin shivered against the touch, and Clementine was fairly sure it had nothing to do with the cold. The reaction made him hunger deep below his gut, like a low, swollen fire. The feeling shared so many similarities to his sexual aching during an erotic fanfic chapter that his subconscious latched onto it, amplifying it tenfold, the term demisexual racing through his mind.

This wasn't about Justin though. It was about his blood and the dozen vampiric urges that were honed on it—skin, and pulse, and scent, and touch. Anything and everything else Clementine might have been feeling was just an unfortunate association. Regardless of whether he was demisexual or not, he didn't want Justin in that way. He didn't.

He couldn't.

Realizing how long they'd stood like that, his fingers beneath Justin's collar, Clementine swiftly pulled back. He motioned awkwardly, clearing his throat. "You had a little something there."

"Must have been a lot of something," Justin replied. His hand tightened, then loosened.

Clem *couldn't* be attracted to him.

He was making things up, inventing these feelings because he wanted so badly for them to be true, even though they weren't. *That* was why he stared at the little cut in Justin's lower lip, the delicate wrinkles around the edges of his tight eyes, the way a few strands of his swept-back hair had fallen in a swoop across his forehead.

"This is the vampire you found? He's definitely a tease."

Clementine startled as the most gorgeous, brown-skinned man leaped down from the balcony above him.

Not a man.

Clem knew it the moment before he saw the teeth, like something in his gut was screaming it at him: this was one of Justin's vampires. He had a pile of small, tight locs tucked sloppily into a high bun, and his wide-collared, long sleeve shirt fell partway off one shoulder, but somehow he managed to look more put together than Clementine did after half an hour of adjustments in the mirror. He bared his fangs like a trophy, not bothering to introduce himself as he slid up to Justin with a palm to his arm greeting.

"Isaiah, hi." Justin sounded like he'd swallowed a bug. "This is Clementine—the pup I've been helping out in the evenings on and off."

"The one you keep texting when you think I'm not paying attention?" Isaiah exchanged a look with him that went far deeper than Clementine could penetrate. "I figured, when you brought him to Mrs. M's. So I thought I'd keep a lookout for any hunters tonight. Since you're so... otherwise *engrossed.*" There was a purr in the back of his voice that felt like the affectionate equivalent of a hiss, a sound so specific to vampires that Clementine wondered if he could learn to make it himself. If he could make it for Justin. If he could make Justin forget all about the way Isaiah was using it, cozying up to him.

It felt like having something stolen right out from under Clementine's nose.

Shame hit him as he put words to the emotion, and he tried to swallow all the feelings right back down. Justin wasn't his—at least no more so than he belonged to any vampire or human in this neighborhood—and Clem had no right to claim him as his singular prey.

Justin glared back down their little side street. "Any sign of the hunters then?"

"They're still doing their usual sweeps of the rest of the inner city, and a woman Santos thought might be Natalie got food off Dove and Hatchet a couple hours ago, but she didn't try to stop anyone or pull weapons." Isaiah hummed. "You think they're really done with us?"

"Natalie was pretty adamant when I fought her. Giving up entirely seems too convenient..."

It wasn't convenience, it was Clementine—Clementine and the information he'd been funneling through Anthony, making sure she didn't have to walk the streets for it, beating it out of whatever poor vampire she came across. Something like pride swelled in his chest, but it was made ugly and anxious by the fact that what he was handing over meant Natalie might still come back someday, once she pinpointed her target. At least innocent bystanders wouldn't suffer in the meantime though, something made clear by just how thoroughly Natalie had stepped back.

And in return, Clementine was getting the rest of his life.

Isaiah and Justin had lapsed into talk of hunter mentalities and general dangers, but they seemed to be wrapping that up in favor of Isaiah mooning over Justin while he patted the vampire's hand.

"If you'd like me to stop by later, just say the word." Isaiah's fangs gleamed despite the low light, and the little toss he gave of his shoulders made the front of his shirt's wide collar shift, flashing more of the smooth, brown skin of his chest.

Justin's gaze followed the motion, rolling down Isaiah's body before darting away.

Clementine felt far too many things at once: a hot tight jealousy alongside disgust at himself for being such a covetous jerk, a yearning in his chest not just to push Isaiah aside but to take his place, paired with a panicked reaction to the desire's strength. He looked away from them both, cold for reasons that had nothing to do with the chill.

Justin's hand wrapped around Clem's arm. The impulse to pull Justin against him was so strong that he had to force himself to be still as he searched for a less predatory response. Touch his fingers, maybe? A smile, probably. Was it still appropriate to bare his own fangs, or would that signal some kind of prey-claiming to Isaiah? Maybe he *wanted* to fight Isaiah. Though the very obvious outcome of that would be for Clementine to lose, and also brand himself a creep in the process.

But Justin was already letting go, slipping past him to take the cart out from his grip. "Let's not keep Mrs. Mendoza up any later."

"Right," Clementine replied, his voice a little rough. He followed as Justin wished Isaiah a good night and set off down the pavement.

A car sped by with thrumming music, taking advantage of the empty road. Laughter spilled from a bar down the block as a small group entered the building, the sound going dim again once the door closed behind them. Every third apartment light was on above, the streetlamps bright, but the shadows of the stoops to their left were deep and the windows dark on either side.

It made Clementine's attention fix on Justin, not exactly fading the rest of the world out, but rather sharpening it to a point, his senses alive with the gentle rush of late night quiet. He could sense Justin's blood from here, the steady pound of it like a song calling his name. When Justin smiled at him, he felt eternal.

He brushed his nails along the underside of Justin's wrist, slipping three fingers beneath the sleeve of his jacket to press against his pulse. They lingered there, heartbeat by heartbeat, and Clementine warred between the desire to pull him close, to taste his blood, his skin, his soft sighs, and to stay that way forever, dwelling in that single perfect moment eternally. For once, Clementine refused to question the feeling. Even if it was just the vampire in him longing for his prey, it set a fire in his chest as bright as the sun, and he was going to bask in it until it burned out, or burned him up.

Damn every other vampire; right now, Justin was *his*.

"Come here," Clementine murmured, his fangs on full display, and he stepped back.

Justin inhaled. His lashes fluttered. He left the cart, following Clementine like a creature enthralled. At Justin's first stride out of the streetlamp's reach, Clem grabbed the front of his jacket. A flash of worry hit him as he pulled— maybe this was too much—but Justin laughed, breathless and rough. "Grabby," he whispered.

"Shush," Clem said, pressing him into the nook between the wall and the door. "Let me touch you."

Justin didn't go entirely quiet, a series of little nonsense sounds leaving him as Clementine fit his fingers in his fine, dark hair, tipping his head back and to the side. The stucco of the wall crinkled as he brushed against it. Justin's pulse thrummed, his bitter scent so intoxicating that it felt dizzying. A car honked down the road, and someone passed on the sidewalk, feet away from finding them there. All of it, together, was perfect.

And Justin was perfect.

His fingers brushed Clementine's hips, fitting into the empty belt loops of Clem's slacks as the rest of him went limp and inviting. Clem pressed his nose to the pulse in Justin's neck first, then found it with his lips, reveling in the shudder that ran through Justin from the mere gust of Clem's breath on his skin. Justin's hands tugged him closer. Clementine leaned into the pressure as he slipped his fangs in, drinking ardently. The soft gasp he received made him yearn for more: to press against Justin, to hold him to the wall as he nipped at his neck, fingers tugging at his hair, Justin's hands beneath his sweater, roaming over skin Clem had never let anyone else touch. The desire filled him, urging him to bite harder, to give Justin enough venom that he moaned like an orgasm and—

Fuck.

The fantasy came into focus with a shock that seemed to latch him up from the inside, the doors of his heart and soul slamming shut in a rush of terror. His fangs recoiled into their sheaths, and he licked the cut closed on instinct alone, trying not to gasp or stumble.

As he pulled back though, his gaze caught on Justin's mouth. And held, not like a question, not anymore, but an exclamation point.

He wanted to kiss Justin Yu. He *wanted* Justin. God, Clementine wanted him so fucking much that it made him ache low and deep and his tongue creep along his lips in haunted anticipation.

He slipped away, shaking out his arms like that might stop his sudden bout of trembling. It felt like an avalanche had been let loose in him, a whole new world opened up. A whole new, terrifying world with a whole new set of rules he'd only ever personally experienced in fiction, dangers that could wreck him—or Justin or whatever blood-oriented thing they had going—lures that might pull him further out of the life he'd worked so hard to grow and keep.

Clementine wrapped his arms around himself, his fingers instinctively finding the spots where Justin's had laid. He was not who he'd thought himself to be. All this time he'd thought he'd been yearning for the impossible, when he was simply... demisexual.

It was so much to take in.

But he had to say something, he realized, could not just keep standing there, staring at Justin's lips and feeling the places Justin had touched him and trying not to collapse under the weight of it all. So he cleared his throat. "Well, Justin Yu, I think you're officially an acquired taste."

"Thank god," Justin replied, hoarse.

And Clementine again, managed not to kiss him.

16

JUSTIN

Clementine had *bitten* him.

Technically, the vampire had been biting Justin for weeks now, but those bites—those were delicate, clinical things, as sterile as Clem could make something that involved skin-to-mouth contact. They came with the pressure of his lips on Justin's wrist, a momentary tender brush of fingers and a blissful little prick of venom, and even then Justin had lingered over every memory, craving their next meeting more aggressively each night. Those bites were little pockets of heaven, veiled views of the fuller, more immaculate experience that surely lay beyond.

But last night… last night Clementine had bitten him like he'd craved it, like he was savoring every moment.

It had been incredible.

The rush, the heat, the way his whole body had already yearned for Clementine even before the vampire had pulled him into that doorway, the way Clem—Clem, whom Justin trusted, who Justin knew was fairly incapable of attacking a human to begin with—had made the moment feel dangerous and daring and exhilarating in a way Justin hadn't quite experienced in all his years fighting criminals and hunters, and abusing the innocent before that. The intensity of that bite had made his skin spark and his dick ache as though Clementine had been edging him slowly toward orgasm all night.

And after he'd freed his fangs, Justin had been half certain, for just a moment, that Clementine had meant to kiss him.

That must have been his imagination. His desire playing tricks on him. His longing for Clementine's mouth and venom not just in his wrist and neck but everywhere else too, caught in his lips and pinched into the tender part of his thighs and tucked ever so excruciatingly into the swollen length of his dick. He had seen what he'd wanted to see. Probably. Maybe.

"Let me touch you."

A giddy shudder ran across Justin's skin. He tried to tap it down, tried to tell himself that he could never have Clementine for more than a moment—he had Ala Santa, and that was where his attention had to be focused.

Already just the thought of Clementine's skin, his lips, his teeth and tongue, was making his current patrol useless— he'd already run through half of *Shane Rates Stuff's* video collection without hearing more than three words, and lost track of the street multiple times. Instead of scouting the east edge of Ala Santa like he'd planned, he ended up mindlessly walking the route to where Isaiah's ground floor apartment was tucked into an alley behind a produce shop. A small bustle came from the place as Isaiah and Mya helped unload clothing-stuffed grocery bags from Mya's ancient SUV, a tired-looking vampire trying in vain to reassure them that it wasn't worth the trouble.

"We got another one?" Justin asked.

Isaiah nodded. "Their name's Soren. Natalie's little gang tripped over them five blocks north of Ala Santa. They were already in between housing this month."

"They don't have anywhere else?" As happy as Justin was to keep taking in vampires, his ability to offer the support they needed was fast dwindling.

Isaiah grimaced. "If the hunters weren't specifically looking for me because of my connections to Wesley and Vincent, they'd probably let Soren crash on their couch for a few weeks, but I don't want to draw any more attention to them, or me, than I have to."

"I understand. Does Soren have a blood source?"

Isaiah shook his head. "Same dealer as most of us, but they've only been able to afford a pint a month, so they've had to do some hunting on the side. Bars and clubs and the like."

That was one more vampire in Justin's neighborhood who wouldn't consistently have what they needed to survive, who'd be placing themselves in danger in the hopes they'd find someone who would consent to the bite. Or else Justin would have to pay for them, find a way to make Clementine's money go even farther than it already was.

As the days passed, it seemed that money would have to go particularly far indeed.

While Natalie and her hunters avoided Ala Santa, they tore through the surrounding neighborhoods with the frenzy of a predator playing with its prey. Each time they circled, it seemed to push a new vampire into Justin's territory.

They were up to something, he was sure of it.

But Isaiah forbade him from doing anything until she made the first move.

So he waited, finding space for the new vampires where he could, praying with every arrival that they'd bring a store of blood with them. By the following week their numbers had nearly doubled. Justin worried that forcing them all so close like this would leave them sitting ducks.

And the more he worried, the more he found himself texting Clementine, the pavement under his feet and DIY videos playing like his personal brand of meditation music in the background.

He shouldn't have been dedicating this much of his time to just one vampire, when the moment Ala Santa needed him he'd have to drop the relationship without a single glance back. He should have told Clementine he had far better options to tease with venom-dripping fangs and give agonizingly soft neck bites to, and dedicated more time to the work that needed to be done in his neighborhood, with *his* vampires—his actual vampires, the ones who depended on him. But the way Clementine's attention made Justin feel was so delightful that his selfishness won out.

For all his growing affection and obvious craving, Clem hadn't stepped beyond their platonic predator-prey dynamic yet—hadn't made a move to kiss him. And Justin was, at least, strong enough to return the favor. They existed in much the same state of suspension as Ala Santa, hovering around the possibility, the point where it would all come crashing down. And it *would* come crashing down, both Ala Santa with its influx of vampires and whatever this thing was between him and Clementine.

But by god he was going to maintain it for as long as he could manage.

And maintain it, Justin did, through every waking hour, from the ironic *good morning* text Clementine sent when he woke every afternoon to the *sleep well* one Justin ended their conversations with as the sun rose. They were just wrapping up another long night of exchanges as the sky began to lighten, the hunter-free winter morning dawning cloudless and brilliant.

Justin snapped a selfie to go with his metaphorical goodnight, his free hand dramatically drawn through his hair and the camera's focus strategically angled for a full view of his neck. He smirked as Clementine's reply bubbles came and went at a flustered pace. He barely had time to glance at the vampire's response though, because another message appeared alongside it.

Isaiah
13th Sprrow Stret Natlie

Fear shot through Justin, turning the fire inside him to ice. He ran.

The commuter traffic picked up around him as he crossed the larger streets, then lessened again to tired pedestrians and the occasional slow car. His heart pounded in his ears and the residual, eternal ache of his shoulder blades hummed in protest. He ignored them and plunged faster, shouting Isaiah's name as he neared the corner of 13th and Sparrow.

He spotted Isaiah immediately, halfway up the side of a four-story apartment complex and still moving. Natalie chased him, her long black braid swishing with each chaotic drag of her body across balconies and up tan stucco ledges. Her holy silver stick bounced at her hip. Two other hunters climbed with her, spread out like they were trying to surround Isaiah.

Any other time it wouldn't have worked. Isaiah was stronger and faster than most vampires, much less a set of human hunters, and he'd been climbing these buildings since before he'd turned. But with the holy silver so near, his grip kept slipping, his muscles shaking as he dragged himself onto the edge of the roof. His foot skidded. Justin felt his stomach rush into his throat for the instant it took Isaiah to catch his balance and dash out of view.

His distressed shout echoed across the roof.

Justin's terror lurched him up the side of the building. Pain speared through his back but he quickly gained on the hunters. Above them, the pink sky was fading quickly to light blue. If the direct rays of the sun hit Isaiah now, with the effect of the holy silver still this close, he wouldn't suffer the slow, building pain of the sun-poison. His would be the death from the legends.

The hunters ascended onto the roof mere seconds before Justin, but by the time he pulled himself over the final ledge, they had already surrounded Isaiah. At least they didn't seem to have noticed Justin yet. They lurked in a twelve-foot circle around their panicked victim, each with some form of holy silver—smaller than Natalie's stick, but still bright and gleaming. A fourth hunter stood in the little doorway that should have been Isaiah's escape from the sun, holding a thick black body-sack like they meant to corral him into it. Isaiah cowered, his sweater pulled over his head and his arms covering his face. His exposed fingers looked raw as a fresh sunburn.

Seeing him this way was agony, like everything in Justin was trying to rip itself apart. He crashed his fist into the base of the nearest hunter's skull, slamming into the flesh there with enough force that the man collapsed. One down.

That caught the others' attention.

Justin bared his teeth and went to work.

This was his neighborhood, his vampires, his people. He didn't hold back, didn't give the hunters a moment to reconsider, didn't feel any pity for the woman who'd scaled the building at Natalie's side as he slipped under a stab from her dramatically large knife and attacked. He sank her, choking, beneath a series of blows to her throat. Two down.

He turned on the hunter blocking the roof entrance, barely feeling the first punch they landed over the roar of his own blood in his ears and the rage boiling beneath his skin. Slamming them into the doorframe, he pinned their knee and cracked the kneecap out of place before letting them drop in a whimpering puddle. Three down. Only Natalie left.

Isaiah fled past him, wheezing something that sounded like a thank you. He paused just inside the building's shadow, still hunched from pain, and motioned for Justin to follow. At the same moment, Natalie lunged at Justin.

He had an instant to react: dive after Isaiah or turn and face the woman who had come into his home and threatened the people he loved.

Justin wheeled on her, already swinging.

He realized his mistake as they danced, trading punch for punch. His back screamed with fury, and the hits he'd taken from the other hunters hadn't been as insignificant as he'd first anticipated. His body ached, slowing him down and fumbling his movements. And Natalie was far from a poor fighter. She might not have possessed extra-human speed and strength, but she was cunning and well-trained. Justin caught a blow from her stick with his forearms and tried to grab the weapon as he'd done in their first fight, but she was smarter now, wrenching it back too quickly and slamming it toward his gut.

He leaped away. His shoulder blades ached, but he cracked his heel into her hip—too slow to do much damage as she retreated.

"You're not a vamp," Natalie panted, her shoulders defensively hunched and her stance wide. "I don't have beef with you."

"But you have beef with *my* vamps," Justin hissed. He lunged at her, landing a blow across her jaw but taking a swipe to his side in exchange. They fell apart again, circling once more.

Around them, the downed hunters groaned and struggled to rise as the first beams of sunlight spread across the roof. Justin had to be done with this. Preferably before he lost consciousness from the pain.

Natalie wiped blood from a split in her lip. "Why do you defend them? They're not worth this. Even the soft ones, the ones you don't expect it from, they're all killers. It's in their blood, thick with our stolen life. It fucks up their heads. I know people who study them; their brain chemistry changes. It gets wrong, makes them kill."

Every new sentence sounded more ludicrous and brainwashed than the last; no logic or sense, only hatred. Justin could do hatred too. "I only see two killers here, and it's you and me."

He launched at Natalie.

Agony spiked through his spine and along his shoulders with each swing of his arms, rebounding on impact. He beat Natalie back, hitting her with such unrelenting force that she went on the defensive. He slipped in close then, tucking his leg behind her knee and driving her to the ground. She scrambled away from him, a mirror of their first meeting. Only this time, Isaiah had almost been taken and Justin felt one wrong step from falling apart.

From the depths of the little entrance building, Isaiah shouted Justin's name. "Behind you!"

A gun cocked.

He and Natalie both went still. The hunter whose knee he'd blown out leaned against one of their companions, a handgun aimed at Justin's chest. Their arm wobbled, but they glared with a conviction that made up for it. He should have been afraid for his life, yet all he could think of was the people he'd let down if he didn't walk away from this. The people Natalie would hurt without him here to stop her. And Clementine.

Would Clementine even know what had happened to him?

"Go, Isaiah," Justin said, his tone an icy calm. "I'm coming."

He didn't pull his gaze away from the gun, but he could hear Isaiah's retreating footsteps down the stairs to safety.

Natalie clambered up, edging around Justin to her armed hunter's side. She gave Justin a look he couldn't fully parse, disgust and contemplation and perhaps something almost like respect. With slow, pained motions, she lowered her hunter's gun. "He's a person. We can't kill him."

"Freak's as strong as them," the hunter spat, shaking harder, but they let her ease the gun away. She kept pointing it at Justin, aimed toward his legs instead. Her companions helped their final member up, and together they fled, taking the same path as Isaiah down the stairs.

Justin followed them at a distance, each step magnifying the aching of his back until his vision had tunneled. As the hunters left the building—gun stashed in Natalie's trench coat—he held the door frame for support. His knuckles went white. The hunters' backs blurred and the busy morning swallowed them up.

They were gone.

So why didn't it feel like a success?

"Justin?"

He turned and stumbled, slumping into the wall in the direction of Isaiah's voice. Isaiah's hands appeared over his, helping him sit. The world faded in and out, in and out, and a joint pressed between his lips.

"Breathe." Isaiah's voice sounded rough, just as tired and worn as his own.

He inhaled, held it. Exhaled. "Thank you."

A choked laugh came out of Isaiah. "Fuck this. That fucking puta'ng ina."

Son of a bitch, he thought Isaiah said. It was still hard to focus through the pain in his back that seemed bent on radiating to a dozen other places, his side and his cheek and his shoulder and his skull. Hard just to keep existing. "You okay?"

"Holy silver is gone so I'll be fine."

He noticed how *I'll be fine* was not the same as being fine now, but didn't have the strength to comment on it.

"I think your new vampire friend was right about them working for Vitalis-Barron," Isaiah said. "They wanted me alive, were trying to force me into their body bag to hide from the sun. I suppose if Natalie was planning to cut me up in little pieces as a message to Vincent and Wesley, then turning me into a sun husk first would make that harder."

"Fuck." It took a moment for him to follow the thought further, his own brain too torn up by the agony still shooting between his shoulder blades. "Could have been both. Give you to Vitalis-Barron as the message? If Vincent and Wesley know what they're doing to the vampires in that lab…"

"Maybe. Wes and Vinny have their secrets, but I didn't ask."

"How did the hunters know to come for you?"

Isaiah shrugged, his shoulder brushing Justin's. "Luck of the draw?"

"They wanted you, you in particular, and your schedule is always shifting—how could they have known where you'd be, exactly at sunrise, when they've barely been in Ala Santa, haven't even talked to any of the vampires here? Luck doesn't cover it."

"Maybe not." On the surface he sounded nonchalant, like the hunters in question were just a gang of bullies trying to rattle some cages, but beneath his casual attitude Justin could see the places where the armor Isaiah had built up all his life was shaking loose. He held his legs tight to his chest and tapped his second finger in a chaotic pattern, each sentence ending in an uncharacteristic huff.

"Now do I get to kill them?" Justin asked.

"I don't know." Isaiah shook his head. "Maybe it's safer for me to leave, just for a little while?"

"And when they hunt you down wherever you go next? Who will be there to protect you?"

Isaiah didn't argue. He slowly, gently, leaned his head against Justin's, nuzzling into his hair. It barely hurt. "Don't kill anyone yet. Don't do anything you can't take back, please. It broke you, last time…"

The insinuation cut Justin to the core, but worse was the knowledge that he'd never put himself together right after Jose's death, or maybe that there hadn't been enough left of him by that point to be a functional person again, to be more than the guardian role he'd taken for himself. "This is different. I'd be protecting my vampires, not—"

"Still, please. For me."

"Fine," Justin replied. He forced himself to let it go. For now. "But you have to lay low. No jobs—I'll pay for everything this month, I'll get more from Clementine if I have to—and no going anywhere without me or a group of humans, day or night. Please. I know it's a lot to ask, but I don't think I could function if—"

"I'll do it," Isaiah agreed. "I'm not in any hurry to have this experience again."

"Thank you."

Justin burned through a large chunk of his remaining drug stash before the pain calmed enough that he could hobble back to his apartment with Isaiah, his jacket over Isaiah's head to protect from the mid-morning light. By the time they arrived, Isaiah still shook from sun-poisoning. He fell asleep beside Justin, and when Justin woke again from the pain, four, then six hours later, Isaiah was still curled against him, drifting in and out of consciousness. Justin ran his fingers through his friend's hair as he smoked and reread his old texts to Clementine.

At least they had planned not to meet tonight.

Justin couldn't imagine pulling himself back down the stairs, much less acting like he was strong and attentive as Clementine bared his fangs. A bite would be nice right now though, along with Clem's venom, and his even voice and precise fingers. Were he someone Justin could invite in, someone he could keep in his life for better or for worse, then he would have told Clementine to come in a heartbeat. He would have let Clem slide off his shoes and climb onto the mattress, curl up at his side and gently suck on his skin as they talked about nothing and everything until the pain dimmed and the world came back into proper focus.

If only he'd ever done a single thing to deserve that kind of tender affection.

He already had one vampire in his life whom he was thoroughly unworthy of, but who had stayed with him anyway. Who stayed with him still. That was more than he could ever ask for.

CLEMENTINE

Dr. Clementine Hughes had spent eight days and sixteen hours not kissing Justin Yu, and that fact was really getting to him. Technically, he'd spent twenty-nine years not kissing Justin, but somehow *that* statistic was worse. Worse still, he was no longer entirely sure *why* he wasn't kissing Justin.

Except that he'd never had a good kiss before, one that wasn't uncomfortable and left him thinking more about the unsanitary nature of it all than anything sensual, and if he tried to kiss Justin only to run into the same problem yet again he thought he might cry on the spot. And if it *was* good, it would make things far harder when it came time to let Justin go.

There was a high probability that they wouldn't work in the long term—Clementine didn't have to be Spock to see that. Justin had an existence that went no further than Ala Santa, and Clementine had a job, an apartment, a family, an entire life, all outside that. But it didn't stop him from wondering: what if he could have Justin, too?

The man was intense, like a bitter black tea but laced with honey and a thoughtful kindness that seemed fit only for him, watchful as a hawk with a sharp memory and the ability to pick up on Clementine's nonsensical rambling even without understanding the basic science behind the more complicated theories. He possessed the same kind of strong elegance as his filigreed tribal tattoos, and wore it like a threat, in his gait and his grin and his rough, dark tone. But it was just as visible in the rare moments that the man gentled himself: the little moans as Clem's fangs sank into his skin and the soft way he cradled Clementine's emotions like they were precious treasures.

And the more time he spent with Justin, the more he worried he'd never get another chance at something like this, that his heart was one and done, hooked on Justin forever now. Soulmates had always seemed like such an alluring concept until he was staring the reality of one down and realizing he'd likely lose them. Somehow, that made finding the courage to kiss Justin *harder*, instead of easier.

If he really did have just this one chance—one chance in thirty years of life, one person who would make him yearn the way he did over fictional couples—then the wrong move could ruin it all. Fitting Justin into Clem's broader life would have been difficult enough without the pressure of possibly losing him anyway.

Odysseus's incessant prodding wasn't helping things, either.

Sissy

I know you said you were not interested in bringing your new boy toy with you next week but how about dragging him to the pre-drinks at my place? As a friend?

Clementine

Will our parents be there?

Sissy

I'm not planning to invite them.

Clementine

So there's a fifty-fifty chance.

Sissy

I can't in good conscience say it isn't so.

Clementine

This just isn't a good time, all right.

By which he meant, it would never be a good time.

If Clem ever found the courage to turn what he and Justin had into something more, there would be no end to the comments. Not about the gender of his date—Odysseus coming out as first a gay man then a straight trans woman had battered down their bias over time—but Justin's lack of college degrees and proper job, his heavily tattooed skin, his criminal past and his impulse to punch first would scandalize them. They'd label him as chronically unsuccessful and a hindrance to the future accomplishments of their son.

He could almost hear them. "Are you sure he's right for you? How do you know he's not just here for your money? Has he been paying half the bills? And there's definitely nothing missing from your apartment?"

Justin would bear the stain of his social status no matter where their relationship went or how pure the man's motives were or how much Clem truly wanted him to make use of the money he provided. Clem's parents would never see him as more than a gold digger.

Despite all that—or perhaps partially because of it—Clem still wanted to watch Justin shine under the glimmering lights of Sissy's parties, to see the look on his parents' faces when the child who'd spent his entire life trying to be good for them—perfect for them—had finally gone off the deep end. To metaphorically, and perhaps literally, bare his fangs at them.

But then his reality would sink in, the one where his vampirism could put him on a table in Vitalis-Barron's lab instead of working at one, and the wonderful human snack he was falling for would make his parents' noses turn up at them both.

So Clementine spent the week texting with Justin, as platonic and casual as ever. He tried not to think about Justin's neck or the way he tasted or the sound of his breathless laughter or how his fingers felt when they ghosted over Clementine's hips or his biceps or his collarbone. Tried not to dwell on the fact that this was his first real attraction in twenty-nine years, how it could very well be the only chance he got for another twenty-nine. He tried so hard, in fact, that he found himself pulling away from the werewolf-AU fanfic he'd been writing for too many years to count and launching headfirst into something with a bit more fangs.

By chapter three, Spock was staring longingly at Kirk's neck while they zipped their way into the unexplored reaches of space. By chapter ten, Kirk was trying not to act like a complete mess from Spock's first bite. By chapter thirty-seven, they were ripping each other's clothes off. Somewhere around a hundred thousand words, Clementine had begun editing and posting chapters on his fanfic account, to an immediate barrage of positive comments—far more than he'd seen on his regular fanfiction. Apparently people rather liked vampires when they were in sexy fictional form instead of demanding space in the real world.

That stung all the more as he realized just how much of his own experience he'd drawn from. Spock's fangs were longer and leaner than Clem's, and Kirk's neck was thicker and pinker than Justin's. They didn't even have the same flavor palette—Clem had made sure of that. But beside those few details, he'd created a near perfect rendition of their vampire-human dynamic without even realizing it.

Eventually one of his readers took notice: an account called 'WagerYou1' with an icon of a bleeding bite mark.

WagerYou1

Sorry this is going to sound creepy af but I'm a human dating a vampire and your fic gives me huge vibes that you have some knowledge in that area.

I'm being told by my boyfriend that yes this is in fact super creepy of me, sorry.

He also says that I should let you know that you don't have to respond to this idiot. The idiot being me.

HighlyIllogicalStarShipping

Your boyfriend is correct on the matter of this being incredibly creepy, but to be fair, you're also correct about my experience. Though, I'm not currently in a relationship, so much as I'd like to be in one. (I am the one with fangs, by the way. I hope I did Kirk justice?)

WagerYou1

Totally dude. (I am assuming dude is chill because your profile says he/him?) Kirk's reactions are on point. The way he instinctively sighs when he's bitten gets 10/10 points right there. Is that based on a specific human you want to be dating? ;)

HighlyIllogicalStarShipping

Yes XP (Don't judge me.)

May I ask, what is it like to be on the other side of a vamp/human relationship like that in real life, outside of the sensual aspects? How do you make it work on a day-to-day basis?

WagerYou1

Real talk? I'm not going to lie, it's rough sometimes. I'm scared something's going to happen to my boyfriend more than I'd like to admit. I'm bi, so I knew I might end up in a long-term relationship where we'd have to be constantly monitoring who knew what and how comfortable we were being out (I'm naturally pretty open about my sexuality but my bf's a lot more private of a person, and he has every right to be) but the vampire stuff is just a whole other level of that. And there's the biting, which is wonderful, but it also requires some extra planning to make sure we're both fed and healthy, especially since our sleep schedules are way different.

But even when it demands more of me than another relationship might, I would still choose it a hundred times over.

I'm asking him to marry me in a couple weeks. I want to be with him for the rest of our lives, whatever trials and joys that might bring.

Clementine wasn't sure what was socially acceptable to say to that other than congratulations, despite how insignificant the word felt and how it did nothing to cover the aching it left deep in his chest. He came back to the thread on and off throughout the week, his heart thudding unusually loud in his chest like it knew something he didn't… or something he didn't want to admit yet.

By Thursday evening—the night before Sissy's party—he was still drowning in the hollow wanting it had born in him as he sat at his lab desk, shuffling aimlessly through his work priorities for the night. He tried to avoid Anthony's gaze from across the room, but the man's face lit up in a way that was all ice and chill and no warmth. The moment he reached the desk, he clamped his hand on Clem's shoulder, his bracelet charm hot against the exposed skin above Clem's shirt collar. "How are things in your neck of the woods? Or your favorite human neck's woods, anyway."

That wasn't even a little bit funny. Clementine slid defensively out from under Anthony's touch. "What do you want, Dr. Hilker?"

"Nothing new." Anthony's thumb brushed the curls at the back of Clem's scalp.

Before Clementine could choose between slamming his chair backwards, fangs out and future be damned, and ducking his head to mutter excuses, his coworker finally pulled away. Not far enough. He scooted around the side of Clem's chair to fiddle with the assorted pens and supplies Clem had perfectly arranged across his desk, along with a single Star Trek pin replica he'd figured he could risk bringing without entirely ruining his authoritative appearance.

Anthony hummed a soft, almost playful sound, like they were co-conspirators and not a man with a broken moral compass antagonizing a vampire who'd been aggressively hitting his own compass on the sides of things to make sure it still worked, and possibly making things worse in the process. Anthony tapped at the Star Trek pin—fuck, his finger oils would be on it now—but then he shifted to grab a marble-sized orb off Clem's paper tray instead.

"God, don't play with that. It emits low levels of microwave radiation." Clementine snatched it back and placed it into the little safety ring it had been sitting in. He was still waiting for a tech on his team to dispose of it, because he could never seem to get around to it himself. The problem was that neither could anyone else.

Anthony's brow lifted. "You working on a new study?"

"A board rep thought we could do something fun with it but it just breaks down our drugs faster." He snorted. "They would probably try to work it into their bottles to put a lower life expectancy on medications if some of the compounds didn't cause minor side effects."

"Motherfuckers." For a moment, Anthony looked like the man Clementine used to know, annoying and competitive but always at least partially on the same team— the man who *was* offering to help him conduct the kind of research that would benefit vampires. "We should be here to make progress, not money."

If only his view of progress was this ethical. "If that's all you need, I have work to do."

Anthony clamped Clem on the shoulder, giving his muscle a squeeze. "I'll see you around, Dr. Hughes."

Clementine lifted his chin, baring the slightest hint of fangs at the man.

He only laughed, and left Clementine to stew at his desk. With every evening spent watching Justin's bitter smirk and every morning confronted by Anthony's cavalier badgering, Clem's guilt had been sitting heavier and heavier in his chest. He hadn't harmed anyone in Ala Santa, he kept reminding himself. He'd given Anthony information, yes, but he'd been careful to keep to the blandest, most superficial details. And nothing had come of it, nothing but safety for Ala Santa and the stability of Clementine's future.

No one had been hurt.

So why, why was he the one hurting a little more with each passing day? With every new piece of information, his lungs felt tighter, his muscles stiffer, his heart more uncertain.

He buried himself in his work after that, all night and long into the morning, using the fully staffed lab to monitor how his team was running and make adjustments to their procedures. It didn't quite eliminate his building dread though. His fear of Sissy's parties wasn't usually this bad, he knew, but with the stress of Anthony's blackmail and his struggles with his vampirism both taxing him this heavily, it made the usual discomfort of a loud, fancy gathering and his parent's ominous disapproval seem like unconquerable things. He felt like he was three wrong moves away from losing the polished exterior he'd worked so hard to maintain—and worse, he was growing so accustomed to not having to wear it around Justin, that the thought of donning it for a few hours of constant conversation from the most critical people he knew sounded like hell.

He didn't know if he could face that.

At noon he holed up in his third-floor office with the blinds pulled closed and a blanket over his head, napping while Star Trek episodes played in his headphones. By the time he returned to the basement chemistry lab, half the techs had already gone to start their Fridays early. And he was still agonizing over the damned party.

Worse, his Star Trek-filled dreams had left him imagining Justin there, what his skin might taste like beneath Clem's lips while pressed into the butler's pantry with the distant sounds of the party creating a slightly unnerving thrum in his ears. Those thoughts made the horrors to come feel softer somehow. Justin's presence, as sharp and bitter as it was, did that to the world. It had been so easy to stand at his side while they'd met and helped person after person back in Ala Santa. Justin seemed to know just how to enter and end a conversation, how to take the reins when Clementine needed him to and offer them back when he didn't, how to ground Clementine in the moment and let him enjoy the chaos of life without feeling as overwhelmed by it all. And god, did he want that tonight.

He couldn't ask for it though. Justin was busy in Ala Santa and he'd never leave his vampires for Clem's sake. But maybe if he just saw Justin *beforehand*, had a few minutes of soothing conversation and a small blood-snack to steady himself, he'd feel calmer. If he could just establish himself in the reality that he had someone like Justin, if only as a friend…

Clementine

I recognize that this is vastly beyond our usual agreement and wildly last minute, but would it be all right if I stopped by at 6pm for a chat? I'd like your emotional support on a matter.

I can come to you, of course.

Justin

I have a meeting with my druggist then actually lol. It should only take a few minutes though.

It'll be in the financial district if that works for you?

Clementine

That would be perfect. I'm just across the freeway.

Justin

At Vitalis-Barron, I remember.

6pm then?

Clementine

Yes. See you then.

The thought of seeing him made Clementine an almost uncomfortable level of giddy. He should not have been feeling like this over a man he had no hopes of maintaining a long-term romantic relationship with. But he couldn't help the effect Justin's steady bittersweetness had on him.

Clementine spent the rest of the day digging through databases and double checking the upcoming week's supply lists, feeling more stable than he had all week. He even managed to hunt down three of the protocol folders that desperately needed updating in the filing room. It helped that Anthony had been distracted with a special project all day, then had left with the regular shift, so he didn't have anyone around to bother him.

The moment his party reminder alarm went off, the full force of his anxiety returned. But it was fine. He'd see Justin, and he'd be all right. He could handle this. Still, as he donned his tailored suit—made from a fabric he'd requested by touch, in the only pattern that didn't feel like it agitated him behind the knees and armpits—his concentration was so lacking that he had to rebutton his black shirt after already having slid on the gold-embroidered vest that went over it. His deep red jacket would have seemed to come from a different outfit entirely if his vest's gilding didn't also run across the jacket's back and cuffs, its bloody color woven like webbing across his little silken scarf and back pocket. With shaky fingers, he ran a miniscule amount of oil and gel through his curls, forcing them in place without letting them fluff or frizz, and hurried back to his upper office for his things.

As he neared the door, Dr. Blood's voice called from behind him, back in the direction of the elevators. His life flashed before his eyes as she spoke.

"Dr. Hughes, a word if you please."

18

JUSTIN

Justin stood on the corner of two unfamiliar streets in the financial district, smoking his last joint under the distant glow of a streetlamp. He was nearly at the edge of San Salud, just south of where the freeway turned to a main street as it curved between the city proper and the lake's boardwalk. Not too far from here, the metropolis ended abruptly in the massive Vitalis-Barron complex that sat along the edge of the forest. Justin never came to this area—usually his druggist would meet him a little outside of Ala Santa in a neighborhood just as rough and poor as his own.

Usually he wasn't asking for a fresh batch this soon, though, or on this short notice.

Natalie and her hunters hadn't returned since Thursday, but he still hated being away from Ala Santa. He'd only agreed because Isaiah was spending the evening with Mrs. Mendoza's elderly queer book club, her doors and windows locked tight, and it was this or wait until tomorrow. He wasn't sure his back would stand that long. The worst of the pain had subsided, kept to a dull ache beneath the drugs.

Without them, he'd be back to lying in bed groaning into Isaiah's hair and thinking about Clementine's soft curls.

His dealer looked distracted as he jogged around the corner. The man's brown hair bobbed in an uncharacteristically lopsided bun above his undercut and his mouth made a worried wrinkle as he checked their surroundings. He must have come straight from work because his badge still hung around his neck. He shoved it into his satchel just before Justin could make out the words on it, but he swore the emblem looked like Vitalis-Barron's. He wondered if Clementine worked with the man.

"Hey," Justin greeted.

His druggist nodded, but didn't quite look at Justin. "Good evening."

They'd never exchanged names, and Justin figured that was for the best. He'd first met the research scientist through a friend of a friend whose very specific prescription had been discontinued. The man had been happy to take samples from Justin for what he'd called *groundbreaking science*, and returned with a drug very specific to the non-human pain receptors in Justin's back. Now he sold them and the necessary joint wraps to Justin for pennies that could hardly cover the fact that he was clearly risking his job to make them.

Justin slipped the ten-dollar bill out of his pocket, exchanging it for a simple brown envelope he tucked immediately beneath his jacket. Usually his druggist relaxed once the trade had finished, but today he seemed more on edge, his gaze twitchy and his mouth tight.

"I need the full period next time," he said. "You're lucky I had the time and supplies to make these, but that's all I can get away with for a while."

Justin grimaced. "What if I could pay you—"

"I don't care about the money," the man interrupted. "I'm making five different customs now, and there's only so much I can finagle out of the company at one time without risking my job."

"And no one else can…" Justin swallowed, too guilty to even finish whether one of the others could wait instead of himself. An unhappy shudder trembled through his back, making it ache despite the joint currently half-smoked between his fingers. He took a drag. It didn't help.

"You're the client I have to put on hold before any of the others. Your problem won't kill you," his druggist said, shaking his head. "It's not fair, but that's life. If I wasn't the only one who cared more about doing the science that matters than making a buck, maybe things would be different…"

"You're the only one at the company you work for who's willing to help?" This was the most they'd talked since they'd first sparked this arrangement, and with each passing second the man grew less contained.

"There's one other associate in my immediate lab who's finally in a place where he should be willing, but one of us has to get this big promotion we've been angling for." He ran a hand along his jaw, his eyes moving across the street. He seemed to be speaking to himself more than Justin. "What would you do, if you'd endangered someone's life to reach a goal that you'd assumed would be worth the harm, but you still haven't reached it yet, so you have to keep pushing, and keep pushing? You couldn't just give up on it now," he continued, like he was answering it for himself, "That would make everything meaningless."

Justin hesitated, his mind wheeling back through all the mistakes he'd made—all the people he'd hurt, thinking it would be worth it in the end. That he'd feel successful and happy finally, when all he'd received was anger and pain and an insatiable hunger that never seemed satisfied, no matter who he robbed and tormented trying to feed it. He didn't think his druggist knew him—knew any of that—and maybe it was all just a coincidence that he'd asked the one person who actually understood. But he had asked. And Justin understood. "You can always stop." He took a risk, clapping the man on the shoulder. "Not sure you can make up for the harm you've already caused, but you can at least stop."

The man grunted, looking unsatisfied. He shook his head and moved back to their normal topic like nothing had happened. "Make this batch last longer. Doctor's orders."

Justin lifted his joint to his lips. "Will do."

With a final flinching look around, the man continued down the street. Probably to wrap around the block before heading back to his car. It was overkill, but for how long Justin continued standing there, smoking languidly like their interaction had been a random meeting between two acquaintances who just happened to run into each other on the street, he understood the instinct well. As the last of his smoke curled into the dark sky, he drew out his phone.

A few texts from Isaiah, a notification for an app he never actually used, but nothing from Clementine.

Justin

Meeting's done. I'm hanging at the corner of Lincoln and Fir so come by whenever you'd like.

He waited for a response. And kept waiting. He checked his phone again after what felt like ten minutes, though the little clock at his screen's corner claimed it had only been three. His message had clearly been delivered, but no *read* marker appeared beside it. That was fine. Clementine was probably driving, and three minutes behind schedule wasn't considered late for most people, even if Clementine *had* been exactly on time for every one of their meetings.

But Justin was not obsessing over the vampire, or his schedule, or his state of mind, or anything else. He would wait for a bit, like a normal friend, then leave. He sent another text for good measure. Then another five minutes after. And four minutes after that. And three minutes after *that*.

Justin

Just checking we're still on for this?

Is everything okay? Let me know if you're coming because I'm not sure how long I can wait.

I can come to you if that's better. Just let me know.

Clearly it wasn't, when ten more minutes passed and not only did Clementine not appear, but he never replied.

Justin
If you don't respond soon, I might come find you.

Justin reread the messages he'd already viewed a hundred times that day, checking whether anything in them had implied Clementine might not make their meeting. The more he scrutinized, the more ominous they felt. Emotional support. A secretive matter. Just across the freeway. Had something happened at Vitalis-Barron?

If they'd finally figured out what Clementine was—if they'd taken him to their basement laboratory and—

Justin had been raring to get back to Ala Santa twenty minutes ago—where he should have been, where he swore he'd have wanted to be—but now his mind, body, and soul were all hyper-focused on Clementine. His shoulder blades spasmed softly under the wave of adrenaline circulating through his veins. Vitalis-Barron's front gate was only a few miles northeast. He could run there in five minutes. Or he could wait five minutes for a taxi to arrive at the dead streets that were the Friday evening financial district. Damn his back. Again.

Justin didn't have to think twice. He sent Clementine a final message—*Screw that actually, I'm coming now*—and took off at a sprint.

19

CLEMENTINE

"Surely your family can't blame me if I steal you away for a few minutes," Dr. Blood had said as she'd led him through the building. She was right about one thing: it certainly wasn't her they'd be blaming.

Still, he'd found himself following without a word, nausea churning in his gut with each step. He'd fought the urge to glance down the hallways for waiting security, so distracted that he'd been sitting in Dr. Blood's office for three minutes before he realized this was some kind of interview.

For the senior associate position.

Oh god.

He'd tried to keep his head on straight, to answer all her casual questions with less detail than his impulse demanded—he'd realized early on that when an interviewer asked what he'd do during a challenging situation what they did *not* want was a twenty-three-step course of action that required excessive clarifications to formulate, as much as the vague sense that he knew what he was doing. By the time they finished, he felt like he'd sweated through his undershirt and worn out every one of the smile muscles he'd been trying to save for the party.

Three steps out of her office and he instinctively reached for his phone. It was back in his car with his bag, he realized. But each clock he passed reminded him just how late he was—so late that his family would be bombarding his phone and Justin… Well, with how much Justin hated to be away from Ala Santa, Clementine had very little hope he'd stuck around. So much for that pep talk and snack. Clem couldn't blame him, though; he was so disastrously late that anyone would have bailed on him by now.

He sped up.

It wasn't quite a run, more of the fastest walk he could reach without further wrinkling his suit. Already the little silken scarf he'd tucked into the collar was coming unfurled. But then, he was already quite a lot unfurled as a person so maybe that was just going to be a theme tonight.

Fuck his parents, and his siblings, and everyone who would judge him for it. *They* did not have to deal with a sudden vampire-turning or a blackmailing coworker or buying blood from a delicious, gorgeous almost-human who would now think that Clem had blown him off. They could all take their little gossip and their back-handed compliments and shove them somewhere he had no desire to think about. He was doing a fantastic job keeping his life together, considering the circumstances.

Clementine hop-skipped to a stop in front of his car. He shoved his scarf back into place, tugged the early wrinkles out of his suit and caught a glimpse of his hair in the mirror. The rush had actually given it an attractive tousle. Not that there was anyone at this party he wanted to find him attractive. Or anyone he wanted to perceive him *at all*.

He was doing this for his family, he reminded himself. For Odysseus and Reginald and his parents. So they would not bring up 'that time you missed Reggie's homecoming party' for the rest of the decade. So really, he was doing it for himself. And still a little bit for Odysseus and Reginald.

They had been weirdly nice to him about the whole demisexual thing, and he genuinely did want to make that up to them. And maybe keep this sudden streak of sibling comradery going, even if he wasn't entirely sure how it had happened in the first place. The moment his car began reading his message notifications though, he fantasized about running away entirely. A seven-message pileup from Odysseus assaulted him, along with one from Reggie and an email—a goddamned email—from his father, which sounded from the preview like it boiled down to 'where the hell are you, traitorous offspring, the rest of your family is here and you are not.'

At the end of it all, a thread from Justin started up. Clem almost shut it off as he sped down the short tree-lined drive toward the road, not sure he could handle the absolute shame it brought on, nor the eventual *never mind I'm out* that was sure to come. He slowed as he reached the lowered pole of the complex's security gate. His anxiety flared at the commotion from beyond it, the guard with her taser out as she shouted at a pedestrian to move away.

The trespasser hunched, his hands up, but his stance aggressive. "I need to get in there!"

Was that...?

No.

It hit Clementine slowly, like his brain was having trouble slotting in the right pieces. Justin Yu was *here*. At Clementine's work. With his tattoos and his swished-back hair and his sharp gaze and bitter smile. But right now that smile was a bare-toothed glare as he pointed over the guard's shoulder, tensed like he was considering knocking her out and being done with it.

He hadn't left. Or he had left, only to come *here*. Looking genuinely afraid for Clementine. As more of his messages played from Clem's speakers, they confirmed it. Oh. Oh *fuck*.

Clementine shoved his car into park and scrambled out, hopping from the momentum as he threw himself over the pole-gate. "Miss White!" He called in a voice that he hoped was just friendly enough not to make her instinctively turn her weapons on him, but with enough authority that she'd keep listening. "I'm very sorry, it seems like there's some kind of mistake here. This man is my friend—I was on my way to pick him up."

She hesitated a moment, glancing at Clem with a mixture of suspicion and relief. She knew him—this was the time of night he'd been coming or going for the last three years she'd worked this position—or at least she knew that he was dedicated to Vitalis-Barron, had a calm demeanor, and hadn't ever caused trouble for her, which had to count for something, right?

Miss White stared at him for a split second, then huffed and slid her weapons away, slowly taking a step back. "My apologies. If I can get a name and contact, I'll add him to the visitor log."

"No, it's fine, we're heading out now anyway," Clem reassured her.

Justin—goddamned Justin—was in front of him suddenly, something rough in his voice. "You're all right?" His hands slid around Clementine's biceps, gripping him firmly, his gaze on Clem's so strong that he seemed to be drinking him in. "Nothing's wrong?"

Clementine's heart fluttered. He tracked the curves of Justin's features, from his long lashes and gentle nose to his lips, pale and taut with strain. Clem swallowed, wrapping his fingers around Justin's arms, thumbs brushing instinctively. "Well, right now the primary thing wrong is that you're trying to break into my workplace's parking lot."

Justin inhaled. As he breathed out again, some of the tension seemed to leave him. He stepped back, slowly, his hands trailing down Clem's arms for a moment longer than was probably socially acceptable and a lot of moments less than what Clem actually wanted. "You *are* all right, then? Vitalis-Barron, they didn't—" He'd clearly put the pieces together but didn't know how to say it.

"My boss just pulled me into an impromptu interview and my family wants to murder me, but everything is more or less the same amount of fine now than it was when I first texted you." Unless he'd fucked up that interview terribly; the interview for the job he needed in order to get his parents off his back and his finances sorted enough to keep paying Justin, but which he was finding more and more that he didn't truly want. He glanced over at Miss White, who still stood at the front of the gate house, looking very much like she was trying not to overhear them. "Come on, we can finish this in the car."

"Sure," Justin replied, but he took some guiding, slipping into the passenger seat only after Clementine pressed against his shoulder. Justin kept glancing at him, first as though he might vanish, then more and more like Justin was actually seeing Clementine: there, alive, healthy.

"Fuck." Justin pressed his hands to his face. "I thought." He looked at Clem again, looked so deeply it brought a flush to Clem's cheeks. "It was just an interview?"

"An interview I never want to think about again." Clem set the car into drive, but he didn't pull forward. Before Justin could ask him if he was sure he was safe, if he didn't want to quit entirely before it was too late, he pushed the conversation—and his thoughts—forward. "You came here for me?" He felt like he was seeing Justin for the first time too. It was beautiful, and terrifying, and he wasn't sure what to do with it. A laugh rose in his chest, bright and breathless. "I'm almost sorry everything was fine."

"No—no, this is better." Justin chuckled alongside him. "I'd take a hundred false alarms instead of one where I find out that you stayed out too long in the sun or had a fatal allergy attack or Natalie tracked you back here or…" He seemed to catch himself then, going quiet.

But Clementine's heart was already a bundle of warm, achy putty that he was pretty sure had molded into the shape of Justin. "I'm touched that you'd… that this… Well, let me just say, my sudden unresponsiveness has lightly inconvenienced the people on my emergency contacts list, and they're hounding me with angry objections that vaguely imply I'm a disgrace to their good name and that whatever worry they might feel over me is disrupting their night."

"You need better emergency contacts." Justin looked truly pissed as he said it.

"My family is, unfortunately, not so easy to get rid of." Though Clem imagined the vampire reveal would do it.

"Is that the mysterious thing you needed emotional support for?"

Clementine cringed. "Yes, right. I didn't know how to explain it over text. They're just a bit much to deal with and I hoped a quick pep talk might help. Or any talk really. You're always so… easy."

"And here I was playing hard to get."

"Easy to *converse* with," Clementine grumbled, but a grin tugged at the edges of his lips and he couldn't help the way his heart leapt and fell. Justin *was* easy; easy beneath Clem's fingers, easy to slip little moans free of with a single dose of venom, easy to make melt in his grasp. Easy to adore. He'd be so easy to kiss too, to give in to, to take home. And so very, very hard to let go of after.

"You know, you can always call me whenever you need to talk about this stuff," Justin said.

It was so sweet of him that Clementine almost accepted automatically, before reminding himself that he didn't have to dance around Justin's feelings like that. "To be entirely honest with you, I'd rather sunbathe than talk on the phone. There's something about it that's always unnerved me. I've grown more capable over the years—my sister calls me constantly—but I rarely feel quite right at the end."

"No phone calls then." Justin nodded. "Is the texting all right?"

"The texting is fine. And if we don't text, I'm not sure how else you'd contact me."

"Carrier pigeon?"

"I only use carrier bats, I'm afraid." He didn't have to sound like he was joking, didn't have to find all the right cues to signal that he meant this to be a funny relief for their current emotional topic; Justin seemed just to look at him and know.

The man chortled, bitter smile stretched wide. "Have you learned to control them yet?"

"No. That's what makes it a terrible alternative to texting. Their messages never get to the intended recipients."

As headlights appeared in front of them, Clementine finally realized how long they'd been sitting on the drive,

Miss White awkwardly back in her booth and the gate still pulled up. He was about to move forward when the approaching car slowed beside his, Anthony in the driver's seat. He waved at Clementine, then paused, his gaze fixing on Justin. His brow tightened.

With his eyes down on his phone, Justin didn't seem to notice, but the way Anthony stared at him was peculiar. The moment passed just as quickly as it had come, though, Anthony pulling forward and continuing toward the complex. Clementine forced his mind not to spiral toward the most absurd reason for his coworker's scrutiny. He wasn't sure whether Anthony had even seen Justin before— he supposed Natalie could have found him a picture? Perhaps he was startled just by the sight of Clementine driving with someone in the first place. That was probably it: shock that Clementine had a date. Not that he *had* a date. Though he certainly had a party to get to.

He pulled out of Vitalis-Barron, quickly trying to calculate which route would get him to his parents' house faster. The beginning of the freeway looped past Vitalis-Barron and circled the side of the city farthest from the lake, forcing him to drive around most of San Salud's circumference in the process, but the straighter shot along the water took him through at least three of the downtown main streets, which would all be bustling at this time on a Friday. He chose the freeway in a snap decision. At least there he could hit the fast lane.

Only after he'd pulled on did it occur to him that he was not the only person in the car. "Oh god, I'm so sorry. I'd love to bring you back to Ala Santa but I'm already disastrously late, not counting the drive. I can pay for a taxi, though, just let me know where to drop you…"

As he said it though, he found he didn't want Justin to go. All the dread and anxiety that he'd built towards this party felt calmer now, Justin's sharp kindness balancing him out. He had told Sissy and Reggie he wouldn't bring his so-called crush—who had since become his *actual* crush. But now that he was staring the night down, all he wanted was to know Justin was nearby.

"Unless," he breached, gently, like he might scare Justin away with tone alone, "you want to come with me?"

"To wherever you're wearing *that*?" His gaze swept Clementine's torso as he said it, looking something between horrified and hungry. He rubbed the side of his neck with two fingers, tracing so absently down his pulse that Clem didn't even think he knew he was doing it.

But Clem knew, knew so strongly that his fangs slipped free. He smiled. "You've never been bit by a vampire in a *suit*, have you?"

"I should get back to Ala Santa," Justin said, though he sounded slightly less adamant than Clementine expected, glancing at his phone like it might provide him a different answer. "And I need another smoke."

"You can smoke first and you don't even have to properly attend the party—it'll be miserable anyway. But they'll have food and drinks and you can chill in a private room, and I'll drive you home when I leave—I'll only be an hour or so. I never stay at these things long. They're a bit hollowing for me."

"Do you mean harrowing?"

"That too. But mostly they just seem to drain my soul like a leech. I tend to hole up in my apartment for a few days afterward to wait for everything to—to settle, I suppose." He'd never told anyone that. He'd gone to great lengths to hide it from his friends and family, compiling excuse after excuse—even going into work instead, because a lab bench and a quiet desk was at least easier than a second large social outing. But with Justin, the knowledge didn't feel harrowing or hollowing, not a thing for Justin to judge or try to fix. It felt like just another part of him. It felt all right.

And Justin, the kind, perceptive man who brought his neighbors exactly what they needed, asked "What would you like me to do?" while smiling his vicious smirk, chin tipped up and fingers dangling off the passenger-side windowsill like he had a joint between them.

All of it together—the sweet and the bitter—caught in Clem's chest. He smiled back. "Honestly, I'm not sure. Even if all you did was sit in the car with your feet up and smoke, simply having you there to return to would help ground me."

It shouldn't have; Justin was just another person he'd have to then talk to after the party was over. But Justin clearly wasn't *just another person* either. He was the sun that Clem so desperately wanted to bask in one more time. The thought of coming back to him after the party felt easy.

They were passing the exit that would have given Justin the straightest shot to Ala Santa, but the man just tracked the billboard quietly, watching it pass. He dropped his gaze to his phone, and his expression loosened as a text came through. After turning the ringer volume to high, he slipped the device away. "All right. I'll stay. I'll come. Whatever you need."

"Should I pay you?" Clementine cringed as he said it. There had to be another way to phrase it, but *should I trade your time for a donation to your neighborhood* didn't sound much better. "I know I'll be taking you away from your work, and I don't want Ala Santa to suffer for that."

Justin tapped the rim of the window, staring straight ahead. "Isaiah can't afford his next blood bag. If you could pitch in a little…"

"Done." Clem shrugged like it meant nothing, when really it meant everything and more. "You aren't offering him your neck for the time being?"

"He already wants me in too many ways I can't provide; I won't complicate things between us further if I can help it."

That twisted in Clem's gut. "So you only let yourself be bitten by uncomplicated vampires who aren't into you, then?"

"That depends," Justin said, lifting his forearm, the sleeve of his jacket tugging back from his wrist. His fingers tightened and loosened, highlighting his veins beneath the skin. "On how much their bite makes me swoon."

Clem's heart beat a little faster. He pulled his eyes back to the road. If he could get through the party, then he could think about that wrist in his mouth, Justin pressed against his chest, their breathing quick and rough compared to the languid draw of every nibble and each brush of skin. After the party.

Even if a strong part of him wanted to know what it would be like to enjoy all of that during the party instead. To have the thrill of Justin's blood and the fantasies of his body just under the noses of the people who'd snub him for it. That part of him just wasn't brave enough.

Not yet, anyway.

Emmelyn and Raymond Hughes' house was *not* a mansion. They were very insulted by the idea that the sprawling two stories of vibrant tan stucco and intricate rock masonry with its sculptured fountain in the front and equally sculptured pool in the back was anything other than a nice upper-middle class home, owned by two nice, upper-middle class people who had both worked very hard at their nice, upper-middle class jobs to make their lives a success. Which made Clementine cringe all the harder as he pulled his car along the sweeping turn-around driveway and Justin's eyes went as wide as Clem had ever seen them.

"I knew it," he muttered.

"I don't live here," Clementine protested, weakly. "Though I did for eighteen years and a few summers, so I suppose that's a weak excuse."

Justin grumbled, "Fancy ass rich kid."

"You liked my money, last time I checked."

That shut him up.

Clementine pulled around a line of electric sedans and sports cars and parked in a gravel, tree-lined side space beside a vehicle that claimed to be both low-emission and a sports car. He sat there.

Justin leaned back in his seat, watching. "You know you can't come back to me if you don't go in."

Clementine groaned. "Can I just stay here instead?"

"Yes. Or we can always drive away, back to Ala Santa; eat take out under the death angel monument."

He wanted so badly to take Justin up on that. "But then I'll hear about it from my family for the rest of my life."

Justin lifted a brow.

Clementine groaned again and shoved open the door. He passed Justin his keys, tugged at his suit, and ran his fingers through his hair.

"You look incredible," Justin said, leaning against the top of the car to watch him.

A flush ran through Clem, settling unnecessarily between his legs. He thought of icy showers and not being admired by the man he was wildly crushing on. It didn't help, but the moment he left Justin behind and stepped into the glimmering world of champagne glasses and sharp laughter and the edged tones of backhanded compliments, his blood seemed to chill back to normal, his vision caving in as jitters filled his gut where the gentle warmth of Justin's flattery had been moments before. He already missed Justin's confident presence, his unwillingness to compromise neither his anger nor his kindness, his perceptive gaze and threatening smile.

Half the party seemed congregated in the wide, granite kitchen that melded seamlessly into a model living room fashioned to support guests on four modern couches and an extra-long wooden table. The rest spilled in groups out of the glass doors onto the back porch, fire pits of colorful glass and heat lamps in elegant shapes spread around to keep the chilly winter from invading the array of cocktail dresses. About a hundred people had arrived already, carrying little plates of hors d'oeuvres and glasses of alcohol as they mingled, their voices ricocheting like bullets over the too-loud music. Clementine recognized less than half of them, though he'd probably been introduced to most at one point or another.

He bounced his attention right over his parents—both talking to the CEOs of companies his father worked with—and searched for his siblings. It was hard to focus on anything for long in a space like this, the overwhelming displays of color, light, and sound seeming to descend on him like a physical presence. Reggie's unmistakable laughter still caught his attention, undimmed by the bright lights and the stuffy atmosphere, but before he could pinpoint his brother through the crowd, a hand fastened around his arm like a vice.

"Clementine Hughes," his sister growled. In her high heels and deep red dress with its lacy top, her golden waves half bundled in an elaborate up-do and her gilded makeup applied immaculately, she looked like Aphrodite come to exact vengeance. She dragged him past the elaborate display of photography from Reginald's travels and through the butler's pantry into the second, closed dining room, where the lights were off and the noise graciously distant. "Clementine Hughes!"

"You said that already."

"Clem!" Sissy snapped.

He cringed, bowing his head. "Yes, sorry. I'm here now. I apologize, I was just distracted—"

"With work, yes." She crossed her arms, scowling. "But you knew this was coming up. You knew it was important to me, if not to Reggie. And, lastly but very much *not* leastly…" She cleared her throat, her disappointment deepening. "You, Clementine Hughes, need to give yourself a break every now and then."

If only she knew how completely opposite this was from a break for him. But with how much she loved this scene— the bustling, shining guests and the glittering atmosphere and the rushing from one conversation to the next—and how much work she put into making each event as spectacular and special as possible, he couldn't tell her that her pride and joy made him want to hurl. Which meant he should sigh and look apologetic and say he'd do better next time, he'd arrive early or he'd stay later, that for once he wouldn't constantly check his phone for work emails or stand stoically at the side of the group whenever a topic he cared about came up, for fear that he'd start excitedly rambling the moment he spoke.

And yet…

Perhaps a bit of Justin still ran in his veins, because the thought of trying to apologize his way out of this made something in him catch fire. He glared at Odysseus right back. "Give myself a break?" he growled, the sound coming out just on the edge of what a human was capable of, the start of a vampiric growl lying beneath. "Since when has this family ever given *me* a break?"

"Here, Clementine! Now!" Sissy exhaled fast and sharp, her expression somewhere between aghast and confused. "I set up this party so that *we* could have a break; me and you and Reggie, together."

"At our parents' house. With their friends, and your law firm, and half the most fashionable businesspeople in San Salud." He tossed his hands to the side, then pulled them back, feeling altogether like he didn't know what to do with them. Like he didn't know what to do with any of this. "Tonight is not a break for me, Odysseus! Not with all of them here, breathing down my neck. You don't understand;

224

you haven't spent your whole damned life having to be perfect! You get everything you want so—so easily."

Sissy went stiff as if he'd slapped her. Her jaw pulsed. "I spent most of my life trying to be masculine enough to pass as someone I wasn't, and I'll spend the rest trying to convince the world and my own damn self that I'm not actually that man I'd faked them into seeing. Easy is not something I have ever known."

Clementine's heart plummeted. Fuck him. "Oh god, Sissy, I didn't mean…"

"I know exactly what you meant, Clementine," his sister cut in, flat and hard. "And you're wrong. If you cared to stick around sometime, maybe you'd get it. Parties like these used to be hellish for me too. But you know what happened when I finally started being myself? It was hard, and it sucked, but it was the best I'd ever felt. The moment I stopped being the person I thought I had to be and started being the one I wanted to be, everything hard and terrible was finally worth it. I can go out there and be happy regardless of the trials, because at least I am *me*." She watched him, her gaze piercing. "What do you want, Clementine? If you didn't have to be perfect, what would you be?"

"I…" His throat tightened, and no matter what he did, he couldn't seem to speak through it.

Sissy shook her head. She took a step back, then another. "Maybe this family and this place isn't what you want. But please, try to find something you do. At least, don't be alone."

He watched her walk back through the butler's pantry, her head held high and each step clicking in her heels, until the sounds of the party drowned her out. Clem felt sick. Sick and angry and like the situation had snapped back to hit him in the face.

"Don't be alone."

But Clementine wasn't alone. He might not have known all of what he wanted—besides his life, exactly the way he'd left it five months ago, which was an unreachable feat now, and one that seemed more and more ominous every time he looked back at it—yet he had one dream his mind had latched onto over the last few weeks. He could prove that much to Sissy, at least.

"If you didn't have to be perfect, what would you be?"

Dr. Clementine Hughes would be happy.

JUSTIN

Justin leaned against the hood of the car as he smoked the ache between his shoulder blades back into submission and tried not to think too hard about Clementine in his outlandish, perfectly-fitted suit with his curls beautifully tousled and his eyes alight. The more his mind fixed on the image, the more he wanted to offer Clementine not just this hour but the rest of the night as well, to let himself be taunted into breaking, then singing Clem's praises until the sun rose.

But Justin didn't have until the sun rose; he'd given himself an hour here, and only because Isaiah had texted saying he was fine. That he'd maintained Mrs. Mendoza would offer him a place for the night was irrelevant, as was the fact that she had enough smut to entertain Isaiah for at least a week. Isaiah had followed that claim with a picture that bordered on flirtation.

But Justin was already with the vampire he really wanted to flirt with.

He'd just extinguished the last of his joint when Clementine burst out of the house like his feet were on fire.

"You're coming inside with me," he said, a growl riding beneath the words. "You asked what you could do for me and it's this."

"I'm not exactly dressed." Justin glanced down at himself: his favorite ripped denim jacket, trim jeans, and a black V-neck that would have been appropriate on a stripper, with his silver crucifix pendant hanging against his sternum. Party material, but for an entirely different sort of party.

"That's the point. I'm making a statement."

Justin lifted his brow. "What's the statement, so I can consent to it?"

That seemed to douse Clementine's anger, turning him almost embarrassed. "That I have better people than my emergency contacts, and these people—this person—doesn't have to blend into a prissy event like this to be worth caring about."

Justin was this person—was Clementine's person. His more desirable emergency contact; his human. That shouldn't have made his chest flutter and his future feel like a weightless twinkle of stars, not with how many other people already relied on him, with how regrettably he'd have to abandon this one vampire the moment his needed him back in Ala Santa. But it was as if that conviction had burned up in the wind, and what remained was every joke, every thoughtful discussion, every shared fear, with each shining memento having forged together into a diamond-solid affection.

He would be the one to shatter before it did.

"For that, you can use me and abuse me." And he held out his hand. "Do your worst, Lemon."

Clementine took it, drawing him off the car. "I'd much rather gently snack on you with adequate reparations, if it's all the same." He didn't let go, tucking his fingers against Justin's elbow. The middle two teased back and forth against the soft flesh there and the veins beneath, the motion turned rough and tremulous by the denim between them.

Justin longed for that fabric to be removed. He longed for a *lot* of the fabric on both of them removed.

"And, if you don't mind, we could, perhaps, give them the impression that we're more intimate than..." Clementine seemed to struggle to find the right word.

"A vampire and the human he's illegally purchasing blood from?"

Clem made a noise in the back of his throat. "Than friends."

It was both not enough and far more than Justin deserved. "I will be whatever you want tonight." He drew his free hand along the back of his neck, little finger flipping against the collar of his jacket and riding up the side of his pulse. "I'm yours." He glanced down at his outfit once more. "But if you *are* making a statement, I think I have an idea..."

Justin strolled into the party like the head of a rival mafia, his shirt gone from beneath his jean jacket and a dozen of the Hughes family's gold and pearl and diamond necklaces dangling against the black tribal ink of his chest tattoos.

The whole event was somehow exactly what he had imagined and nothing like it at all. No over-polite staff in black outfits. Instead, delicate little food parcels were arranged on elevated platters along a bar, each pre-plated on their own individual faux-crystal circle. Miniature replicas of European and Southeast Asian landmarks were arranged among them with labels denoting how each taster related to its specified country of origin.

He swiped a small plate of Filipino pancit off its pedestal, plopping the whole mix of stir-fried rice noodles and vegetables into his mouth in one go. The betrayal he expected never came. It wasn't exactly the variety he'd suspected he'd have found in the country itself—he'd never been, though Isaiah had made a few trips to visit family there prior to turning—but it tasted like it came from his best friend's own kitchen, the arrangement more elegant and the portion size vastly too small but the flavor and texture acceptable. It irked him to watch his home life consumed by this fancy, chittering crowd of tailored suits and tiny dresses.

Even if there were fewer white faces than he'd expected—
which wasn't saying a *lot*, since his expectations hadn't been
high—he wasn't sure they deserved this.

No, based on Clementine's descriptions of them, he was
sure they *didn't*.

From the confused and lightly amused way most of them
looked at him as he passed, his certainty only grew. Every
momentary glance made him feel like he was interrupting
something, brows wrinkled and mouths quirked. At least it
seemed their judgment was reserved for his looks and not the
way he had his arm wrapped through Clementine's. Justin
had the physical strength and biting smile to face the bigotry
around him head on, but he still felt uneasy if he had to turn
his back on potentially hostile strangers while displaying his
sexuality. He'd heard enough stories, seen enough bruises in
his youth. But this crowd didn't seem the sort to throw
punches. He figured tossing money at the wrong laws did far
more damage than a fist to the face, though.

Justin fiddled with one of the borrowed necklaces. He'd
promised to give them back after, but as they moved through
the lavish kitchen, he quietly snuck a pair of their dainty
crystal salt and pepper shakers into his pocket. A trophy for
his time and a very tiny middle finger to the owners of the
house.

Clementine grew stiffer with each step, strangling the
stem of his champagne so hard that it looked like it might
break.

Justin lifted onto his toes to brush his lips to the vampire's ear. "Look at these assholes," he scoffed, perhaps a little overdramatically.

But it seemed exactly what Clementine needed to hear. He turned his head, his chin brushing lightly against Justin's temple. "Fuck them, right?"

I'd rather fuck you, was not the revelation he needed to slip right now, whatever his feelings toward Clementine's current state of dress. "Do you think they'd know a good time if it bit them?"

That got a laugh, not as bright or full as Clem's usual, but still genuine, the curve of his mouth turning ever-so-slightly to a smirk. "There's someone else I'd rather bite… right under their noses, maybe." His gaze slipped to Justin's neck, then focused past his shoulder. His nose wrinkled, his posture tensing. "Speaking of the devils."

He turned toward the demons in question, gently guiding Justin with a hand at the center of his back. The light but steady touch brought a hunger, its aching so deep that it nearly masked Justin's usual misgivings over having anyone but Isaiah touch the muscles near his shoulder blades. Clementine's pressure was so perfect, gentle and sure, Justin relaxed under it, breathing gratefully out. He dragged his fingertips against Clementine's hip as he diverted his attention to the couple meandering toward them from the wide porch doorway.

The devils indeed.

He could see Clementine in both of them. The woman's perfect loose waves held the same golden glow as Clem's and she mirrored Clem's delicate nose and the way he always lifted it, like the distance was letting them both look a little closer at the world. Clem shared the man's strong jaw and his contemplative eyes, his hair silver now but the curls still cresting around his ears with the seeking, tousled manner that Clementine's did. The way they surveyed Justin though—if Clementine had dared to look at him that way the day they'd met, he'd have offered the vampire the other end of a stake instead of a business deal.

"Good evening, Clementine." The woman's smile felt every bit as much a threat as Justin's usual grin, but her gaze kept dragging back to the necklaces Clem had borrowed for Justin, like she didn't know quite what to do about it. "Nice of you to finally join us."

"I hope we weren't inconveniencing you," the man added, moving seamlessly from staring at Justin to ignoring his existence.

He pulled a little closer to Clementine. The vampire's hand slid down his back. It cupped his hip, and Justin's mouth went dry. They weren't a couple. But the fact that Clementine wanted his parents to suspect their son had come here with Justin made him proud. Maybe he couldn't actually be with Clementine, but for this one night he could pretend.

"Justin, these are my parents, Emmelyn and Raymond," Clem said, looking solidly to Justin before letting his gaze flit back to the disgruntled pair in front of them. "Mother, Father, this is Justin Yu. I'm so sorry I was late; traffic picking him up tonight was a little worse than most days."

"It's nice to meet you both." Justin grinned, baring his teeth so wide they both flinched. "I can see where Clem gets his hots from."

Clementine made a sound that could have been a laugh, covered quickly by his throat clearing.

His mother looked like he'd force fed her a spider. "*Doctor* Emmelyn Hughes," she corrected, glancing at the necklaces again.

"It's a pleasure," droned Raymond, looking very much like it was anything but. He switched his attention immediately back to his son. "Odysseus didn't tell us you were bringing anyone."

Clementine shrugged so casually the motion looked almost wrong on him. "We'd originally thought he couldn't come. It was a last-minute thing."

"I would have assumed you'd postpone your dating life until Dr. Blood selects the new senior associate. Seeing how close you are to it."

"I have time for both."

"But not for this Sunday's Cancer Research Brunch?" Emmelyn asked. "We were very disappointed not to see your RSVP come in yet. You know how hard it is on the schedulers when you tell them you'll be there so late like this."

The pressure of Clementine's hand on Justin's waist increased just enough for him to feel the change. On top of having to deal with his mother at the brunch event, it was also during a prime time for sun-exposure. Clem had probably been turning down their daytime engagements for weeks now and praying they wouldn't put two and two together.

His voice wavered as he began to reply, "Well—"

"This Sunday?" Justin cut in, playing with one of the golden chains around his neck as he leaned into Clem's side as much as he dared. The solid presence of him sent a delicious shudder down Justin's spine. "Babe, wouldn't that conflict with the charity sale after Mass?"

Clementine turned his face toward Justin's, close enough now that their space felt singular. "Right, we've had that on our calendar for weeks."

"Weeks," Raymond muttered.

"Well," Emmelyn said, like she was going to continue, but her gaze bounced between her son and Justin's fingers on the borrowed necklaces, and the words seemed not to come.

Her husband stepped in for her. "How... nice."

"It really is." Clementine agreed, so enthusiastically that Justin worried maybe he was overselling it, but his parents seemed too confused to notice. "We haven't gotten a chance to see Reggie yet. I'm sure you'll excuse us while we look for him."

He pulled Justin away from the Hughes parents without a second glance. It was such a power move, both parents staring speechless after them, until Emmelyn finally hissed under her breath, "I swear that looks just like my—"

Justin glanced back, baring his teeth in a smirk terrible enough that she swallowed the words.

"Was that all right for you?" Clementine whispered as he stepped onto the porch.

Justin swore the vampire's lips brushed his skin, and he had a flash of what it might be like for Clementine to tug on his earlobe and nip at the soft skin just behind it. A shudder ran through him, bright and blissful and hungry. "It was brilliant." His voice came out husky. He cleared his throat, trying not to think too hard about the warmth and confidence radiating from the vampire at his side or the pressure it built within him. "Your parents really are shit, aren't they?"

Clementine groaned. "They're... complicated. But yes, in this they are the absolute worst. And I'm finally ready to say: fuck that."

A few other guests tried to talk to Clementine, asking after Justin in ways more gracious than Clementine's parents, but he politely brushed them off with growing confidence, winding Justin through the swelling crowd with a hand always somewhere on Justin's person—his elbow, his biceps, his wrist, his hip. Even without his parents to taunt, the connection seemed to ground Clementine. To ground them both.

The darker landscape of the yard left more room for each other, but they stayed nearly as close as they had in the house, so near that when Clementine playfully slid two fingers into the cuff of Justin's jacket, Justin had only to lean in and turn just so, rising onto his tiptoes as though looking out over the scenery, in order to get Clementine's mouth mere inches from his neck. Clem growled, teasing, but a little impulsive too. When Justin glanced back at him, the vampire lifted the edge of one lip, slipping his tongue along the side of his fang.

Justin's nerves lit up. He swallowed.

"There's someone else I'd rather bite... right under their noses."

What would it be like to be bitten here, to feel the rush of the venom while surrounded by these strangers and their sideways glances and unsated curiosity? His heart thudded faster. He wanted to know; he wanted to feel Clem's fangs in him like a dirty secret.

As they passed a table of assorted desserts, Justin plucked up a chocolate thing with an Eiffel Tower on its name card. He bit off half of it, pausing for a moment to relish the dark, sweet substance melting on his tongue. Clementine moved to take one for himself, but Justin stopped him with a palm to his waist.

"Mh, try this one." He gave Clementine just enough time to look up, before lifting the treat to Clem's lips.

A flush brightened Clementine's cheeks but the tug at the edge of his mouth was absolutely devious as he opened for Justin. The way the vampire worked over Justin's finger and

237

thumb made the head of his dick ache so hard he had to hold back a moan. Clem made the sound for him, swallowing once around the tips of Justin's fingers.

Justin could still feel Clem's fangs out. Gently, he pressed the pad of his thumb into one. He just caught the change in Clem's expression, his pleasure turning to shocked ecstasy. Venom hit Justin like a rush. In his current mindset, with his desire so aroused and the colorful glass fires twinkling about them and the distant thrum of the music, it felt like floating, like drifting off in his own world where it was just him and Clementine, lost in each other.

It lasted only a moment, but the instant it was gone, he needed another hit.

Clem gave Justin's thumb a final suck and let it go. The little grin that lingered on his lips was like a second rush. Clementine clearly wanted this too; wanted it from Justin, even if it had taken time for the feeling to develop. Or perhaps it was that time that had made it all the better: that they'd known each other first as people, before they'd finally come to this.

Even if this *was* just for the night.

Clementine stepped toward him, and Justin found himself moving in too, their feet overlapping, their gazes glued.

A man jogged up behind them at a pace uncharacteristic of the rest of the party, bumping into Justin with a tiny, "Oops, my bad," as he tried to grab five different dessert plates at once. He paused as his gaze slid up, and a huge smile spread across his face. "Clem! You made it!"

Clementine cringed, but unlike the anger and pain that had come with his flinches from his parents, this seemed more a reaction to the overall exuberance. "Reggie," he cleared his throat, "Meet my—my Justin."

Where the resemblance between Clementine and his parents had been uncanny, it took work to see the ways these two were related. Reggie was built like the traditional representations of Vikings compared to Clem's slim figure, his long auburn curls holding just a shimmer of gold in the firelight. His nose looked like it had been broken at least once, offsetting his much too fashionable glasses, and he had the kind of crooked smile that never really went away.

"Dude, I thought you said he wasn't coming?" His attention seemed to leap from one piece of Justin to the next, taking in his sorely underdressed outfit, his bare chest, and the bundle of borrowed necklaces that bounced against his finely detailed tribal tattoos. The grin already taking over Reggie's expression widened further. He shoved his desserts clumsily into a leaning stack against his broad chest and held out a hand. "Reginald Hughes, doctorate in dumbassery and sibling embarrassment. The lone jock of this nerd-infested family. How I have *struggled*."

"He's always like this," Clementine explained wearily.

Justin didn't want to like the man—he was part of this family who seemed to so actively disregard Clem—but as Reginald took his forearm and pulled him into a full embrace, he was pretty sure that ship had sailed. He laughed, clamping Reggie on the shoulder, and began helping the man consolidate his desserts to one plate. "Good to meet you. So, this is your party?"

"According to Odysseus." Reginald shrugged. "She did all the work, bless her. I'm just here for the food. And the fame. And the girls, if they're into that."

Clementine grunted, giving the tiniest eye roll. "He's a self-proclaimed thirst trap. Has about ten million followers."

"What can I say? They like my abs!"

Maybe Reginald wasn't Justin's type, generally speaking—he wasn't sure anyone else *could* be so as long as Clementine was standing beside him, with his tall, lean frame tucked perfectly into his gilded suit and his elegance wrapped for the moment in a devastating, almost devilish confidence—but Reginald certainly looked like he'd have incredible abs.

"Some of them follow you because they like the travel photography." Now *this* woman *had* to be Clementine's sister. Just as slim and tall, with a facial structure less refined and her nose more robust, she slipped into the conversation like she belonged, not simply in this one, but in any conversation she chose. She wrapped one arm around Reginald's shoulders for a light squeeze as he reassured her.

"Nah, I still think that's just you," he teased.

Odysseus—what was it with this family and kids' names?—turned her attention to Clementine and Justin. Her gaze sharpened and she crossed her arms, her lips pressing into a curious pucker as she surveyed them. When she finally spoke, her voice revealed nothing. "So this is him, huh?" But she wasn't looking at Justin at all. Instead, she watched Clementine pointedly.

He stared right back at her, two minor deities locked in a battle beyond mortal understanding. "I don't know yet. I'm still figuring things out."

Her expression softened into affection and pride. "Well, still, I like it."

Clementine released a breath. "Thank you." It didn't sound like the acceptance of the compliment, but something deeper and fuller than this single bizarre conversation could ascribe. "And I am truly sorry. I really didn't mean—"

"I *know* what you meant." She said it with such gentleness yet force, a phrase like a hug, and it seemed to wash over Clementine just so.

His eyes gleamed with unshed tears, and he smiled softly. As his lips pulled back, a hint of his fangs poked out, and he closed his mouth again. Odysseus didn't seem to notice.

Reginald grabbed Clementine's arm with one brawny hand so firmly his champagne spilled. "Did you see the photo display Sissy made?" He took the glass right out of his brother's hand, downing it in a chaotic swig that dumped half his bite-sized treats off the plate at the same time. "There's this one picture," he continued like there had been no interruption, "that I took in London—I've got to show you. Sissy blew it up and I swear in the background there's that guy you like from Star Trek..."

Justin watched Reginald pull a stunned and grumbling Clem across the increasingly crowded yard with a wave and a laugh. He was pretty sure of all the villains here, this was not one Clem needed rescuing from. He prepared to grab another dessert from the table and follow them, but Odysseus cleared her throat, stepping into his way. He'd given the look she now wore too many times himself not to know what it meant.

This was a schemed tag-teaming, then. So be it.

He sighed and tried to offer the woman something that wasn't just a baring of teeth. "We're not actually together."

Odysseus lifted one brow. "That's worse."

Justin cringed.

"He likes you." Her voice went soft in a dangerous way, her long legs bringing her so close to him in a single step that her towering presence sent an instinctual chill up Justin's spine. "Whatever this is you are both playing at, he is *not* playing."

"I know," Justin admitted. He tried to look away, to focus on anything but the distant bob of Clementine's golden hair as he and Reggie stood before an elaborate framed collage of travel photos, Reggie's every motion huge and exuberant while Clementine seemed like he was trying to curl into an embarrassed ball in the most dramatic and nonsensical way possible.

"So the question is, do *you* like *him*?"

That wasn't a question—at least not to Justin. In what world wouldn't he fall for Clementine? If there was one, it was so far removed from this reality that he'd no longer be himself. Justin's chest ached, a slow steady burn that seemed like it would grow until it consumed him. His feelings for Clementine weren't the problem, but who Justin was. Perhaps it was those very unfortunate faults that had turned him into the kind of person who would fall so far and fast for a gorgeous, naively generous vampire in the first place. The version of him who loved Clementine could also never be worthy of him.

"Ah." Odysseus nodded. "You do like him. Yet you say that you two aren't together? Or, what was the word: *actually* together?"

"We're friends, but we're not—we haven't. This is just to fuck with your parents."

"I saw you before Reggie interrupted. Nothing that extravagant is just for the parents."

Justin felt like he was being put on trial for all the secret little yearnings tucked deep in his chest. Part of him wanted to punch something and be done with it, but his smarter half recognized this wasn't a situation that could be punched out of, and Odysseus was not actually the person he wanted to punch. If he was honest, he suspected the person he really wanted to punch was himself.

Odysseus seemed more than happy to oblige his self-flagellation. "So you're acting this out with no intention of carrying through? If you're pulling each other's hearts around and thinking that you can just slide back to normal afterward, then you might be able to recover from that, but he won't. He doesn't give himself to people like this. He's more sensitive and trusting than he looks, and if you are taking advantage of that, I will find out, and I will make your life a legal hellscape."

Justin grimaced. "This was *his* idea," he protested, weakly.

"Because he's a fool for you, and he will take everything you give him without considering the long-term detriment." Her tone softened, turning almost questioning. Pleading. "But you like him. And he likes you."

Justin could almost hear the rest of her question: *so why not?* He swallowed down the yearning of his heart. There were so many reasons why not. He had his neighborhood and his vampires—the ones that weren't Clementine; his debts to repay. But all of those things mattered less right now, compared to the biggest one: "I don't deserve his love."

Odysseus gave him a look so full of emotion—annoyance, pity, anger, love—that it felt like a physical blow. "This is the most vibrant I've seen my brother in months—maybe years. I don't give a fuck what *you* deserve. You are good for him and *he* deserves that. What he does not deserve is to have it ripped out from under him."

Justin couldn't find a reply over the pain that bloomed in his chest, warm, bright, and terrible.

"Those necklaces are certainly a look," Odysseus added, and he wasn't sure if it was an inside joke or a threat.

Then Clementine was there again, strolling through the crowd with Reggie at his side, the firelight gleaming in his golden curls and his long fingers gently tapping in time to the music. As they reached Justin and Odysseus, though, Reggie's attention caught on someone coming out from the house: a pale-haired man who could have been mistaken for a fairy prince on a cover of one of Mrs. Mendoza's romance novels, his delicate features pinched in haughty distaste and his suit so immaculately embroidered that it had to be custom-made. Reggie's face lit up, and he shouted clean across the yard.

"Yo, my man! What's up!"

The man in question's expression didn't change but when Reginald ran at him, he let himself be smothered in a side hug with the kind of resigned affection that made Justin think it was a typical greeting.

Clementine scowled, and his fingers laced with Justin's, sending a tingle up Justin's arm. "Come on. If we're roped into a full conversation with Reggie *and* my boss's son, I might have to fake my own death."

"Reggie's friend is your boss's…"

But the wannabe fairy prince's affiliations didn't seem all that important compared to the hand that Clementine was sliding along the small of Justin's back, and the heat of his breath in Justin's hair. A shiver ran straight through his body, settling as an ache between his legs. If only those long, delicate fingers of Clem's would slip a little lower, sneak beneath the fabric of his jeans, if only—

He breathed out, trying just to enjoy the desire without letting it run to places he could never go. It was hard, with

Clem's mouth at his ear, and the urge to tip his head until his neck was bared for Clem's teeth making every other desire hotter and blissfully painful.

"I'd much rather focus on you," Clementine whispered, the gentle music from the speakers fading out to make his voice agonizingly crisp.

A band started up on the corner of the wide patio and Reggie hollered in excitement.

As though with one mind, Clementine and Justin both drew away from the dessert table, into the cleared patio where a few couples had already started swaying to the beat. Odysseus caught Justin's gaze. He swallowed down the guilt. Clementine *had* chosen this. He had chosen to enjoy the moment despite whatever heartache came of it. And Justin had to respect that decision, didn't he?

Clementine pulled him forward, each motion turning to a graceful glide as he twirled Justin to the rhythm of the music, the Hughes's borrowed necklaces shifting against his sternum. The two of them shimmied and bobbed, not following any particular steps but still building off each other as though they knew each other's bodies like their own, could feel the push and pull of the other through the invisible twine of fate that had brought them together in the first place; two so different people, so made for one another. It was freeing— just existing with Clementine, lost in the music and the happy concentration on Clem's face and the feeling of his hands occasionally brushing Justin's arms.

The song turned to one with a slower rhythm, enticing and dark. Beside them a pair of women giggled, the smaller, more curvaceous one swaying her partner in an embrace with too much soft kissing and ass squeezing to be anything but romantic. Their openness calmed Justin's initial fears that the party might judge him and Clementine for their overt affection. He still didn't *like* these people, but Odysseus's taste in guests could certainly have been worse.

Watching another couple flirt didn't usually stir things in him. Tonight though, with Clementine before him, so polished yet so recklessly undone at the same time, Justin yearned for what the two women had, soft and slow and sensual. He slipped closer to Clementine, then closer still, cupping his palm to the vampire's hip. Suddenly they were together, brushing in time to the music.

The buttons of Justin's jacket skimmed against the front of Clem's suit, their feet making room for their stances to overlap as they swayed heel to toe, heel to toe. His pelvis didn't quite meet with Clementine's, and the anticipation of grinding against Clem was almost too much to bear. He lifted his chin, turning his face just enough to keep their noses from bumping as they shared each other's air, the same as they shared their time, their space, their beings, Justin's life source having dripped red so many times from the vampire's lips.

Clementine's palm slid once more against the base of Justin's back, low enough that Justin could feel his pinky cupping into the crack of Justin's ass. He didn't rest it there long though, drawing three fingertips up Justin's spine, light enough that it soothed the low level of pain that always buzzed beneath Justin's skin. Clementine's arm tightened around him as that pressure trailed across his far shoulder, over the bundle of borrowed chains and along Justin's neck, Clem's arm wrapping so firmly around him that one light tug would pull them flesh to flesh. Justin inhaled, his whole body alight.

Clem set every one of Justin's nerves off with a pinch to his pulse.

The sharp little pain rolled through him, so like a bite that it made him ache as though he'd had teeth sunk into his flesh. He tensed beneath the feeling, accidentally leaning into Clementine's chest. "That's cruel," he whispered, the words coming out like honey and gravel through his tight throat.

"But you liked it." Clem's body continued shifting in rhythm, and their hips met properly for the first time, dragging a sensation from Justin's dick like vibrant sparks against a satin-black night. As Justin pushed back, Clementine sucked in a tight breath, rough and hot.

"Perhaps." Neck still stinging, Justin tipped his face up, tilting his head until Clem's breath was on his skin. He hoped Clem could feel the pounding of his pulse. "But if you don't offer me the real thing soon," he teased, dark as his smirk, "then I'm going to taunt you until you have no choice but to attack."

Clementine leaned over him, so tense he seemed a band about to snap. Each exhalation felt heavier than the last, a weight building, until finally he whispered, "Someplace darker and less loud."

He drew back, fingers lacing with Justin's as he guided him out of the slow-dancers, past a fire pit where Reggie regaled guests with a story, the fairy prince son of Clementine's boss to his left and a gaggle of enraptured women all but hanging onto his knees. They moved past a mini bar and a planter of roses, past another fire pit occupied by a woman and an androgynous person chatting as they brushed ankles. It all seemed secondary, hazy snippets of life that locked him and Clementine into their own glorious bubble. The sparkling backdrop of laughter and music thrilled up Justin's spine and back down through every aching sliver of his being.

Grass squelched under his shoes, and Clementine tugged him into a misshapen veil of willow branches. Through their dark shroud he could still see pieces of the party, licking flames and the bright lights of the house, but individual people turned to indistinct blurs. Clementine was just as vague in the darkness, the touch of his fingers tantalizing as he tucked Justin against himself. His hand slipped along the rim of Justin's jacket, fisting into the dense fabric. He held there, taut to the point of shaking, like he wanted something that he couldn't quite take.

Justin needed him to take it though—*needed* to be *taken*.

Desperate, he dragged his fingers up the back of the vampire's neck, tangling them into his curls, and led Clementine to his neck.

Clem's lips met his skin first, but his mouth opened in an instant, his whole body pressing into Justin's as he bit down. His venom burst through Justin's mind in a wave that lifted him up and set him on fire. He shuddered, gasping like a final breath.

This was religion, he thought—this was the way his god smiled on him, not in a cathedral of people who thought less of him for who he loved, but here beneath a willow, tangled in another man, giving away a piece of his life in a chorus of little moans. Love and sacrifice and desire and exaltation all wrapped into one. It was his hands in Clementine's hair, so soft and loose and smelling of vanilla with a hint of almonds, and it was Clem's grip on him, teeth inside him, his free hand making itself less free by the moment as it wrapped around his thigh, climbing higher.

Clem's thumb brushed the curve where his leg met his crotch. It dragged forth a gasp.

Shaking from the sheer intensity of the thing that pounded through him, an unearthly feeling with a presence of its own, no longer just an emotion but a possession, he burst free the top button of Clementine's suit vest and slid his hand across the silky fabric of his shirt to grasp at Clem's nipple. Clem growled, his teeth sinking deeper with a fresh rush of venom.

Beyond their little world, two high, young voices grew nearer. They buzzed in the back of Justin's mind, but didn't register as any more important than the other background chatter until the beam of a weak phone light flittered across the willow branches. Clem yanked his teeth out. Perhaps nothing else caught in the glow, but his fangs must have, sharp and bright and perfect, because a shriek came from one of the passersby.

"Vampire!"

The cry sounded more giddy than afraid, nervous laughter bubbling after, but it seemed to echo along the nearest edge of the party, turning darker with each transfer.

"Clementine?" The call burst between it, followed by confirmations. "He took Clementine!"

It wasn't the truth, not in any way it was laid out. Clementine had led Justin here. Clementine had fed on him. But it was Justin their memories produced, Justin they had been skeptical of and Justin they were all too willing to fit into the role of vampire.

And thank god for that.

Justin could feel the glorious brush of Clem's tongue over his bite mark and he tried to let go, to face the chaos mounting behind them, but his head swam, his blood still figuring out what it was good for beside a lover's feast. The venom coursing through him was still bright and hot, turning his attempt to cover for Clem into a bitter, sultry snap. "Fuck off, he's mine."

How he wanted that to be true, or better yet, for it to be Clementine's truth too; to be the one Clementine would sink his fangs into forever, to be claimed publicly and in excess. But it was just a cover, as much a game of pretenses and pretend as everything else they'd done so far. And it seemed to be working.

He could make out the charge of feet across the grass, and the rustle of the willow branches behind him as the party took it hook and sinker.

"Get away from him!" someone shouted, suddenly much too near for comfort.

Justin turned in time to see the tiered metal plate holder swung at him like a bat, but not fast enough to stop it. He barely recognized the man who wielded it—someone who had looked at him with curiosity or suspicion, he couldn't remember which—before the makeshift weapon crashed into his back. Pain bloomed through his spine and across his shoulder blades, where it turned white hot. It seemed to leak into his soul, burning out everything that he was.

Then he remembered nothing.

21

CLEMENTINE

Justin collapsed into his arms.

Clementine caught him on instinct, his mind still reeling.

This had been going so well, so gloriously perfect, like a dream he hadn't dared let himself fully engage with, much less live out. He'd taken his life into his own hands, held Justin in his arms. The whole time, Anthony and Natalie had been so far from his thoughts that he almost believed it could always be like this, Odysseus's parties turned from awkward battles to bearable, occasionally joyful proceedings with Justin at his side, Justin to come back to at the end of his day at Vitalis-Barron, maybe even the senior associate position to choose whether to claim or turn down on his own terms and not for his parents' attention, the extra cash not going towards blood payments but directly to the charity work he and Justin would do together.

And Justin; all of Justin. His body warm and hard against Clementine, his bittersweet scent flooding Clem's senses as he swallowed the man's blood in hungry, sensual drags. His fingers on Justin's thigh, Justin's grip around his nipple, the strain in his pants pleading for release.

And then came reality.

"*Vampire.*"

It should have been him they came for, but of course it wasn't. Of course it wasn't their perfect Hughes doctor, buttoned up to look just like everyone else here, normal and nonthreatening. Instead, they targeted the one person who didn't quite fit in: the unknown party, an easy option to ascribe all their worst fears to.

As far as attacks went, this one shouldn't have been so traumatizing. Clementine had barely felt the impact of the blow through Justin's body pressed against him, only the way he'd gone stiff, then limp as though he'd been cracked in the back of the skull instead of cautiously batted in the meaty flesh of his shoulder-blades. Clem didn't have time to dwell on that now though, not with the crowd still growing, their gossip gaining speed by the moment. It wasn't all nasty, wasn't all bad even, some of the protests defending Justin, if only by claiming that Clementine was with him by choice. But whatever it turned into, Clem didn't want to still be here for it, holding back his fangs and playing into their biases just to save his own skin while Justin—oh god *Justin*—

In his arms, Justin gave a weak groan. His lashes fluttered.

Fuck.

Someone tall and broad pushed through the willow branches toward them—Reggie, maybe—but Clementine scooped Justin up against his chest and barreled out of the spotlight. The crowd parted with muffled gasps and concerned exclamations. He ignored them all, carrying Justin at a steady jog across the patio and through the house. Only one person followed.

Her high heels clicked as she sprinted across the foyer, the skirt of her dress bunched in one hand and the pinned strands of her half-updo falling sloppily around her panicked expression. "Clementine!"

He didn't stop—he couldn't stop—his heart in this throat and his fangs halfway out from the traces of Justin's blood still lingering in his mouth. Sissy didn't stop either though, shouting his name again with increasing authority. She tore after him out the front door, the cobblestone entrance not slowing her in the least. If he could just run faster without fear of hurting Justin, without fear of giving himself away...

"We can help him, Clementine." She rounded the front of the house, following them toward the parked line of expensive vehicles. "If you love him, then his vampirism doesn't matter."

If you love him—like there were prerequisites on it. Some goal to meet before the alleged vampirism was made tolerable; not even accepted, just shoved into a corner to be ignored.

Justin groaned again, a mumble leaving him that sounded like Clementine's name tangled with a curse. Clem's car beeped open from the presence of its key in his pocket, but he had to tug twice at the passenger door, Justin propped against his chest on wobbling legs. It finally came open with another beep, and he helped Justin into the seat. Justin collapsed, his half-mast eyes glazed over. But he was conscious. That was good, wasn't it?

"Clem, please, you're scaring me!" Sissy slowed behind them, close enough that he could hear her gasping. "Tell me what's happening. I can help."

The offer felt like a slap, so harsh and fast that Clementine hadn't been expecting it—hadn't been expecting something so mundane to hurt so badly. She had liked what she'd seen earlier, had accepted the man he was trying to be, appreciated him even. But Clem wasn't a man, not in the linguistic sense, not the second half of the word for human. He was a vampire.

He would *always* be a vampire.

There was no normal version of his old life he could reclaim now, no going back, no pretending it hadn't happened. Whoever Sissy accepted as her brother, that person wasn't real. She didn't know him, and there was no way he could be certain she'd ever want to.

Suddenly he couldn't run anymore. He turned so fast the world blurred, a hiss rising in his throat. "I'm scaring *you*?" he shouted right back. "My god, Sissy. Someone hit my—my Justin hard enough to do this and *I'm* the one scaring you."

Odysseus's shoulders heaved with each breath, but she pressed them back, meeting Clem's gaze firmly. "They were trying to defend you, Clem. It was an unfair reaction, but they don't know Justin, or how much he cares—"

"*Defending* me." Clementine choked on the word.

Defending him, when he should have been the one who'd taken that blow. Defending him, only because they couldn't perceive a reality where he was the thing they feared. Defending their perfect Dr. Hughes Junior, who would have to keep being all the more perfect, all the more human, just to *keep* them defending him.

Beneath the rage he felt hollow. And Sissy, despite all her social prowess, just stood there, not knowing, not seeing.

"Clementine," she began.

He couldn't stand here while she told him she'd make this all better, while she made it seem like everything could work out if only he opened himself up. "I know you've been through some tough shit, okay, and you think that if I'm just myself, it'll be better. But not everyone is that lucky." He pushed the passenger door, the whole car rattling as it shut. "I have to go. I can't be here, I'm sorry. I thought this could work for me, but it—it isn't—it can't."

Sissy reached for him, but he slipped around the front of the vehicle, too fast, too agile. He didn't care. He should have cared—this was the life he wanted, and his sister one of the few people he truly did want in it—but right then it seemed like if one thing was going to crash down, then everything else might as well come with it. The driver's side handle bent under his grip. He shook as he climbed in, yanking the belt so hard it refused to move once, twice, then he gave up and started the engine.

Sissy knocked on his window. He could hear her through the glass. "You shouldn't drive like this, Clementine! Let me take you. I won't even talk," she pleaded, "I'll just drive."

"Get away from the car." He cracked the window as he said it, one eye on his sister and one on the half-conscious man in his passenger seat.

Odysseus sounded genuinely panicked now, her fingers grasping uselessly at the door. "Please, wherever you need to be, I can take you there."

"I don't need your help, Sissy!" It came out in a rumbled growl, too deep and snarled for human vocal cords, his teeth bared and his hands clenching the wheel.

And it was true. It wasn't true. It was—Clem didn't know.

He had been avoiding her help so long, he didn't know what he needed, or wanted from her, or where those two things coincided.

But it made her step back.

Her hands fell limply to her sides, her expression going slack. Then shocked. Then *distressed*.

That's when he finally felt it: his fangs fully extended. She was staring at them. She knew.

He closed his mouth as his heart pounded, turning the world to a rush around him. People called both their names from nearer the house now, but Sissy just kept staring, her fingers slowly lifting to her chest, curling against her heart. Her lips moved in something like a curse.

Clementine sped out of the driveway so fast the wheels bumped over one side of the curb. Justin made a pained sound from the passenger's seat.

"Oh god, I'm so sorry," Clem whispered.

He wasn't sure if Justin could hear him. Somehow he'd gotten his seat belt on, but his eyes were pinched closed, his jaw so tight that Clem worried for his teeth. He still had no idea what to do about that; find a doctor? Take him back to his Ala Santa family? Was Justin the kind of almost-human who would find most hospital staff demeaning and obtrusive? Would they even know what to do with him? Not-quite-humans who weren't vampires or werewolves were so rare, or else so much better at hiding what they were than their blood-dependent and cyclically obligated neighbors, that the way they were treated when they did appear ran the gamut from cordial acceptance to complete rejection.

As he put his parents' house behind them—he'd deal with that later, the fallout, the repercussions, it was all less important than Justin in that moment—he headed for the city, taking the main road that would bring him past his own neighborhood and one of the city's bigger hospitals before finally reaching the turn toward Ala Santa to the west.

"Justin?" he asked, trying to keep his tone soothing despite the panic threatening to tear sharp claws through his insides. He was pretty sure the only reason he hadn't thrown up was that he was driving. "Justin, please. I—I don't know how to help you." It felt like he was pleading with a corpse.

Oh god, what if Justin was dying? Maybe he *should* have let Sissy help, or at least called an ambulance.

"I'm okay," Justin muttered, so low it sounded like a mistake.

It was a mistake. "You're clearly not okay, dammit."

Justin laughed at that. It was bitter and rough and it lasted only a moment, but it eased some of the terror mounting in Clementine's chest. "No, I'm in... pain." It sounded like every word he spoke was a spear driven through his chest. "But it's normal. I'll get over it."

"This doesn't sound normal," Clementine protested. The car hit a pothole, and Justin's consciousness seemed to blink out for a moment, coming back with an expression of sheer agony. "We can't keep driving."

"Home," Justin managed.

He looked about three seconds from passing back out. Ala Santa was a thirty-minute drive through, the last fifteen over some of the least upkept streets the city had. If Justin expected Clementine to take him there, watching him pass out and return in an endless cycle of pain... He couldn't do it. Clem shook his head. "We're almost there. Five more minutes, just hold on."

Living so far across the city from his work suddenly felt worth it, just for this. Still, that five minutes grated on him, every slow car and speed bump and crack in the asphalt sending a shock of anger and fear through his chest. Justin's consciousness came and went, there as Clementine pulled into the underground lot and gone as the elevator carried them up, returning long enough for him to hold himself against Clementine's side as Clem opened his door, only for him to collapse again as they stepped into the hallway.

He barely protested as Clementine set him on the couch and helped him lie down, removing his extra bundle of necklaces and propping up his knees.

"This is not... home," Justin grumbled.

"For tonight it is."

He grunted in response, and felt along the front of his jacket. His hands shook.

Clementine slipped his fingers under Justin's, helping retrieve a small box from his inner pocket. Inside, two joints had been rolled already, tucked beside a familiar-looking baggy. These were from a laboratory—not an illegal basement operation or even a re-sold pharmacy stock, but a traditional chemical lab, the design around the hazard symbols exactly the same as the ones Clem used. The drugs within were like nothing Clem had ever seen, though: flakey, iridescent strips that had the same chemical sweetness that mixed with Justin's more earthy, bitter scent.

"Can you..." Justin mumbled.

It took Clementine a moment to realize what he needed. "Right, yes, of course."

He wanted to dig through Justin's pockets again just for an excuse to touch him, but the man still looked so pained that he sprinted across the room to the kitchen instead, grabbing his own little fireplace lighter and igniting the end of the joint. Cradling the back of Justin's hand, Clem slid it between his fingers and helped guide it to his lips. Justin trembled in his grasp, but he managed a deep inhale, holding it so long with his eyes closed that Clementine's panic started to wiggle back through his stomach before Justin finally breathed out.

"Is that better?"

"It will be," Justin replied. "Give me a few minutes."

Clementine did. He kneeled beside Justin, supporting the man's hand in one of his own, and softly, ever so softly, he found himself brushing his fingers through Justin's hair. They weren't faking being a couple for the party anymore, he reminded himself. They weren't even conducting their newfound feeding ritual of light touches and devious teasing. Justin was just here, more vulnerable than he'd ever been before and utterly alone with Clem. Playing tenderly with his hair felt right.

It wasn't sexual, exactly—or it was more than sexual, more than romantic, even. It was the only possible outcome, the epiphany, the epitome, the ascension. It was a promise that he was there and would keep being there for as long as Justin needed him.

Justin didn't stop Clementine. He didn't look like he wanted Clem to stop either, slowly relaxing beneath the motion as the agony lines around his face eased. Or maybe that was just the drugs finally doing their job. By the time Justin had dozed into a less volatile state of half consciousness, the continual soft buzzing of Clem's phone finally dragged his attention away. He slumped onto the ground with his back against the couch and cautiously checked his notifications.

He couldn't count them all. Three calls from his parents. Worried texts from at least fifteen different people, including three he hadn't even realized were at the party, but most prominently from Reggie, who'd interspersed a few calls of his own.

No one seemed to know that he was the vampire.

Half of them were concerned for his safety, half apologizing for the poor reaction to his vampiric date, half trying to drag gossip out of him, half affronted that he'd run off in the first place, and he couldn't be bothered to figure out where the Venn-diagrams of all those halves overlapped yet. Later maybe. Or never. He didn't give a damn about nearly all the people who'd messaged him. It was the one person who hadn't that he cared about most.

Nothing had come in from Odysseus.

He pressed the phone to his forehead, his chest tightening in a dry sob. God, he'd fucked this up. Was she trying to figure out how to talk to him? How to tell the others? How to quietly step out of his life? He couldn't imagine her being cruel, but there were many things beside cruelty that could cut just as deeply.

The empty bar at the bottom of their thread—the last few messages a continuation of their crow conversation—stared into him. He typed out *hey Sissy*, then *I'm sorry*, and *I know I should have told you*, then a series of messages that rambled off into nonsense, but he deleted each version as soon as it was written. In the end, he kept it brief.

Clementine
Hey?

He waited for dots. And kept waiting.

As he sat there, he felt the curls at the base of his skull shift, then a more purposeful draw of fingers. Tiny, loose brushes and little tugs as Justin's fingers caught on the tangles. Clementine closed his eyes, and let his shoulder relax. It felt so right. In a moment where everything else was so very, very wrong, it felt like stability.

This was a promise too, he thought, though he didn't know of what yet.

JUSTIN

Justin had never felt better—contextually speaking. He had also never felt worse. The pain spearing through his back had the aggressive presence of velociraptor's teeth constantly sinking and resinking into his spine. When he moved, it worsened. When he breathed, it worsened. When he thought about it too much, it worsened, and when he stopped focusing directly on it for too long it turned into a jealous lover deliberately sensing the wane in his attention and throwing a fit over it. So in that sense, Justin felt about as bad as he possibly could have.

But considering all *that*, he had never felt better. He had a pleasantly molded, but still firm, velvety-cushioned couch beneath him, his third joint half smoked in one hand, and Clementine's curls in the other. The vampire had given up with his phone a little while ago, and tipped his head back against Justin's waist, his eyes closed as Justin ran his fingers in little spirals through the soft golden hair. The locks had protested at first, but now they flowed loose and free beneath his touch.

As he lay there, Justin let his attention wander, trying to force it somewhere beyond the pounding assault of his back. He tried to guess the cost of the pretty, dark wood coffee table and the massive TV across the room, mounted above a glass-rock fireplace. The same as he'd been charging Clementine for blood, or more? Or less? He couldn't begin to fathom.

A double door took up most of one wall, both of them pulled open to reveal a neat office with a large desk and a long, organized shelf of what looked like sci-fi nerd paraphernalia: figurines on plaques and signed posters of spaceships and a collection of DVDs that had somehow outlived the takeover of streaming services. With the number of salt and pepper shakers currently occupying Justin's apartment, he was hardly one to judge. At least Clementine's private hobbies weren't associated with eccentric grandmothers.

On the other side, the room turned into a cute, open-space kitchen with a granite island and a high table near the curtained corner windows, an orchid blooming in the center. If Justin tipped his head enough, he could almost see down the hall to the front door, where he was pretty sure they'd passed a bedroom upon entering. Or a sex dungeon. He'd been too out of it to tell the difference.

But he suspected it was the first, which meant that despite the elegance and expensive furnishings, Clementine's apartment was... well, certainly not humble, but not what Justin had imagined either. For someone with thousands of extra dollars to spend a month, he'd have expected a penthouse or a miniature version of the elder Hughes mansion, but this was *almost* normal.

"Nice place you've got here." His voice came out graveled and rusty, and he gave a little cough that he regretted instantly.

"Oh?" Clementine made a tiny sound like he was coming back from a daze, but as he blinked he focused again with his usual intensity. "I rather like it. The more spacious floorplan lets in a lot of sun... which isn't very useful these days."

Now that he'd mentioned it, Justin noticed just how thick every curtain was, all the blinds closed and an extra blanket thrown over the biggest window of the office. "It's a shame. Even when I thought I wanted to turn, that was the one thing that almost held me back."

Clementine sighed. "I miss it."

"You could always buy yourself a mansion with faux-windows and shine heat lamps through them. You have the money for it."

"Like a blacked-out version of my parent's house?" Clem gave snort, but then he laughed. "I *might* have had the money for some fake sunlight if I wasn't already paying a fortune for someone's blood."

There wasn't any bitterness in the statement, his tone teasing and his hand lifting to poke Justin's side so gently that it didn't even bother his back—at least not any more than the incessantly screaming muscles were already bothered. But it still stirred something in Justin's gut; his own bitterness, poisoning himself. "Would you really prefer buying that instead of me?"

He wanted to say that if the vampire did, then that was fine too, that he'd always have Justin's blood, always have Justin, that Clementine's mouth on his skin and the little pulses of his venom were more than payment enough. But Clem's money had gone to those who needed it and Justin had so many new vampires to support. Back in Ala Santa.

Back where he belonged.

"No." Clementine shook his head adamantly. "I have spare portions of my paycheck *because* I don't feel like I should spend it on myself. I was already giving most of my spare money to charity, and letting you do that for me is..." He seemed to struggle to find the word, and in the end his throat just bobbed, and he waved a hand around the room. "This is already everything I need—more than many people have—and adding luxuries to it feels callous when someone across the city can't replace their broken fridge or—or buy their kid diapers. I don't have to worry about a second mouth to feed and I won't have kids to raise and send to college. It's just me here, and I have all that one person requires. Well, except the sun."

There was so much in that response for Justin to linger over. His chest warmed with it and burned from it in turns. Clementine was a good person, a genuine person. And Justin had taken advantage of him.

But it wasn't quite the same anymore, was it? They were in this together now, because they both wanted to help the people of Ala Santa. It was like Clementine had *agreed* to be exploited. Justin should have thanked him for the money, told him how important this was and how much he appreciated it and how even more of his help would go even farther.

Instead his mind diverted to the next available topic and clung there. "You don't want kids?"

"I love kids, don't get me wrong. And they've always been expected of me, because Sissy already set herself up to be the doting aunt, so our parents just assumed I'd get around to it once I reached senior associate. But I've never been able to imagine my life in a picket-fenced house with two children and a dog. It's been a long time since I dreamed I could have a spouse, though, and that..." He trailed off. Justin wished he could see more than the sliver of his profile, could tell the exact way his brow was furrowing and read the thoughts buried beneath. "Well, life changes and it changes what we want out of it, I guess." His shoulders bounced. "Did you always want to be a vampire protector?"

Guilt squeezed around his heart. He had wanted a lot of things in his younger years and helping anyone but himself had been very low on the list. "No, that... that was an accident." An accident he'd caused. He'd killed the king and now it was only right that he wore the crown, thorns and all. "I never thought much about a spouse or kids, but I've always had a family, just not a nuclear one, and that family included vampires. For a while, I stopped appreciating their love and support, and it only served to hurt us all. So now I just want to care for them in return, the way I always should have."

There was one vampire in particular he found himself caring for more and more—it just happened to be the wrong one.

He trailed his hand along the back of Clementine's neck. Clem turned his face, letting Justin's fingertips trace the edge of his jaw, like they were the contented couple neither of them had foreseen in their futures. They weren't. Not when Justin already had a place he owed himself to, body and soul, the only marriage he deserved. But they could pretend for a few more hours.

Clementine gave a sad smile. "Ala Santa really seems to love you. It's brilliant and beautiful and I'm not certain I could ever be enough to achieve that kind of affection. I've spent my life trying to act as perfect as possible and the only relationships I have to show for it are two parents who still pinpoint my every insufficiency, and a sister who took one look at my fangs and is ghosting me for it."

"God, I'm sorry. I didn't realize…"

"Yes, well, it is what it is," Clementine replied, sounding very much like he wanted it to be anything but. "I have Reggie too, I suppose, though affection with Reggie is like a flash flood. It's exuberant and gives no fucks to whether you deserve it and then it goes on an eight-month trip around the world where it momentarily forgets you exist. He's just like that."

"I'm going to be harsh as fuck here, but Clem? Your family is shit. The way they treat you is not your fault." Justin took a long drag of his joint. "Those people in Ala Santa who care about me—the ones I count as my family—if I had to *earn* their affection, I'd never measure up either."

"You're so easy to love, though; all your confidence and how you know exactly what to say and what each person needs. It should be physically impossible to disapprove of you."

Justin snorted. "I haven't always been like this. God, Lemon, during my teenage years, I was the devil. I felt like, after everything I was suffering, that I had a right to whatever I wanted. I was cruel and reckless, as strong and fast as I am now but my pain was just starting to be a real problem, and I had no way to deal with it but to take out my frustration on others. I stole and harassed and beat the shit out of anyone who tried to put up a fuss. And I... I did the very worst of that and more, to the family who loved me the most." To the vampire who'd been there for him when his pain first started, cared for him through all his blind anger, his incessant theft, and abusive aggression, as he'd fruitlessly attempted to cover up his growing fear and agony—and to the woman who'd forgiven him after, taken him back in without a second thought. "I'm not a perfect person, not even a half-way decent one. And they kept me anyway. Somehow they just kept loving me." That should have made his guilt easier to bear. It should have, but it didn't. It wasn't them he needed forgiveness from.

"Whoever you used to be, I still think you're incredible now." Clementine said it so softly that it was easy to ignore. "You deserve their love, Justin."

Because he didn't understand the full extent of what Justin had done. But as he watched Clementine, with his eager attention and his open affection, Justin didn't know how to explain it. So he redirected. "Your sister's still not answering?"

That seemed to distract Clem well enough. He checked his phone again, even though it hadn't buzzed since the last time. "No."

"She might come around. I didn't react the best when Isaiah first turned either, and I'd been practically *raised* by one. It's shitty, because you vampires are the ones who are hurt most, yet we humans still feel like it's about us far more than we should, and sometimes we act thoughtlessly because of it. But that's what makes us people, isn't it? Our ridiculous, illogical emotions."

"You're Kirk," Clementine said, like that was supposed to mean something.

"I'm what?"

"You're—" He laughed. "It's nothing, just Star Trek. It's silly, really."

"That's what all your sci-fi stuff's from?"

A light flush bloomed across Clementine's cheeks. He ducked his head. "I said, it's nothing."

"It looks like a great collection."

"A silly collection, you mean," Clem insisted.

Justin strained through the pain in his back, lifting himself up enough to turn onto his elbow so he could look at the vampire properly. "You keep saying that, but it doesn't make it true."

"No, I really. It's just a weird little—a thing I liked."

Justin decided to go a different route. "Shame. Nerds are *hot* these days."

Clementine's mouth bobbed like a fish.

If Justin hadn't been in such pain, and they hadn't been definitely not a couple, he would have taken advantage of those gaping lips: pressed his tongue between them; made Clementine moan. Instead he shrugged. "There's nothing more attractive than a handsome vampire explaining his nerdy passions while wearing a rumpled suit in the middle of the night."

"Yes, fine, I fucking love Star Trek. But not *that* much. I just collected the merch and run a couple forums. And sometimes I write fanfic."

"Fanfic?"

He went red all the way to his ears. "It's nothing."

Justin grinned. "When do I get to read it?"

"You *read*?" Clementine managed to sound absolutely shocked while still looking like the incarnation of a tomato cherub.

"I listen to DIY videos when I patrol, and an audiobook might slide in. Sometimes. Occasionally." He had technically meant to try them out since he'd failed to keep up with his favorite Batman x Superman fic, but it just never happened. He waggled his eyebrows at Clem. "So if you could just—"

"I'm *not* recording myself reading my own fanfic."

"Why not?" Justin had barely asked the question when Clementine's face answered him, his obvious embarrassment combining with the way his gaze flickered almost instinctively down Justin's body and he drew his legs closer to his chest. "Oh. *Oh.*" Justin cackled. "No, now you *have* to read it for me." His smoking joint still clutched between two fingers, he tipped his head and rubbed up the side of his neck. "It might make my blood taste better."

"I'm going to go tie myself to the roof and wait for sunrise, now, thanks." Clem stood, walking pointedly toward the hallway.

"Clementine? Clementine!" Justin laughed again. "I've never seen Star Trek before! You don't think there's someone here who would watch it with me?"

Clem stopped, his face scrunched in the prissiest, most sophisticated pout Justin had ever seen. "That's cruel. You know I can't possibly refuse you."

"I know." He was pretty sure Clem meant his *you* in the general sense of *people asking to watch his favorite show with him* and not Justin as a specific person—a person who was a little bit in love with him—but the idea of Clementine being that into him sent a thrilled shiver down his spine, light and ecstatic enough to dim the pain for a moment.

"He's a fool for you, and he will take everything you give him without considering the long-term detriment."

Justin's good humor faded a bit.

Clementine didn't seem to notice. "What do you prefer, movie or show? Preferably we'd start from the very beginning but we don't have time for that tonight. Unless you plan to come back."

Justin ignored the invitation, despite how his heart tugged toward it. This was not his place. He already belonged to Ala Santa, and he'd tied himself too thoroughly to Clementine as it was. Which was definitely why he was leaving… in the morning. "Whatever you want, I trust your judgment. Let me just—" He tried to sit up properly, but as he did it felt as though a thousand spears shot through his back. Fuck, he was three joints in; he should not have been hurting this badly.

He held himself in place, focusing on his breathing, then pulled himself up with excruciating slowness. Clementine watched him with an expression bordering on fear. For a moment, Justin almost wished for Isaiah instead, wished that he could have hidden this part of himself from one more person. But he didn't. He *trusted* Clementine.

He trusted him, even with this.

Still he hesitated as he fiddled with the lip of his jacket. "There's something I need you to check for me. I can find a mirror if it makes you uncomfortable but…"

"Anything." Clementine said it so purposefully, like he'd truly considered every option one by one and decided they were all acceptable, whatever Justin might ask of him. He'd do it.

275

It made Justin's heart ache.

"He's a fool for you... without considering the long-term detriment."

Fuck them both—what hell were they putting each other through? Justin deserved the torment that would come after but Clementine didn't. Clementine deserved love. He deserved someone who cared enough to let him down now, while there was still time to do it softly. If there was time left for that.

But the longer Clem stared, his expression so earnest and contemplative, the more Justin wondered if they might find a way forward instead. They had made it work so far, Clementine coming to Ala Santa every few days to spend an hour just after dusk, both of them texting constantly in between. That could continue, but with soft kisses atop the angel of death and frantic thrusts against the alley walls, Clem's hand over Justin's mouth to cover his blissful screams and Justin's blood turning the vampire's moans soft and ragged.

And then what? When he wanted more of Justin's time, wanted him to be a proper partner, and Justin had to say no for the sake of Ala Santa? When he was in danger for real, across the city, and Justin had to choose again: this vampire or the ones he already belonged to...

Then would come the heartbreak.

Odysseus was right, it was better to do it sooner than later. Maybe Justin had been good for Clementine this one night, but he wouldn't be for the rest of their lives. This night was all they had. This night, made worse by the fact that when the sun rose, Justin needed to be back in Ala Santa, protecting his vampires once again.

Sooner than later.

Clementine lowered himself before Justin, looking up at him, his fingers sliding around Justin's where they worried the edge of his jacket. "What is it?"

The tremor that ran through Justin felt like a revival. Sooner than later, but not now. Not yet. He needed more time like this, goddammit. He breathed out, and gave in, to his desires, to Clem, to their long-term detriment, to a future where he hated himself even more than he already did, just so he could feel a little less like he deserved that hatred for the moment. "The pain is coming from my back, obviously, and the drugs I've been smoking are to help ease it, which you've probably figured out."

"They're custom made." Clementine seemed to have more to say, but he closed his mouth, settling into a stiff silence. "I suspect—and correct me if this is inaccurate—that since you're not fully human, this pain stems from some non-human aspect of your genetics?"

"Yeah." Justin looked down to Clementine's hands still loosely fitted over his. Neither of them had said anything. It was easier than the impossible. Than the long-term detriment. "It's simpler just to show you."

He turned with his hips, slowly, achingly swiveling his body to face one of the armrests. He'd taken his shirt off earlier, but the way he'd have to bend to remove his jacket seemed like a marathon when each movement still hurt this badly. "Help me?" he whispered.

"Always," Clementine replied, as gentle as his hands.

Justin wanted so badly for it to mean forever.

23

Clementine

This was not how Clementine had imagined his first time pulling off Justin's clothes. After the night they'd had, he'd been certain it would happen in a breathless moment, their hands in each other's pants, Clem's dick hard and his knees wobbly, his vision tunneling with desire. This was none of those things. It was hesitant and tender, Justin's posture so strained and Clementine's attention so fixed on not hurting him that it almost stopped being sexual at all.

Almost.

There was still something about the sight of Justin's bared skin, even in this unfortunate context, and the fact that he'd had been willing to hand over control to Clementine, to be this vulnerable before him, that pulled at Clem's heartstrings, resting like a warmth in his core. He took off his own suit jacket, glad he'd tailored the outfit specifically for comfort, and settled on the couch behind Justin, one leg folded beneath him and the other tucked against Justin's thigh. Their calves brushed. He hooked his ankle over

Justin's and cupped his hands around the fabric at Justin's sternum.

With slow, delicate motions, he drew the jacket off. The backs of his fingers brushed over Justin's shoulders, then down his arms, outlining the muscles as he went. Justin's inhale quivered. He shrugged, pulling his wrists out of the sleeves and letting the jacket drop around his waist.

Justin's back was bare of tattoos. They curled along his triceps and peeked from the base of his neck, and a pair of wavy lines flowed over one hip, but that was where they ended, cut off from the lighter skin of his back, untouched by ink or sun.

It was not bare of marks though. A thick scar tore through the muscle on the right side of his waist, and a bubbling white knot like a decades-old burn marred the flesh at the outer edge of his left deltoid. And between his shoulder blades …

The sight alone made Clementine cringe in empathy. From the place where his ribs met his spine, spiked spindles of something much like bone ran beneath the oddly translucent skin, most as small as a fingernail but a few large enough that each movement seemed to poke and prod their tips into the muscle. No wonder he was in such pain. It shocked Clementine that he could run and lift and fight in the first place.

"Is there bruising?" Justin whispered, like he was afraid the growths in his back might hear.

"A little." Clementine tried to keep his tone calm, while his mind raced through what they could mean for Justin in the long term. Was it cancerous? Would it *kill* him? Oh god. Clementine felt hollow suddenly, his heart beating too fast. "It seems..." He had to swallow to get the words unstuck. "It seems to be primarily where you were hit. I can still mostly see through it to the little bones—do you have a term for them?"

"My mother called them spurs." Justin fiddled with his silver crucifix pendant, the last bit of his joint still clutched between two fingers. "If it's just a little bruising then at least the bleeding was minor."

"Justin," Clem started, but the question didn't come. "Oh god, how do I ask this?"

Justin exhaled, and as though he could read Clementine's mind, he answered, "They've been growing slowly all my life. I don't know what will happen with them. My ancestors who shared the trait have been very good at dying from other causes before they reached their forties." It sounded like he sympathized with them. "It's a remnant from my mom's side of the family—the legend is that they were wings once. There's no proof, but somehow we're associated with them anyway. The site of the spurs, I guess, looks like someone's torn a pair of angel wings off. Made a devil."

"Wings..." Clementine muttered. Something clicked. "That ghost tour we scared off back when we first met, they mentioned the angel statue we met at was based on a mythical figure who haunted the region, killing people. Does that have anything to do with it?"

"That monument was inspired by my great-grandpa, yeah. But it was a pox that did the killing, not him. Whatever genetic mutation we have made him immune to the plague. He was trying to *help* the victims." Justin's posture turned aggressive and he winced as his muscles tightened. He relaxed slowly, and Clementine could feel the same anger ripping its way through him, too. Even if the people to blame for this pain were long dead, their sentiments remained. "Back then the city was just a village for the people who worked the lower-class jobs at the sanitoriums on the lake edge. They knew what he was doing, and they called him an angel for it, but the wealthy sanitorium residents didn't understand, or didn't care."

"I'm sorry. For all of it, the past and the present." Clementine drew his thumb over the crest of Justin's waist, trying not to think too hard about the softness of the man's skin or the way it might feel to wrap his arm all the way across Justin's chest, burying his face in Justin's neck and just breathing in his scent. "Is there a way to learn more about the spurs? To find a therapy or a cure or something?"

"Perhaps if there were a hundred thousand people with it. Even ten thousand. But I'm one of so few, at least in the States. Fixing me isn't profitable. Dissecting me, maybe, but not fixing. I only have the drugs I do because of a crazy happenstance."

"That's awful." If there was a way to use Vitalis-Barron's lab to help Justin... It was such a risk, but Anthony had already agreed to help him conduct his own secret research once one of them filled the senior associate position, and it might be worth the danger if he could save Justin from further suffering. "Is there something I can do to help with the pain?"

"I wouldn't mind some of that Star Trek." Justin hesitated, his jaw tight. "And..."

"Yes?" Anything. Always. He wanted to keep saying it, until his own life shifted to accommodate.

Maybe it was possible. If he continued working with Anthony, and he got the promotion; if he could be the person he wanted, *and* a vampire, and keep enough of his old life while taking in parts of this new one with Justin. Even if his relationship with Odysseus never fully recovered, and Justin wanted to live in Ala Santa, he could still maintain the same bright, successful existence that he always had, but with a bit more of what he wanted in it—so long as he had the stability Anthony was offering him: the high paying job, the hiding of his vampirism in his professional life, the continued support of his family. And Justin.

If only Clementine could bring himself to ask for more from him.

And he *wanted* to ask for it, for a real relationship, because being with Justin—that felt right. Watching over his shoulder, hearing his breath turn ragged, feeling his muscle tighten under each touch and knowing that he trusted

Clementine with all of this, with his blood and his life and his pain and his pleasure, it seemed right. Clementine felt, for once, like himself, emboldened and heart beating and living so thoroughly in the moment.

"Touch me." Justin said it low, not pleading but *taunting*, as though he knew that Clementine could deny him nothing. "Touch me like you do when you're savoring the hunt. Like you want to make me last until the sun comes up."

"Touch you like a vampire?" Clementine whispered, remembering the evening two weeks ago when they'd sat on the angel monument, and he'd told Justin he wanted to experiment. Well, this was also an experiment, wasn't it? Their whole night had been, and Clem never wanted it to end.

"Exactly." The smirk peeked through in his voice, a beautiful, sharp thing, dark as it was bright. It paled as he continued, "The nerves around my spine react well to easy caresses. It's like when you run your hands over an itch? It settles the pain for the moment. You have to be gentle with me, is what I'm saying."

Clementine drew his fingers lightly over Justin's waist, up the curves of his back, slowing as he neared the man's shoulder blades. "How is...?"

Justin made a tender noise. "Perfect," he whispered.

So Clementine kept going, memorizing the softness of his skin, the crevice of his spine, and the star-shaped malformations, as though by assigning a width to each he could keep them from growing. At the top of Justin's shoulders, he cupped his neck and leaned forward. With the faintest brush of lips, he slipped a fangful of venom into Justin's skin below his jaw. The sound of delight and desire that escaped him was a delicacy as delicious as his blood.

Clementine licked the pinprick closed with care, trailing his fingertips down Justin's spine. "Would you like to lie down? That seems more relaxing."

"That would be incredible," Justin said, hoarsely.

As they repositioned, Clementine caught his expression, such a mix of yearning and joy and pain and something almost like heartbreak that it caught in Clem's chest. He let Justin lay across his lap with a pillow propped beneath his head and two more under his ankles. The pressure of his chest on Clementine's thighs was solid and warm, and each inhale reverberated between them like an echo.

Clem started the show. As they watched, he traced absentmindedly across Justin's back, letting the tender motions become second nature and his skin as known as Clem's own. Justin sat up sometime around the end of episode number three, dozing in and out between a few more joints, but he leaned against Clementine, and he didn't protest as Clem continued to touch him, tracing his tattoos—his hands, his arms, his stomach, his chest, filtering fingers through his hair on occasion, so enthralled that he lost track of entire scenes just to delight in the pressure of Justin's body and the way he reacted to the gentle caresses, so casually contented, like this was how they were meant to be: Justin existing while Clementine doted on him. As the hours passed, though, he noticed other little bruises beside those around Justin's bone spurs, tender points and blotches of purple that seemed to have nothing to do with the attack at the party.

Fight marks, Clementine finally realized. His gut twisted. As their current episode rolled to the credits, Clementine's fingertips lingered over one of the spots on Justin's side.

Before he could ask about them though, Justin's phone chimed. He glanced at it, then scowled and caught Clementine's hand, drawing it off his skin. He gave it a soft squeeze, lingering there like he was struggling to let it go, before he finally pressed it gently into Clem's lap.

"Isaiah's asking when I'll be back." He stood, not looking nearly as pained as the last time he'd tried, and he managed to pull on his boots and jacket by himself, but each movement was rigid and calculated.

"You're still hurting," Clementine protested. "At least give it a few more hours." A few more hours for what, Clem didn't know. For Justin to feel better, for Clementine to savor him, for him to find a way to ask for what he wanted. For them to become something more.

"The sun will rise soon; I should never have stayed this long in the first place." Justin shrugged stiffly. He began to walk, awkward but purposefully, toward the hallway. "The pain's receded enough. If I can move, I can fight."

"Why?" Clementine stood. "What good will you be to them like this? You won't last ten seconds. The hunters haven't even targeted your vampires in weeks; they can survive without you for half a day."

Justin went still, and when he spoke next, it was so rough that it seemed made of gravel. "They almost took Isaiah on Thursday morning. I only let myself attend your party because he's promised to lie low, but if they come for him in the day again and I'm not there... They found him so easily last time, I can't be certain they won't again."

"They... no." It couldn't have been. They had been leaving the vampires in peace, relying on Clementine's information, waiting to see if their target was even there, if— "No, they can't have, they said they were just looking for..." For their target. Which meant their target was Isaiah.

Who happened to be Justin's best friend.

Clementine felt lightheaded, the world too loud and the space inside his body too small suddenly. His knees gave out, planting him back on the couch. He'd given Isaiah's work hours to Anthony when Anthony had made it sound like he was confirming that Isaiah had nothing to do with Natalie's target, and now...

Distantly, he could hear Justin asking,

"What do you know?"

The suspicion in his voice tore a hole through Clementine's chest. The night had been going so well, so amazingly, incredibly well that Clem had almost convinced himself everything could work out well so long as he had Justin, but now... Whatever they had—whatever potential their relationship still hadn't reached—it might end like this, a crash and a burn and a final explosion, because Clementine had fucked Justin over without even realizing it.

A part of him wanted nothing more than to bail, to quietly stop working with Anthony and leave Justin none the wiser. But he couldn't bear that. Justin—beautiful, bittersweet Justin, who'd been willing to break into Vitalis-Barron for Clem, who'd nestled beside him all night, letting Clementine explore his skin with wandering fingertips—he deserved to know. Even if it destroyed them both.

He would just have to trust that Justin would understand—Clem had meant well. He'd never wanted anyone to be hurt, much less Isaiah. Much less Justin.

Still, his heart pounded in his ears and he couldn't meet Justin's gaze as he said, softly, "I think I know how they found Isaiah."

24

JUSTIN

He could still feel the lingering brush of Clementine's fingers, the way that touch had seemed to curl up in his chest with him, rooting him to the moment. It had made him worth something, for a night. Between its tender grounding and Clem's soft adoration, Justin had almost convinced himself this wasn't doomed to end, that he could have it all—his vampires and Clementine, and no one would get hurt.

But as much as he'd procrastinated and doubled down on his excuses, his vampires were still in danger. And Justin had let Clementine's misplaced affections lure him away from them, only for Clem to treat his attempt to leave as if it meant the world was shattering. Maybe it was. Beneath the memory of Clem's fingertips, Justin could feel a breaking deep in his chest, even if he couldn't quite tell what had caused it yet.

"I think I know how they found Isaiah."

Justin's knees wobbled, and he wasn't sure whether it was from the pain still aching through his back, making his world tight and dark, or something else. Something worse.

Clem swallowed, then started again. "You remember how, when I told you I worked at Vitalis-Barron, no one there had realized I was a vampire? Well that... that changed."

Dread coiled in Justin's gut.

"One of the other researchers, a man named Anthony Hilker, he figured it out—or he already knew, I don't know. I think perhaps he was just waiting for the most opportune time to tell me. Opportune for him, anyway," Clementine continued, so still and tense beside the couch that he looked like he might drift apart from the reality of the apartment, from the hours they'd both spent there in lavish relaxation. "He's dating the hunter you've been having problems with, Natalie. They're together."

"What the fuck..." Justin could see where this was going, like falling into a telescope, and he wished he could scramble back, wished the peace that Clementine's care had granted him wasn't turning quickly to fear.

Clem glanced at him, then away, his expression tight. "Anthony realized that I was buying blood from you, and he threatened to tell Vitalis-Barron about my vampirism if I didn't provide him with information to pass on to his girlfriend. Information on you, and Ala Santa. So I... I did."

Each word was a dagger that sliced its way through Justin. His heart thudded, pounding a rhythm into his pain, and he had to press his hand to the wall for support. He'd suspected the hunters were getting their information from

290

somewhere, but Clementine... not Clementine. God, not him.

Every time Clem drank from him. Every little baring of fangs and brush of fingertips and long, honest conversation, everything they had gone through tonight, and all the while Clementine had been selling him out.

Justin had the impulse to throw himself at Clementine, to drive a fist straight through his perfect face, to watch him stumble and fall and bleed the way Justin felt his soul do within him. But he couldn't. And he knew, like he knew every crack in his neighborhood's pavement, that Clementine could betray him a thousand times over and he would never be able to. All the affection and emotion Justin had built for him over the weeks—all the ways Clementine's care tonight had made him feel momentarily like he could deserve something this beautiful—all that could shatter and die, but it couldn't be excised.

It would rot there in his chest ceaselessly, stinking for all eternity.

Even now he could feel it, pulling closed his lungs and crawling up his throat. "How could you?"

"It's not all bad—it's what made the hunters back down in the first place; they didn't have to corner your vampires for information, because they had me." Clementine looked so expectant as he said it, so goddamned ignorantly optimistic. "They only really cared about one specific vampire—the one they associated with the death of Natalie's mentor—but they were going to fuck up all the others to get it and I... I thought this was better. Fewer people get hurt and my identity stays secret and I—"

"You spied on me for them! You sold out my vampires."

His vampires, the ones Justin should have been focusing on all along, should have been tending to instead of being here. "That's your community. People like you. Suffering, because of you. You were selling them out for a *job*."

"It was my life!" Clementine shouted, his expression cracking. Weaker, he repeated, "That job is my life."

The selfishness, the denial—it wedged in Justin's chest. He felt himself shaking distantly, like it was happening to someone else. His back ached from it, the agony of the party replaced by this new engulfing hurt, as if the pain in his heart was seeping through his spine and carving a hole between his shoulder blades. "You didn't think to even tell me what was happening? You could have come to Ala Santa, I would have protected you, but instead you—you fucking—"

The little scoff Clementine made sounded almost like a sob. "Come to you? And what would you have said? Leave my job? Give it all up for the chance to scrounge for survival with hunters breathing down my neck? I can barely afford your blood as it is!" He breathed in, and *there* was the sob, trying to cut into Justin's heart anew.

"But you're going to now, aren't you?" He demanded. "You're quitting Vitalis-Barron, getting the hell away from Natalie and her boyfriend?" For an instant he was almost hopeful that they could turn this around.

But Clementine swallowed and looked away. "No? I don't know. I *need* that job, Justin. But I'm not going to tell Anthony or Nat anything about Ala Santa ever again. Please believe me on that."

Justin felt like his hearing was going, a buzz starting up behind his ears, inside his head, but Clementine kept speaking.

"I made a mistake, I know, but I was never trying to hurt anyone. Please, after what we just went through, you must know I would never do something I thought would harm you, or anyone you loved. And I can fix it! Let me make up for the damage I caused, please," Clementine begged, stepping toward Justin, each stride a hesitant, hungry thing. "We could work together. I could use my position to help your vampires." Clementine wavered like he was about to drop to his knees.

Justin almost wanted to see him there, to watch him grovel. To have an excuse to forgive him. To cradle his head, fingers gripping into those lovely golden curls again, and wrench his face up, a little vengeful and a lot possessive, and tell him that he was Justin's—always now, and that meant forever, so together they would make this up to Ala Santa.

But Clementine looked away instead, and he whispered, tensely, "It was just a mistake."

"A mistake." Justin repeated, hollow. A mistake was not the terror in Isaiah's eyes, or the burns still healing across the tops of his hands. A mistake was not the black body bag the hunters had brought for him, or the way Clementine had known, all along, that fate was coming for someone, even if he hadn't known who. Justin could almost see the doom that would have befallen Isaiah had he not been there: the capture, the torture, Isaiah's dark, thick vampire blood that would look so much like Jose's as it spilled.

Justin's skin crawled.

Clementine was not his, not his vampire, not his anything. He had known from the beginning that this was always going to end, even if he'd tried to forget it for a few desperate hours. If it hadn't come down to this, it would have come to something else. Clementine had just made it so much easier by proving how bad Justin's relationship with him was for Ala Santa.

That hardly meant it didn't hurt though; Odysseus had been right about that. Maybe it *was* better that they were getting it over with now. Maybe this whole revelation was for the best. "This wasn't a mistake, Clementine. I've screwed over enough people to know what betrayal looks like." He stepped toward the door.

"No, please…" Clementine whispered, reaching out, like he was a ghost running on impulse now. "I don't want to lose you." Their gazes met then, soft and consuming, the desperation in Clem's eyes tearing into Justin's heart like a knife.

This—this was why Justin shouldn't have come here in the first place, shouldn't have let himself fall so hard and so fast, because he wanted nothing more in that moment than to reach for him back. It tore him apart to turn toward the hall. "I already belong to Ala Santa."

Every step he took toward the door made his back vibrate with pain. He didn't slam it on his way out, but he didn't look back either, quietly fading out of Clementine's apartment with a flare of dread and melancholy like he was truly the angel of death after all. He was halfway down the elevator before he realized he'd forgotten the second half of his last blunt on the table. It felt like he'd left behind a lot more than that.

25

CLEMENTINE

Clementine felt numb.

He could still hear the click of the closing door as Justin vanished beyond it. Could still feel the burn of his glare, made all the worse by the hints of longing that had shown through. Could still smell him in the final joint he'd left, half smoked. But inside, Clementine was numb.

He slumped to the floor. His head rang. His chest hurt. The roof of his mouth felt irrevocably dry and the top of his throat pulsed behind his jaw.

This was heartbreak, he realized.

He'd lost Justin. Truth be told, he'd never really *had* Justin, not the way Clem wanted him, but he'd lost what they did have through one terrible, senseless misstep. Clementine wished he could be angry at Justin for abandoning him because of a single mistake, but in the corner of his broken heart, something else bled, dark and tender: guilt.

"I've screwed over enough people to know what betrayal looks like."

It wasn't like that, he wanted to scream. He had done nothing to deserve the fangs that sprouted over his canines, nothing to deserve the awful choice between his life as it was or his dedication to a man and neighborhood he'd barely known at the time. But still... he'd made that choice, with his own conscience, and held it there as a secret, like all the other private facts he knew he would be judged for. And that meant the repercussions of his actions were his to bear.

Clementine Hughes was not perfect. For all that he'd tried, his life was still coming down around him; since turning, he'd pulled his broken pieces back together, only to watch them each crack again, one by one. Now the final shattered fragment was his relationship with the only person he'd ever desired, romantically or sexually. And that person was *Justin*. His Justin, bittersweet and perceptive, dangerous and compassionate, deserving of so much more than he seemed able to accept for himself. Justin who'd now been hurt by Clementine's egotism.

Clem had to make that right somehow. He had to get Justin back, or try, anyway.

Slowly, he managed to pull out his phone. His hands shook. He flipped to his texts; still no response from Sissy, and Reggie seemed satisfied with his vague explanation that he'd wanted to get his date somewhere quiet as quickly as possible, and Justin...

His most recent message was still the last one he'd sent before trying to storm Vitalis-Barron's gates for Clementine.

Goddamn him.

Clementine curled his legs against his chest. He typed and erased, typed and erased, but everything he managed seemed too impersonal. What he wanted, was to have Justin before him, to let him see the remorse, feel the change in the air when Clem's breath hitched and hear the thud of Clem's knees against the ground as he groveled. For all that he'd learned to convey over text, he didn't know how to transmit that, not without turning it into a thousand-word story.

An impromptu apology fanfic didn't seem serious enough for their current crisis, though. Instead—teeth grit and fingers shaking—he clicked the call button. It rang, once, twice, a third time, each unanswered bell sounding doom in his heart. Finally, the voicemail tone sounded with a snarky *Hey, it's Justin, I'll get back to you soon* in a tone so sharp and kind that it welled tears in Clem's eyes. He lifted the butt of the phone to his mouth.

"So I uh, I know I said I hate calls, but I figured you would probably rather hear this than read it, or that it would mean more in my voice or something. Though you probably don't want to hear from me at all. And I get that. But I—I just wanted to apologize, properly." He inhaled, shuddering.

It should not have been so difficult for him. This was Justin, after all; he'd witnessed Clem at his messiest, and he already knew the truth of what Clementine was struggling so hard to admit. This wasn't to enlighten him of Clem's imperfections, but of his recognition and his regret. And he wanted—needed—Justin to know that he was sorry, for every mistake and every willful misstep too.

Dr. Clementine Hughes was done being perfect.

He was ready to be good.

"I fucked up," he said, simple and straightforward. "I fucked up royally, and I'm truly sorry. I really did think I was doing something useful, even if it was awful. But it *was* awful, and I understand that now. If you hadn't been able to save Isaiah, I don't think I could live with myself. So if I can do anything to help, please let me know. Or if what you want more from me is to never see me again, then"—his voice cracked there, and he had to breathe out long and slow to get it back—"then I'll do that instead."

He pleaded in his mind as he said it though, begged the wider universe for Justin not to take that route. Even if Clementine never got to touch him again the way he had that night, or be trusted with something so vulnerable as the space between Justin's shoulder blades, or taste his bittersweet blood, or—fuck. His *blood*. Whether Justin forgave him or not, Clem was going to need to feed again in forty-eight hours.

He cursed out loud, covering it with a cough after. "Sorry, I just realized, if I could get the number of a blood dealer, that would be most helpful. And preferably if you have someone who doesn't charge any more than you. I know that's unfair of me to ask, but I can barely afford your blood with my current bills as it is. That's part of why I need to keep my job so badly—why I need this promotion. And it's selfish, I know, because I have so much more than your vampires. But they don't deserve to choose between blood and a life either. None of us do."

The words burned, angry and righteous in his throat. Despite his responsibility in the hunter's attack, he was still far from the only one at fault. But Justin knew that well enough, had already condemned those sources with tooth and fist. This message wasn't about them.

"Anyway, I just wanted you to know that I'm sorry, and that you're worth more to me than how I've treated you. I should never have kept you in the dark about Anthony's blackmail or made excuses for why I caved to it. And if you don't give up on me, then I promise I will be the kind of—of friend that you deserve."

Clementine ended the message there. It felt like he had just hiked Mount Everest and dove the Mariana trench and been flung headfirst into outer space from a canon. He wasn't entirely sure how he lived through it.

He didn't mean to sit and stare at his phone. That wasn't healthy, and he didn't expect a response, but he couldn't seem to force himself to move any longer, the sheer act of breathing requiring more effort than he seemed to possess. But it meant that he was watching their text thread the moment Justin's typing bubbles popped up. They vanished, popped up, then vanished for what felt like an eternity, until finally a simple message came over.

Justin

I'm not going to just let this go, but I'm willing to hear you out.

How are you with video calls? I'm flat out of carrier bats right now.

Something broke in Clementine's chest and his inhale turned to a mix of a sob and a mutilated laugh. This was not forgiveness, not yet. But if Justin was offering him the chance to earn it, Clem was ready to work harder than he had for anything in his life. He initiated the video call from his end, tapping his knee incessantly as the ringtone cycled once, then twice. Finally Justin picked up.

"Hi. Sorry, just getting out of the cab." He sounded calm and contained, but as he leaned against the wall of a stucco apartment building with a grunt, his face told a different story: tight and flushed with irritation. As he stared through the screen, though, Clementine swore he could still make out that terrible, wonderful yearning from earlier pinched beneath it all.

"God, I'm sorry. I'm really, incredibly sorry. Please, I meant it when I said I don't want to lose you—to lose your friendship." It was more than that too, but if friends with their little experimental touches and bites were all he got—even if Justin no longer permitted those vampiric additions from him—then he still wanted Justin, *needed* Justin. "Let me make this up to you. Please."

"And if I say no?"

"Then I'll... I don't know." Clementine tried not to think too hard about that possibility. "I won't ever work with Anthony and Natalie again, though, and I can stay away from Ala Santa if that would make you feel safer. I just need that job's paycheck and a blood source, and I'll figure the rest out as I go."

Justin looked away from the screen, rubbing a hand across his face. "You're really staying at Vitalis-Barron just so you can pay for blood?"

"Not only that but..." Clementine thought of Anthony's offer to start up vampiric research under the company's nose, and his heart twisted. But the lives of the vampires around him weren't worth sacrificing, not even for the chance of bettering their future. Medical science had been down that road too many times before and created rules of ethics because of it—even if those laws didn't apply to vampires. "Mostly to pay for your blood, yes. And I *want* to keep paying you what you're worth. If you'll let me, that is."

"Yeah, so—fuck." Justin grunted, looking absolutely wretched.

Clementine wanted to reach through the phone and pull him close, but at his next words, the feeling stuttered in his chest.

"This is still not forgiveness, but I guess then I have something to admit too..."

JUSTIN

Justin felt more miserable than he had in a very long time, which was saying something considering just how badly his back had hurt him eight hours before. His physical pain had been made worse by each bump and jolt of his taxi ride here, but as he stood at the edge of Ala Santa, staring at Clementine through their video call, that ache was far outweighed by the strain on his heart and the throbbing through his soul.

Even this far away, with a screen between them, he still wanted to reach out and pull Clementine close.

Since leaving, his mind had been in chaos, torn between the knowledge that he'd made the right, and only, decision, and the yearning to run back and unmake it just for another moment of Clem's undeserved adoration. He'd thought being in Ala Santa would settle things, but then had come Clementine's apology, sincere, if a bit adorably analytical, and containing everything that would have broken Justin had they been back at Clem's apartment. On top of all that, was Justin's own guilt.

He'd had a hand in this. He hadn't made Clementine choose the way he had, hadn't brought the hunters here or been the one to blackmail Clem, but he knew, when he was being more honest and rational, just how many cards were stacked against Clementine. And Justin had put one of those cards there himself.

Goddammit.

It didn't mean he had to forgive, or to let Clementine back in, but it felt wrong not to be honest after Clem had just revealed his own misdeeds and followed them with a sincere apology. If Justin didn't take him back, he would find out the truth soon enough anyway.

"My blood…" Justin sighed, groaned, and started again. "The truth is, *no* blood is worth what you're paying for mine. I've been overcharging you. You looked like you were from money—you *were* from money—and so I figured you could afford it and there's so many people in Ala Santa who need that cash and I—I guess I have a dozen other excuses if you want them, but really it was just shitty to you, and I'm sorry. Though, for the record, not as sorry as you should be. But I contributed to the problem, so… there is that."

Justin forced himself to watch Clementine's reaction, the little tightening of his brow and the parting of his lips. But the indignation he expected didn't come. Instead, Clem's shoulders began to shake, then the softest wet laughter came over the speakers.

It almost scared Justin. "Are you okay?"

"Yes, fine." Clementine shook his head and the corner of his lips quirked into an ironic smile. "We're both a mess, aren't we?"

Justin snorted, but some of the heaviness in his chest settled. He tried to ignore the way it lightened his heart too. "That's just being alive, Lemon."

"I've been living among mannequins for too long, then," Clementine muttered. He seemed less tense now though, and that settled something in Justin, too, like the tender acts of the night had bound their emotions together. "How much *does* blood cost? For reference."

"Six or seven hundred. Five if you're lucky. More than most people can comfortably afford, but still." Justin tipped his head back, but he lowered his gaze to Clementine's, searching as though between his golden curls and his tender expression and the little fangs he hadn't retracted since leaving Sissy's party Justin might find the answer to all of his problems.

Here was this vampire who had fucked up, but was trying to fix things. His blood ran as dark and red as Isaiah's and Jose's, his fate just as precarious in a world that was cruel to him and then told him it was his fault. Maybe Justin couldn't take him back, but he could still let him fix things for the other vampires he'd hurt. "Do you really want to make up for it all?"

"In any way I can. I didn't want anyone to get hurt," Clementine said. "If I can stop that in the future, I will, even if it means telling Anthony to go fuck himself."

Justin shook his head. "No…" Maybe he still wasn't ready to forgive Clementine, but he didn't want Clementine to put himself in that level of danger if he could help it. Besides, Justin had another idea, a way to make this mess worth the trouble it had caused. Then, would their broken hearts be worth something, too? "What if you keep telling Anthony about Ala Santa, but you tell him what *I* want him to know instead. We lead the hunters on a wild goose chase, give them just enough to make them think they're getting somewhere without letting them cause any harm."

"Yes," Clementine replied instantly. "Yes, anything." He laughed again, dark and harsh. "God, I should have told you about the blackmail from the beginning. We could have been doing that all along."

Justin wanted to agree with him, but as he opened his mouth, he found that he couldn't. He'd used Clementine's deceit as a barb back at the apartment, but as he envisioned their relationship around the time the hunters had first backed off, he realized with a gut-wrenching certainty that without the affection that had grown between then—this dangerous, painful cord—he never would have dared ask for Clementine's help like this. "If you had, I probably would have told you to fuck off. I liked you, and your money, but letting you anywhere near Ala Santa if I knew the hunters had access to your knowledge would have been a risk I couldn't take. It wouldn't have been anything personal but… now I know you. And I trust that you won't fuck me over a second time." He could feel the ghost of Clementine's fingers dancing over his spine as he said it, and he hoped he wasn't wrong.

"Thank you for giving me another chance. I'll make this up to you."

"Yeah, well, if I ever so much as suspect you're working with the hunters again, I'll stake you like the vamps of old."

"I'll peel my ribs back to aid your work." Clementine sounded so utterly sincere that it took Justin's breath away.

His anger was still there, his hurt, his fear, but his heart still squeezed as though that single statement was the most romantic thing anyone had ever said to him. It probably was. Justin forced himself not to let it tear his guard down too far and bared his teeth in return. "Sleep well, Lemon."

"You too," Clementine replied. And for a moment they just stared at each other, stared into each other, like there was something more there; something they were just beginning to grasp.

When the call ended, Justin couldn't remember which of them had finally pressed the button.

He walked the rest of the way to Isaiah's apartment in an exhausted fog, his head vacant and his boots heavy. His back felt like fire and his soul like ice. Everything was going to be fine now, he decided. Not perfect, but at least they could find a way to get the hunters off his vampire's backs, and then perhaps he and Clementine could go back to being friends. *Just* friends. That was all they were ever supposed to be, no matter how much the knowledge sank in Justin's gut like a rock.

As he reached Isaiah's apartment, he found the door cracked open, the bustle inside spilling out into the alley as two of his vampires sprinted around the car, a blood bag half tucked beneath one of their coats. They looked panicked. Justin went cold with a dread that wiped everything else from his mind in an instant.

Ignoring the screams from his back, he tore into the little first story apartment.

The open front room and kitchen had been cluttered with the belongings of new vamps over the last couple weeks, their duffels and trash bags spilling into the hallway toward the bedrooms. The space was crowded with more vampires than were technically living there, though, along with a couple of the neighboring humans, voices tight and raised. Someone cried.

"What—" Justin began, but before he could ask the question, the throng parted for him.

Marcus knelt beside the couch, a bruise blooming across his left cheek and an unhappy sheen to his skin that almost resembled a sunburn. Paola leaned against them, whimpering as Isaiah inspected an angry, blistering welt that ran from her jawline down her chest. A third injured vampire—one of their newer refugees, Soren—lay on the couch, their olive skin a ghostly pale and a towel held to their arm, soaking in the slightly darker, thicker blood that vampires possessed.

One of the blood bag retrievers rushed up to them, helping them bite directly into the freshly acquired bag. At the little kitchen table squished into the corner, a human had a tourniquet on, slowly draining her bright red life source into a mug.

"Is this everyone?" Justin asked, breathless.

Isaiah's head shot up. "Yes. We're all alive."

Thank God. He had the usual impulse to cross himself. "What happened?"

"Natalie and one of her gang were looking for me again, I think. But when they found Paola and Soren instead they..."

"The hunters tried to take them," Marcus spat. "They would have, too, if they had better numbers or prep, or if I hadn't been near enough to call for help."

So they had escalated after all. It was Isaiah they wanted most, but it seemed they'd grown bored of waiting, perhaps deciding that if they took enough vampires they'd get to the one they wanted eventually.

"Why didn't you call *me*?" Justin wasn't sure what he felt; offended, alarmed, furious maybe.

"The threat had passed." Isaiah stared at him, a long hard look he couldn't read, or perhaps just didn't want to. "The hunters left. You deserved a night off, and we were handling it." He looked away; looked to the vampire hovering over Soren—a pink-haired butch named Whitney who'd been one of the first to arrive.

Something seemed to pass between them, passed, in fact, around the whole room.

"We can't keep waiting for you, Justin," Whitney said. "Even if they all have holy silver, there must be *something* we can do to protect ourselves. If we place all our safety on one—one human—" She stumbled over the word, seeming to know it wasn't quite right, but she kept going, "then sooner or later you're going to go down, and we'll go with you."

"I'm not going anywhere." The words were out of Justin's mouth before he could think through them, a bond he'd been locked in since he'd first accepted this chance at redemption. But it was still the truth. He'd already decided that his night with Clem would be a one-time event. He belonged to Ala Santa, to its humans and its vampires. "Last night was a... It's not happening again. I'm here for you." He was here for *his* vampires, even if those words brought Clementine to mind more strongly each time he thought them, the last glimpse of him over the phone screen pressing through the pain of his betrayal with an affectionate warmth. Shaking his head, Justin focused on the two hurting in front of him. Hurting because he wasn't here to stop it. He pursed his lips toward Paola and Soren. "How are they?"

That settled things, at least for now.

"Paola got hit by that damned holy metal stick, but the wound seems stable now. Sofia Lim is coming back with something to stitch Soren's arm up. With some blood, they should be all right." Marcus gave Paola's shoulder a squeeze. "We'd run out last night. Thank fuck our dealer is selling from the empty storeroom on Dove this weekend, and we caught Sofia on her way back from the hospital. She just happened to have a fresh batch of phlebotomy supplies with her." He pursed his lips toward the human donor, one of the vamps offering her a cup of juice.

There were so few humans with the desire to give, and hardly any of those were comfortable letting a vampire directly bite them to receive the blood-rejuvenating chemicals through the venom. It made stockpiling blood for an emergency nearly impossible. The fact that everything had lined up so perfectly today was a fluke that might not come around again.

"All right." Justin nodded.

It was sheer luck that everyone had escaped with their lives. But the hunters would be back. If this proved anything, it was that feeding their next move through Clementine wouldn't be sustainable for long. Next time, Justin was going to be here to stop them. He was going to put an end to this.

As Sofia finally returned and the frantic tension in the room calmed to a subtle dread, he slipped out to the alley. The sun was already rising beyond the apartment complexes, forcing vampires across the city indoors. Into hiding. He pulled out his phone once more, navigating to his thread with Clementine.

Justin

Scratch what I said earlier, I don't want to drag out the hunters' attack.

I want to lure them where I want them and fuck them the hell up so bad they never come back.

You in?

Clementine replied barely a moment later.

Lemon

Always.

CLEMENTINE

Clementine took his second chance and held on tight. Whatever it meant for the two of them—whether they could come out the other side as anything more than awkward friends—Justin still hadn't let him know, but after all the pain Clementine had caused him, he was eager to do whatever he could to make up for it. And helping Justin meant Clementine had a reason to keep texting him.

Their plan was simple: get the hunters where Justin wanted them, and give them a very, incredibly hard time. Its linchpin was to film the whole thing, focusing on the faces of the hunters and their connections to Vitalis-Barron. If the beating wasn't enough to convince them to leave, hopefully stoking suspicion against them would shame them out of the area for good.

It took an hour of back and forth to get Justin to admit that in order for that to work, they'd need actual vampires to act as bait.

Clementine

Otherwise, it will look to the camera like a bunch of people showed up to an apartment and you randomly beat the crap out of them. We'll already be up against anti-vampire sentiments as it is, so capitalizing on how heroic you are for saving the defenseless vampires is our best move.

Justin

But what if I WANT to randomly beat the crap out of the hunters?

I can't risk anyone else getting hurt.

Clementine

You'll be there to defend them.

I see that Paola, Marcus, and Isaiah already volunteered via the group chat.

You literally can't back out now.

Clementine sent him a shrugging emoji like the topic was closed, and Justin only spent forty five minutes aggressively complaining about it, and trying three times to pull the plug, before giving in.

Justin

I want both alleyways blocked then.

Clementine

Deal.

Now came the hard part: convincing Anthony to fall for it. The lying didn't trouble Clementine—half his life had been a lie for as long as he could remember, and every piece Justin hadn't wormed his way into was doubly so now that he had his vampirism to hide—but convincing Anthony in such a way that wouldn't immediately pin him as a double agent the moment the ruse was up... That would be a feat. Somehow, he'd do it—he'd have to, if he wanted to keep his job.

Because Clementine wanted this job. He wanted this life. He did.

Staring at his work desk in the communal lab office, with its stacks of regulation and protocol binders, and so many experiment results he needed to sign off on that he probably wouldn't make it into the lab itself for another four hours, he was still certain this was what he wanted. At least a tech had finally picked up the microwave radiation bobble from his paper tray. He nudged his little Star Trek pin to straighten it, but at the sound of footsteps he jerked, setting it off-kilter again.

He expected Anthony, but he realized the click-click of the tile sounded far too much like heels just in time for Dr. Blood to enter the space with an impenetrable smile, tight and professional. "Dr. Hughes, what a pleasant surprise."

Or the start of his long and painful death, he reasoned. Maybe his interview had gone so badly that she'd realized he was a vampire by the sheer force of her disgust.

Instead of dragging him to the basement though, she invited him to her office once more. He was reliving the nerves of their interview two evenings ago so strongly that he almost missed when she officially offered him the senior associate position.

With just one word, Dr. Clementine Hughes could be head of Vitalis-Barron's microbiology department, second only to her and the CEO.

It was the position he'd been both dreading and pining for. Accepting it would mean working more daytime hours, but he could get around that by coming in before dawn and leaving after dusk. No one would question him; he'd be the boss after all. He could even make a few blood bags go missing, set aside space for a project or two that wasn't strictly on board. So long as he covered his tracks well enough, no one would question it.

He would have his job, his life, and so much more.

Which was why, when the time came for his answer, the words that escaped his mouth were, *he'd think about it.*

He'd *think* about it. As though thinking about this job, this life—making it work for him even as a vampire—hadn't been racing around in his mind for nearly four months straight. He knew plenty well that if he said yes, he could accomplish everything his parents wanted for him, everything that would keep him elevated as the worthy middle child who still just barely fit into his shining family of extraordinary people, and still do a lot of good at the same time. And yet…

And yet.

For all the anxious joy the promotion should have provided him, he couldn't stop thinking of the last glimpse he'd had of Justin over the phone on Saturday morning and his message still sitting unanswered in Sissy's thread. He found he couldn't care less that his parents hadn't stopped berating him for bringing a vampire to their house—for letting one bite him in public of all places—and Reggie's third ice cream meme in a row was almost comical, but he already missed Sissy, even her goddamned phone calls.

He was too scared to add another text to their thread though, too scared he might see it not go through at all. So he plunged even deeper into helping Justin instead.

He'd scooped up the half-blunt Justin had left on his living room coffee table and started it through a series of analytical procedures the night before. Now he stood in his managerial office—the big, private one on the third floor—and stared at the results of Justin's drug sample. Their chemical makeup was not nearly as surprising as the fact that the database had given him a pre-established name for the compound: CP007. Which meant someone here—someone at Vitalis-Barron—had already run this very drug...

Clementine startled as the elevator down the hall dinged open. He carefully slid the results back onto his desk and stalked toward the office's tinted glass door, half expecting another surprise visitor. He poked his head out nonchalantly at the same moment that Anthony tried to step in. Their noses brushed, air sharing space for half a second before Clementine jerked backward.

Anthony grabbed him by his sweater collar. "You said you'd be here fifteen minutes ago."

Fifteen minutes ago, Clementine had been in Dr. Blood's office. But Anthony didn't need to know that yet, not when he looked ready to bite Clementine's head off.

Anthony pressed them both into the room, letting the door close behind them. His hair was out of its usual bun today, laying in limp brown locks down to his shoulders, and it seemed grayer in the low light, the slight wrinkles around his eyes compounded by his glowering. He wore no tie, his collar open and his shirt unbuttoned to a depth that Justin would be proud of. He was a mess, but the kind of mess that almost looked good on him.

Except that he was currently still grabbing Clementine's sweater with his holy silver charm dangling uncomfortably between them. Even that small piece of the metal hanging inches away from his bare flesh was enough to leach out his usual strength, leaving his muscles protesting weakly and his skin tingling like he was a human lying out at the pool without sunscreen for too long. He gave a halfhearted tug against Anthony's hold, baring his fangs.

"Let go of me, Anthony."

By technical standards, Anthony did, uncurling his fingers from Clementine's sweater, but his palm still rested pointedly across Clem's collarbones, and his glare hadn't lessened in the slightest. "You were with... Justin, on Friday night?" he sounded almost hesitant as he said it.

"Yes?" Dread knotted in Clementine's gut, but he couldn't place exactly where it came from. "And you sent Natalie into Ala Santa because you knew he was gone, didn't you?" It was only a suspicion, one his guilty conscience had obsessed over after learning what she'd done that night. "You said only the vampire connected to her mentor's murder would get hurt, but last night she expanded her reach. She went after innocent people."

Anthony waved a hand. "You know our hunters bring in vampires regularly and you're well aware of what we do to them in the basement—what Vitalis-Barron would do to *you* if they discovered what you were. Yet you're here still, making the whole system run. So don't come at me about innocence."

That hurt more than Anthony's silver charm ever could. Clementine had his reasons for staying—besides, he wasn't making Vitalis-Barron run, *it* was running *around* him, and would keep running whether he took the company's money or not. But Justin had been right when he'd said that working with Anthony was betrayal. And if he had been right about that, then...

Clem curled his fingers around the sides of the desk behind him, as though that might ground him enough to clear away his sudden rush of uncertainty. This wasn't the time, or the place to be doubting himself. He and Justin had a plan to enact. He could worry about the moral

319

repercussions of his job once he was certain he was going to be able to keep it in the first place.

That meant playing this right: not too aggressively ethical but still enough himself that Anthony wouldn't suspect. Clementine wrinkled his nose. "I'm not the one whose job is to bag and torture them," he retaliated, scowling. "It doesn't matter now anyway. You scared Justin so badly that he's shipping all his vampires out of the city tomorrow night."

Anthony went still. "What?"

Clem shrugged. "He's borrowing a blacked-out van, I think."

"Where are they leaving from?"

"Why do you want to know?" Clementine asked, baring his teeth. Anthony seemed to suspect nothing.

He swung his charm on its long chain, pulling it up between his fingers to hold it like a spike, clenching one of the tiny bat's wings. Its heat increased as he stepped back into Clem's space. "I like you, Clementine, I do. But I'm not going to be messed with."

"Or else you'll finally tell Vitalis-Barron about me, I'm aware," Clementine grumbled, but he flinched away from the burn of Anthony's holy silver charm all the same. "All I've been told is that they're congregating at one of their apartments."

"I want an address."

"You don't even know if the vamp Natalie's after will be there yet," Clementine snapped. "Unless she's decided her

320

vengeance is against all vampires…" He didn't have to act aghast—it was just as easy to be hurt; hurt and ashamed and angry.

"Think of it this way," Anthony's mouth flipped to something grin-like, but too clipped and jagged for any kind of joy, a thing that made Justin's bitterness look tired and lonely. "How much more will Justin Yu care about you once you're the only vampire he has to protect?"

For all the ways that sickened Clementine, there was something in those words that his heart still leapt for—not to be the *only* one Justin cared about, but his *one and only* all the same. His most important, his person, his treasure. For Clementine to be his soulmate the way Justin so positively felt like he was Clementine's. At least, to have the chance at that, if Justin was willing to let him back in.

Some of that yearning must have shown on his face, because Anthony's grin widened. "There's one other thing I'm going to need from you." He played with his holy silver charm absently, still standing so close that Clementine instinctively leaned away from the heat of it. "You must have seen Justin smoke before? I want you to take the drugs he rolls into his joints and dispose of them."

Clementine's stomach sank. Their conversation had been leading Anthony exactly where Justin wanted him, but this—this they hadn't planned for. And the way Anthony demanded it crawled in pinpricks across Clementine's skin. He knew what Justin's drugs meant to him, and how limited his supply was. How hard it would be for him to get more on short notice. Because…

Oh god. It hit Clementine slowly, painfully, the sting of the holy metal feeling more and more like it was peeling layers of skin off his face by the moment, but the tighter his grip around the edge of the desk grew, the more the paper with Justin's drug results pressed into his palm.

"You're the one supplying him." It all added up, how certain Anthony was that he could pull off using Vitalis-Barron's money and equipment under their noses, how shocked he'd looked when he'd seen Justin in Clementine's car—seen the man he was making custom drugs for sitting beside his coworker. He must have put two and two together since then. "You're not just open to making drugs behind the company's back with me. You're already doing it, for Justin and for god knows how many others."

"I supply the kinds of people this company would let die. If no one else is willing to help them, then I will. I'd think you of all people would understand that, now more than ever." He sounded sincere in his commitment. And sincerely a hypocrite.

Clementine scoffed. "Yet you're going to let a group of vampires be killed by this very same company." He tried to shift farther to the right, away from Anthony's charm, but the man slipped a leg between his, pressing him in place with a thigh.

"Sometimes you have to sacrifice something now for a better future," he said. "How do you think we got this far in the first place? Doctors and scientists used to be brave—the *heroic* age of medicine, they called it. Now we're so confined, by ethics, by capitalism, by fear. Where is the real scientific progress anymore? We have more technology and more knowledge than ever and yet we retread the same paths over and over. I'm doing something new—offering research to people who have never had it before, discovering what no one else has." He leered closer, his fingers wrapping once more around the collar of Clementine's sweater. This time the exposed charm between his fingers nearly brushed skin. "And rewards like that, they require risks. Exactly like you are going to do for Justin. Because if his pain takes him out of the way, then Natalie can't hurt him."

A chill ran down Clementine's spine as he pictured it: Justin, laid out on his couch the way he'd been two nights ago, drifting through a haze of pain with nothing to help cover it up. It wouldn't happen the way Anthony was describing—Justin would call the whole thing off if he thought he couldn't fight. But it wasn't Anthony's demand itself that concerned Clementine. He could find a way around it, he was sure, stage something with Justin's help. It was the repercussions that would come after: the ability Anthony would now have to deny Justin his drugs whenever and however long he liked. That thought burned through Clementine with a protective rage.

Anthony must have taken his revulsion for resistance, because he laughed, an edge to the humor. "Should I give you another reason?"

For a moment he seemed to draw back, but as he did, he reached with one arm behind him.

Clementine could feel the holy silver even before it came free from the back of Anthony's pants, a towel sliding off its long metal form. The bulk of it seared through Clem's skin, seemed to scream into his soul like it was tearing him apart molecule by molecule. His knees gave out as he lifted his arms instinctively, wrapping them over his face. He huddled on the floor, trying to scoot backward, but he only ended up under his desk, bumping his back into the wooden panel that ran through the center.

A whimper left him, turning quickly to a sob. "You've made your point!"

The holy silver didn't lessen, the pain didn't subside.

"I have always wondered what would happen with enough holy silver exposure," Anthony's voice came like fingernails on a chalkboard through the burning agony, branding itself into Clementine's skull. "Whether it can burn past the skin, past the muscle. What is it inside you that reacts so violently? Would it happen even in your bones, do you think?"

The idea made Clementine sick with panic. He tucked his head deeper into his arms, curling against the wood to keep as much of his bare skin covered as possible. "Anthony, please!"

Eventually, he would have to let Clementine go—he needed someone close enough to Justin to acquire those drugs. So Clementine held on, trying to think not of the pain, but of Justin. Of his dedication, his protection. Clem wished desperately that he could be in Ala Santa, could be with Justin instead—that was all he wanted, to feel Justin's skin beneath his fingers one last time and see the stress and tension ease off him. If Justin's pain was anything like this, he deserved all the gentleness in the world.

And since the moment Clem had chosen to work with Anthony, there was a chance—a chance of his own making—that Justin might never allow that closeness again. The knowledge felt nearly as miserable as his silver-induced pain, a nasty, violent thing that curled up through his chest and squeezed like it was trying to rip the sob from between his lungs. There had to be some way to show Justin that he was truly sorry, truly his in every sense of the word, convince him to accept the tenderness Clem knew he so desperately needed, in whatever form that might take.

Friends, lovers, or something in between—Clementine didn't care. In this moment of agony, all he wanted was to hold Justin in his arms once more and ease him of his pain, transfer it into Clem's own body if he had to. He wanted that, and he held to it, gritting his teeth and clinging to the desire like a lifeline.

Finally, the holy silver retreated. Clementine felt like he was catching his breath for the first time in hours, a sharp, nasty inhale that made even the inside of his lungs burn. He still couldn't bring himself to move, as though his body were in shock, tensed to the point of cramping. Lifting one arm, he managed to blink up at Anthony, staring at him with newfound horror.

Anthony didn't seem to register the look, or if he did it meant nothing to him. He leaned over the side of the desk, the holy silver stick still somewhere atop it. "Well, what will it be? This will happen regardless of your help. Your choice is whether Justin will be out of the way beforehand or has to be put out of the way in the process. You'd be saving his life, probably. Let him be in a little pain now, so you both can have a brighter future."

Clementine had to say yes and find a way to fake disposing Justin's supply later, but at the moment he only cared about one thing. "After this is over, you'll keep making drugs for him?"

"Or you can do that yourself." Anthony's voice was congenial again, as casual as if they were chatting at the coffee maker. "I know Blood's giving you the senior associate position, and my offer still stands. You could even promise to produce Justin's drugs in exchange for his blood on demand—a live-in snack, perhaps? I'm sure you two could arrange something more practical for you, once he doesn't have any other vampires to tie him down."

The thought of Justin being his—living with him—under those circumstances went so contrary to everything he wanted that it turned his stomach. It took all his strength to keep up the ruse, to confine himself to a glare and not launch for Anthony's throat with his fangs out. "Fine," he spat.

"Now let me up." He knocked on the bottom of his desk, swearing he could feel the holy silver even through the wood.

Anthony laughed, and the metal blazed into view once more. "Send a video when you're done," he said as he tucked the stick away. "I expect it within the hour, or *you* can expect this batch of drugs to be Justin's last and a very different job offer from Dr. Blood on Monday morning." And as though this was his office, he handed over Clementine's coat and motioned him out.

Clem had no way to refuse him. He managed to rise, to walk out into the hall, and board the elevator, his coat clutched to his chest. The moment its doors closed behind him, he slumped against its side. His legs shook. His throat caught.

He was alive. He was alive, and Justin's plan was in action, and the hunters wouldn't even be expecting him when they arrived tomorrow. This was good. This would have been good, anyway, if the moment Natalie returned here broken and bruised, Anthony wouldn't be far less likely to believe anything Clementine claimed, and all his threats would be made real.

Clem would just have to find a way around that. For Justin's sake.

With his anxiety still riled but the threat now three stories above him, Clementine found that Justin was still all he could think about, as though the only way to stop his shaking hands was to run them across Justin's skin. As though seeing Justin melt beneath them might make their unstable future seem a little brighter.

As though together, they might just get through this.

He couldn't wait around and hope that what he'd done so far was enough to redeem him. If Justin wanted him to prove himself, then he would—in all ways. He would offer anything, everything, so long as there was a chance Justin might accept even a shred of what Clem had to give.

28

Justin

"At least stay for half an hour." Isaiah tugged gently at Justin's arm, guiding him onto the barstool.

Justin slumped there, less in surrender and more to get out of the way of the trio of drunk humans who were trying to pass in front of them with another round of brightly colored shots. The Mexican music thudding through the place had the same electric vibrancy, the mix of dim orange and toxic neon lights giving everything a slightly odd glow that turned the guests into monstrous, beautiful things from another world, and made the assault of sandals glued and stapled and tied to every available surface look almost majestic. The bright pairs arranged to form a pride flag against the far wall were barely distinguishable as their correct colors.

Half an hour here at La C's was just as likely to kill someone as relax them, but at least it would be a joyous death.

"Why do you do this to me?" Justin grumbled, as though he hadn't been half in love with the place—in all its equally ridiculous iterations—since he was thirteen.

"You are the one who refused to let us go to the Fishnettery until the hunters are dealt with." Isaiah waved across the tight, chaotic room to where a couple of Justin's other vampires were half-hidden behind a column covered in flipflops. "This is the next best thing."

"The hunters are exactly why I *shouldn't* be here."

"If they take your vampire's bait, they won't risk launching such a large-scale attack without the benefit of the sun."

He's not *my* vampire, Justin wanted to protest, but his heart clung to the idea like a damned traitor. And he had to admit he was still worried about Clementine, and the state of their plan, and whether he was possibly making a huge mistake luring the hunters here in the first place. Whether trusting Clementine with this was another huge mistake, or whether that mistake was not taking him back in full force, not having him here with his breath on Justin's skin and his affection to ground him, to make him feel like he was worthy of love for a few minutes more.

"Besides, you need a break even more than the rest of us—and stress watching how-to videos from the rooftops doesn't cut it." Isaiah fit his hand around the back of his barstool and drew light circles over Justin's shoulders.

His muscles loosened under the touch, but it only served to remind him of Clementine's fingers, the way he'd treated

Justin's skin as though it were precious. As though *he* were precious. He shook his head, trying to dislodge the thought. "I *like* the how-to videos." And he'd progressed so far past the ones he might actually use to help his neighbors that the sheer act of watching them was as much a guilty pleasure as Clementine's attention had been. "Besides, the pain is a lot better today."

That was not technically a lie. The facts were, independently, that his back felt much better than it had Saturday morning, and that he'd had to smoke through five days' worth of his drugs to get it there. Isaiah simply didn't need to know that last part. Though he sure side-eyed Justin as if he did.

Justin gave him a half-smile, preparing to protest again, when someone new stepped into the bar.

Justin should not have noticed from across the crowded room, except that he would notice Clementine anywhere, like a string inside him was pulled taut whenever the vampire was in sight. His whole being stirred, from the flutter of his heart to the warmth in his chest, the tingling goosebumps along his limbs and the ache between his legs. Every part of him yearned despite his better judgment.

It didn't help that Clementine was spectacular. The odd mix of dim fluorescence and neon glow from the bar's lighting would have washed out anyone else, but it transformed Clementine into an urban deity, pinks and greens cascading along his gilded hair and his tailored jacket flaring in time to his steps, the knit sweater luminescent beneath.

Justin hadn't forgiven him, not fully, and this half hour for himself was not meant to include the one vampire he was supposed to be keeping at a distance. But boy did he yearn for that anyway, heart and body and soul.

Clementine's face hardened as he surveyed the room, twitching away from the brightest of the lights and the thrum of the speakers. When his attention finally fixed on Justin, he visibly relaxed. It was precious, the way his tension eased and his face lit up, and Justin tried to ignore how much that trust and adoration meant to him. Clementine adjusted his jacket with three precise motions, chin lifted and eyes half lidded, and wormed his way through the crowd like one touch from them might infect him. With La C's cleaning schedule, he was probably half-right.

His gaze swept down Justin as he neared, a flicker of unreadable emotion tugging at his lips. He slipped into Justin's space, close enough to touch, and murmured in a low, vampiric tone, "Hey. Sorry for just appearing like this. I don't know if you want me here, but Marcus told me where you were, and I…"

Justin was pretty sure a piece of his soul ascended. He fought the feeling, but it was a half-hearted battle, Clementine's physical nearness decimating the defenses he swore he'd honed during their previous day of texting. He couldn't let himself be lured back to that quiet, romantic space they'd built in Clementine's apartment, but perhaps he could still lust, could give Clem a peek inside without tearing down the entire wall.

Besides, they were here in Ala Santa, on Justin's home turf, surrounded by every reason he couldn't submit to Clementine's full adoration. Justin *would* pull himself away the moment his vampires needed him. He would put them first, regardless of how beautiful Clementine was or how much he might grovel.

"You're not a convict on parole, Lemon." He bared his teeth and tried very hard not to lean into Clementine's presence. "Fuck, you really can't stay away from me, can you?"

It was meant to be a joke, but the desperate honesty with which Clementine answered and the breadth of emotion behind it took Justin's breath away. "Never."

Clementine leaned in further. The slight whiff of his vanilla fragrance reached Justin over the bar's sweaty stench. Clementine's fingers brushed Justin's back in slow, steady draws. With each motion, Justin thought his heart would stop. Even through the fabric of his jacket, the touch was enough to send an earthquake trembling through him.

The force of Clementine's affection was dark and sweet and as intoxicating as his venom. It slipped into Justin's bloodstream so fast and hard that he felt himself caving to it before his right mind could tell him not to, lingering on the weight of Clementine's fingers like they were a lifeline.

Justin hadn't forgiven him, though. He kept trying to remind himself of that, and it felt like looking for a hole he'd already filled, like he might notice the freshness of the dirt and dig his anger and pain back up. He didn't *want* that anger and pain though. He wanted *this*.

Isaiah cleared his throat and stood, not quite meeting Justin's gaze. "I'll be around if you need me."

Justin couldn't gather his strangled emotions fast enough to stop his best friend's departure, leaving him wishing Isaiah could have carried away every sensation his body was feeling in that instant because he wasn't sure he could let go of them otherwise. So much for keeping up the wall. He tried again—unsuccessfully—to force his focus elsewhere. "How did your chat with Anthony go?"

"Great, yet terrible." Clementine made a stiff, small sound. "He took our bait, but he's realized that you're reliant on the drugs you smoke. He told me to destroy them. Which shouldn't be an issue; if I get a good look at them I can make something that fits the part enough to pass on video, and you'll just have to act like you're in pain the further we get into the morning in case they send someone here to check. But once you do beat up the hunters... he'll suspect that I've lied to him. And he won't be happy."

"I'm sorry." Justin's heart twisted. It was just a job, he reminded himself, something he'd hoped Clementine would give up for weeks, but now that it was staring them down, threatening to abolish Clementine's agency and force him into a place he didn't want to be, Justin wished for any other outcome.

"I'll find a way to play it off," Clem assured him. "I'll make it work. It'll be fine." But for all his feigned confidence, he looked worried. He tugged at his sweater, shaking his head. His gilded curls bobbed and settled. "God, it's not important right now. I don't want to think about it. I just…" He lifted his gaze, staring into Justin like he'd seen the light for the first time in days. And he smiled, a look so deep and layered that Justin couldn't see through to the emotion beneath. "I just want you to know that you have been the best part of my life for weeks now, and that I'm going to give you back everything you could ever want because of it."

Then Clementine dropped to his knees, like a prince asking for a pardon.

And Justin found he'd already granted it. Sometime between their fight and the moment Clementine walked through the door, he'd let everything he knew of Clementine confront every hurt in his chest and found that the memory of Clem's affection won out, again and again and again. Between the two of them, it was Justin who didn't deserve this love, not Clementine.

But Clem seemed determined to give it all the same.

Justin's legs had been loose and wide, the toes of his shoes tucked into a low rung on the barstool to keep from dangling, and Clementine barely had to press them apart to fit his shoulders between him. His gaze stayed locked on Justin's as he propped his chin on the edge of the seat. Justin swore he could feel the vampire's breath even through the fabric of his jeans, and he strained for it, all the blissful

335

warmth of Clementine's words turning to a needy ache. God, Clementine was going to murder him, right here and now. Justin would be the first of his lineage to die early, not from heroism or overdose, but from *wanting*.

He tightened his fingers, but he couldn't seem to stop Clem, couldn't look away from him. Like he had been tied to the railroad tracks, like he had to wait for the train to hit. It was all he could do just to keep from burying his hands in Clementine's hair and begging for something—anything that would close the remaining space between them.

"Does running a con always turn you this demonstrative?" He managed to tease, his voice thick and low.

"I think that's been the result of this whole weekend. It's proved a lot of things to me." Deliberate and precise, Clementine turned his lips to the pulse that ran through Justin's leg and nipped at it with blunted teeth. "Like that I'm yours; your hopeless addict."

Addicted. That's certainly what this felt like, an incessant, impossible pull to have more of Clementine, to accept more, to *become* more. Forgiveness or not, they weren't supposed to be doing this again, but here they were, closer than last time, twisted up in each other in a way that was going to be hell to peel apart, and yet Justin couldn't say no, not when Clementine traced his fingers up Justin's leg, dragging his nails absentmindedly over the seam along his thigh, cupping across the top and firmly gripping down as though to hold

Justin in place for something to come. Justin's body was responding with a reckless enthusiasm.

Clementine clearly noticed, a subtle smirk tugging at the edges of his lips. He slipped his chin closer, his nose coming a hair away from brushing the seat of Justin's increasingly fuller pants, and leaned his face into Justin's inner thigh like he was committing his soul on the altar. Fangs out, he whispered, "Take from me, please. Drain me dry."

Justin felt like he was about to turn metaphysical, ascend into heaven or fall to hell.

He didn't know what part of Clementine he could accept, not for long and certainly not forever, but he understood the request nonetheless, deep in his bones and heavy against the front of his pants and pounding like blood through his heart. *Please.*

Someone had to be seeing this—even as crowded and dim as it was, Clementine kneeling with his lips practically pressed to Justin's lap wasn't exactly subtle—but it made the moment electric with a delicious kind of danger, their lust and love on full display. So slowly, as though at any moment he might finally find it in him to withdraw, he drew his fingertips along Clementine's forehead, treasuring the softness of his skin, then pushed back a few stray curls. "What if I don't want you drained but rather carved open for me? I'm no vampire. All I have is a stake and a prayer."

"You have something else, too." Clementine lifted his head.

"What is that?" Justin held still, letting his fingers drift down to Clementine's jaw and along his cheek until they caressed his lips.

"My heart, for your pleasure." Clem's mouth parted against Justin's touch with each word. "I told you I would peel back my ribs for you and I meant it."

Justin watched him with a tight inhale, then another. "Prove it, then."

He trembled as he slid his pointer finger into Clem's mouth. Clementine didn't pull away. Justin wanted almost to close his eyes, to feel the moment more perfectly, the pound of the music and the warmth of Clementine's mouth and the roll of his tongue as it teased, but he couldn't force his gaze off Clementine. His fang slipped into Justin with a pinprick of pain, a tingling rush of venom following.

A blissful sound left Justin, so soft that the music and the chatter should have drowned it out, but it seemed to do things to Clementine, a vibration like a purr rising in his chest. Justin pressed his finger a bit deeper into Clem's mouth, flipping to run the pricked, still bleeding tip over Clem's tongue. Clementine sucked it once, purposeful yet gentle, and Justin finally withdrew.

Clementine licked his lips after. "So, will you have me back?"

Justin wasn't sure what exactly he was agreeing to—there was little he could agree to in the first place, when he had Ala Santa to return to in the morning—but the truth came unbidden, his voice rough and the gravel of his lungs more pronounced. "Always, my Lemon."

Clementine's smile grew, fathomless and as bright as the sun. It stole Justin's breath and, at this rate, he was afraid it wouldn't be long before Clementine could take whatever else he wanted with it.

29

CLEMENTINE

Clementine should have feared rejection—that he would offer up everything only to be denied again, held forever at a distance, both their heart strings pulled into breaking. But on his knees before Justin, Clementine was fairly certain there was no other place he'd rather have been. He had never been a church-goer, but he wondered if this was what penance felt like, heart open and body willing.

When he'd first entered the bar, it had been a struggle to keep himself moving. La C was a small place, tucked a little lower than the main street, its windows too high and squashed and its door heavy. The smell of fried food and sweat had wrinkled up his nose in a way that was half off-putting and half addictive. Fifty or sixty people filled the place, along with a ridiculous number of sandals hanging off every surface. The dimness of the neon lighting set his head spinning. The music was lively and the customers jubilant, cheap tablecloths piled high with buckets of loaded fries and a variety of colorful drinks that Clem was pretty sure also covered parts of the floor beneath him. The whole environment had made him feel wrong, like all his limbs were sized just a bit differently than they had been all his life. He'd held himself tight and close, trying to take up as little space as possible.

Then he'd stood before Justin, and the rest of the bar—the noise, the bustle, the slightly too loud music and off-colored lights—all faded into a distant blur. His anxiety still coursed under the surface, but, as he'd hoped, Justin had drowned it out with his skin and his smile, half bitterness and half honey. When Clem had dropped to his knees, the heat of his own breath returning to him with the earthen musk of Justin's scent as he'd offered himself up until it seemed that Justin was dangling over the edge of a cliffside—then what remained of Clementine's worries had faded away.

It had felt so natural, so easy. Like the sensual playacting for the ghost tour and the teasing they'd done over the last few weeks, but beyond simply the sensory; it felt now as if Clementine had offered every dusty corner of his soul for Justin's pleasure. With his attention this fixed on Justin, the openness was suddenly second nature, as though this was what he was made for.

Clementine was made to give himself away.

Anyone could see him here, groveling, Justin's finger in his mouth, but Clementine found he didn't care. Or he did care. He just cared the wrong way, the pucker of Justin's lips and the tightening of his jeans more delicious where anyone might be watching, seeing just how far Clementine would go for Justin. Just how much they wanted each other.

And oh, how badly Clementine wanted this. Even knowing the danger that lay before them, he could not stop wanting this so thoroughly that it ached all the way through him.

"*So, will you have me back?*" Clementine had asked.

"Always, my Lemon," Justin whispered.

Always. It wasn't *forever* when they said it—Clementine knew that well enough—but it was *of course*, and *yes*, and *forgiven* all wrapped into one. When things were most terrifying and most unstable, that was all Clementine required. Only this. Only Justin: his heart to cherish and his body to adore.

It seemed so beautiful and impossible until Justin shook his head, breaking the spell. "Of course I'm happy to have you, while we're here. So long as we have the time. What's this new drug disposal Anthony's demanding? Shouldn't we focus on that first?"

The world came back in a rush, too loud, too present. Clementine's stomach twisted. He didn't want to face their future yet. As selfish and as awful as it was, he needed another minute just to bask in Justin's forgiveness and pretend his *always* was eternal. "Not yet. If I send him the confirmation too fast, he'll be suspicious."

Justin gave one of Clem's curls a tug. "Well, get up at least. You don't know what else has been on that floor."

Clementine laughed, his chest helium light. He stood, cringing as the shin of one of his pant legs momentarily stuck to the ground. "Frankly, I don't *want* to know." The back of his mouth went sour. "You should probably have washed your hands before fingering my mouth."

Justin's smile widened. "Oh, don't worry, I haven't touched anything but you all night. Though, considering how many of this place's drinks end up on the floor, I'm told they are actually quite good in recent years."

"You're told?" Clementine settled on the stool Isaiah had abandoned and leaned against Justin's arm, drawing light circles over his back.

"I don't drink anymore." Justin shrugged, looking almost defiant. "I never did like the taste to begin with, but I found even the effects are less and less appealing with time."

"That's fair. I don't like tuna fish or horror movies," Clementine offered, adding his own shrug to the mix. "And you could not force me on a rollercoaster on pain of death. Unless, maybe that rollercoaster wore denim?" He leaned closer and fitted his head on Justin's shoulder, like he was going to snap at his denim collar, or perhaps something just beyond it.

Justin's muscles eased, his neck extending, bare and vulnerable, before his lips quirked and he shoved Clementine gently off. "Hey," he called down to the bartender—a Hispanic man finishing up a neon green drink with two umbrellas and a miniature sandal hanging off it. "What do you have for my vamp here?"

Like the old woman from the convenience store down the road, the bartender didn't even flinch at the mention of what Clementine was. "The margaritas go great with half an ounce of blood, if he's into that?"

Clementine stared. Blood, as in *real* blood?

Blood in their drinks, their vampiric customers allowed to exist fully as themselves—it caught in Clementine's chest, warm and full, and ached there. This was a neighborhood Justin loved, a neighborhood where they took care of their vampires, where they had worked hard to create bubbles of joy and peace. And he had played a part in Natalie's attacks on it.

Well, he was doing something to make up for that now, at least.

Justin gave the bartender his typical smile, sharp and dangerous. "Get him one of those. On me."

"I can cover it—"

"No, you can't. I have all your money, remember."

"Not fair." Clementine tipped his head toward Justin's ear, palm pressed to his lower back. "I'm still buying *your* blood later tonight…"

Justin caved against him, his eyes nearly closing as his hand slid over Clementine's thigh, gripping the inside like he was trying to ground himself with it. "You know you have me at your fang-tips any time you're in the neighborhood, payment or not."

Clementine's chest rumbled, a soft, vampiric purr vibrating like a hum at the base of his throat. He fiddled gently with the shorter sides of Justin's hair and drew his fingers down the man's neck to play with his jacket collar.

"What if I want you now? What if I want you, here, beneath my lips? In my mouth…"

Between the words and the subtle brush of skin on skin, a visible change came over Justin, his gaze less focused and his breath shallower. He leaned into Clementine's touch, letting Clem's palm press flat against his neck. "Here?" He smirked, bright and bitter and taunting. "In front of everyone?"

"Bloody margarita," the bartender coughed, delivering the drink and turning away with a smirk.

Justin lifted the glass like a toast between them. Then he raised it to Clem's lips.

Clem opened his mouth. The bright burst of citrus and the sharpness of the alcohol and the blood all worked perfectly together. As Justin had once implied, it didn't matter that the blood wasn't to Clem's palate. The other flavors masked its blandness, leaving just his body's instinctive pleasure over its mere presence.

As he took the glass for a proper drink, he watched Justin, letting himself feel every ounce of the longing that had built in him over their weeks together, savoring every curve and angle of the man he'd grown so close to: his dark hair swept back, his narrow eyes turning his irises black in the dim lighting, the ink of his intricate tribal tattoos tucking around his neck and cutting the bared top of his chest into its well-formed muscles. His silver crucifix pendant gleamed against the base of his sternum.

Clementine set his drink down and caught the little cross between two fingers, letting his skin brush Justin's with each twist and turn. He pressed to the edge of his seat as he did, their thighs riding together, their feet tucked close. Justin moved with him, shifting forward like they were two magnets increasing their attraction the closer they grew. Their seats tilted to accommodate.

Clem slipped his free hand beneath the edge of Justin's jacket, feeling along his ribs with a thumb. He felt Justin quiver.

His chair tipped and jerked as someone bumped it from behind, and the foot he'd looped through Justin's seat kicked out instinctively to catch himself. Justin tumbled forward, spilling into him in such a dramatic colliding of hips and chests that it would have been as romantic as it was comical, if not for the way Justin winced as Clementine caught him under the arms.

He gingerly found his footing, giving Clem a bitter smile that bled tension.

Clementine's heart caught in his throat. "Your back?"

He grimaced. "I should take a quick smoke."

Clem figured it was the most explicit admission of pain he was going to get.

Justin paused as he stepped away, two fingers reaching, then brushing Clem's jawline. They pulled back just as quickly. The heat of their attraction hadn't vanished, but in the distance between them it seemed to transform into something else, an aching so deep that Clementine could barely perceive the scope of it. Justin shook his head. "I'll be back."

As he left, Clementine felt pieces of himself slide apart, his anxiety rushing into the cracks. He tried to nurse the rest of his margarita, but his stomach twisted, nausea building with each sip. His foot tapped against the floor completely out of time to the music. It sounded like Spanish pop.

Around him, the bar carried on as usual, loud with joy and packed with people who seemed to care so fully for each other, vampires and humans alike. It was wonderful and beautiful and so undeserving of the hell that had set the neighborhood in its sights. Without Justin there to distract him, though, Clementine felt like he was going to implode from the sheer amount of noise and chaos and utter lack of hygiene.

He tucked himself as close to the bar as he could without touching it, distracting himself by counting the random assortment of jars and bottles on the wall—a variety of liquors and syrups, salt and sugar, something flakey and cream-colored, and an iridescent shimmering substance labeled *edible glitter*. He squinted, his mind turning. In the right proportions, those last two could almost look like...

He waved down the bartender, putting a hundred-dollar bill on the counter before the man finally shrugged and left him to scoop portions of the ingredients he wanted into an empty shot glass that he covered and slid carefully into his pocket. The cup clicked against something solid—so solid that for a moment he could feel it through his sweater—but when he pressed his fingers in he found nothing at the pocket's bottom. He headed for the bar's entrance. The bustle seemed to chase him out, louder and rowdier and creeping under his skin.

As he neared the door, Justin pushed back through it, the last remnants of a joint in one hand and his little drug tin in the other.

Clementine caught his elbow. "Can I see them now? I think it's about time."

Justin flinched. He pushed the case into Clementine's hands. "Just be careful, they're all I have."

"Yes, of course." Clementine swallowed down the fear that they might be all he ever received again.

Justin must have assumed that Anthony knew about his drug dependence from local rumor—he certainly smoked enough in public for all of Ala Santa to realize he needed them. Clem would have to reveal how much worse the truth was; that Anthony and his dealer were one and the same. But there was nothing either of them could do to change that now and Clementine wanted—needed—to give Justin one slice of happiness, one tiny eternity that would still be so much less than he warranted, before he finally broke that news. Justin deserved not to have his night ruined just yet.

Before morning, Clementine was going to show him that he was worth all the love Clementine had to offer, in whatever form he'd accept it.

Drugs in hand, Clem made a beeline for the bathroom. It was a single stall with signed walls and a dirty floor—the least sanitary place for a drug transfer, but it would have to do. He locked the door behind him, but even that couldn't quite shield him from how the loud, rowdy place had crept under his skin. He wanted to sit in the dark, in the quiet, and feel the pressure of Justin's body against his until the chaos of it all drained back out of his soul.

Soon.

His hands shook as he switched Justin's drugs for a passable combination of the bar's stock. He kept the camera fixed on the toilet as it flushed, pouring the substitute from Justin's tin and into the already spiraling water. He sent the video. The text came through not thirty seconds later.

Anthony Hilker
I knew I could count on you.

Clem almost wilted against the counter before remembering just how disgusting it was. The easy part of the Anthony dilemma was down, but the hardest part was still to come: the morning, where they'd find out whether this had doomed him and Justin both.

Before then, he was going to give Justin something wonderful to remember him by. They both deserved that much, at least.

30

JUSTIN

Justin felt like he was being pulled apart in the most exquisite way possible, drawn between two things he so desperately wanted, desperately *needed*. His daily guilt was an internal war on its own, but not even the regret and shame he'd lived with the last decade could match the current battle happening somewhere between his head and his heart.

He ran both hands up his face and through his hair, trying not to be so keenly aware of every step Clementine took toward the restroom. Every breath he breathed. Every little pinch of his lips and gleam of his eyes. The way his fingers moved, precise and delicate, but sturdy too, and the way they had felt as they brushed Justin's skin, the exact and perfect rhythm they might find if they reached between his legs. He could still feel the ghost of Clementine's breath as he'd settled his chin between Justin's thighs. Even after he'd stood, Justin hadn't been able to form a single linear thought for what felt like minutes.

He wanted Clementine with every ounce of his being, to taste him like Clem had so enthusiastically been tasting

Justin for weeks now and to settle quietly beside him after, to talk of futures and pasts like they had purpose. But Justin's past was a wreck, his future already indebted. He had said that he'd take Clementine back, but in truth Clem was only his in the way of a god: awesome and unreachable beyond the most fleeting of moments.

"Well, you certainly found your tease." Isaiah leaned against the bar, lounging long and feline with his nose lifted and expression slack. "He's a catch, though; I'm impressed. If I could have followed someone that hot and that enthralled with me into a bathroom, you wouldn't be seeing me for the rest of the night."

"I need to be alert in the morning."

"*Half* the night then. In your apartment, perhaps? Beds are multi-purpose, after all; you *can* sleep in them when you're finished." Isaiah ran his hand over Justin's shoulder, drawing it down his chest in a way that would have been flirtatious had he not been telling Justin to fuck someone else as he did it. "All I'm saying is, you wanted some fun with a vampire who wasn't from Ala Santa, and here you have one. So why are you holding yourself back?"

"I…" Justin knew why, a thousand reasons that boiled down to a single, deadly point. But how many were relevant right now? In the morning they'd all come crashing back in, but for the moment…

Isaiah sighed. "I'm telling you this as someone who loves you: I think you should go for it. At least until the sun comes up."

Until the sun comes up—Justin could not believe how amazing that sounded, how much his body screamed for it. Perhaps one night would curb this, sate his hunger just enough that he could go on living, protecting his vampires without constant fantasies playing in his head. And then whatever happened between himself and Clem—all that had to happen, to turn Justin's focus back where it belonged— would at least leave them both with one night to remember.

Just until the sun came up. And the hunters arrived.

Clementine emerged from the bathroom. He scanned the bar, his gaze focusing on Justin with an intensity that seemed almost dangerous.

Justin pushed himself out of his seat, pressing determinedly through the crowded space. People began parting for him, chairs scooting back and heads turning. They were watching, a charge moving through this room of friends and acquaintances and likeminded strangers—of family.

As he met Clementine in the middle of the bar, he pressed one hand to the front of Clem's chest, palm on his heart, nails biting in. "Would you peel your ribs back for me now?"

Longing tightened Clementine's features, and he whispered, "Always."

Maybe *always* could just be always. Maybe it didn't have to mean forever.

Justin's fingers latched onto Clementine's clothing with a mind of their own. His whole being seemed to run on

352

instinct, on every coiled band Clem had so masterfully wound up, as though Isaiah's push had finally released them.

Clementine's brow tightened. His mouth opened, a word already forming. But Justin didn't listen.

He kissed.

Head tipping and body pressing forward, he caught whatever the vampire was about to say on his own tongue, tasting it with a ravenous delirium that shoved Clementine backward, thrusting him against the nearest table. There was no crossover, no hesitation, no instant where it went from his kiss to *their* kiss, it just was, as though it had been so at the beginning of time and would be so at the end of it too, both of them with equal weight and will and lust, and beneath that, something deeper, pounding like a sun in the center of Justin's chest.

He ran one hand up Clem's neck, seizing his curls and holding his head as Clementine consumed him with deep, frantic kisses. His tongue caught on Clem's fangs and he relished in the sharp prick of pain and bliss as they cut him open, the vampire sucking so fiercely that the wound closed again in an instant. Justin ached between his legs, his dick hard against his pants, begging to press against Clem, to press *into* him if he would allow it, the rub of their hips an agonizing taunt that shuddered greedily up his spine.

Clementine's arms tangled around him, long lean limbs grabbing and dragging, pulling him closer at the same time that Justin pushed, pushed him back until he was sitting on the table's edge with one of Justin's knees propped against his thigh, Justin sitting half in Clementine's lap as they devoured each other. He swore a drink spilled and someone might have cursed, hollers and shouts of his name echoing through the space, but it all felt like a buzz of color and adrenaline, edging him forward.

Every run of lips and teeth set his nerves alight and stoked a fire in his core, his whole body sensitive to each touch and grasp and moan from Clementine in a way that seemed impossible, as though their very cells were in tune. He didn't stop—couldn't stop—until his head swam, his lungs crying that the tiny inhales he was taking between Clem's lips weren't enough. As the kiss finally broke, they came apart in each other's arms like half-shattered vases, their pieces intermingled. Justin rested his forehead on Clementine's temple, Clem's breath on his neck, hair in his hands. Soft laughter came from him in breathless heaves as he clung to Justin in turn.

The world spun around them, but through it Justin could still make out the general chaos resuming throughout the room. Anywhere else they might have been kicked out already—anywhere else, Justin wouldn't have exposed his back to a potentially hateful world in order to kiss another man to begin with—but here enough people knew him that the bar's reaction was a mix of congratulations and amused annoyance, Isaiah smiling with a melancholic fondness, while at his side Marcus rolled his eyes and crunched on a bite of his salad. Justin yearned to press closer to Clementine still. The nearness of Clementine's thigh beneath him and his narrow hips just begging to be straddled made Justin ache viciously, but he forced himself to slide off instead, pulling Clementine up with an apology to the group whose table they'd commandeered.

The woman—Lydia, was it, or Cynthia, maybe—at the nearest seat seemed to be trying desperately not to meet his gaze, while her androgynous date winked suggestively, and teased, "I was hoping you'd give us the full show."

As much as Justin's body lit up at the thought, he was pretty sure *that* display would turn La C into a completely different kind of bar, one the owner—and most of the customers who knew him—wouldn't appreciate without prior warning. That didn't mean their show had to *end* though, just move to an audience of two. Wherever this heartbreak was taking them, he was already committed.

"Let's get out of here." He wanted to beg. He wanted to drop to his knees or strip off his shirt or spill a vein to lure Clementine in, whatever it took to make Clementine want him with the desperation that Justin wanted Clem. But as Clementine's gaze met his again, he knew it was irrelevant— he was fairly sure no one had or ever would look at him the way Clementine did just then, like he was trying to consume Justin through sight alone.

"Please." Clementine glanced out across the room. He swallowed, and his brow tightened. "This place is too loud and just—yes please. Take me somewhere. Take me home with you."

It seemed unreasonable how little the chilly night air did for Justin's painfully thick erection, but what it couldn't dim, the subtle but growing pain in his back was sure taking a whack at. He considered having another smoke, but the five blocks to his apartment wouldn't be long enough to burn through an entire joint, and he wanted his full attention for Clementine as soon as they arrived.

The vampire walked beside him, not quite hand in hand, but close enough that every third step their fingers brushed. After all the touches they'd shared and that perfect, aggressive, endless kiss, those tiny blinks of skin on skin shouldn't have done such stupid things to Justin as they did. Neither should the light, loose quirk of Clementine's lips have, nor the almost imperceptible bounce in his normally steady step.

"I'd never—" Clementine started, then shook his head. "God, that kiss was incredible. It really can be *that* good."

Justin lifted a brow, smirking. "So I'm the best you've ever had?"

Clementine rolled his lips, his gaze snapping toward Justin, then away. "Truth be told, you're the first I haven't bailed out of. Kissing has always seemed like such a lovely, sensual thing in my mind, but the act of it never quite functions. The moment saliva comes into the picture, it makes me want to retch—someone else's bodily fluids in my mouth? It's not appetizing."

"Of course it sounds gross when you say it like that," Justin grumbled. "You drink blood though, which is technically a fluid of the body, you do know that?"

"Yes! And can you just imagine how hard this all has been for me?" He waved one arm, fingers splayed like he didn't quite know what to do with them. "Until you grew on me, anyway."

"Wait," Justin put the pieces together as he said them, only realizing how blunt it might sound once it was all out, "So this means you've never done anything like that before? Never?" It had been ages for Justin—years between each hookup, and none of them were with people he'd had been interested in seeing after, which had been the whole point and one he was aggressively failing at this time around—but sexual acts weren't *completely* foreign to him, at least.

Clementine shook his head, his curls bobbing. He didn't look embarrassed by the fact, though. If anything, he was beaming now, a bright, proud expression that made Justin want to swoon into the nearest lamppost and pull the vampire down with him.

"Have you..." He wasn't quite sure how to ask it, so he just slid the word out there as a question. "Sex?"

"Not personally, but I will bet you the meager rest of my savings that I've written twice as many creative and kinky erotic scenes this month alone than most people have lived through." The way he smiled, Justin got the feeling it wasn't meant to be an overstatement.

That knowledge made him entirely hotter than should have been possible in this cold night air.

Clementine's shoulders bounced as he continued. "But I… I suppose a part of me always doubted that sexual interactions could truly feel the way I've learned to write them. That we aren't all making it up, portraying what we hope for and not what's real. Because every other attempt I've made has always been so distressing, gross and stiff and even when I thought I was turned on, the moment our lips met, my desire would vanish. But this was—it was *real.*" He sighed like he was filling Justin's depleted lungs with his own breath. "Sorry, I'm rambling."

"You're beautiful," Justin whispered back. "I mean, yes, and I love it. Keep, keep doing that. I like to listen."

The vampire gave a tiny laugh. "You're the first."

"Everyone else has been an oblivious fool then," he replied. "Do you know why this kiss was different?"

"I think it's because I'm demisexual." Clementine said it like he was testing out the word, but as it lingered between them, a little smile grew across his face. "And possibly grayasexual and demigrayromantic, too? At least, some combination that makes my attraction rare and take time to grow when it finally does. Like what happened with your blood. When we met, you tasted of nothing special, but then our relationship deepened, and now there's nothing I'd rather have in my mouth more than you." He accented the innuendo with a seductive slip of his tongue along his lower lip, sliding it around his fangs as he pulled it back into his mouth with a smirk.

Justin felt himself tremble, his hard dick begging to be the thing Clem put in his mouth next. It would have to contain itself... for one more block. "Hold up, you're saying that you liked me for my personality first? My dear Lemon, I am seriously questioning your sanity."

"Don't be ridiculous, you're wonderful, Justin."

He gave a scoff. "I wouldn't go that far."

"No, stop. You like to listen to me ramble, so I'm rambling." Clementine said it with such force that Justin couldn't object, couldn't stop him as the words spilled from Clementine's lips and drove like daggers right into the center of Justin's chest. "You aren't perfect, but what of it? Who is? Certainly not me, for all my damned efforts." He snorted, before seeming to come back to himself, his smile dangerously soft. "What you are is loyal and practical, observant and thoughtful. You are the kind of man who gets attacked by a vampire and *offers* to feed him. You love the people of this neighborhood with such genuine attention and devotion that despite the pain you've caused them in the past, they truly adore you now. And you do all of this—all of it—thinking that it means nothing. You, with your incredible blood and your incredible kisses and your incredible—occasionally bitter—personality, you are wonderful."

He stopped, facing Justin, the street around them caught in a bubble of pure quiet against the distant hum of other blocks, the darkness broken only by the orange lamplight at their side, gilding Clementine's curls and casting him in bronze as he reached out. Justin's breath caught so tight within his chest that it seemed ready to burst as Clem cupped the side of his face, staring at him with something so much deeper than lust or hunger, something that saw inside Justin's soul, and found that it was good.

"You are wonderful," Clementine repeated, "and I just think you ought to know it."

Justin's head felt light and his knees weak, and he realized only belatedly that he still hadn't taken a breath. He wasn't sure he'd ever be able to take one again, not while Clementine's palm still rested so tenderly against his face and his gaze held Justin's like a match to brittle timber. Wonderful. Clementine Hughes thought he was wonderful. And had used the word *ought* in a romantic soliloquy.

And Justin couldn't—he didn't—this wasn't—

He turned his face, and the air came rushing back, the world sharpening once more into focus. This was no longer merely the grounding affection that made Justin feel like he might be worthy of love once more, but rather an adoration that transcended the senses, that brought him instantly back to their night in Clementine's apartment, only stronger and surer and deeper, an ocean where a lake had started—the very thing he was not supposed to be doing with Clementine any longer. But now that they were here, Justin didn't think he could ever go back.

Clementine stared, brows tighter now and lips parted a hair.

Justin caught the vampire's chin between his thumb and fingers. He tipped it down to press a light kiss to Clem's mouth, ending with a lower lip tug that made Clem whimper. Another little moan followed it as he rolled his hips against Clementine's just once, letting a single shock of bliss tingle through him at the pressure of the equally hard presence in the vampire's pants. "This is my building," he whispered.

"It's very nice." Clementine's voice sounded deeper and softer suddenly.

"You're not even looking at it."

"Well. Yes, fine." He still didn't pull his eyes from Justin's, but he slipped two fingers into Justin's back pocket. "As long as it has walls and a bed, it'll do."

Justin laughed, leading him up the stairwell. "That's good because it doesn't have much else. Well, besides… you'll see."

It was an old building so far as San Salud was concerned, sixty years at least, with its cement steps chipped and its doors a little crooked. The metal railing outside his second-story studio apartment had rusted to an unsafe degree and the walls were so thin he could hear the old woman snoring two floors above. He had to give the lock an extra shove to open it.

"Please don't judge me," Justin said, feeling strangely sheepish. The last time anyone had been here, he swore he hadn't owned *this* many salt and pepper shakers.

They filled the bookshelf and topped his humming mini-fridge and cluttered the kitchenette counter, little old antiques mostly, each one more bizarre and outlandish and adorable than the last, making haunting rows in the dimness. They were, as he'd implied, just about the only things worth seeing in the rundown room. The queen-sized mattress managed to cover only half the cracked wooden floor tiles. He was pretty sure the bathroom still had toilet paper, and the closet's broken rolling door revealed his collection of gray, white, and blue V-necks with such similar designs that they were nearly the same shirt. From beyond the single, curtainless window the streetlight shone so brightly that he didn't bother to turn on the single lamp that sat on the floor.

Clementine's brow lifted. "You have a problem."

"I stopped collecting them, I swear. People just give them to me now." Not that he didn't keep and cherish every last one, all the way back to the very first pair, a prank gift from Jose on his thirteenth birthday, the comical angel and devil shakers now missing shards from when they'd been painstakingly glued back together twice. The collection was, if anything, the one piece of happiness he felt he truly deserved; weird little pieces of other people's lives that had been discarded, now loved again under his care.

Clementine snorted. "The shakers are odd but kind of cute, honestly, excluding that pair you stole from my

362

parents; you should definitely throw those out. The problem you have is with everything else. Or, specifically, the lack thereof."

"I'd rather spend my money helping the people who need it more." As he said it though, he couldn't stop thinking of the way lying in Clementine's apartment had seemed to take a weight off his soul. Clem's home was a lived-in place, and his was just a storage unit for a collection he was barely even here to enjoy. He tried to box that feeling back up with a grin. He was already giving himself another luxury: a night with Clementine. One night before a return to his duty. And then... well, then he'd have to wrangle his heart back into place.

"Besides, I only really shower and sleep here." He nudged the door closed with his foot, slipping into Clementine's space in the process, and bared his teeth like a challenge. "And sometimes I think of you, and I do one other thing."

Clementine reacted to him like a predator to a wounded prey, pulling him closer by the small of his back and the cheek of his ass, his smile revealing the full length of his fangs. "No more teasing."

Justin's exhale held a shudder, his nerves lighting fresher and fuller than ever. He pushed Clementine back, directing him toward the mattress with hungry kisses and gentle shoves. Somehow their shoes came off along the way, their jackets dropped into a crumpled pile that Clementine jerked away to fix before Justin caught him by both hips, grinding fully against him like he was trying to bring them both to climax then and there. Clementine's attention rekindled so hot and bright that it seemed like they were the only two things in all the world.

The thralls of their lust felt gentler now, though, each hungry grasp thoughtful and each nip of teeth deliciously tender. And despite his best attempts, it warmed Justin, melted him, turned him molten in a way that produced a shuddering ache between his legs with Clementine's every little sign of pleasure. He wanted Clementine, wanted to take him apart moan by perfect moan, but more than that he wanted to treasure him, to put him back together again until he knew every piece of Clementine's soul and could care for it with the devotion of a priest for their god.

There was no blasphemy here, only beauty and love, a blissful sacrifice.

Justin slipped his hands beneath Clementine's sweater, fingertips dancing along soft skin as Clem sighed. He was all tight muscles around delicate bones, more crevasse than curve. Even the few little hairs beneath his navel were so fine and light that they felt silken under Justin's touch. He roamed upward, tugging Clem's sweater off as he went. Clem's light skin was untouched by the ink and scars that littered Justin's, a few small moles along one of his ribs and his nipples a stiff, aroused pink that made Justin lick his lower lip. He rolled his thumb over one and Clementine whimpered.

Clem's hands tightened, one around Justin's hip and the other in his hair, and he pressed his mouth to Justin's once more. Justin felt a sharp tinge of pain as Clementine's fang caught, followed by a rush of bliss that he swore hit him stronger than any bite that had come before. The groan it dragged from him seemed formed from the base of himself, resonating with the rest of his aching desire, and he wanted—needed—Clem's teeth in him and himself in Clem, to turn from two tugging, yearning things into one being, if only for a moment.

He shoved Clem backward onto the mattress so hard that Clem's fangs clipped Justin's mouth again, leaving him with the metallic taste of his own blood. Clementine stared up at him in only his slacks and socks, propped on his elbows with his golden hair tousled and the front of his pants straining so hard it looked deliciously painful. Justin grinned, lip still seeping. A visible shudder of hunger rolled through Clementine.

Justin dropped casually to his knees between Clementine's legs, trying to ignore the lance of pain the sudden motion shot through his back. Clem lifted to meet his mouth as he leaned in, the vampire giving one ruthless suck to Justin's cut lower lip. Justin groaned, or maybe cursed, he wasn't sure anymore, and he found the front of Clementine's pants like his limbs had a will of their own. He tugged free the first button and slipped his fingers inside them, following the soft trail of hair down to the firm length of Clem's dick. Clementine jolted against his palm with a shocked cry, hips thrusting so hard that his shoulders bumped Justin's chest. His fangs sunk into the crook of

Justin's neck, hooking into muscle with a burst of venom that had Justin tightening his grip without thinking, a lightheaded rush of power crackling like fireworks behind his eyes.

Clementine whimpered, subtle in Justin's arms but each muscle tight as a cobra about to strike. His fangs withdrew suddenly, mouth still pressed to skin as he whispered, "Justin?"

"Hey, Lemon." Justin stroked him once as he murmured it, relishing in the inhale it forced from the vampire. But beneath it he was stiff suddenly, and Justin realized why with a jolt. "Oh, god, this is your first time. I'm moving too fast." He sat back on his calf as he said it, withdrawing his hand to rest it against Clementine's stomach. "I should be asking what you want."

"It's all right." The vampire sat up properly, his legs still splayed around Justin. With his pants unbuttoned, his dick made a silhouette against the front of his white briefs, so thick and taut it was hard not to stare at. Slowly, Clementine leaned in, his gaze raking up Justin's body. His mouth found Justin's jawline in little thoughtful nibbles with just the blunts of his original human teeth. "What I want is to know if all of you tastes this good." He hummed, the sound turning nearly to a purr as it rumbled in his chest. "And then you can play around with those wonderful hands of yours. If you'd like that too?"

Justin wrapped an arm around Clementine, fingers moseying down from his lower back to slip under his pant-line. "I want to know what it feels like inside you."

"Please refrain from cutting me open. Vampires are resilient, not invulnerable."

"Fuck." Justin leaned his head against Clementine's, still trying to decide whether to groan or laugh.

"Sorry, I couldn't help myself," Clem said, tracing along the front of Justin's pants with two fingers, light and just a little painful and absolutely disastrous in its effects on Justin's dick.

"I should really just fuck you and get it over with," he grumbled.

"Well now, if *that* was meant to be sexy—"

"Dammit, Lemon." He laughed, grabbing Clementine's ass in retribution. He was rewarded with a squeak and he shifted his grip, pressing provocatively into Clementine's crack. "What I want is to slip my fingers inside you one by one, until they fill you up and make you writhe, until I can feel each tightening muscle as you come around me."

"You could write a halfway decent fic like that." Clem's voice sounded husky, his breath shorter.

"Can you act yours out?"

A growl snapped out of Clementine, and he grabbed the rim of Justin's jeans. "Maybe if you'd lay down already."

Justin laughed, letting Clementine push him gently backward. The space between his shoulder blades protested, forcing him to shift positions three times in order to find something suitable, but by then Clementine was already kneeling before him, head bowed like a convert in prayer. Justin had a flashback to the bar, of Clementine's chin resting on the seat between his legs, then reality took over full force as Clem caught the lower edge of his shirt and the front lip of his pants. He pressed them apart like he was peeling Justin open, exposing him from the tattooed crest of his lower pec and the tight stretch of his abs, down his navel and over the curve of one hip to the lowered line of his dark briefs.

The sight looked like it was doing even more unimaginable things to Clem, his eyes raking across Justin's body hungrily. Sliding two fingers along the crook from his hip toward his crotch, Clementine continued to unravel him, until Justin's anxious dick had almost slipped free of its own accord. There he stopped. Justin groaned. His body begged for the reveal, for the chill of the air and the blessed exposure and the feel of lips and teeth, the way Clementine would take him so precisely with his contemplative mouth like his orgasm was an experiment. Instead, Clementine left him like that, straining against the puckering rim of the fabric as he smiled, fangs glinting in the grainy lamplight.

He bent, pressing his lips in thoughtful kisses to Justin's hip, and worked his way down the crevice between Justin's pelvis and his thigh. The more tender the skin grew, the more teeth Clementine gave, turning just painful enough that Justin had to bite his own lip to hold back a cry. He forced himself not to shudder or buck, closing his eyes until the first prick of skin finally brought a surge of venom with it. He moaned. Clem fed in little drags and nips, a more teasing version of the intoxication from his earlier bite, but every bit as wonderful and terrible. Each break of skin made Justin ache, and when Clementine drew his thumb in little circles over the barely contained length beneath Justin's briefs, he trembled like his soul was coming apart inside him.

"You're such a tease," he moaned, the statement more pleading than any please ever could be, even if he wasn't quite sure what he was begging for yet—to come or to linger here, trapped in this exquisite tension for all time.

Clementine paused, blood on his lips and a trail of red forming slowly along the path toward Justin's crotch. With excruciating slowness, he licked up the trickle of blood and over his latest bite mark, sending shivers up Justin's spine. "I'll devour you in my own time." Clem's gaze slid up Justin's abs to where the lip of his shirt had settled. "If not your ribs, you could stand to peel *something* back…"

Smirking, Justin drew up his shirt the rest of the way, shifting in the few lurid twists of shoulder and neck that his back pain would allow before he could finally drag it over his head and toss it to the side. Clementine reached beneath Justin's legs to his ass, lifting him with vampiric strength as he tugged Justin's pants off. Justin's briefs had slipped half-off now but still, somehow, they held him in by the tip. Clementine made a sound, quizzical and delighted as he stared.

Justin spread his legs wider, tucking one arm behind his neck. "If you're going to taste *all* of me…"

"Hold still then," Clem grumbled, pressing a hand to Justin's hip and the other...

With the other, Clementine held Justin's dick in place, still just barely trapped beneath the fabric as he brought his tongue to the exposed side and licked. He made that same sound again, deeper and fuller this time, the slightest vibration from his vocal cords working its way into his motion. It sounded like a revelation. It *felt* like one too, every slide of his mouth as he explored turning to a feral hunger inside Justin.

Clementine freed Justin's tip, finally, taking it into his mouth, and Justin's world tightened to the pressure of Clem's lips and the caress of his fingers, to each drag of his mouth and the white rush of excruciating bliss with every roll of tongue and slide of throat against the head of his dick. His motions were just as perfect and precise as Justin had anticipated, but wild somehow too, shifting and recalibrating like Clementine was tuned to Justin's every ache and flutter, dragging him to the brink without letting him fall over.

As Clementine slid the edge of his fang along Justin's dick though, the burst of venom that followed made him totter so far forward he had to force himself back by sheer will. He managed to lift a hand to Clementine's wrist, gripping like he might lose his resolve if he didn't.

"No—wait. I want to come at the end, in case this is the only one I get," he said, as if by holding this out, he might make it last forever. "Can I have you, first?"

"You can have me always," Clementine whispered.

And with him, Justin suspected that wouldn't be nearly long enough.

31

CLEMENTINE

"I want to come at the end, in case this is the only one I get."

The only one for now, he meant. Not the only one forever. It was not an implication that what they had wouldn't last long enough for a second night, a second round even.

Clementine had to believe that. He was still reeling from their first kiss, even now that they'd come so much farther. He thought perhaps he'd never stop, he'd spend the rest of his life with a piece of himself locked in that moment, and another in this one, and a third when they finally—

He didn't need to start imagining it, because he was going to live it. Every touch, every bloom of blood, every moan that sprang from Justin's lips was already more immaculate than Clementine could have dreamed, anyway. He'd written these things, sure, dwelled so close to them at times that he'd had orgasms that felt like an ascension, but there had always been a little discomfort in the back of his mind, a terrible dark worry that no matter how much he yearned to experience all those things in his own life that they would always dissatisfy him. That every kiss would feel forced, half of him unable to stop fixating on the awkward sensation of saliva just inside his companion's mouth and worrying that his partner would grow hungrier with each brush of lips just as he was growing less and less inclined to continue, more and more inclined to run for the hills and live the rest of his life under a rock.

And then Justin had kissed him.

The moment their mouths met, Clementine's brain had short-circuited right past every anxiety and revulsion and straight to *oh god, fuck, yes.* It hadn't stopped screaming that since. He swore he'd never been this hard before, never been this comfortable with his mouth on someone's skin, their being mixing with his. And it was all because of Justin—compassionate, aggressive, bittersweet Justin who was delicious and wonderful—Justin who was now naked before him, easing him out of his boxers like he was paying tribute to a god.

It was so easy to expose himself for Justin, so easy just to lay there, stretching his arms above his head and one leg spread wide, and just *be* beneath Justin's gaze, letting Justin take in every crook of him in a way no one else ever had, from the points of his fangs to the desire that was already beading at the tip of his cock. Justin settled between Clementine's legs, and Clem ached like his body was already hollowing out a space for Justin, inviting him in with a desperate shiver as he displayed a tiny bottle of lube and a pair of condoms.

"Full disclaimer," Justin said. "I think Isaiah slipped these into my back pocket at La C's. I can't vouch for their hygienics."

"I'll worry over that tomorrow," Clementine replied, and he probably would, but right now all he could care about was having Justin inside him, being filled by him with both blood and body.

"Have you ever..." Justin started but swallowed.

Clementine had to fight not to roll his eyes. "I have toys, and fingers. I know what it feels like to be anally penetrated. I'm a twenty-nine-year-old virgin, not a sacred statue."

Though Justin was certainly watching as though he gazed upon something holy, each motion as thoughtful and reverent as though he was preparing to dedicate his hands and tongue in worship. It was the opposite of what Clementine had come here for—he had come to *give* his adoration, not to receive it—but Justin wore an expression of perfect contentment, of a peace so deep Clementine could have drowned in it, so full that this felt like giving back just as much as anything before it had. And it thrilled him that he *could* give this to Justin, his body as a temple of exploration, for this man and this man alone.

Justin shifted Clementine's legs up and apart, and, fingers protected by one of the condoms, he spread the lube across Clem's opening with such gentle teasing that it lit every nerve in Clementine's body. As though discovering something mystical and eternal, Justin pressed his fingers in.

It turned out that while Clementine knew what it felt like to be penetrated, he also *didn't* know what it felt like in the least, because never had it felt quite like this—the brilliant, measured chaos of having someone else in control, of submitting to the slide of Justin's fingers and the way he sought Clementine's internal pressure point with a gentle ruthlessness that had Clem tipping his head back, freeing the little sounds he'd always smothered when doing this alone. Each glide brought a fresh wave of delight and vulnerability. To have someone else touch him this way for the first time in his life, someone he trusted, wanted, cared for so thoroughly that it turned from a violation to an elation—it set him on fire. He let the feeling take him, until it was too much—too much and not enough.

"You—" Clementine cried, tipping his head back as his muscles clenched and released, clenched and released to the motion of Justin's fingers. "Inside me."

"That's not very eloquent, my Lemon," Justin mused, as though he was prepared to keep going like this all through the night. Goddamn him, Clementine was sure he'd come a dozen times by sunrise if he did, and if their uncertain future wasn't waiting for them then, he'd have jumped on that in an instant.

Instead, he bared his fangs, gasping between them. "Think of me, tight around you, shuddering under your weight, of filling me up with your—"

"Fuck you," Justin cut him off.

And he proceeded to do just that, climbing onto Clementine and entering him in one smooth thrust to the hilt, turning it into two and three and four and then Clementine lost track as Justin's fingers found his hair, and their mouths met in a momentary dance, each of them breathless and shaking against the other. Clem held onto Justin's hips, his sides, his shoulders, egging him on, until that suddenly wasn't enough.

With the utmost care, he pressed Justin back and beneath him until Clementine could ride him, setting a blinding, frenzied pace. As he did, he pulled Justin's neck into his mouth. He could feel Justin's orgasm as he bit down—could taste it in his bittersweet blood like a shot of lightning straight to the soul. Clem drank him down, riding him through it until his own peak hit, white hot and ascendant. It lasted an eternal moment, and lingered with warm, sparkling tingles as he relaxed.

Languidly, he licked closed the bite and pulled himself off of Justin. He collapsed at Justin's side, perfectly full and utterly drained all at once. "Was that everything you could have wanted?"

Justin responded by rolling up against Clementine's side, an arm stretching across Clem's stomach and his head propped on Clem's chest as he moaned, slow and contented. His other hand played aimlessly through Clem's curls. Clementine was vaguely aware of his cum slick between Justin's torso and his, but he almost didn't care to do anything about it. This already felt so right, so perfectly, exactly as it should have been. Even as the afterglow faded, Justin's nearness, his subtle, humble affection, was everything Clementine had ever wanted.

Justin tugged on one of Clementine's curls, and asked in a tired, low murmur, "How was it for you?"

Clementine smiled. "You continue to be the best thing I have ever experienced."

"Me?" Justin grunted.

"Yes, you."

Justin shifted to look at him, a slight scowl on his face, but as he lifted onto one elbow, something clearly triggered in his back. His expression tightened in pain and he lowered back down, stiffer and slower. "I should smoke," he grumbled, but made no move to get up.

Clementine slipped his hand lower, trailing it along Justin's spine in the firm but gentle caresses that had eased his agony during their previous night together. Justin's drug tin was still in Clem's jacket pocket; he hadn't asked for it back yet. It seemed so far away now though, and he would have to make Justin move in order to retrieve it for him.

In the silence, Clem's mind couldn't leave the thought of Justin's pain alone, its needlepoint focus letting in all the shit he'd been avoiding. He still had to tell Justin about Anthony. There were only so many hours he could put it off, and the longer he waited, the harder the bomb would drop.

He tipped his head back onto the mattress, staring at the dark ceiling. "Hey, so, remember back at the bar when I said there was more, but I didn't want to talk about it?"

"What's wrong, Lemon?" Justin sounded, reasonably, concerned, though a hint of forced humor came into his voice as he added, "Do I need to get my stake ready?"

"No—god, I hope not. I tried to do what I thought was best for us, for the plan and for Ala Santa, and I just don't know…" He breathed in, feeling the weight of Justin's arm across his chest, the pressure of his presence, and Clementine reminded himself that they had been through worse and come out the other side, together. "The researcher who's been making your drugs… it's Anthony. And he knows now. That's how he realized how much of a benefit it would give Natalie in her hunt if you didn't have them for even just a night. Once you beat the shit out of her, he'll know I've likely been playing him. And he might decide to take that out on you. By withholding your prescription."

Clementine wanted to believe he could spin things well enough that he'd get Anthony back on his side again—maybe if he took enough pain, volunteered himself for Anthony's personal research, Clem could convince him that he was worth keeping around. He shuddered at the thought, and Justin's body echoed his with a ragged tremble.

"Fuck." Justin had to know the odds of everything working out, and he clearly didn't put much stock in them. He shook, inhaling a fast, shallow breath, and he curled against Clementine's side. "I need those drugs…"

"I know." Clementine held him, lacing his fingers through Justin's. "And I'll find a way to keep getting them for you, I promise." He kissed Justin's hand tenderly before tucking it against his heart. "I *promise*."

"Thank you," Justin whispered, a hitch to his voice. It went low and dark as he added, "I can't protect Ala Santa without them."

Clementine sighed, squeezing his hand. "You know, you should have them not just for Ala Santa but for yourself. You deserve to live as fully as anyone else."

Justin grimaced. "You have to stop saying that shit."

"What *shit*?" Clementine felt the shift in his own body, the flair of anxiety that always came with his social confusion. This didn't feel like the same conversation they'd been having.

"This—" Justin waved his free hand uselessly. "This nonsense. About how I'm decent and deserving and the best you've ever had." He sat up, suddenly, his legs tented over Clementine's thighs and his free hand tucked to his chest as he stared away from Clem, toward the night. "You can't just keep—keep—"

"What?" Clementine sat up himself, bringing his body closer to Justin's. "I can't be kind to you? Tell you the truth?"

"But it's *not* true. That's not the real me." Justin shook his head. "You don't *know* me, Lemon."

That stung, and a bolt of panic followed it, like a stake levied over Clementine's heart. His impulse with anyone else would have been to laugh it off, to pretend it was his mistake. But with Justin all he felt was a dam opening, emotions pouring free, like that might fix the feeling that something had just fallen out from under him. "Right, so I just spent weeks thinking of no one but you, held you through your pain, and just fucked you into delirium, but I don't *know* you."

Justin groaned, offering him one small, frazzled glance. He looked, for a moment, just as panicked as Clementine now felt. "I didn't mean it like that."

"Then how did you mean it?" Clem snapped. "Is this you or is it not?" It wasn't a real question—he had seen Justin in every possible light, his anger, his pain, his exhaustion, and his love, always his love, shining through even the most stringent of his bitterness. But there was also clearly a part of Justin he still didn't understand, couldn't predict. He held Justin's hand tighter. "I know you, Justin. What I'm still trying to figure out is why the closer we get, the more you push me away after."

"I know," Justin sounded utterly and thoroughly miserable. "I know, and I'm sorry. I shouldn't have let it— god, I'm so sorry."

"Shouldn't have let what?" It crept in on Clementine slowly: the realization that he already knew, had known since before he'd even kissed Justin. Always had never meant forever. Maybe it had only meant tonight.

Justin breathed in, then out, and he looked at Clementine, longing and regret in shifting proportions across his face. "You will always, *always* have a place among my vampires." Agonizingly, finger by finger, Justin withdrew his hand from Clem's. "I'm honored that I got to be your first, but I'm not worth being your forever."

It was like Justin had pulled every fear straight from Clementine's soul and thrashed him with it. Simply being unwanted—that would have hurt. But this was worse. "You're worth that *to me*." It felt so obvious, so necessary, that he didn't understand how Justin couldn't see that. Clementine had pulled up his ribs, bared his heart, and still Justin refused to get it. "I don't want to be one of your vampires, Justin. I just want to be *yours*." And fuck, Clementine did. He wanted that more than he wanted his old job, his old life, maybe more than he wanted life itself. "I would upend my entire existence for you. And you don't owe me anything for that, but I'm still here, offering it, and you can't even look me in the eye." He felt himself leaning forward, trying to lodge himself in Justin's line of sight as though that would make him suddenly be seen. "Tell me you don't want me."

"I—fuck, who *wouldn't* want you, Lemon?" Justin swallowed and it caught in Clementine's chest like a dagger. "But..."

That single word came down like a stake, and after such a fast descent into this terrible revelation, Clementine didn't know how he was meant to survive it.

32

JUSTIN

"He will take everything you give him without considering the long-term detriment." Justin could hear Odysseus's words from the party, sudden and sharp and more pointed than a knife. *"Because he's a fool for you."*

And Justin had let that happen, over and over again. He had told himself *just once more*, convincing himself that this time would finally be enough, and now that he was staring the truth in the face, all he could see was how awful he'd been. And how wrong Clementine was to think him anything better.

Fuck, how did Justin make him understand this?

Clem was still staring, his brow tight and gaze pleading, his lower lip red from use. It scared Justin just how much he wanted to lean in, to take Clementine's mouth tenderly in his and tell him always, that he always wanted Clem. Always, and forever. He forced himself to look away instead.

"It doesn't matter how much I want you, because I can't have you." He tried to wield the knife with care, to find the gentlest words to let Clementine down, but he didn't think there were gentle words for something like this, only serrated ones, rusted and toxic. "I can't be in a real relationship, much less one where I care this goddamned deeply and I feel this fucking good. I want to ignore everything else for you, I want to give up everything for *you*, and that's the problem, because my first commitment must be to Ala Santa."

But Clementine made a sound like he still didn't understand. "Can't you have both, Ala Santa and me? I would never ask you to give up everything—anything—for me. I understand how much you love this neighborhood and I want to help you in that. We could keep doing what you've been doing, together."

It sounded so perfect, so simple. So impossible. Justin shook his head, like that would extricate the pain in his chest. "I don't deserve the life you're describing."

"I don't believe that—I *won't* believe it," Clementine snapped, fangs bared, but whatever anger he had in him seemed closer to tears than violence. "Even if it's not a romance you want, even if it's just not a romance with me, and you're trying to let me down easy." His voice caught and broke and reformed again, each word lodging into Justin's heart. "Even then, you still deserve to be cared for with the same unconditional attention that you care for everyone else in this neighborhood."

"I forfeited my right to that a long time ago, Lemon." He'd entombed it in the ground, a line of ashes beneath a guardian angel in that packed micro-cemetery where Mrs. Mendoza's family had been buried for a hundred years, where Justin's final remains would have been scattered too if he hadn't betrayed their family so thoroughly that he couldn't conceive of taking up the same space as the vampire he'd murdered. His jaw ached, and he fought not to swallow, again and again until his throat went raw.

"Why? Because you beat up and stole from them as a *kid*. Haven't you given back enough to make up for that?"

"I *can't* give enough back! I can't give Mrs. Mendoza back her son; I can't bring Jose back to life." His lungs tightened around the words. He hadn't meant to say it, but it hung between them all the same, hung within him too, an ulcer that seeped between his ribs where his burnt-black heart lay. "I can't—I can't unkill him. Nothing I do will be enough for that."

"Oh." Clementine was silent for long enough that Justin finally had to look at him. When he did, he found Clem so close that he couldn't extrapolate his expression from the tight edges of his features and the glimmer over his eyes.

"Tell me." Clementine leaned forward further still, touching the tips of his fingers to the flesh above Justin's heart, his breath hot on Justin's lips. "Let me know you, please."

How the hell was he supposed to do that, Justin wanted to ask, how could the one day every cell of him was inextricably linked to, and the thirty years of buildup and fallout surrounding it, how could that all be exposed so candidly? But he supposed he already knew the answer.

Clementine had shown it to him, had demonstrated it himself, one rib at a time.

One rib at a time.

So with excruciating care, Justin bared his heart.

"Jose was a vampire, the oldest in Ala Santa by years turned, the one who took care of them all, made sure that they all got by, together. He raised me, after my mom died—him and Mrs. Mendoza—but the more my pain grew, the more I lashed out at them. I took out my self-pity on a lot of people, but I guess I felt like Jose could handle the worst of it, since nothing I did ever seemed to break him. He was just there for me, always goddamned there for me, and I—I think maybe I hated him for that, because he was someone I could never be."

Clementine looked like he wanted to say something at that, but he didn't, and Justin continued.

"I was in such constant agony by the time I turned nineteen, that I demanded he turn me, in the hopes it would take the pain away. That was the first real time he'd refused me anything; said it wasn't worth the risk of losing me if it went wrong. But that risk was what I wanted all along, I think, the chance that maybe everything could be over with, and I—" Justin could feel the knife in his hands still, the way his voice had gone hoarse from shouting, even as Jose's was as soft and gracious as ever. "If he had only fought back." The anger that spilled out of him was all at himself, himself, staring down as Jose bled. "A cut for a cut, I told him, that if he didn't turn me, either I'd bleed out or he would. Stupid, fucked up me, I thought I'd just call for help once he gave in, but by then it was too late." Justin swore a part of his soul had died with Jose's final breath, and there was nothing he could do to resurrect it. "They saved me and took me back after, Mrs. Mendoza and Isaiah and the other vampires. They fucking shouldn't have, but since they did—since I'm here and Jose isn't—I have to make up for that. I'll never be enough to fill Jose's shoes, but I have to try."

"Justin…" It was every coo of his mother when he was a child, every one of Mrs. Mendoza's loving reprimands and Jose's undeserved blessings, every time Isaiah had said his name like it was a prayer, and it was more, rounded at the edges by Clementine's aristocratic voice and brimming with the eternity's worth of love and lust they'd just shared. "What you did was terrible. But you were a kid, a desperate kid in pain. We're all living an existence we don't deserve; we all have been given too much or too little and sometimes both at once. And wherever we can't change that, we just have to do our best with it, to take care of those we love—and that should include ourselves. It has to include ourselves. We all deserve that, at least."

Each word knocked the wind out of Justin anew. He couldn't find a response, not one he hadn't already given. He didn't deserve what Clementine was offering. He didn't. *He didn't.* He couldn't… The thought congealed in his chest, a lump he couldn't push through.

Clementine reached for him, slow and soft. He barely flinched when Justin yanked away. Instead he settled there on his knees, hands folded in his lap. "You said that I don't know you, but I think it's you who doesn't know the man you've become." He spoke with all the tenderness in the world, and that made it worse somehow, as though the gentler the words the deeper they dug. "All of this self-denial is punishment for the sins of someone who hasn't existed for a long, long time. And that helps far fewer people than you think."

A chill ran down Justin's spine. "I'm doing good for my neighborhood."

"You are, often and beautifully, in ways that Jose would be proud of," Clementine said. "Much of what you do for Ala Santa is incredible. But some of it is just to hurt yourself."

Justin couldn't handle this: the pity. The love. The lies or the truth or whatever the hell Clementine was telling him at this point. Any of it.

Justin shouldn't have brought him here. He had to make that right, as fast and firmly as he should have the first time Clementine asked to touch him, now, before it cracked him apart. Before his ribs came off.

He had pulled them up but instead of a stake he'd received a caress. And he couldn't abide that.

When he spoke next, his voice felt like it was made of gravel. "It shouldn't matter what I choose to do to myself. I'm not yours to take care of."

Clementine looked as though Justin had cut his last shard of hope from his chest with a butter knife. He wrapped his arms around himself, so small suddenly, bare and pale and alone. "All right," he whispered.

Justin could barely recall Clementine scooping his clothes off the floor and slipping into them, but somehow he was standing at the door, staring back at Justin like he was seeing God for the first and final time.

"I'll always want you, Justin. Not just always, but forever. I will keep wanting you forever—know that."

Forever. The word cut into Justin. He wanted to reach out, to turn, to assure Clementine that he wanted that too. He just couldn't have it. Whatever Clem thought, Justin wasn't Jose.

He wasn't.

All his striving, all that he gave back, and he had still gone and torn out the heart of the very next person who'd given their all for him. And despite all of that, Justin still wanted to lead him on a little longer, to take just a bit more of the grace he offered.

Luckily, Clementine was already gone.

In his place sat the little tin filled with Justin's pain medication.

Justin swallowed at the knot in his throat, but it did nothing. He ran his hands up his face instead, grabbing onto his hair as he stared at the ceiling. A wet spot had been spreading in one corner—how long had he missed that? How long had he been letting himself enjoy Clementine instead of committing to his responsibilities? When had a paycheck turned into a heartthrob?

A spear of pain shot through his back as he bent to pick up the container Clementine had left. He crouched there, one hand on the door, the other on his drugs, waiting to feel all right again, as though that were possible. He rolled a new joint with shaking fingers, lighting it and dragging in a long breath. It tasted odd, flatter and tangier than the usual chemical sweetness, but it *had* been assaulted by La C's bathroom air. He opened his window, staring aimlessly at the street as he smoked. He couldn't think of Clem. But he couldn't not think of Clem either.

So he just leaned there, eyes half closed.

And he wept.

At the start of his second joint, he should have noticed something. If his eyes hadn't been so grimy, his glasses too far away. If his thoughts hadn't been so scrambled in Clementine, in his touch, in his adoration, in the way his expression had contorted into something haunted and hurt as Justin had told him off. If he hadn't been so torn between scrubbing clear all signs of Clementine from his life—from Ala Santa altogether—and scrambling out the door after him. If he didn't have the vampire's voice as an echo in his head.

"I would upend my entire existence for you."

"You're worth that to me."

"All of this self-denial is punishment for the sins of someone who hasn't existed for a long, long time. And that helps far fewer people than you think."

Justin's traitorous gaze went to the first set of shakers in his collection, to the pieces missing between those glued back into place. He felt himself in the little figurines, a hole where the devil's chest should have been and one of the angel's wings too ruined to be called a limb any longer. He'd thrown the first at Jose, exactly two years after he'd received it, screaming that the new pain meds did nothing. The other had dropped when he'd come home from the hospital four years after that—home to the Mendozas', flowers for Jose's memorial already cluttering the kitchen—as he'd frantically shoveled everything left from his old life, the life that had murdered Jose, into a trash bag. Without Jose's reassuring guidance, he'd cut his hands trying to gather the broken pieces, until Mrs. Mendoza had wrapped her arms around him and rocked him slowly.

"Rest, my son," she'd whispered. "You can rest now."

But her son was dead, and the boy she held hadn't known how to make her see it.

That boy still existed, stronger than Clementine knew. He was very much still there, hurting in such bitter, slicing pulses through his chest, like his heart was trying to stab itself on his own ribs, kill itself with the cage that was meant to be its protection.

At first it nearly masked the pain in his back. As the ache between his shoulder blades grew through the end of his first joint, he tried not to worry. Over the last month, he had become so dependent and the pain so severe that needing a second in a row felt commonplace.

He rolled it, lit it, and returned to his mulling.

But nothing changed. Or, it did change, but the wrong way—the pain got worse. As he pulled out the container for a third try, he paused, kneeling beneath the ungainly orange of his old lamp, and scrutinized the drugs Clementine had returned to him. They were still his, certainly.

But something looked *wrong*.

Panic did seize him then, the tight, terrible thing that he'd felt when Clementine first told him that Anthony and his drug dealer were the same. But this time there was no Clementine to curl up against, to promise him the world as though he was someone worth being cared for. Justin dragged his phone from his pocket and dropped to his knees on the mattress. He hesitated only a moment, his finger lingering over Clementine's name—his Lemon; *his* goddammit—before he hit call.

33

CLEMENTINE

Clementine was crying.

It wasn't loud, or forceful, not the sobs and hair-pulling and deep soul screaming that every ounce of him felt inside, just one tear, then another. He wiped each away before they could blur the apartment steps. The click of the door closing behind him still rang in his ears.

He wanted to look back, just to chance one final glimpse through the window, even knowing it would hurt. It felt like everything from now on would only ever hurt. Justin *wanted* Clementine. He just wasn't willing to *have* Clementine, so he might as well never have wanted him at all.

God, had he been so foolish to think that what they had was turning into something more?

Clementine's feet carried him absently down the quiet street, each purposeless stride born from the sense that if he stopped moving he wouldn't be able to force another step. He didn't know where he was going anymore—back to his car? To Isaiah's, where they were meant to prepare for the hunters' arrival soon? It didn't feel right to leave Justin alone for that, but he couldn't stop hearing the last thing Justin had said, that excruciating denial of Clementine's love, uttered so rough and sharp it had seemed meant to stake straight through his heart: *I'm not yours.* And Clementine had made it so easy for him.

He *had* been a fool.

Without Justin, he didn't know what he wanted anymore, but he knew he had to leave, now, before the ragged screaming in his chest managed to burst its way free.

As he walked, the world beat and bled around him, a thrumming thing that disrupted his usually keen directional instincts, until he was on a street he couldn't quite remember. He couldn't stop moving, though. He couldn't, one block, then two, then four, telling himself with each step that he just had to get out of Ala Santa. Then he could collapse. Somewhere out of Justin's view, out of his territory, somewhere Clementine was no longer even a little bit his.

He turned down the first alleyway that looked vaguely like the one he and Justin normally met in, but instead of an angelic statue at the end of its micro-cemetery, there stood a dead tree, half fallen against the apartment building to its right. A dim lamp light blinked eerily through its branches. Clementine shifted closer to the wall of the alley, arms wrapped around himself.

As a door swung open at his side, he jumped, nearly stumbling into the person who'd stepped out. He received a hiss from between a pair of delicate fangs.

Clementine's own fangs slid out in response, but all he managed was a faint, "Sorry," as he stood there, awkward and tired and unable to summon an ounce of aggression.

It seemed enough to quell the other vampire's annoyance though. The stranger lifted his hand in a gesture of peace. His nails were painted a shade of blood-red to match the lace shirt beneath his leather jacket. With his dark hair slicked back and his stern Mediterranean features, a single diamond hanging from one ear, he looked like a modern interpretation of the old vampire mythology: beautiful and deadly. His smile only added to the effect. "Seems we're all on edge tonight."

Clementine nodded. His legs tingled, but now that he'd stopped, they felt rooted in place, caught between everything he couldn't have and everything he had to lose. He crossed his arms again to give them something to do. "Are you one of Justin's too?"

The stranger scoffed, closing the door behind him. "I'm no one's anything, love."

"It's not safe in this neighborhood right now," Clementine warned. "I'd be gone before sunup."

"I wasn't turned yesterday." On the front of the door he'd come through, the stranger began drawing a symbol with a piece of chalk. As he did, he asked, "You're here for blood, then?"

Blood?

As the vampire's chalk made one swoop, then another, Clementine recognized the symbol for a single droplet, like the emoji Justin often used while texting. Clem's heart seemed to break all over again, each tiny shattering replaying at impossible speed. He would have to find a new source of blood soon—blood that wouldn't be rich and delicious like Justin's, wouldn't come with his soft sighs and the feel of his skin, wouldn't make Clementine ache between his legs. Blood from a source that didn't fuck him like he was holy, then tell him to find someone better.

He swallowed back the tears draining from his throat, and asked, "Are you the blood dealer?"

"Hardly. He'll be setting up shop inside." The stranger narrowed his eyes, his gaze drawing down Clementine's body. His lips twitched into something that could have been a smile or a sneer, where that space between seemed the whole point of the expression. "I haven't seen you around. Where've you been buying?"

Clementine took a step back. "I—I'm not. I mean," his voice caught, "I had someone, but I think he's…" The pocket of his pants vibrated. He drew his phone out on instinct, his fingers shaky. Justin's name showed across the incoming videocall screen, overlaying a picture of his bittersweet smirk. "He's calling me."

"Ah. *That* kind of someone." The stranger nodded, and his brow lifted as they stood there. "Are you going to answer?"

"I don't know." He wanted to—he wanted so badly to hear Justin's voice, to see his face, to hope again. Yet he couldn't seem to swipe. "I adore him. I—I think I'm ready to give up a lot of things I've spent my life holding onto, for him. But he won't accept that. He doesn't believe he's worth that kind of love."

The screen went dark again.

One missed video call from Justin Yu.

The other vampire sighed, tucking his hands into the pockets of his fitted leather coat. "Stranger to stranger? I'm still pining for a guy I met one time, four months ago, and he's probably forgotten I exist. Love is imperfect—it's downright fucked up sometimes, honestly—but you can't manhandle it into shape and you can't force anyone to be yours."

"Then what *can* you do?"

The stranger shrugged. "I'm still figuring that out." He paused, then fiddled a black card out of his wallet, handing it over. "If you do end up needing blood, text this. I'll get you covered."

Andres Serrano, he/they, freelance acquisitions. Clementine thanked him with a nod. As he tucked the card away, he thought for a moment that his hand brushed something hard, but at the bottom of the pocket he found nothing.

From inside the blood seller's door, someone shouted Andres's name. He turned for the handle. Before he could step inside, Clem replied.

"You just keep loving them, I think, in whatever way is best."

"If you say so," Andres shrugged, but as he vanished behind the door, Clementine swore his expression changed, his aloofness sliding away to reveal the same deep dejection and strangled hope Clem felt himself.

And the love, he thought. Buried beneath it all, there was still love.

That felt like the answer, painful, but bright too, and hopeful in a way that nothing else was. He could keep loving Justin, even if he failed at everything else. He could keep showing him what he was worth, and even when it wasn't enough, at least Clementine would know that he was bringing something true and beautiful into the world.

That was what being good was, wasn't it? Not perfection, not success, but devotion and kindness and, if he had to, the ability to finally let go.

But Clementine wasn't ready to let Justin Yu go, not yet. Perhaps not ever.

He drew out his phone, steadying himself against the gentle buzz of it whirring away again. And this time he hit accept.

The screen opened to a darkness impenetrable from Clem's side of the screen and the faintest "Hey" from Justin.

Before he could keep speaking, Clementine cut in, so loud and strong he surprised even himself. "I refuse to give up on you," he said, not caring that his voice was drenched in emotions too thick and wet to parse, or that it echoed down the alley, a one-sided declaration of devotion. "I meant it when I said I'll want you forever. You *are* mine. Whether you claim me or not, you are mine to care for and mine to protect, mine to adore and mine to pardon, and you can push me away if you must, but my love is not going anywhere."

For a moment there was silence, but for a subtle pounding in Clementine's ears, and then his phone speaker gave a scratchy whine.

"Clementine? Sorry—can you hear me?"

Clementine's heart sank. He hadn't heard. He hadn't heard, or he hadn't wanted to hear.

The screen lightened as Justin stepped in range of a streetlamp, the silhouette of his apartment behind him. Each step he took appeared stiff and pained, his jaw set.

Clementine knew he was meant to be acting as though his drugs were destroyed, in case the hunters sent in a spy ahead of time. Still, his voice caved as he asked, "Justin?"

"There, I think you're back." He *sounded* pained, too, and as he moved by another light, the rigidity of his movements made Clem wince, each line of him too harsh and fragile.

A chill rolled over Clementine's skin. "What is it?" He had no mind for making dramatic promises anymore, only for living them out, in whatever way Justin needed him to.

"It's my drugs."

Clementine was already running down the alley, back the way he'd come. He still wasn't certain of his own location, but some part of him knew where Justin was, pulled there as though by a red ribbon tied to the last rib in his chest. His vampire speed sprung him forward at a rate that no human could have met, much less sustained, but in that moment he didn't care who saw, who knew, who judged, so long as it brought him closer to Justin.

"Did you do something to them when you took them out?" Justin's tone was pleading, not accusatory, and the glance Clementine managed at the phone screen showed his brows tight and his eyes wide. "Please, if you know anything..."

"No," Clem gasped, not from the effort of the run but the strain on his heart. "I have no idea—Justin, what's wrong with them?"

"They aren't working."

"Not working," Clem repeated, like that could get the statement to make more sense. Another block down, he recognized a side street enough to cut up it toward Isaiah's apartment. That seemed to be where Justin was heading now.

"I went through two full joints and nothing."

Clementine shook his head. "You roll them daily, they should be stable against anything I did—air, limited light," he kept his voice down, lifting the phone's butt to his mouth. "I even sterilized the container I temporarily moved them to as best I could. They should be fine."

"Tell that to my back."

"God, Justin, I don't know what else to do. I'm sorry."

As he said it, he rounded the final corner, dodging the set of dumpsters and sprinting into the alley outside Isaiah's apartment. On the other end of the street, Justin appeared. He looked even more desolate in life, not simply in pain but in misery too.

"I'm so sorry," Clementine whispered again. Call still running, he rushed to Justin, throwing his arms around him as gently as he could, mouth in Justin's hair and apologies bubbling like a stream between his lips.

Justin remained stiff in his embrace, and as Isaiah's door opened to their right, Justin disengaged himself so awkwardly that Clementine felt something tear in his chest. His vision blurred around the edges. He forced himself to step back.

Justin stared at him, his fear and pain almost palpable. "If not you, then what happened?"

Clementine pushed his hands into his pockets to give them something to do. "There's nothing that should have…"

But as he said it, his fingers bumped something—the small, solid object he'd sworn he'd knocked into twice already tonight. Again, he found nothing at the bottom of the pocket, but as he withdrew his hand, his thumb tapped it once more, just beneath the fabric. His blood went cold. Carefully, he peeled the flap of his coat open, to the little pucker of material that made a makeshift secondary pocket on the inside. Tucked into it by a piece of lab tape was the microwave radiation module he'd left at the end of his desk last week.

"God," he whispered. But this was clearly the work of no deity, just a sociopath with a doctorate. He turned to the open doorway, two other vampires now peeking out behind Isaiah. "Get me a thermos."

For a moment no one moved, then they all burst inside, too fast to track. By the time Clementine entered the apartment, Isaiah had a metal water bottle ready for him, its green exterior paint chipped and the rainbow flag sticker nearly rubbed off.

Clementine slid the microwave radiation orb into the bottle and capped it. "We'll have to get rid of it later."

Justin watched him in horror. "What was that?"

"It's from Vitalis-Barron's labs. Anthony probably slipped it into the flap behind my pocket when we were at my office earlier. He must have suspected that I wasn't going to betray you, but he knew that whatever I did, I'd be near you. Near your drugs. The long-term proximity breaks down their active ingredients."

Clementine could see the understanding bloom across Justin's face. They had planned to lure Natalie and her friends into a trap, but that trap relied on Justin's ability to fight, and without him, the hunters would have the advantage. And they would keep having it, for as long as Anthony felt like denying Justin, perhaps until every last vampire had been seized from within Ala Santa's borders.

"Puta'ng ina," Isaiah cursed, slipping close to Justin to make the gentle soothing motions between his shoulder blades that Clementine so longed to.

Justin didn't seem eased by them the way he usually was. "There's no way to turn back its effects? To get my drugs working again?"

"No." The word came out rough and agonized, though it held only a fraction of the grief Clementine felt. "I'm sorry."

Justin pressed his palms to his face, his shoulders trembling once beneath Isaiah's hold. He dragged in a breath, long and bitter, and dropped his arms to his sides. "We can't lure the hunters here if I'm not strong enough to fight them—we have to stop this."

Clementine lifted his chin, trying to project Justin's unyielding confidence. "Stopping them will be impossible at this point. We can move the vampires out, but that will only delay the inevitable."

"Then we delay it!"

"No," Isaiah cut in, and around him the other vampires agreed—four of them, with a fifth appearing in the hall to the bedrooms. Their belongings were piled around the living space, from trash bags to duffels, a sleeping bag rolled up on the couch and a blow-up mattress half-deflated in one corner. "We've all come because you've been protecting us. Let us protect you now. They did this to you and we will finish them for it."

But Clementine knew it was not so simple as that, not when they were vampires and the hunters were humans. A heroic defense by a non-vampire like Justin might have gained them traction online, but portrayals of vampires fighting against humans was a normality, and the vamps' success a regular fear of the wider human populace.

"They'll have holy silver, Isaiah. They'll destroy you," Justin replied, his face tipped so close to his friend's that they nearly touched. His teeth pulled back in something that had no resemblance to a smile. Clementine could see the love in that expression, though, and Isaiah threw it right back at him, not with longing or lust for once, but a fierce devotion that seemed to give everything and ask for nothing in return.

Clementine loved him for it.

But Justin was right: the vampires couldn't fight back, not on their own. They weren't the only people in Ala Santa who loved Justin, though.

Clementine stepped forward, not between Justin and Isaiah but into their midst, brushing the tips of his fingers to their arms. "I might have a better idea, if you'll listen."

Justin didn't hesitate. "Always."

But he did step back. Stepped away from them both.

For a moment, Clementine felt like he could still hear his own admission, his own promises echoing back from that blood dealer's alley, and Justin had again refused to acknowledge them. But Clementine was here regardless, here for Justin whatever the cost.

And he was counting on the fact that he wouldn't be the only one.

34

JUSTIN

For all his bravado, Justin could feel the fight trying exceptionally hard to abandon him.

His pain drugs were unusable, everything he had, everything he was likely ever to get from Anthony Hilker, all gone in one night. Back at his apartment, Clementine had promised he'd find a way around Hilker's skepticism, but now Justin wasn't so sure. If the man had already suspected Clem enough to do this, Anthony probably wasn't going to let Clem waltz back into Vitalis-Barron without repercussions.

That was all assuming the new plan worked, anyway, and Justin didn't lose all of his vampires come morning.

Without them, he wasn't sure he deserved his drugs anymore. He had already been living on borrowed time, anyway.

"All of this self-denial is punishment for the sins of someone who hasn't existed for a long, long time. And that helps far fewer people than you think."

Justin grimaced, trying to dislodge Clementine's voice from his head. The shudder only managed to shoot fresh pain along his spine.

Isaiah shifted the steady, gentle motion of his hands, lifting his chin from Justin's shoulder. He said nothing, only watched Justin, scowling softly. Justin tried to grin back, letting all his fear turn to sharpened points and angel wings.

Across the apartment, the rest of his vampires were preparing for whatever was to come. After a long and aggressive debate, they'd decided to stick—mostly—to the old plan, but with a few extra volunteers. Justin never would have permitted any of them to act as bait, if not for the plan Clementine had proposed.

Somehow Clem, who of all the people here knew this neighborhood the least, had also been the one to see them for who they were—perhaps had seen all of Ala Santa for what it was exactly *because* he'd spent his life among people who didn't hold the same love and unconditional loyalty. And Justin's vampires had backed him up.

Now it was the darkest part of the night, the endless, quiet wait before the dawn, and they worked with Clementine like he was one of their own. Watching him and Marcus board up the apartment's one primary window, seeing him smile and laugh and joke in ways he hadn't with the guests of Sissy's party, warmed Justin's heart. But it also terrified him, just how well Clementine could fit here, could fit into his life. Could keep pulling him from his debt forever.

Isaiah watched them both—him and Clementine in turns—a scowl fixed on his face.

"What?" Justin grumbled.

Isaiah shook his head. His scowl, Justin realized, held only confusion and contemplation, the former vanishing quickly. "You love him."

Love.

"You can push me away if you must, but my love is not going anywhere."

Justin had heard every damned and beautiful word Clementine spoke over that video call like a shot to the chest. And he had waited so long, so long trying to find a way to deny Clementine with a tongue that wanted only to worship him and lungs that refused to breathe any air but his, until finally Justin had taken the coward's route and pretended not to have heard at all.

Like it had a will of its own, his gaze fixed on the lines of Clementine's face, the certainty in his jaw and the deliberate way his fingers moved as he shifted the nail he was attempting to hammer, a wedge of his golden curls sticking out farther on the right side of his head. He may very well have given up his future for this, yet here he was, choosing them over the only life he'd known.

And Justin could see all too clearly where this new path might take Clementine, and how selfishly easy it would be to entangle their futures, always, and perhaps something a little like forever. If Justin could disavow his promises to Ala Santa.

"All of this self-denial is punishment for the sins of someone who hasn't existed for a long, long time."

Deny Ala Santa, by no longer denying himself.

Justin swallowed. "And you got this love theory from that how again…?"

"The lemon—"

"That's my nickname for him, thank you."

Isaiah rolled his eyes. "The *clementine* isn't even from Ala Santa, yet you keep staring at him like he's the world and you're not sure whether you're the moon or a meteor. I can't imagine anything but love would do that to you." His solemn expression turned loose, a little happy but a little sad, too. "He makes you look… tender, I suppose. Like you've taken a breath for the first time in ten years."

Justin knew the decade reference was just an outrageous number meant to over dramatize, but it twisted in his chest like a knife.

"Much of what you do for Ala Santa is incredible. But some of it is just to hurt yourself." That accusation had stung with irrational irritation before, but as the bitterness faded it left its uncomfortable truth behind in a crust that Justin knew would take time to chip away. And he had to chip away at it. If he could bear it.

"It's a good look on you. And as much as it pains me, I would support you two—not just for tonight. If you won't have me, then you grab that beautiful vampire and you let him tease you forever."

Though Justin ached at the pain in Isaiah's voice, something in his marrow seemed to buzz at the thought, an impossible, incomprehensible feeling rushing through him like thunder and fire and ice. He tore his attention away from Clementine, trying to focus on the here and now, his body in this place, pain still aching between his shoulder blades with every motion. "We have to live through the morning first."

"And then?"

"Then... we'll see."

The morning came in slow, tense silence. Once all the possible work had been finished, Clementine seemed not to know what to do with himself any longer. Justin watched him draft and redraft a message to Odysseus—in case the plan failed spectacularly, he said—and once he'd hit send, he began to pace with such a deliberate routine that it hurt to watch, each stride exactly the same distance, each turn grinding down the floor in the same place, his jaw set and his chin up. When he finally stopped, he went so still that Justin fought the urge to check if he was alive. That, at least, was an easier battle than the one Justin had with his desire to grab the vampire by the front of his sweater and pull him close, to brush at his hair and press taunting kisses along his jawline, to lure him into the bathroom and fuck him until neither of them had any room left for fear. To simply talk with him.

That desire was the worst by far because every time Justin thought of it, he did not think he could stand for anything less than to bare his heart once more, and he still did not know what he'd be showing Clementine if he did. They had already flayed each other to the brink of heartbreak, and Justin couldn't risk that again.

So every time Clem gave him the opportunity, he looked away.

Justin thought he'd finally break under the strain of Clem's mere presence when the sun finally peeked over the horizon and the warning call came.

"A white van," Marcus relayed, "Coming up Jackson Street, four blocks. Three now."

The vampires were on their feet instantly, all eight of those he'd let stay springing into action as Justin followed far more slowly, groaning with every movement. Ten hours without his medication and already each step made his vision tunnel, a constant scream filling the back of his mind and stealing what little of his attention remained. He positioned himself near the door all the same. If he could knock even one hunter down before they incapacitated him, then he would suffer it happily.

His vampires scurried behind furniture barricades, retrieving weapons and pulling up hoods. Clementine tucked himself into the hall, his phone ready. He nodded to Justin. Justin nodded back.

Through the strategic slits of the window boards, he could make out the deep, blue-tinged shadows of the alleyway against the glimmering early sunlight that sparkled down the main street. Then tires screeched.

The van stopped just outside the front entrance, and a few moments of banging later, the door crashed inward. Justin slammed his fist straight into the first hunter's jaw. Pain shot through his back—more pain than the hunter was likely feeling—but it was a pain he knew well, a pain he could push through just a bit longer. Just one more punch. One more.

The fight turned to a blur around him as five more hunters spilled into the room, wearing vests beneath their coats that looked meant for bullets, not the blades and fangs of the vampires. It was all Justin could do to stay on his feet, to hit back more than they hit him, to not flounder as one after another of his vampires screamed and whimpered and shied away, their bodies reacting to the two bastons of holy silver Natalie held and the smaller charms the others carried. Within the chaos of the fight, the hunters attacked systematically. Natalie plunged in to leave a vampire wailing and incapacitated with her bastons, then gave room for her partners to wrap a bit of holy silver around the overpowered vamp's neck as they were bound and gagged by a tuft of fabric.

Marcus and Paola fought together, nail and fang, but welts appeared on their skin and their battle cries turned limp and hollow as the holy silver was clamped to their necks. Isaiah was caught with a demonic shriek, his hands over his head and his bun half-fallen. Ana Lee went down next, then Soren, Mya and Whitney barely managed to hole themselves up in the bathroom. And Clementine... Clementine was thankfully absent.

No matter how hard Justin tried to get to Natalie, to force her attention onto him, someone else always stood in his way, ready to leave him gasping through his back's agony, time seeming to jump around him as the hunters progressed. But he was not his vampires' greatest weapon, and he never had been.

Justin was just one man, in pain and exhausted. But he had a neighborhood. A family as massive as a single heart could hold.

As the hunters dragged their first victims out of the door, Justin heard them, a chant like a choir rising up from the cracks of their old streets and filtering through the cemeteries, scattering the feathers of the angel of death. They stormed around the hunters' vehicle, ordinary humans who'd rallied behind a series of texts and phone calls and fists pounding on their front doors in the early morning darkness.

"Our vamps belong here!" they shouted. "Our vamps belong in Ala Santa."

They waved hastily formed signs with slogans like *don't take our vampires* and *cruelty to vamps is cruelty to us all.* Clementine stood at their forefront. Behind his focused expression beamed something like pride, his phone aimed at the faces of the hunters emerging with their victims. Around him, others filmed, too, cameras lifted beside protest boards. They could only hope that the pressure would be enough to force the hunters down—force them out of Ala Santa for good.

Natalie stumbled out the door and into her panicking crew, a whimpering Soren in her grip. Her face drained of color as though a vampire were stealing away her blood, her attention flashing between the crowd and the half dozen vampires they'd caught and back to Justin, still hunched and panting behind them. He locked eyes with her.

He could see the understanding consume her as her gaze jumped from person to person—humans planted in the sun, prepared to stand in her way, to push back regardless of how hard she shoved. Whether or not they could tie her party back to Vitalis-Barron, the fallout Natalie would face if she was caught harming humans in the process of her vampire captures would not be worth a couple of potential lab rats.

Her fingers peeled off Soren and she jerked away like she'd been stung.

"Get in—just get in the van," she called. "Abort!"

Hope surged in Justin's chest.

But her voice was hoarse, and half her team seemed not to hear her. One of them reached for the gun in his belt as he continued lugging Isaiah toward the car, out of Justin's view. A bullet fired. Then another.

Justin couldn't see where they landed, but the effect it had on the crowd was immediate, screams and dropped banners, people shoving their loved ones out of the potential line of fire.

No.

"Stop!" Natalie shouted. But she couldn't contain her team anymore, could barely shove forward fast enough to follow her hunters as they charged the van, pulling guns on the remaining protestors in aggressive desperation, their bound victims still dragged and carried and forced along with them. Justin barely caught sight of Isaiah's panicked expression as one of the hunters tossed him into the back of the van.

Justin sprinted after them. The world tunneled, turning to an impressionist painting of sparks on black with each painful wave that rolled through his spine. He was already stumbling by the time he reached the apartment door, slumping instinctively into it. The van tore down the alley as the human protestors scrambled to help each other out of its way. A trash truck backed across their path, blocking that end of the tiny backstreet as the driver leaned out, shouting the protestors' chant.

The van squealed to a halt. It began to reverse.

There was nothing to stall it this time, no other vehicles to come to their rescue. The protestors were already spilling past Justin to attend to the remaining three vampires or help their battered neighbors out of the way. Beside him, Mrs. Mendoza howled into her phone for her no-good-lazy-too-short supply driver to hurry up with the truck, but by the time it reached them from down the block it would be too late. He could see the path the van would take, backing out of the alley and turning, speeding off with his vampires. With Isaiah.

Clementine still held his camera up, secretively aimed toward the incoming vehicle, one arm over his head as he charged into the sunlight. He called to Justin, hand extended, and together they followed the van. It shifted back into drive as it hit the main street, nearly colliding with Mrs. Mendoza's delivery truck before taking off eastbound.

"We're losing them," Justin shouted, staggering to Clementine's side.

Clem wrapped a supportive arm around his waist. He bared his fangs, his eyes bright, the light touch of the sun making his hair gleam. "At least we know where they're going."

Clem drove with his visor down and a delicate silken scarf he'd tugged out of the glove compartment wrapped clumsily around his neck and lower face. When Justin had protested that he'd still get sun-poisoned, he'd only shrugged. Between them, the most massive beach umbrella Justin had ever seen bounced up and down against the center console with each bump.

Justin cursed through his teeth, tightening his grip on Clem's still-recording phone as he shot off a text to Odysseus at Clementine's command. "In case we don't come back," he insisted. "If we vanish, someone with legal knowledge should have evidence of where we were headed. She'll do something. Even if it's not *for* me, she's good like that."

No response came back though—at least none that Justin noticed.

The backs of his eyes stung. His toes tingled. Something hot and itchy seemed to creep around the base of his spine. Those were the things he focused on, instead of the agony flaring through his back and pounding like war drums in his head. The world skipped in and out of focus, but through it all he knew one thing: they were running out of time.

They caught up to the hunters' van at the eastern edge of the financial district, but as they raced down the final stretch toward the entrance of the Vitalis-Barron research compound, they were still no closer to rescuing anyone.

"We have to crash into them," Justin commanded.

To Clementine's credit, all he said was, "Where?"

"Under the big bridge. It can't be in the sun or the holy silver—" Justin inhaled sharply as a fresh wave of pain hit him. His reality jolted, muddling Clem's reply, but the freeway overpass and its last chance at shade was looming closer and closer, their speed increasing since they'd reached the edge of the commonly used roads.

"Now?" Clem asked.

"Now!"

As Justin spoke, the van's front passenger door swung open. Natalie leaned out, pistol ready. Clementine gave a guttural scream and swerved the car. They hit the hunters' van at an angle.

Clementine's car jolted, the back half lifting into the air as the van twisted, then tipped, Natalie's body tumbling out in a blur. The pressure of Justin's seat belt caught up to him just as his fear did, the flood of terror keeping him conscious for one final second before their own vehicle arched, the front passenger side bumping violently into the road's side wall, and everything caved in.

35

CLEMENTINE

Clementine's car creaked against the long streak of paint and crushed cement its front passenger side had carved into the road's wall. Hisses and pops came from the mutilated hood as his massive beach umbrella slowly fell through the shattered gash it had made in the windshield.

Clementine moaned, taking stock of his limbs. Two legs, two arms, one pounding head. He managed to unclick his buckle. After pushing the remaining bit of pole from the beach umbrella out the broken window, he went for Justin's seatbelt.

As it released, Justin slumped forward, hissing in pain.

Clem cursed and reached for him. "Are you okay?"

"No," Justin grunted, lifting his head to squint through the broken windshield. "But I will be. Once we save them."

Clementine could see the van, lying on its side three yards from the bridge's protection, its back door flung open. Within, Justin's vampires were righting themselves as best they could with their hands still bound, Isaiah at their lead. So far, it seemed their captors were all trapped or unconscious. But the vampires were just as trapped, Clementine knew. So long as the holy silver was strapped to their necks, the few yards of sun that blocked them off from the rest of the world might as well have been a brick wall.

Clementine flung himself from the car, helping Justin out afterward. His every flinch and whimper was painful, and the way his eyes rolled at his first step onto the asphalt made Clementine want to scoop him up and carry him home. He leaned on Clementine like he would crumple without the support, half tucked into Clementine's arms already.

Clem should have said no to the crash, thought of something better—something that wouldn't have hurt Justin like this. But there hadn't been enough time.

There still wasn't.

From outside the wrecked car, Clementine could see what else lay between them and the van. Just beyond the bridge's shade, Natalie pulled herself from the street by one leg, favoring the other where it twisted at the knee. Her face looked ghostly, a long gravel-filled scrape ruining her forehead, and when she met their gazes, the rage that shot across it was almost piteous.

Clementine felt Justin stiffen alongside him.

"Behind the wheel," Justin muttered, and Clementine glanced back at where he'd helped prop the still-filming phone against the front wheel of their car, before realizing it was the van wheel that he meant, and the dark form of Natalie's pistol.

It was too far into the sun for the vampires to make a grab at, but if Natalie noticed, and she chose to run for it...

For now, she seemed to be struggling just to stay standing, scowling like she wanted to murder them by sight alone. Like she wanted to murder Clementine especially. "Fucking bastard, you *set us up.*"

Clementine was so focused on her that he startled when it was Anthony's calm and controlled voice that answered.

"Fucking bastard, indeed." He must have known they were coming, and rushed down Vitalis-Barron's driveway to reach them, but he looked as contained as ever, half a smile at his lips and a document neatly curled in one hand. His gaze traveled the scene and casually he moved towards Natalie, staying just out of range of the bridge's protective shade. "I'd expected *something* dastardly from you, Clementine, but certainly not *this.*"

"Anthony," Clem hissed.

"Fuck you," Justin spat the curse, trembling in Clementine's arms.

Anthony's attention shifted to him just briefly, sympathy that could have just as easily been genuine or completely fabricated shifting across his features. "No hard feelings, Justin. I hope you know this is purely business."

"Puta'ng ina mo."

Anthony only lifted a brow. As he came up beside Natalie, he wrapped his arm around her, muttering soothingly into her hair. For all her anger, she melted against his embrace so openly that it hurt to watch.

Anthony kissed her forehead and turned his attention back to their surroundings. His gaze caught on Isaiah, where the vampire hovered at the end of the van's shade, his tiny locs loose around his half-bare shoulders as he breathed in pained, panicked gasps and wriggled against his bonds. Anthony hummed to himself.

"This is some mess you've made," he said. "But I want to believe we can all still walk away with something here."

Every second they let him prattle was a second lost, but with Justin still unable to walk on his own and too much holy silver nearby for Clementine to risk the sun, there was nothing else they could do. Then Anthony held up the paper he'd carried there, revealing a familiar system of lines, and Clementine could focus on nothing else.

"See, I have the last copy of Justin's drug formula."

Justin cursed again, clinging to Clementine with such force that it seemed he was the only thing grounding Justin in place. He clung back, like that could hold them both together, as Anthony continued.

"I can burn it, *or* you can have it, along with whatever's left of your life that you haven't botched, and my help in the drug's production, if you trust me enough for that," he said. "In exchange, you give Nat and I the one vampire she originally wanted, the one you promised us. We won't even hand him over to Vitalis-Barron. I'll take him myself, use him for all the same valuable science that you wanted done for vampires. Natalie will have her statement of vengeance, you and Justin will get your lives, I'll get my research, and that pretty specimen"—he glanced at Isaiah once more, one half of his teeth baring in a smile—"will probably even live through it. In fact, I'll do my best to make sure he does, which is more than Vitalis-Barron will offer him."

Give up Isaiah. To Anthony's experiments. For Justin's medication. The idea encircled Clementine's mind, a terrible, incalculable thing he wasn't sure how to compute.

But Isaiah took one glance between them, from Anthony's winning smile to Justin's pain, and said, "I'll do it. Give Justin his meds, I'll do whatever you want."

"Like hell you will, Isaiah." Justin spat back, almost dragging Clementine into the sunlight with the force of his leaning. "I'll go the rest of my life in agony before I lose him."

"I was not asking you," Anthony said. And he looked at Clementine, no different than if he'd been requesting to run a sample off a piece of lab equipment that Clem's team had been using that quarter. "This was *our* deal, Clementine."

"Because you were blackmailing me," Clem objected, something almost like a laugh tightening in his throat. "Did you ever really plan to tell Blood about me? Or was this your game all along, to see how much you could poke and prod me before I broke?"

"You want the truth, Clementine?" Anthony shrugged. "At first, I did hope that turning you would get you out of the way, but I cared more just to see if I could do it."

A cold rush crashed over Clem, the sounds of one car, then another whipping across the freeway above echoing oddly in his skull.

Anthony kept speaking, his words oddly distant suddenly, "I almost tested it on myself, damn the risks, but I thought hey, why not kill two birds with one stone? If your work slipped or if Blood found out, or if you died during the turning, it would have left me with the senior associate position, and on the rare chance you pulled everything off, you'd be more amenable to the kind of research I was doing."

"You... turned..." Clementine found himself sinking. His grip on Justin tightened.

"No," Justin breathed, and at least Clementine wasn't the only one failing to wrap his head around it.

Anthony was human—he was standing in the sun like it was nothing. He couldn't have... he couldn't...

"How else did you think it happened?" Anthony snorted. "Alone in the lab, getting drugged by your own coffee, right after Dr. Robinson's retirement announcement? I slept with holy silver around my neck the first week, convinced you'd come for my throat. But you never even *suspected*."

"You *did* this to me?" The nausea building in Clem's stomach burst like bile at the back of his throat. He'd been right: he'd never deserved this.

It wasn't his fault. He hadn't fucked up protocol or carelessly fallen asleep on the job. Anthony hadn't even targeted him for being anything more than convenient and good at his job. There was nothing Clementine could have done to see it coming or prevent it. The understanding, finally, after so long overthinking and worrying, should have consoled him.

Instead, it made him feel hollow and bitter. Whether he'd deserved his vampirism or not, it was still ugly and traumatic and unchosen, and he shouldn't have had it forced on him. He could hear that sentiment echoed by the vampires in the van, their fear not enough to overwhelm their horror at his situation. Clementine was one of them, after all. For all their differences, he was still a vampire, and that left parts of him that they would always understand, many having also faced the terror of turning unexpectedly, the trial of trying to adjust to a world which no longer wanted them... an old life taken from them with nothing they'd done to deserve it.

But vampirism wasn't something *anyone* deserved. It just *was*.

And it was a part of them, Clementine realized, a thing that bound them together and a huge part of who they were, and for all the pain the world had inflicted upon them for it and all the work that was still to be done, he found he could hate Anthony for turning him, but Clementine could not hate being a vampire.

He could only do his best with his own vampirism and strive to support the vampires around him.

Anthony was still talking, though, answering Clementine like this was merely a question of facts. "It was incredible, actually. I wasn't sure it would work. You were an experiment, in a way. The basement had recently lost a specimen and I was able to collect the venom sac before the body was disposed of. I injected and drained you in doses, to be safe. It took you far longer to show any signs than I anticipated. At the end there I thought I would run out of venom."

The way the man spoke of it, he could have been recounting a typical drug development instead of the initial desolation—and eventual transformation—of a life. It made Clementine nauseous. He could not truly hate being a vampire, sure, but he could certainly hate Anthony for the carelessness and cruelty of his part in it.

The same dismay and anger split across Justin's expression, and Clementine had an instant to revel in the ferocity of it before that adoration turned to horror as Justin tore out of his grip, throwing himself into the light.

36

JUSTIN

It was simple:

Justin Yu was in love with Clementine Hughes.

And this man before them—this heinous piece of shit who called himself a scientist and made custom prescriptions for the poor and needy while experimenting on his own coworker without permission—this man had risked Clementine's life, upended it, and used that to blackmail him. Therefore, he was going to die. Justin's drugs be damned; if he could rip the spine out of Anthony Hilker's body now, he would never complain about his own again.

That pain seemed like nothing suddenly, the impending darkness choked back by his sheer determination as he lunged forward.

Through the midst of his tunneled vision, he could see Natalie moving too, but he didn't care—he could take them both down, turn them to matching blood pulps for the horror they'd put his vampires and Clementine through. Clementine, who was only his vampire because of these people's cruelty.

Too late, he realized that Natalie wasn't coming toward him; she was moving away. Toward her pistol.

She swept it up as Anthony stepped back, her aim rising to meet Justin's heart.

Behind her, Isaiah was already moving, half his shoulder shoved into the sun, but Paola pinned him in place with a snarl, and it was Marcus who charged forward, flinging himself at Natalie from behind. He crashed into her back with a feral shriek so inhuman it could have come straight from legend, sinking his fangs into her neck and tearing.

Natalie's pistol fired, but the bullet kicked into the pavement at Justin's stumbling feet—Justin's collapsing feet—and as he dropped to the asphalt, the recoil chucked the gun from Natalie's grasp entirely. She crumpled onto her injured leg with a scream. Marcus let her go. He took a step back. Toward the van's shade.

The holy silver around his neck gleamed. Justin had just enough time to panic for him, to feel the growing reaction of his flesh as though it were happening to Justin himself, as a crust of red and black ignited along Marcus's skin, starting beneath the holy silver. It left the flesh beneath it ashen, a charred husk from the fires of Pompeii. He lurched back again, but the process was too fast, too deadly, too consuming.

It spread across his chest, searing off the bulk of his clothing and drawing a gurgle of decompressed air from him before it shot down his legs, stilling them permanently. When his gaze met with Justin's for the final time though, the pain in it faded. His terrified expression stilled in rings of red, finishing him off like a flame going out, and what remained was a fierce acceptance.

Marcus's body toppled. It broke apart as it hit the ground.

From inside the van, Paola sobbed.

It felt like a sound straight from Justin's chest, a wailing thing of bitterness and guilt and anguish. Someone had to pay for this. It should have been him, he thought, numbly. It should have been him.

Natalie bled from Marcus's bite as Anthony held the wound. Justin could still reach them, probably, maybe. If his legs would work again. If he could force himself to his feet.

But he couldn't. There was too much darkness closing in, his lungs no longer seeming to draw air, a cry of pain like a banshee echoing through his spine. His foot dragged on the asphalt as he tried to pull it under him. It bumped Natalie's fallen pistol, and carefully, he lifted it up. Still lopsided on the ground, he pointed it at Anthony.

The man's head shot up, fear flashing across his face for the first time, and Justin felt a burst of his original anger returning, burning brighter and hotter for the pain of Marcus's loss.

"You ruined Clementine's life," Justin whispered.

"Did I?" Anthony snarled in return. "He was doing just fine before he threw his lot in with your people. He had his fancy suits and his impending promotion and a pretty neck to bite, and that glorious vampiric strength and immunity to boot. What I did only made him better."

"*Better?*" Justin hissed.

But Clementine cut him off. "Anthony's right—my life isn't ruined."

Justin trembled as he tried to glance back, the pistol still tight in his grip and his head reeling beneath a dozen different kinds of pain: emotional, mental, physical, spiritual even—for what god would have created something so beautiful, so good, as Clementine and placed him into this hell?

He looked paler than ever, hovering at the edge of the shade, but his voice was full and rich over the distant hum of sirens. "But everything I've accomplished is mine alone. It's not because of anyone, it's not about anyone else at all, and it sure as hell doesn't excuse any of the shit you've done, Anthony. I would *happily* throw that all away for these people." He sounded so certain. So determined. "Leave them, please, Justin. We know who we're here for."

Justin followed Clementine's gaze to the back of the van, a dark hole against the morning. And he was right. Fighting with Natalie and Anthony at this point would only delay what really mattered, only keep them from those Justin loved.

They were so close—Isaiah, Paola, and Ana Lee, with Marcus's ashen body still laying across the asphalt. Justin tried to pull his legs beneath him, to crawl, even, but the agony of his back wrapped around him like a black hole, every last bit of strength used up. The call to unconsciousness roared in his ears. Here he was, nothing but a gun. A gun against the sunlight. "I can't..."

He could never leave his vampires. But he couldn't save them either. However hard he was trying, however much of himself he gave, how many punches he threw, it wouldn't be enough.

The front of the van rattled, one of the hunters screaming within, and from up the Vitalis-Barron drive, Justin could make out an incoming assault—whether security or scientists, he couldn't tell. They were almost out of time.

"I can't," he repeated.

"Not alone," Clementine replied. He held his ruined umbrella—mangled down the middle and the stand bent too awkwardly to be kept in place by only one person. Slowly, he extended his hand. He flinched as his fingers met the light, his flesh reddening, but when the crust that had consumed Marcus didn't burst along them, he pressed forward. "Not alone," he repeated, "But maybe together."

Justin reached for him.

He was closer than Justin had thought, their fingers sliding together like time and space had broken just for them, and Clementine pulled him up with his vampiric strength, drew him as close as a lover—as a second half of a whole. Justin slumped into his embrace and Clementine took the pistol from him, replacing it with the umbrella.

Between both of Justin's hands and one of Clem's, it finally held, its broken top stretching at an awkward, elongated angle above them but still plenty large enough to cast a wide shadow against the rising sun.

Together, he and Clementine stepped into the light.

It took effort to keep the shelter properly in place, properly together. Its shadow spread beneath them on either side, providing two long, jagged arches of shade as though a winged being were flying above, an angel coming to the vampires' rescue. Ana Lee stumbled out first, tucking her shorter body beneath Justin's to help hold him up despite the shaking of her limbs and the massive red welts bubbling around the holy silver on her neck. Isaiah propped his elbow under Clem's, helping him hold their shelter up. Paola huddled against them from behind, like it was their solidity that held her upright now that her partner was ash on the ground.

Together, they staggered back to the safety of the bridge in a shadow shaped like wings.

As they stepped into the shade, the umbrella fell, Justin nearly collapsing with it. Four vampires were there to hold him up, clutching him tightly as he ripped the holy silver from their blistered necks and flung it aside.

At the Vitalis-Barron gate, security guards jumped from their cars, racing toward the crashed van as a scientist trailed behind. Their presence made Justin anxious, but during the commotion, a few random citizens had stopped their cars on the other side of the bridge as well, possible witnesses if Vitalis-Barron tried to interfere. So far only a single human had dared to get out, her phone to her ear as she explained,

"A crash, yes, but I think—I think they're vampires? I don't know!"

The sirens were getting closer.

They could wait for the emergency vehicles to arrive, but five vampires in a crash with a highly respected pharmaceutical company—its humans trapped, unconscious or dead in the van, and another bleeding from a drastic bite as her boyfriend carried her toward safety—with no proof of what had transpired? Justin did not like their chances. Their best bet was to leave, to hide the Ala Santa vampires away and hope that Vitalis-Barron found it more beneficial to cover the whole incident up rather than twist it to blame the vampires.

But they'd come in Clementine's car, and by the look of its crunched hood, it wasn't going anywhere soon.

As Justin debated the possible repercussions of stealing one, a stylish blue SUV weaved through the growing bystander crowd across the bridge from Vitalis-Barron's gate, aggressively honking people out of the way. Justin's body prepared for a fight, his tension shooting a fresh wave of blinding agony through his spine. But when his vision cleared, he found Odysseus at the wheel.

She burst from the driver's side, her heels in one hand and a pocketknife in the other. Her hair was disheveled and her floral pink-and-green blazer rumpled, but she stormed toward Clementine like she was a goddess of vengeance. And of love.

"Sissy—" Clementine started, breathless, but she shook her head.

"Get inside, all of you. Hurry, hurry," she said, snapping the vampire's zip-tied bonds with her metallic pink pocketknife and ushering them all toward the car.

"My phone," Clementine muttered, glancing back at the wheel of his totaled car.

It was gone.

Justin's gut sank. In all the chaos, anyone could have snuck up to grab it, but there was nothing that hanging around could do about that. "It's just a video."

Isaiah and Clementine helped him maneuver into the back seat between them while Paola and Ana Lee piled in behind as they checked themselves for any remaining holy silver. They all blinked and huddled inward as the car drove into the light. Only Justin looked back.

The Vitalis-Barron security team had begun ushering the random onlookers away from the crash, someone in a slightly more professional uniform hurriedly digging through the van like a secret agent as the lab technician tried to wrestle what remained of the ashen vampire corpse into a black bag. Anthony and Natalie were nowhere in sight. Dr. Blood's protocols must have leaned toward covering up situations like this, then. Return them to the status quo.

As he watched the technician dismantle Marcus's ashen form, his stomach roiled with nausea and anger. That blackened husk had been his life-long friend just minutes ago, sacrificing himself for Justin—for all of them. It felt wrong to leave his body to the modern-day wolves. But it was too late to go back now. Too late to turn back any of this.

This was not the status quo after all. That implied an evenness, a stability. This was the continuation of something terrible, and the stabbing of the knife again and again into the same wound did not become irrelevant simply because it had been done before. Anthony had denied Justin his pain drugs, the hunters had violated a place of safety, and Marcus had died because of it.

"God, Marcus," Justin whispered.

"I'm sorry." Clementine slid his hand into Justin's lap, gently pressing against him. His fingers on one hand were raw from where he'd held them in the sun so close to the van's holy silver, and they shook faintly.

Justin clutched the uninjured ones. His grief hit him like a physical pain. He tucked his head into Clementine's shoulder and forced himself to breathe through it. "He was my responsibility, I should have…"

"He *chose* to save you," Clementine said, gently. "He believed in you. He *wanted* you to live."

"I'm not worth his sacrifice."

"Is anyone truly worthy of someone else's death? But you have *always* been worthy of his love and his blessing. Besides, you brought his community together and kept them safe. You've given everything for them. If there *was* someone deserving of his sacrifice, it's you. There's not a vampire in Ala Santa who doesn't believe that."

Justin didn't know what to say. His heart still retaliated, told him to bite back, to deny. He was still that boy who had killed Jose, after all, and he felt the guilt of his failures regardless of Clementine's gentle words, felt it as a violent, bitter thing that wrenched his heart in two. It told him to pull away from Clementine, to wallow in his grief alone, where he belonged. But as he felt himself slipping, Clem held him all the closer, mouth pressed into his hair.

"You're worthy of all our love," he repeated. But Justin heard something else in the statement: all their love, yes, but that of two vampires in particular, one who'd loved him unto death and the other who'd offered to love him for life.

Justin inhaled, sharp and fast as a sob. "I don't feel like it."

"You don't have to."

37

CLEMENTINE

They held each other like that for the rest of the trip, over each bump and through every sunlit intersection. Clementine's nerves seemed to catch fire, burning and screaming from the middle of his back to the tips of his pinkie fingers and the base of his heels, a constant feverish shaking descending soon after. The other vampires were suffering similarly, their situations made worse by the deep holy silver burns on their necks.

"Where to?" Odysseus had asked.

Before Isaiah or Justin could respond, Clementine had said, "Home. To Ala Santa. Isaiah's place, on Miranda Street, please."

Sissy hadn't questioned further.

Clementine still felt the tension between them, the things they hadn't yet said to each other. He felt it even more strongly with Justin. The nearer they came to his neighborhood—their neighborhood, even if Clementine's attachment to it was still a small, brittle thing, vicariously acquired but holding tight for all he was worth—the more Clem worried.

The way Justin held him now, as entwined with him as they could be in the backseat of a moving vehicle, seemed so purposefully affectionate—he had pulled Clem as close as he had Isaiah, who shivered on his other side, nearly in his lap. But that could just as easily be his instinctive response to coping with the pain, a thing that he would choose to deny himself again the moment they were back on his home turf. He had been ready to murder for Clementine, but that didn't mean he was ready to be loved by him.

The long shadows that had swathed the alleyway outside Isaiah's apartment in life-giving shade earlier had nearly retracted by the time Sissy pulled her car up to the door. The huddled, anxious residents sprinted out to help their fellow sun-poisoned and blistered companions, two of them wrapping their arms around Clementine to hold him up as his shaking knees threatened to give out. They lowered him into a kitchen chair from the nearly-dismantled barricade before moving on.

They helped Justin stagger in after him. He caught the doorframe, and paused there, half in light, half in shadow. His gaze connected with Clementine's.

Clementine's heart caught. He pressed his palms to the side of his chair, preparing to leverage himself back up, to go to Justin, if that's what he needed.

But Justin lifted one hand, motioning him to stay. He seemed to hang there still, wavering between the past and the future, between never and forever, until slowly, he set one foot into the dark. His legs quaked as he stumbled to Clementine, the expression on his face so set that it was hard to look at, hard to wonder over, not knowing whether to worry or hope.

As he reached Clementine's chair, he dropped quietly to his knees.

Clem hardly breathed as Justin settled there, between his legs, looking for once as small as his short, lithe body and not the fierce soul it held within. It felt like the inverse of La C's in every way, the tension cool between them instead of hot, their roles reversed, Justin the supplicant and Clem waiting in suspense, waiting not for affection or fire, but for a verdict.

Quietly, Justin said, "You were wrong, I think. I am still the kid who did all of those terrible things."

Clementine's heart dropped, and he leaned forward, elbows on his knees and his legs wide. "No, Justin—"

"Shh." Justin reached up, his finger pressing to Clementine's lips. It drifted, gently, tracing the top one, then the bottom, and Clementine trembled against the touch. "You were right too, though. While that boy still exists, and he always will, he's a better person now. He's good, or he's trying to be." Justin took a breath, and Clementine could see the war inside him, but it raged a little less bitter and bloody than before. "Maybe… that can be enough."

Hope bloomed in Clementine's chest, warm and light, and he could barely breathe as Justin cupped his head. He turned his face into Justin's palm, his lips to Justin's wrist, and inhaled. Justin shifted his hold, gently pressing Clementine's fangs into his flesh.

Clem couldn't stop the desperate sound he made as he was met with Justin's bittersweet blood. When he drank, the drag of his mouth over Justin's skin felt light-years different from their first bite back in the micro-cemetery, every ounce of hesitation gone, every thought fixed on Justin's pleasure even as his senses delighted in the taste and feel of him, the way his free hand trailed along Clem's thigh and some of the tension in him eased. The delighted sigh Justin gave made Clementine yearn, the ache in his chest intensified by every desire coursing through his veins.

As Justin withdrew his wrist, Clementine dragged his tongue over the bite, savoring the lingering taste of him, and it took everything in Clementine not to promise him the world in exchange for the chance to do that one more time. Instead, he whispered into Justin's palm. "So, what does this mean?"

Justin tipped his head up, guiding Clementine's down with a handful of his hair. "That I don't know if I deserve a lot. But I know I deserve you." He demonstrated by kissing Clementine, one hot, sharp press and tug of lips on lips. Clementine met him with joyous abandon, but Justin pulled back almost immediately. "Fuck, that sounded like an insult—I didn't mean—"

Still reeling, Clementine laughed. "Imperfect me, the lemon."

Justin's bitter mouth pulled into such a smirk that it made Clementine ache for those lips on him, taking him in, making him whine. "What I'm trying to say is, if I haven't fucked this up too much, will you still have me?"

"I'm already yours, ribs peeled back, heart bared," Clem murmured, and dragged Justin's face back to his.

He eased them into it this time, slow and molten, making each motion linger as his heart shot fireworks through his chest. He was Justin's. Which meant Justin was his. Two impossible facts, so simple and so perfect.

They were made for this. Him and Justin. Together. He could feel the longing on Justin's lips, in his touch, in his very breath, a thing far beyond the physical and more potent than anything Clementine could have imagined.

Justin finally pulled back, draping his arms over Clementine's lap and staring up at him like he was the world *and* he was Justin's, and like Justin was in utter awe of those facts. He cupped his fingers over Clementine's.

Clementine kissed the backs of them. His brain protested suddenly, and he ran his tongue unhappily over his teeth a few times. "Your skin wasn't clean."

Justin laughed, so quiet it was barely visible. "You seemed to be enjoying me anyway."

"Yes but now it's all I can think about," Clem grumbled.

"I'll wash first next time."

"Thank you." Clementine hesitated only a moment before adding, "I feel I should inform you that you are not allowed into my bed with your clothes on, and I mean that both in the sexual manner and in the sense that my bed is a clean space that can only be enjoyed immediately after washing, and that includes any fabrics you bring into it." He had never told that to anyone before. It always seemed such an odd desire, an imperfect thing. And he had no idea whether Justin would understand it, but he found that didn't matter. It was a part of him. And he was, while not perfect, still good.

That smirk returned, so devilishly beautiful that it ate Clementine alive. "I can live with that," Justin replied, "so long as you'll be joining me in some of these mandatory showers."

"Will you be washing my hair?"

Justin made a sound then, tight and hot and like he was imagining so much more than just his hands in Clementine's hair. "Keep this up and I might drag you straight into the bathroom."

Clementine chuckled, but he glanced out the front door, to where Sissy's car still waited. "I think I might already be spoken for." The thought of leaving Justin didn't hurt quite so much, though, when he knew there would be a coming back. Perhaps even an eternity worth of them. "Are you going to be all right here on your own tonight? With your back as it is?"

Justin grimaced. "I have plenty of people to care for me. I'll survive. *Painfully*, but I will. And... so will Ala Santa."

"We'll all look out for each other," Clementine agreed. Between their entire neighborhood and the funds that

remained in Clementine's bank account and all the love that
Justin had cultivated over the years, they would find a way to
take care of one another. "What about your drugs, though?
What if I could still—"

"Don't you dare go anywhere near Anthony or Vitalis-
Barron. They're both too dangerous. I want you more than I
want those meds." Justin smiled, all warmth and light and a
bitter longing that felt soft and delicate now. "Besides, maybe
I deserve a little rest? Now I *have* to take a break. Read some
of those books Isaiah keeps recommending me. Watch more
Star Trek. You know someone who could help me out with
that?"

Clementine knew exactly how to respond. "Always, and
forever."

Sissy was still there.

She had driven Clementine to his apartment, letting him
curl up in the back under a spare blanket Isaiah had offered,
and said nothing. Asked for nothing. And she was still here,
scowling at all his curtained windows like her glare could
scare the need for them away.

Clementine could feel the final tingles of his sun-shakes
wearing off as he uncapped them both a drink—a lager for

him and a cider for Sissy—and handed hers over without question. They stood in silence for a minute more, staring at the covered window and sipping their alcohol. It occurred to Clem that for her, it wasn't even the middle of her waking hours. But then, she looked nearly as tired as he did.

"You could have told me." She froze, lifting her fingers off the side of her bottle. "No, let me rephrase that: why did you feel uncomfortable telling me? What can I do to fix that?"

Clem was crying. He didn't realize it at first, one salty bead rolling over his chin and dropping onto the back of his hand, but as he noticed, a sob broke free with it.

"Sissy," he whispered.

He needed to say more, but the words wouldn't come. Unless maybe, maybe he didn't need to say more—not to this. Odysseus hadn't been the one to make him feel uncomfortable; the world had, its hatred working itself into Sissy in little ways she probably hadn't even noticed. Little ways that he expected his sister would be happy to confront, if he was willing to point them out to her.

And he had done the same thing to her—had ignored how she of all people would understand such a major life change, a change that made others wrongly question her validity, her worth, her personhood. He couldn't change the harm they'd caused each other. But they *could* fix it, together.

Starting with him. "You should know that phone calls are a special kind of hell for me. I hate big parties. And anything too loud or chaotic. If there are too many different kinds of lights in the same space I feel, I don't know, claustrophobic in a way? I love orchestral metal but I tried to attend a concert in undergrad and I couldn't force myself to leave my dorm room for a week after. I don't hide at work because I'm afraid to have fun, I hide there because it's calming. I know what everyone is doing and why, and I can just sit and listen to my music and relax to something routine. Until now I have cared far too much about trying to earn a position that will make Mom and Dad proud, despite it likely taking me farther from the parts of the work I enjoy, but what I *do* enjoy—the things that I stay late for—those make me happy."

Sissy wrapped her fingers around her bottle. She looked as though she was trying very hard to keep the distress off her face and failing. Clementine's immediate reaction was to pull away, to frame everything he'd just said as a silly whim that she should ignore. To present himself as exactly what she wanted from a brother.

But that distress wasn't aimed at him, he realized, not in the ways his brain wanted to assume. Perhaps she was less distressed that *he* was her brother, and more that she'd been asking him to *be* that brother without understanding the pain it caused him.

She shook her head, reaching like she might caress the side of his arm. At the last moment, she slipped her hand behind her back instead, her gaze dropping. "It was academics that I never truly wanted. The law grew on me once I started my practice, but the parties I hosted and the elaborate vacations, those were what truly satisfied me. I had always just assumed…"

"And I always just hid the truth."

Sissy gave a laugh that turned quietly to a scoff. "Fuck our parents! You shouldn't need to impress them with a job, or cater to my party whims, or be willing to tolerate anything that makes you uncomfortable just because it's what I, or they, or anyone else wants." She shook her head and looked at him again, finally, purposefully, her expression so warm and determined. "Clementine Hughes, you are impeccable. And you should not have to be."

Clem swallowed against the lump in his throat, his heart taunting him with a thousand different hurts at once, a thousand different joys bundled into a tight, hot mess that felt like he'd need years to unpack. He lifted his bottle, sucking in a breath, and whispered. "I'm allowed to be a lemon."

Sissy clinked her cider to his beer, smiling fiercely. "You are allowed to be a lemon!"

The end of her cheer was interrupted by Clementine's front door clanging against his hallway. Reginald hollered. "Lemons! Should I have brought lemons? Did I miss the memo?"

Clementine hid beneath his palm. "You called him?"

Sissy just smiled deviously and shrugged.

"No lemons?" Reggie asked, his auburn curls bouncing against his back as he power-tumbled into the room, glasses askew.

Clementine groaned. "It's just me, I'm the lemon."

"Yeah you are! You freshen up everything."

"Thanks Reggie." He grumbled the words but he found he meant them.

Reginald had grown up the baby in a household of seemingly perfect, golden-haired intellects, yet he'd stumbled into success just by being his outrageous self, and Clementine couldn't instantly throw off his jealousy of that. But he could see it clearly now, for all its pain and cruelty. It only served to hurt them both.

And perhaps... perhaps there was more to Reggie's persona too. Perhaps all of them were being less of themselves than they wished. Clementine tapped his beer to the one Reginald had taken it upon himself to pull out of the fridge. "I'm a vampire now, by the way."

"Oh, dude, that's why your curtains are closed." Reggie laughed, but as he took a swig of his drink, his face fell. "Shit though, that must suck?"

"It's been hell, to be honest. But it sucks less now." A fresh tear slipped down his face, only half sadness this time, and half that wonderful, aching presence in his chest full of the love and acceptance of his siblings and Ala Santa and the way the callous dismissal of the rest of the world seemed even harsher and more terrible by comparison.

Sissy lifted her hand again, hesitantly. He didn't give her the option to pull away this time, sweeping her into his arms and burying his face on her shoulder as he cried. Her chest shook, and great heaving sobs broke out of her, seeming to spur on Clem's own weeping.

He batted her arm playfully. "Why are *you* crying?"

"My brother is *hugging* me," she sniffled.

Reggie's larger body all but barreled them over as he tackled them in a smothering embrace. "Both your brothers! Sibling hug!"

Clem could feel the claustrophobia of too much touching creeping up on him, but for a moment this was still perfect. This was still *good*.

They were all laughing by the time they pulled apart, Sissy and Clementine both wiping away tears. Reggie fussed over his smeared eyeliner no longer looking invisible while Sissy taunted him that the whole point of makeup was that it *wasn't* invisible and Clementine tried to pull himself out of the shock that Reginald had been *wearing* makeup without him realizing it.

As their teasing sobered, Clementine realized there was more to be said still. And it would not all be easy. "There's some stuff you should know though, about my life now... and Vitalis-Barron."

He thought the hard part would be explaining the situation, but it turned out that was easy compared to the effort it took to convince Reginald not to charge right out of the apartment on a hunt to crush Anthony Hilker's skull in. He was pretty sure the only thing stopping Sissy from vowing to do the same was her extensive knowledge of the law, and Clementine's assurances that the man would have nothing more to blackmail him with now that his vampirism was revealed. Vitalis-Barron and its basement laboratory was their more pressing issue, and the far harder one to solve.

Odysseus went dark and stoic as Clem spoke of it, tapping her manicured nails in an irregular pattern. "Without that video to prove where the hunters were headed, there's no easy route to come after them, but... I'll keep thinking." She drew back her lips like a vampiric baring of teeth. "And if they lay a metaphorical or literal finger on you, I will eat them alive in court."

"I'll be all right, Sissy. But thank you." They both knew it was a hollow promise. So long as Vitalis-Barron hunted vampires and San Salud's laws let them wiggle their way around the repercussions, every vampire in the city was at risk, even if the danger to himself was minimalized by his status and family.

His family was a problem all on its own though.

For how aggressively his siblings had vowed not to let things change between them—or, at least, to only let them change for the better—he had no doubts that his parents would not react so positively. His call with them confirmed it well enough, littered by awkward pauses and remarks of, "how could you do this to our family" and "I cannot believe you decided to bring this up now, right before your mother presents at the Clayton Health Symposium." They did not bother to ask how he was feeling, how he had been living, what they could do to help him adjust. It wasn't about him at all, he realized. None of their subtle insults and micromanaging ever had been.

"Fuck our parents!" Sissy had said.

He didn't have that courage yet. But he suspected neither did she, not at her core. Perhaps they would learn it together.

Between the physical and emotional strains of the day, he fell into bed as soon as he hung up the phone, too little room left in his soul to keep dwelling on them.

Clementine was still mostly asleep when the buzz came at his door.

He threw on a robe and retracted his fangs, then realized it didn't matter. There was no one to hide his vampirism from now. He squinted at the viewing camera, struggling to understand what he saw beyond: the director of Vitalis-Barron's San Salud research branch waiting patiently in the hall.

"Dr. Hughes," she called into the speaker. "I'd like to speak with you, if you'd be so kind. I'm alone." As she said it, she lifted her hands, turning a slow circle. Clementine saw no signs of weapons, though perhaps she hid a holy silver charm or two beneath the cuffs of her fitted outfit. "Your mother escorted me past your doorman."

Escorted in his mortal enemy, then left without even bothering to reprimand him—that was possibly a new low for her. But he was still fairly certain his parents preferred him alive.

Slowly, he opened the door, his fangs bared.

Dr. Blood strode into his hall like an ambassadorial queen in her tailored and embroidered pant-suit, her gaze skeptical behind her fine glasses and her dark hair long and luscious. She was an aristocrat for the modern era; American royalty, made complete by yachts and Ivy league degrees. Her son had looked almost like the myths of the fae during Reggie's homecoming party. Clementine's soon-to-be-ex-boss looked *exactly* like one now.

She clicked her tongue against her teeth as she surveyed the room, her gaze finally landing on Clementine.

He drew back his lips, straightening as much as his worn body would let him. "Pleasure seeing you again, Dr. Blood. If you're here to bring me to your little basement torture racks, I hate to inform you that you're four months late."

"Three months, four weeks, and a day, Dr. Hughes. You have not been, shall we say, *subtle*," Dr. Blood replied. "But I was willing to overlook certain *changes* to your availability and so forth because of the superb work you've done for our company. What you did today, however, I will not stand for."

She had known. Clementine felt his stomach fall, his muscles weakening in shock instead of the silver's effects. She had known he was a vampire and let him keep working—and promoted him, even. Perhaps if he begged, he could placate her, worm himself back into her good graces. If he could turn a blind eye to the cruelty of her research and the hypocrisy of her ideals.

And that was something he found he could not stomach for another moment, no matter the price. "They were good people, and what you're doing is immoral."

"What I'm doing will define the human species for the rest of time." Her words snapped, not with emotion or anger, but with a determined sharpness, a thing almost like pride. She stepped toward him, her gaze flashing down his chest like she was seeing through to the organs within, where his heart thrummed a mile a minute. "I could have you killed, Dr. Hughes. Do not presume that beneath my power, nor my principles. But it would be messy, and I rather like your family; I consider your parents friends, and your brother has always had a balancing influence on my son. However affronted they may have become over your current state, they still love you, and I'd like not to grieve them by your loss."

He could feel the implications in her words, the thin line he rode upon.

"So, I am choosing to let you live." She glanced around the hallway once more as she turned, giving a huff. "And I have a final job offer for you, if you're interested."

"Get out," Clementine snapped.

"It's a *good* offer for someone in your... state. If you are half as brilliant as your parents make you out to be, you will listen."

If her work and her morals did not disgust him enough, that alone would have been all the reason he needed to say no. He bared his fangs then, a hiss under his breath. "I said, get out."

She wrinkled her nose. "As you wish. Though I cannot imagine this is a place you'll be able to kick people out of for much longer." As she turned toward the door, she called back. "Go, amuse yourself with your little vampire colony— that's what they call a group of bats, is it not? When you tire of playing the hero and are ready to perfect the world, let me know."

Clementine wanted to hurl something at her back. It took all his control—and all his logic, repeated in his head in a voice that sounded a lot like Spock's—to quietly watch her leave. He locked the door behind her.

The only excellence he needed could be found, not in the perfected cruelty of Vitalis-Barron, but in the goodness of a caring little neighborhood with cracked walkways and a dozen vampires just doing their best to survive. Clementine would spend the rest of his life helping those vampires, if he could. And he thought he knew just how he wanted to start.

38

JUSTIN

They held a spontaneous memorial for Marcus at dusk beneath the angel of death's monument. It was small, half humans and half vampires—only Marcus's closest connections. But it was sweet, too, as sweet as it was bitter, a terrible yet beautiful pairing of lovely stories and tear-stained cheeks and their shared anger toward Vitalis-Barron's hunters.

At the end of it, Mrs. Mendoza took Justin's hands. She cradled them in her delicate, wrinkled ones, and her eyes shining as she smiled at him. "*Anak*, my son, rest. You've done enough. Jose would be so very proud of you."

Justin cried then.

Her words couldn't take away the guilt that he carried—not for Marcus's sacrifice or for Jose's murder—nor the pain of their losses, but it settled something in his chest. Another broken piece mended. A hundred left to go.

"Thank you, Lola," he whispered in return. *Thank you, Grandma*; the words sounded different now than they had the last time he'd said them, his voice deeper and fifteen years older.

Her eyes fogged over too.

As the memorial broke up, Justin swore he caught sight of the receding trench-coat that Natalie Deleon always wore. With the pain in his back though, he couldn't run after her, couldn't fight her even if he did. No one else saw her, though, not among their group nor the human patrol who'd formed to keep an eye out. Finally, gratefully, he texted a goodnight to Clementine.

Even tucked safely into Isaiah's bed and surrounded by his Ala Santa vampires, sleep was harder to come by than Justin expected. His back screamed from every possible position and he drifted through tense dreams only to wake gasping, nerves trembling, not quite able to remember what he was so scared of. He played a series of DIY videos to try to soothe his mind. After the fourth attempt failed, he went looking for the Batman x Superman fanfic he'd fallen behind on a while back and found its last update had been longer ago than he'd thought—five and a half years—and all that remained was the note from the author explaining they'd taken it down. It hadn't been their best work, they said, and they were ashamed of it now. The knowledge tangled inside Justin, uncomfortable but thoughtful too: that he could adore a thing that someone else was ashamed of.

An imperfect lemon.

He set the phone back down.

Around him, his vampires still slept, all but Isaiah, who watched him with a tight brow. His hair fell free, the tiny locs curling gently and bundling where they hit the bed. The two of them weren't quite touching, Paola pressed between them, but Isaiah reached across to squeeze Justin's wrist gently.

"You were calling for him before you woke. For Clementine," he said, so soft the words were like a heartbeat.

Justin cringed, not at the act as much as the implication. It was not Isaiah who Justin's subconscious found his comfort in any longer. He looked away, then back; neither focus felt any less awkward. "It looked like you two were getting along earlier?"

A crook came into Isaiah's irrationally pretty mouth. "He seems nice, and he's certainly easy on the eyes. And he makes you happy." Sighing, he leaned back. "Maybe I'm just hoping that if he grows to want me, then you'll both…" He drew a breath, sharp and harsh. "I'd be so good to you, you know? I'd do anything for you, for both of you. Whatever you wanted from me, you'd have it."

"I know," Justin whispered. Isaiah was beautiful. And he was gentle and loving, when he wasn't being a drama queen. He'd have been as amazing a partner as he was a best friend. But as amazing as Isaiah was, that relationship wasn't the right relationship for them.

Isaiah seemed to read it in his expression. He nodded, his gaze lifting to the ceiling. "I understand."

"Clementine needs a friend though. I think you two could be good for each other."

"We probably would." Isaiah's tone filled with longing. "But I likely won't be around enough for that."

"You're leaving?" Justin felt his voice crack a moment after his heart did.

"I have to stop pining after you sometime, right?" It sounded like a joke, but the sorrow leaked through, hints of something pained beneath it. "Soren is taking over my spot here. Their little hole got taken over since they've been gone."

"And you?"

"I'll find something. Wesley and Vincent said they'd let me hang if I get too desperate, now that it seems we've finally convinced Natalie that revenge won't go well for her."

"But you'll be safe out there, right?" Justin couldn't continue the thought with words, but he felt it in his chest: *safe without me.* Everyone was going to have to be safe without him, if the pain in his back stayed this way. His gut still reacted to that, telling him he hadn't done enough for them yet, he couldn't retract his protection, much less ask for theirs in its place. But he hadn't asked. *They* had offered.

It was time to stop punishing himself.

"I'll be safe, Justin, I promise. And I'll be in touch, so you don't have to worry. We'll meet at La C's for a bucket of fries when I'm settled again. You can buy me a drink for old times' sake."

"All right," Justin said, but in his heart a fresh wave of grief flooded through. He had thought his sorrow over Marcus's death was deep, but this felt endless, an infinite, aching thing like a grave that pulled in all that surrounded it. It wasn't for Isaiah though, not really—as much as Isaiah leaving would hurt, it was right, too; he deserved a life of his own, a life Justin couldn't give him. The grief was for himself. For everything he had built here, the family he had worked so hard to maintain. How easily it all fell apart.

His instincts still told him to try and force it back together. But this wasn't bad. It wasn't an end, just a new chapter, one that now included Clementine, and vacations, and finally letting in all the love that was offered him.

A new text scrolled across his screen.

Clementine
I feel as if a train ran me over.
I may sleep for the rest of the night.
I just wanted you to know so you don't worry.
<3

The little heart broke Justin and put him back together again, stronger and warmer and happier than before.

Justin
You're sweet :)
I'm also pissed you can sleep. I'm too distracted.
I miss you already.

Clementine
I'll come by tomorrow night.

And who knows, maybe I won't leave after ;)
In the meantime, do you want an erotic gift to doze
off to?

Justin
Nudes?

Clementine
Absolutely not.
I have something better though.

Justin waited, more and more curious as the seconds passed, until a link appeared. He checked that no one else might be watching—Isaiah seemed to have drifted back to sleep—and clicked it. He could feel the smirk that spread across his face as the page opened.

His Perfect Nemesis, an Omegaverse alternate universe fic by HighlyIllogicalStarShipping.

He was going to need a significantly less populated mattress...

Justin tried his best to savor the fanfic, moving through it a few chapters a night—usually in his own bed, but occasionally in Clementine's. It took all his willpower not to constantly check in with Ala Santa whenever he left his neighborhood's borders. When the impulse became overpowering, he'd remind himself of Mrs. Mendoza's voice and her hands gently squeezing his.

"Rest, my son, you've done enough."

The more time that passed without a reappearance from Natalie, the easier that rest became. His fears faded as his vampires continued to thrive, the hunters slinking back into the wider city. Returning to hunting individual, lonely targets, he suspected. It was not progress, exactly, but it let Justin sleep at night. At least, when the pain didn't keep him up.

It was always there, always limiting, always shooting or pounding or coursing its way through him, and as his grief and anxiety waned, it remained to fill the space. But so did other things.

Justin was never alone in Ala Santa. His relaxed schedule didn't change that. If anything, taking more time for himself gave him better opportunities to connect with his neighborhood, his mind freer and his schedule far more open. After ten years of rushing from one house, one shop, one vampire to the next, he now spent hours just sitting with the people he loved, talking about the past and the future and sometimes about nothing at all.

That was what he had missed while taking care of the people of Ala Santa—he'd missed being one of them, missed the joy of being there, not *for* them, but simply *with* them.

Missed the impact of their love. This, more than anything, was what it meant to rest.

While he adjusted to his new life, so did his boyfriend. Only Clementine—the absolute tease that he was—refused to tell Justin what he was working on, maintaining that if it all came to pass, it would be a happy surprise. One Justin would love, he promised, on pain of staking, ribs peeled back and heart exposed. Justin knew it had something to do with the old thrift shop, but try as he might, he could not get Clementine to tell him what he was up to there.

It was tantalizing.

God, did he love that vampire.

He almost canceled his scheduled weekend visit with Priscilla and James when Clementine announced that the thrift shop's new iteration was finally about to open, but Clem had refused to let him. "Go, enjoy yourself. You missed their wedding, after all. I'll always be here when you get back."

"Forever," Justin clarified.

"Exactly."

It certainly felt like forever by the time he returned, an hour early, his back only functional because of the electric scooter Priscilla had rented for him during their weekend of outings. While he could walk without help, the aid cut down significantly on his pain and the sheer fatigue that came from forcing himself through it for hours at a time. He was still daydreaming about purchasing one himself—second hand, of course—when he stepped into Mrs. Mendoza's convenience shop.

"You leave for three full days and this is all you bring me?" she scoffed, spreading out the used copies of old lesbian pulp fiction in front of her. "Terrible! Anak, you are a disgrace!"

Justin grinned at her, his bared teeth part affection, part threat—a threat of more affection, anyway. "In that case, I can take them back."

"You can say that to my face!"

"I'm standing right here, Lola."

"Do not sass me." His adoptive grandmother huffed, collecting the books back up and reverently placing them on the shelf behind her. Above them stood her collection of pictures: her late husband in the photo with her, her friends and relatives surrounding them. But closest on either side were Justin and Jose. It felt right now that their pictures were so near, both to each other and to Mrs. Mendoza. That they were family.

It was exactly what Jose would have wanted. And for perhaps the first time in his life, he was ready to truly live into Jose's memory, in the way his old guardian would have hoped for him.

"Why are you here still?" his Lola barked. "Go kiss that tall vampire of yours!"

Justin left as fast as his back would let him.

39

CLEMENTINE

From the moment the idea had hit him, Clementine had known exactly where he wanted to build it.

He vowed he would do the old thrift store justice, its history of redistribution carrying on in a new way—one he was certain Jose Mendoza would have approved of as well. Reggie and Sissy worked tirelessly at his side, their wallets and connections getting him places his fangs wouldn't have allowed. Through the long nights and the tears, he would stare out its front windows, across the street at the angel of death, the monument's wings extended and its arms outstretched toward Clementine in a blessing. Its silent salute kept him going, even when he couldn't bring himself to tell Justin what he was doing for fear that he, too, would get his hopes up only for everything to fall apart. Clementine's hopes were high enough for the both of them.

With the pizza boxes and stacks of board games from its Clementine-approved christening party all neatly tucked away, he'd stood with his siblings and fellow vampires on the street as the pinks and teals of sunrise burst around the sky, the first rays falling across the new sign above the door, installed the day after Justin had left to visit his friends. *Jose's Blood Bank for Vampires.* It was beautiful.

And that glitter of light was all the fanfare it seemed they would get.

The Ala Santa residents who had already been donating to their vampires came, along with a scattering of those who had wanted to but never felt comfortable without the professional setup that a blood bank provided. But just one neighborhood's participation wasn't enough for an entire city of vampires in need.

Clementine sat behind the front desk as the sky darkened, not sure if the shakes rattling his shoulders were from the evening of indirect sun or just his own frustration piling up. He flicked mindlessly from Justin's texts to all his saved emails full of receipts and budgets and dreams. On a whim, he opened the chat he'd been having on and off with his vampire-dating fanfic reader.

HighlyIllogicalStarShipping

I know your blood is already accounted for but if you have any ideas on how to get humans interested in donating to my new blood bank I'd love to know.

WagerYou1

Wait so you put together an actual blood bank FOR VAMPIRES?

No fucking way.

Please confirm if I've misunderstood because I just gave my fiancé a heart attack with this news.

Oh shit he found your website.

Dude this is epic. You are killing it.

If I didn't have a pair of fangs in my neck right now I'd come check it out in a heartbeat.

He says I shouldn't message while he feeds, the nerve ;)

Clementine hadn't really expected anything to come of it. When the bank opened for draws the next morning, he'd stood in the back, the curtains still down for the sake of their one vampiric phlebotomist. He hadn't heard them until the front door opened: masculine voices, echoing down the street.

A line of thirty men stood outside.

He wanted to cry. Not just men, he realized as one by one they entered: queer men, with rainbow bracelets and bisexual pins and a variety of other pride accessories. They had all come. For this.

Clementine opened his messages with a whole new kind of shaking, his body still not quite believing it wasn't a dream as he snapped a pic of the incoming group and sent it to WagerYou1.

HighlyIllogicalStarShipping
Did you do this?

WagerYou1

Sorry I couldn't make it myself yet. I thought I'd stop by after work when my fiancé can join me.

I might have gone a little out of control with my marketing spiel ;)

But no one else wants our blood donations, so I think we all figured, fuck it. If you'll take it, we'll show up.

We just want to do something good, you know?

Clementine did cry then, a thin film of moisture that collected along his lower lids, making the whole world sparkle. They were really doing this; and it was working. He couldn't wait to tell Justin—he'd be home again soon, just in time for the good news.

A final message from WagerYou1 appeared, this one a picture of two people in their early 20s, a Latino with a massive grin and a pale, sleepy-looking vampire, his head tucked onto the other man's shoulder.

Clementine stared at it. They looked weirdly familiar.

Oh god. They *couldn't* be... the couple who'd broken into Vitalis-Barron back in October? There was no way. Clem had been in a haze of fatigue and fear at the time, he had to be remembering wrong.

He was still reeling over the weird coincidence when one of the men from the front of the room stepped out of line and interrupted him with a cough.

"I'd like to donate."

A weekend away should not have been long enough to make Clementine's heart stop at the sight of Justin, his hair flopped a bit to one side and tucked behind his ears, and his collar turned up around the tattoos that curled onto his neck. His bitter smile held all the sweetness in the world, bright and warm and a little timid for once, and the gleam in his eyes showed just what he thought of the sign out front.

"I want to donate," he continued, sounding husky from emotion, and he fiddled with the collar of his jacket, the tips of his nails casually tracing along his pulse. "Except, I'm kind of only here for my specific vampire. You think you could get him my blood?"

Clementine's voice cracked to match. "Our policy is that all blood donations and vampire recipients remain anonymous to each other. But since this place is half yours, I believe we can make an exception."

Justin closed the space between them, catching Clementine's mouth with his own. He kissed in a way that would have seemed soft—almost hesitant—if not for the fire that clearly lay beneath, his face tipping and his teeth catching hard on Clementine's lower lip. Clem bit back, drawing blood that no longer tasted of chemical sweetness, only Justin's natural bitter, earthy tones. Justin trembled against him, his mouth widening to let Clementine feed from the inside of his lower lip as he sighed.

Someone sitting in the donor's chair to the left of them whistled. The sound seemed to sparkle through Clementine, everything going twice as hot, three times as intense.

466

He licked between Justin's lip and teeth, gripping Justin's hair and tugging his head back a little in order to reach. Their saliva mingled, tingled red with Justin's blood as it beaded in the corners of their mouths. Clementine found he did not care in the slightest.

Justin clung to him, laughing. "You—you did all this? And *here*."

"Mrs. Mendoza thought it would be an honor to his memory." Clementine thoroughly believed her—he'd heard enough stories of Jose by now, of how he guided his community, cared for his vampires, tried to raise Justin up to be just as kind and thoughtful and selfless as himself and fully succeeding in that, even if it only came about after his death. "It's not the kind of medical science that I'm used to, but there's a nice big room in the back that I'm hoping can be transitioned into a lab soon."

"It's beautiful. Jose would be so proud." Justin looked around like he was seeing the place for the first time. A shine crested the edge of his eye and he wiped at it, laughing once more, rich and deep and full.

"I'm glad." Clementine's throat clogged with the same depths of emotion. "What do you think of filling this place with that shaker collection of yours? I was thinking little wall shelves with glass, themed per phlebotomy seat? Though perhaps we'll keep the copulating animal sets at home."

"You perfect lemon," Justin muttered. "I could fuck you senseless right now if I didn't need to sit down here really soon."

Clementine took hold of his elbows gently, concern overriding his lust for the moment. Overriding, but not eliminating. He smiled. "Would you accept a bed?"

"Your bed? Always."

40

JUSTIN

Justin had never loved Ala Santa more.

With the spring rain, little strips of green grass had started sprouting through the cracks in the pavement, stretching toward the darkening sky as though reaching for the last orange glow of the evening. He swerved his electric scooter to dodge a defiant yellow flower and it bounced as it rolled over a bump. His back gave a sharp jolt of pain and the last bag of supplies in his scooter's nearly empty cart rattled in complaint. He'd handed out the rest already—despite the half-hearted relief he got from this new regimen of drugs Clementine had made for him, he still found the scooter to be a life saver during his check ins. Worth every penny they'd spent, though he still wished that money had been able to go elsewhere.

The surprise charity deliveries were the only thing he did regularly now. A team of his vampires and the local young people patrolled a bit in his place, just to be sure they spotted any new hunters before those hunters spotted them. So far, their streets were still blissfully free of them.

And thank god. With how many vampires were regularly coming in before dawn and just after dusk to collect donated blood, it was imperative that they wouldn't be snatched off the streets as soon as they stepped out. The local black-market dealer wasn't too happy with them, but that was a problem for another day. And for more heads and fists than just Justin's. Whatever came their way in the future, they would all figure it out together.

The newest of their four phlebotomists held the blood bank door for Justin on her way out for the night, the homemade smoothie in her hand swirled with a deep red that smelled faintly metallic beneath the fruity scent. Between shifts like this, the main space room was strangely empty, almost haunting with its tinted windows and its high-backed chairs and IV stands, like a church after the last priest had gone home. Something surreal and faintly holy.

Justin parked the scooter off to the side of the door. His back protested the shift, but he gave it a moment, breathing through the ache as he lowered himself into the chair behind the front desk. There was probably work he could be doing, but he could hear Clementine finishing up in the other room. Justin settled for one of *Lace and Leather*'s sewing tip videos and fiddled with the vampire salt and pepper shakers beside the computer, enjoying the moment for what it was.

He almost didn't hear his boyfriend when Clem finally emerged. "Try this one."

Justin closed the video and leaned slowly back in his seat, eyeing the little tablet as he took it from Clementine's palm. "It's not going to turn my bone spurs blue again?"

"That was a completely harmless reaction." The vampire grimaced. "At least, I think."

"Your confidence overwhelms me," Justin grumbled.

He popped the tiny pill into his mouth and swirled it beneath his tongue, letting it drift back and forth there. This one tasted a bit more of the chemical sweetness that imbued Clementine's closest attempts so far. Without the original formula or the high-end ingredients of Vitalis-Barron, Clem was struggling to form an exact recreation of Anthony's pain drugs on the limited setup he'd bought for the back room of the blood bank. It probably didn't help that he was determined to move away from a smokable substance to a patch or a tablet.

As Justin swirled the final residue of the pill beneath his tongue, Clementine wrapped both arms around his chest from behind.

He nipped gently at the side of Justin's neck without breaking the skin. "I think it's time you let go of your studio and officially move in with me."

Officially move out of Ala Santa—by one whole street. The little well of panic the thought brought Justin felt like an old companion, its strength slowly diminishing each time he battled through it. He focused his thoughts on the little place Clementine had found, the small, cute space full of modern touches and indirect sunlight that didn't bother Clem

471

terribly even in the day, its front windows wedged beneath such a large balcony that they could leave the curtains open for most of the morning to enjoy the view of the complex's quiet, tree-filled courtyard. It was perfect, and it was theirs, and it was already filled with the quarter of his salt and pepper shaker collection that hadn't gone onto shelving displays around the blood bank.

And Justin wanted to live there. But even his longing couldn't entirely fight back the deeply buried fears he'd let grow through his heart over the decade.

"We won't even be in Ala Santa anymore," he whined, brushing his fingers through Clementine's hair.

Clem laughed. "By one street. We agreed this place was worth it when I signed the lease. Besides, you already practically live there."

"And if our vampires need me?"

Clementine had heard his objections before, but he didn't sound frustrated, didn't tell Justin he was supposed to be over this already. Justin adored him for that. "The neighborhood watch hasn't failed them yet." He traced his fingers down Justin's chest as he spoke. "Besides, you have a vampire right here who needs you far more than they do."

"Do you really?" Justin tipped his head back until he bumped it into the top of the seat, igniting a ripple of pain in his back that seemed to bulldoze through the medication. He gritted his teeth. Maybe it was time to shift their focus from perfecting his drugs to finding a surgeon willing to take him on. Soon, maybe, but not right now. Right now all his attention was for the weight of Clementine's breath on his skin and the way his lips felt as Justin rolled the pad of his thumb over them. "Just how much do you need me?"

"Absolutely, excruciatingly, always." As he spoke, he pressed his nose against Justin's neck, letting his teeth scratch at Justin's skin with each word. Justin could feel the edges of his fangs, hints of trailing venom tingling tauntingly across his nerves with no bite to release it into his bloodstream.

He groaned, slipping his fingers through Clementine's curls, trying to nudge the vampire's fangs into him. "Always as in forever?"

"Forever and infinity." Clementine fiddled with the lip of Justin's pants, his teeth pressing teasingly against Justin's neck, and still he sucked and pinched, refusing to break the skin. It made Justin ache, his mind so flooded with the need for his boyfriend's bite that he could barely focus on anything else. "Always as in I love you. Always as in I'm yours. Always as in you're already enough."

"You hopeless romantic."

As Clementine parted his lips to respond, Justin gripped his hair, pulling Clementine's mouth against his skin hard enough to finally break it. A flash of pain accompanied the bite, then a burst of venom that rushed blissfully through him. Clem gave a startled noise, but it turned to a moan as he sucked. The drag of his tongue over the wound made Justin shudder in all the right places. Clementine's fingers slid beneath Justin's pant line, traveling to the citrus flower tattoo Justin had recently added to the crook below his hip.

Each tender circle made Justin ache for that touch a little lower, a little more centered.

Clementine murmured, bending to kiss the center of Justin's sternum, leaving an imprint of blood behind. "Your turn to be hopeless."

"I'm always hopeless for you." Justin moaned. "You very, incredibly good, exactly right lemon. I would wash my hands a thousand times a day just in case I get to stick them in your mouth once, and leave a thousand loud bars with you for the chance to hear you whisper softly to me, and let you shoo me out of all my 'untouchable' fabric every time our sleep cycles align because then I get to be all that much closer to you as we dream."

"I love you too." Clementine sounded hoarse with emotion, and he tugged at the hair between Justin's legs in a way that made Justin want to beg and scream all at once. Then the vampire made a noise in the back of his throat. He went almost still but for two fingers still fiddling just an inch away from where Justin wanted them. "I was thinking about some of the things I'd been killing myself to conform to, the phone calls and the bars and the parties, and I realized that those aren't problems with me, they're just who I am. So, I did some research, and it turns out that perhaps the reason I'm… the way I am is I might be autistic? Or I have OCD. I'm neurodivergent, at any rate. And that's all right." He sounded hesitant, a little withdrawn, and Justin realized suddenly how much strength this must have taken him to stop seeing this part of himself as a failure and instead view it as something worth understanding.

"I'm glad for you." He turned his face to kiss Clementine's temple. "And whatever kind of neurodivergent you are, I am happy that I have the you that I have. I happen to think he makes for an incredibly good you." Justin lowered his voice then, adding a rumble to his already gravelly tone. "Your deviously precise fingers are precisely in the wrong spot though."

"Really?" Clementine hummed. He pressed his hand deeper into Justin's pants, closing in on him with such delicate roughness that it drew a grunt from between Justin's teeth. "Better?"

Breathlessly, he replied, "You should have left the curtains drawn."

"The windows are tinted." Clementine stroked as he spoke.

When his boyfriend's thumb rolled over the head of Justin's dick, little stars flashed behind his eyes. He was not quite out of it enough not to notice Paola and Whitney pause to wave at them from the sidewalk though. A ragged chuckle left him as he waved back. "Not *that* tinted, Lemon."

Clementine laughed with him, giving him a gentle squeeze before withdrawing his hand and turning his attention back to Justin's skin, tugging the collar of his low v-neck to the side to nibble on his shoulder. "That's fine. I like us both well strung out before coming, anyway."

They'd already had their fair share of sexual escapades in public, but the blood bank was off limits. The front room, anyway. And the one Clementine had converted into his lab. And the phlebotomy storage closet. And the blood bank's fridge room.

The tiny back office, however...

He almost recommended it, but he wasn't sure he'd get his boyfriend off his neck long enough for them to move.

"How much do you want for a pint?" Clementine nuzzled the soft skin behind Justin's ear, a purr building at the base of his throat.

"Only everything you have." He smirked, trailing his fingers up and down his boyfriend's arms. "And everything you are."

"Only that." A soft, musical laugh left Clementine. He cupped Justin's chin, lifting his head to press a delicate kiss to his lips. "Then I promise you everything I have and everything I am, to repay each drop of blood I drink from you tenfold."

As he said it, he brushed his fingers through Justin's hair in such a gentle motion that it felt like every wall and lie and self-destructive piece of barbed wire Justin had wrapped around himself over the course of his life was being drawn aside until the vampire could see straight into Justin's soul. And there he worshiped. Justin stared back at him—at his boyfriend, his soulmate, his always—and couldn't imagine there was anyone else he would ever feel so tenderly towards. "Being with you is payment enough."

"Be with me, then." Clementine smiled.

"Always, and forever." Justin pressed his lips to his boyfriend's, the slow and curious start of the kiss turning deeper and more seeking as Clem leaned in.

They both startled as Justin's phone rang. A spike of pain shot through Justin's back, fading more slowly than it should have. It seemed the new drug wasn't quite right yet. Justin twisted uncomfortably to slip the phone out of his pocket. He felt a drop in his chest at the sight of Isaiah's name for the first time all month. If Isaiah was calling now, then it had to be important.

He showed the screen to Clementine, who swiped for him.

"You're both seeing this, right?" Isaiah asked the moment it connected. "Tell me you're watching it now."

"Seeing what?" Justin asked. Clementine gripped his shoulder.

"Open any San Salud social media tag right now. Just do it." Isaiah seemed to take a breath, and Justin swore he could hear him tremble in the silence. "Vitalis-Barron is on the news."

THE END

The story continues…

If you'd like to read about Clementine's first meeting with Wes and Vincent, or Clem and Justin getting handsy on vacation, check out the free bonus content **available through my newsletter**, linked on my website!

Three months ago, a vampire exchanged a business card for hasty life advice from Clementine...

"You just keep loving them," the blonde vampire had said, smiling like he'd solved something.

But love? That was Andres's whole problem.

He had fallen hard and fast for the feather-cloaked journalist he'd spent a single evening with at the Vitalis-Barron costume gala—for his sharp smile and fierce intellect and the vulnerable way he'd shuddered when he'd learned what Andres was. He should have been focusing on the atrocities he'd learned of that night, but here he was daydreaming instead; half in love with a man he would probably never see again. A man who could have condemned him, but had rescued him instead... and might have unknowingly saved so many of San Salud's vampires in the process.

Andres will return in book three, where he plays cat and mouse with an enthralled human journalist who made the mistake of letting him live.

HAVE YOU READ BOOK ONE?

Find out how WagerYou1 and his now fiancé first met in this cute, steamy, and heart-tugging friends-to-lovers romance…

OTHER BOOKS BY D.N. BRYN

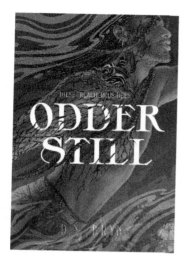

ODDER STILL

A lonely eccentric navigates an anti-capitalist revolution where both sides want to dissect him for the sentient parasite latched to his brainstem.

This slow burn, M/M romance features murderous intrigue and a Marvel's Venom-style parasite-human friendship in an underwater steampunk city.

OUR BLOODY PEARL

After a year of voiceless captivity, a blood-thirsty siren fights to return home while avoiding the lure of a suspiciously friendly and eccentric pirate captain.

This adult fantasy novel is a voyage of laughter and danger where friendships and love abound and sirens are sure to steal—or eat—your heart.

D.N. Bryn is part of The Kraken Collective—an indie author alliance of queer speculative fiction committed to building an inclusive publishing space.

If you're interested in more queer vampires, check out *Stake Sauce Arc 1: The Secret Ingredient is Love. No, Really.*

Once a firefighter, now a mall cop, Jude is obsessed with the incident that cost him his leg and his friend, five years ago. He is convinced a terrifying vampire was involved, and that they haunt Portland's streets. Every night he searches for proof and is about ready to give up... until he runs into one—a fuzzy, pink-haired vampire named Pixie. Cuddly, not-at-all scary, Pixie needs his help against his much deadlier kin. Stake Sauce is a perfect blend of dark and amusing, while giving a wide space to trauma healing and found families.

Printed in Great Britain
by Amazon

25814382R00280